BRIGHT EYES

TO CHRISTINE,
FOR FLYING THROUGH IT ALL.
THROOM!

SHUTTERCLIQUE #1

BRIGHT EYES

ACTION! ADVENTURE! ROMANCE!

WRITTEN BY

DAVE NEAL

NOSETOUCH PRESS

CHICAGO · PITTSBURGH

BRIGHTEYES
THE SHUTTERCLIQUE #1
© 2024 BY DAVE NEAL
ALL RIGHTS RESERVED.

ISBN-13: 978-1-944286-40-8
PAPERBACK EDITION

PUBLISHED BY NOSETOUCH PRESS
WWW.NOSETOUCHPRESS.COM

FOR MORE INFORMATION, CONTACT NOSETOUCH PRESS:
INFO@NOSETOUCHPRESS.COM

CATALOGING-IN-PUBLICATION DATA

NAME: NEAL, DAVE, AUTHOR.
TITLE: BRIGHTEYES
DESCRIPTION: CHICAGO, IL : NOSETOUCH PRESS [2024]
IDENTIFIERS: ISBN: 9781944286408 (PAPERBACK)
SUBJECTS: LCSH: SUPER HEROES—FICTION.
GSAFD: FANTASY FICTION.
BISAC: FICTION / FANTASY / URBAN.

SOME ILLUSTRATIONS MADE USING ARTWORK
BY ALEXANDR SIDOROV ON ADOBE STOCK

COVER & INTERIOR DESIGNED BY CHRISTINE M. SCOTT
WWW.CLEVERCROW.COM

THE SHUTTERCLIQUE #1
BRIGHTEYES

KABOOM!

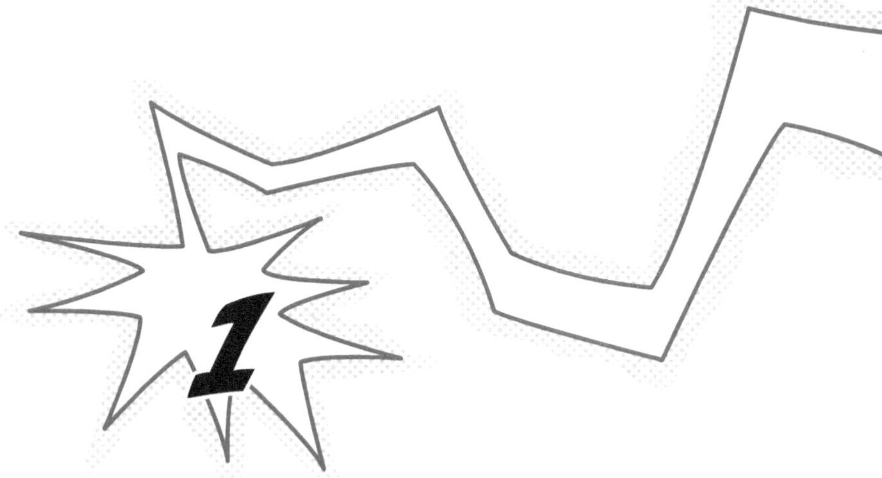

You'd never know it, because both of us operate clandestinely, though from opposite sides of the same coin: he's the supervillain, and I'm the superhero.

What you're thinking (maybe), something along the lines of a weary sigh at the prospect of yet another superhero story, made worse because you're reading it and not watching it on a screen or reading it in a comic book—excuse me—graphic novel.

Okay, I get that. What you're reading is my very classified memoir, which I have put out there for people to read and decide for themselves what's what, because there's been a lot of back and forth where I'm concerned. I live in infamy.

But the reason I've been tailing the Leveller is because he's a bombmaker. He's a radical revolutionist. I didn't say "revolutionary" because I think the Leveller is only in it for the explosions. His official line is this warmed-over "Smash the State" ethos, and while his targets usually fall within the realm of industry and government, he's really more about the boom. His ideology isn't fully coherent beyond a desire to kill as many people as dramatically as possible.

He's been working for about five years as the Leveller. Former military. Canadian, in case you were curious. He's from

Quebec, so I think he has a lot of separationist anxiety that flows into his work.

Bombmakers don't typically have long lives, owing to the inherent risk in their line of work. The Leveller's good, however. Maybe not so good as to garner attention from the Affiliates, but he's no slouch.

What he's doing right now is rigging a high-rise to collapse in downtown Chicago. It's a new building under construction, the Strathcart Building, intended to revitalize the flagging Streeterville neighborhood, saddled as it is with so much generational wealth and expensive properties. It'll be one of those multi-use buildings, servicing both the rich AND the powerful.

Inasmuch as I understand what Leveller is about, he's striking a blow at the heart of the capitalist class that rules society. Bring down the Strathcart Building and issue a prepackaged statement claiming responsibility for it. This is what he's planning, to raise his profile within the Crime League. I'll tell you more about them later, but this *isn't* officially a Crime League project; rather, it's a side gig. Ergo, whether or not he gets away with it, the League won't be implicated. That's how the League operates. They're very slippery that way. Remember that for later.

Oh, you're wondering who I am. Shame on me for not introducing myself already: I'm Cameraman.

Who am I? I'm Mitch Paulsen. You don't know me. I've built my whole life around *not* being known, on being more infamous than famous. That's *my* superpower.

But seriously, I'm Cameraman.

I'm the one who's always watching. And, yes, I was briefly part of the Affiliates. That's right—I belonged to the greatest, most powerful team of superheroes in the world. I was a member for three whole years. Not because I believed in them, because I didn't, and I don't.

No, I was just keeping an eye on them. What can I say? It's what I do. Maybe it was a mistake. In hindsight. Before then, I could simply lurk in the shadows and do my thing undisturbed.

I was never a marquee hero—not like Tandem, Wingman, Ms. Fit, or even the Knack. They're all what I consider "camera ready" heroes. The camera *loves* them. The media loves them. The public adores them. They're the ones that have their action figures for sale in stores and online.

I'm not an action figure; I'm a covert action figure.

I'm stalking Leveller *because* he's beneath the notice of the Affiliates. Why? Because he doesn't have superpowers. He's a skills villain, and I'm a skills hero, so I get where he's coming from. We have to do more than the supers to make our mark.

What I'm doing right now is disabling each bomb he places after he arms it. Yeah, defusing bombs was a thing I taught myself, but mostly I just watch what he does to arm each bomb and I reverse those steps. He's not set up countermeasures because he thinks he's gotten the drop on everybody.

What he didn't expect was that Cameraman was watching him. I'm wearing my specialized Camerman suit, which lets me be as invisible as I want to be. I adapted it from some military tech I'd gotten my hands on years ago, never mind how. It's my own thing, now, made to my own exacting requirements.

I don't know why I let Leveller get as many of his bombs placed before I finally confronted him. Maybe I just wanted him to attempt his deadly threat so I could show the Affiliates what they missed out on.

As far as bombmakers go, the Leveller is an artist. Each bomb is carefully constructed, each one is impeccably placed, and were I not there, maybe nobody would find them, except for the supers who have super-detection abilities, and even they might not get them all in time. Or maybe Rad Lad would flit down and do a localized EMP burst to frag the bomb electronics, or Speedo would super-speed around and disarm them in a few seconds. Something super-spectacular. However, they're not here; it's just me.

By the time we're on the nineteenth floor, I'm thinking the Leveller is getting suspicious, figuring out that I'm tailing him. I can tell the way he looks around himself while wrapping up this bomb. He may not know it's me, yet, but he might suspect *someone* is onto him.

His costume is mostly body armor—a metallic grey outfit with an old Gothic "L" on his chest in white, surrounded by a black circular bomb with a short fuse. He wears a protective utility vest with plentiful pockets for equipment and he's got two bandoliers that have a variety of grenades hanging on them. His helmet's got a pair of eye slits and no visible mouth and has twin spikes that arc upward in a "V" shape. Those are antennae, tied to his radio detonation bombs he's so fond of using.

Another thing about Leveller I sympathize with is he's operating alone. I imagine with mad bombers, it's hard to find partners who'll willingly work with you on projects. I'm only halfway joking. Superhero and supervillain work can be lonely and thankless, I can attest to that—it's far better working with a partner, but good partners are hard to find.

People all think you're insane to begin with, and without the benefit of powers, which at least can impress and terrify the normies, skills types *always* have something to prove. The work has odd hours—honestly, who would be voluntarily creeping around in a construction site after hours if not a supervillain and a superhero? Only criminals and cops can relate to this lifestyle.

The Leveller whips his head around, left and right, lingering in a way that makes me think he's got some optical scanning gear in his helmet, not unlike the heads-up display I have with my own rig.

He's probably scanning thermographically, trying to make out heat patterns, trying to find me. But I anticipated that, am keeping enough distance between us that if he's looking my way, he's just seeing an ill-defined blue soup, because I'm hiding behind a wall at distance and am using one of my periscope cams to peer at him around the corner. One of the benefits of my own knowledge of optics is that I know what someone might use against me.

Leveller paused about twice as long as he had at the others, which means he knows I'm somewhere, and he's wary. Maybe he did a scan on his other bombs and saw that I'd disarmed them. The question is what his next move will be. I have to hand it to him for keeping his cool so far. Then again, as a bombmaker, avoiding temperamental outbursts is probably essential.

I didn't have long to wait, as he lobbed one of his grenades in my direction. Leveller's loadout was a blend of fragmentation grenades, concussion grenades, flash grenades, smoke bombs and chemical grenades.

This one spat out a plume of smoke, and now I knew what play he was making, here. Does he suspect it's me tailing him? I do have a reputation. Criminals hated me because I was this wraith who'd find out their secrets and spill them to the wider world. The harder a criminal might seek to keep their criminality secret, the greater the rush I got exposing them.

My greatest hit list covered all sorts of power players—CEOS, mayors, police chiefs, military officials, gangsters, televangelists, senators, representatives, sheriffs, celebrities, sports figures, city officials, etc. Nobody doing bad stuff was safe from me.

"Come out, Creep," Leveller said through his voice modulator that translated his French-Canadian into English. "I hope you brought some friends."

He was just trying to goad me into revealing my position. The smoke wasn't a bad choice, because if I moved through that, he'd see the outline and just start shooting.

I decided to play his own game back at him, taking one of my flashbombs and tossing it at him. They land with a cutely tinny sound, are bouncy by design, veritable catnip for the curious, drawing the eye on a 1, 2, 3 and then the flash. It's a blinding flash, even if someone has a protective helmet. I've designed them that way.

In that moment, I charged from my position and raced toward him across the smooth construction slab. Keep in mind,

I'm invisible while I'm doing this—I have a four-way switch on my suit, and invisibility is one of its modes I like best.

The Leveller draws a gun, a submachine gun, and, no doubt blinking away the spots from my blinding bomb, is trying to target me to fire. My suit is bulletproof, but bullets still hurt if they hit, so I swept his legs from under him as I batted the submachine gun aside, which fired off a burst that chewed into the concrete overhead. Bits of shrapnel and dust fell on us as we struggled.

Critics of my work think I'm some simple lurky voyeur, but I see myself as a two-fisted recon guy, and I've tried to develop my skills (that word again) to allow me to at least fight well enough when I have to.

I gave Leveller a punitive backfist with my armored gloves and I heard the satisfying crunch of his helmet to know that I've mucked with whatever digital display he's been using. Hearing him curse, I knew I had bothered him more than he expected. His Leveller eyeslits—designed to protect him from his own bombs—don't serve him so well without the HUD.

He brought his submachine gun down on my back, or where he thinks it is, since he can't actually see me. I felt it, because he lucked into the spot between my armored backpack and my armored shoulder, right at the joint. Nothing some physical therapy sessions couldn't fix.

It's my turn to curse, and I threw an elbow into his face while keeping that submachine gun off to the side, where it can't cut me in half.

Then we're on the floor, desperately spinning around as we tried to get leverage on each other. This close, I'm very aware of the brace of grenades he's sporting, as they clattered against me. Neither of us were street brawlers, so it's not an elegant fight, but it *is* a desperate one.

"Stupid Cameraman," Leveller said, and I heard the gritting of his teeth. "I'm going to *end* you."

"Yeah?" I replied.

Not the best riposte, but I was wanting to end this quickly. I carried a stun baton, but I'm wary of using it and somehow accidentally setting off the pile of bombs he was carrying. Instead, I grabbed the gun and gave it a nasty lateral twist, which broke his trigger finger, and made him cry out. I kept twisting and he tumbled. This was where some knowledge of Hapkido helped, because I kept that hand of his stuck with his gun and gave him another twist and turn until he cried out.

"Alright, Psycho," Leveller said. "Enough. I surrender!"

Yanking away his gun and tossing it aside, I pulled out some zip ties and forced his hands behind his back, securing them. I started to take off his arsenal of bombs, but he stopped me.

"I'd be careful with that, eh, Cameraman," Leveller said. "Some of my bombs are rigged to blow if improperly removed."

Supervillains always had things like this. Contingencies were the lifeblood of supervillainy.

I dialed up Affiliates Central on my helmet phone and was routed to Tag Team, who was apparently on-duty that night. Tag Team was basically an okay guy. I didn't exactly have a problem with him. In fact, he'd be the perfect guy to remove the handiwork of the Leveller. Tag Team could make duplicates of himself.

"Tag, it's Cameraman," I said. Tag Team's polite reply made me feel like he'd been briefed on me in some manner, probably after what had happened. "I've caught the Leveller, who placed a score of bombs in the Strathcart Building."

Tag Team was all business, as I'd expected him to be.

"Are they on a time fuse or radio detonator?" Tag asked.

"Radio, but I disarmed all of them," I said.

"All except the last one," Leveller said, thumbing his detonator switch from behind his back, and I was kicking myself that I'd neglected to consider that.

The explosion was a big one, but because Leveller hadn't finished rigging the entire floor the way he had the others, what it did was knock Leveller and me across the unfinished floor, perilously close to the edge, our ears and heads ringing.

So perilous was our perch that Leveller and I went over the side, and I was foolishly still holding onto him as we plummeted. I knew for a certainty that as well-designed as my Camerman suit was, it would not protect me from a nineteen-story fall. I disabled my cloaking screen, not wanting to meet my end as some aesthetically pathetic flickering mass on the ground.

But I didn't have to worry about that, because Tandem appeared and saved us, flying in and catching Leveller and me. Tandem is like a god, better seen than believed—his suit is a mix of red, white, and blue, with a blue "T" at his chest, and white leggings and red shoulders and a facemask. His cape is red, with a white circle and that blue "T" upon it.

Seeing Tandem made me think of Victoriana, who'd been my girlfriend and partner, the one who'd gotten me to join the Affiliates in the first place. She was another heavy hitter the way Tandem was—powerful, green-haired, red and white costume with a red cape with a stylized white "V" that was on the front, too. She was amazing. I wish she was here. That was in my head as Tandem rescued me.

"Got you, Cam," Tandem said. "And you, Leveller."

Gentle as fate, Tandem got us to the ground, while I was still on the phone with Tag Team.

"Eh, Tandem's here," I said.

"Yep," Tag said. "I buzzed him the moment you called. You're damned lucky Tandem was in town, Cam."

Tandem was impressive as hell in person. He towered over both Leveller and me. Should I explain Tandem to you right now? Would that be appropriate? I'll talk about Tandem first, because Victoriana was still too painful for me, even a year later.

Tandem was a unique superhero, in that he was a gestalt being made up of a brother and sister who were individually superpowered but could form a third hero between them—Tandem. The siblings were Fusillad (the brother) and Lassitude (the sister). They were fraternal twins, and, weirdly enough, could form Tandem, who could alternately present as masculine or feminine, depending on their mood. The origins of their strange power were highly classified.

Believe me, I tried to uncover this, but it's a very closely guarded secret, and neither of them have breathed a word about it. I always thought the two of them had to have a very bizarre psychological profile, since they existed both as their independent selves and the composite Tandem.

Both Fusillad and Lassitude had legitimate, envy-inducing superpowers of their own that made them credible superheroes as individuals.

ALIAS: FUSILLAD

REAL/ASSUMED NAME: AUSTIN HARTLAND
HAIR: BLUE
EYES: BLUE
HEIGHT: 5'10"
WEIGHT: 187 LBS.

POWERS: *FUSILLAD POSSESSES AN ARRAY OF SUPERPOWERS, INCLUDING:*

• **ENERGY BEAMS:** *FUSILLAD CAN FIRE ENERGY BEAMS FROM HIS HANDS OR EYES, CAPABLE OF CUTTING THROUGH PLATE STEEL.*

• **ENERGY ABSORPTION:** *FUSILLAD CAN ABSORB ENERGY (INCLUDING KINETIC ENERGY) IN EXCESS OF A NUCLEAR DETONATION, WHICH HE CAN THEN USE TO FIRE ENERGY BEAMS, GENERATE FORCEFIELDS, ETC.*

• **SUPER-SPEED:** *FUSILLAD CAN MOVE AT SUPERHUMAN SPEEDS, DEPENDING ON THE AMOUNT OF ENERGY HE'S ABSORBED.*

• **FLIGHT:** *FUSILLAD CAN FLY AT UP TO SUPERSONIC-SPEEDS.*

• **GESTALT:** *FUSILLAD CAN MELD WITH LASSITUDE TO MANIFEST TANDEM.*

THREAT LEVEL: 9/10

* * * * *

ALIAS: LASSITUDE

REAL/ASSUMED NAME: ABIGAIL HARTLAND
HAIR: BLUE
EYES: BLUE
HEIGHT: 6'0"
WEIGHT: 222 LBS.

POWERS: *LASSITUDE POSSESSES THE FOLLOWING ARRAY OF SUPERPOWERS, INCLUDING:*

• **SUPER-STRENGTH:** *LASSITUDE IS SUPERHUMANLY STRONG, EASILY ABLE TO LIFT APPROXIMATELY FIVE HUNDRED TONS.*

• **INVULNERABILITY:** *LASSITUDE IS IMMUNE TO MOST FORMS OF PHYSICAL AND ENERGY DAMAGE, AT LIMITS AS YET UN-KNOWN.*

• **ENHANCED SENSES:** *LASSITUDE HAS SUPERHUMAN SIGHT, HEARING, TOUCH, TASTE, AND SMELL, THE LIMITS OF WHICH AREN'T ENTIRELY KNOWN.*

• **LIFE SUPPORT:** *LASSITUDE DOESN'T NEED TO EAT, SLEEP, OR BREATHE, ALTHOUGH SHE'S CAPABLE OF DOING ALL OF THESE THINGS AT WILL.*

• **GESTALT:** *LASSITUDE CAN MELD WITH FUSILLAD TO MANI-FEST TANDEM.*

THREAT LEVEL: 9/10

* * * * *

ALIAS: TANDEM

REAL/ASSUMED NAME: NONE
HAIR: BLUE
EYES: BLUE
HEIGHT: 6'6"
WEIGHT: 280 LBS.

POWERS: *TANDEM POSSESSES SUPERPOWERS, INCLUDING:*

• **ENERGY BEAMS:** *TANDEM CAN FIRE ENERGY BEAMS FROM THEIR HANDS OR EYES, CAPABLE OF CUTTING THROUGH PLATE STEEL.*

• **ENERGY ABSORPTION:** *TANDEM CAN ABSORB ENERGY (INCLUDING KINETIC ENERGY) IN EXCESS OF A NUCLEAR DETONATION, WHICH HE CAN THEN USE TO FIRE ENERGY BEAMS, ENHANCE THEIR STRENGTH, CREATE FORCEFIELDS, OR HEAL.*

• **SUPER-SPEED:** *TANDEM CAN MOVE AT SUPERHUMAN SPEEDS, DEPENDING ON THE AMOUNT OF ENERGY THEY'VE ABSORBED.*

• **FLIGHT:** *TANDEM CAN FLY AT UP TO SUPERSONIC SPEEDS.*

- **SUPER-STRENGTH:** *TANDEM IS SUPERHUMANLY STRONG, EASILY ABLE TO LIFT AN UNREVEALED NUMBER OF TONS, BUT OBSERVED TO BE WELL IN EXCESS OF A THOUSAND TONS.*

- **INVULNERABILITY:** *TANDEM IS IMMUNE TO MOST FORMS OF PHYSICAL AND ENERGY DAMAGE, AT LIMITS AS YET UN-KNOWN.*

- **ENHANCED SENSES:** *TANDEM HAS SUPERHUMAN SIGHT, HEARING, TOUCH, TASTE, AND SMELL, THE LIMITS OF WHICH AREN'T ENTIRELY KNOWN.*

- **LIFE SUPPORT:** *TANDEM DOESN'T NEED TO EAT, SLEEP, OR BREATHE, ALTHOUGH THEY'RE CAPABLE OF DOING ALL OF THESE THINGS.*

- **GESTALT:** *TANDEM BENEFITS FROM THE CONSCIOUSNESSES OF BOTH FUSILLAD AND LASSITUDE, WHICH RENDERS TANDEM IMMUNE TO TELEPATHIC SCAN OR ATTACK.*

THREAT LEVEL: 10/10

"Thanks for the rescue, Tandem," I said. I might resent not having superpowers, but I never forget my manners. And, to their credit, Tandem managed the right amount of graciousness.

"Glad you were keeping tabs on Leveller," Tandem said, while Leveller glowered at us both. "Who knows what he might have done if you hadn't been here, Cameraman."

"Just doing my job," I said. I've recovered myself, and acknowledged it, not wanting to be stuck babysitting Leveller until the authorities arrived. I ran off and reengaged my cloaking screen, vanishing from everyone's gaze except for Tandem, who knew exactly where and who I was.

Seeing Tandem up close like this brought back memories of Victoriana in a big way, but I'm not going to open up about that just yet. I'm sorry, but it still hurts too much. Let me work through it and I'll tell you about it, I promise.

KRAKK!

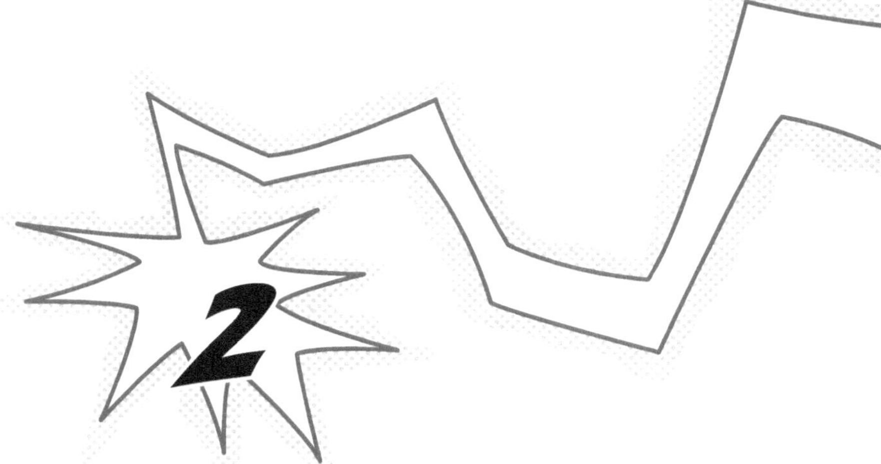

Live by your wits? Use your powers of observation? Take solace in your finely-honed, hard-won skills? That's what we normies tell ourselves in a world where *they* are busy being extraordinary. What're mad skills when faced with someone who can break down a wall with their fists? Or even someone who can fly? It's one of those things I often ask myself.

Naturally, the media fawned over Tandem thwarting Leveller, with news crews arriving. I'm thinking Tag Team probably gave them a call, or else one of the oily Affiliates PR super-people like Lynn Credible. Either way, there was Tandem and the petulant Leveller without his helmet, looking like the sour-faced Québécois he was.

"The Affiliates were able to stop the Leveller before he brought down the Strathcart Building," Tandem said, pointing to Tag Team, who was posing with a group of himself in front of the pile of bombs *I'd* already defused. His costume was black and orange, one of those half-and-half numbers, the orange above the black bodysuit. His logo was two "T's" that formed a ligature.

Would they mention me? The smart money was that they wouldn't because they would rationalize that I didn't want my profile raised, and they wouldn't want people to think that the

Affiliates were relying on someone like me to do their jobs for them. Better to think that the supers had this one.

"While one of the bombs detonated on the nineteenth floor, I'm happy to say that nobody was harmed," Tandem said.

"The Affiliates are eternally vigilant," Tag Team said. "The Leveller's going to be in prison for a long time."

I turned off the broadcast before they could say more. And I know what you're probably thinking: "That's just sour grapes, Paulsen. You wish *you* had superpowers, you envy them theirs, and that's why you don't like the Affiliates."

However, you'd be wrong. That's not how I roll. I made my own way, on my own terms. I'm a detective, and I detect things. I saw things others hope to keep concealed. I found out things nobody wanted to be discovered. I made sure the proper authorities knew about them. When that wasn't enough, I'd leak the information to those who *would* break the stories. I had a group of trusted journalists with whom I worked. Sure, I did their jobs for them, but the ones I knew, they would leap at any story that had legs. I don't even know how many Pulitzers I helped people get, and I didn't care. Let them have their prizes; I was going after the bad guys, and, more importantly, *they* knew I was going after them.

As a superhero, I've never killed anyone. I've never busted down a wall, either. No, the way I worked was quiet and sneaky because I'm the surveillance guy. They knew who to go to when they wanted something uncovered. Little old me, the guy without any superpowers. Except for one, I guess:

I do have a photographic memory. Appropriate, right?

So, when the former lead singer from the Dreadful Yesterdays darkened my door, I knew I was in for something worth seeing.

You might know her by another name: Decibelle.

My office was in downtown Chicago, Near North Side, otherwise unassuming, right above Flying Saucer Videos. Yes, it's a front, or was supposed to be. Back in the day, I'd stocked it with obscure films, not imagining it'd become a hipster hangout over the years, one of those destinations people would drop by to snag a wicked tee shirt or pick up some obscure flick they'd learned about on social media. I paid two employees to work there—Molly Hatcher and Stan Kirby. They're good kids, and because I'm a bad boss, they pretty much get to do what they want while there, and it all works out.

I hated social media, but I'd made it work for me more than not. Cameras were everywhere. Electronic eyes were on everything. The smartphone pretty much killed professional photography, and I still get pissed about that. Photography used to be an art and a profession. Photojournalism was a thing. And sure, professional photographers could still eke out a living if they were particularly mercenary.

Sorry for the digression, but photography's important to me. Years back, I made decent money—cover money, yeah—as a fashion photographer and an art photographer. You might see some of my work here and there. It used to amuse me, like my alter ego as Mitch Paulsen, fashion photographer, which let me get around, where I could do my *real* work, as Cameraman.

That's why Decibelle was here. Desdemona Bell. That's her real name. She's trying to disguise herself, but I saw her coming long before she rang my doorbell. She looked the same— the stray lock of magenta hair peeking artfully out from under the black beret she's wearing, the big black sunglasses, the black faux fur coat, the black gloves, the magenta lipstick.

I'm thinking she turned up because the other Affiliates talked about my surfacing to deal with the Leveller. For all of their media puffery, I'm sure that Tandem and Tag Team told them that I'd called them about the Leveller.

Desdemona and I were friends, as far as that went with superheroes (don't even get me started on how tangled it can get between superheroes). Maybe this counted as a wellness check on her part, seeing if I was okay after what happened. I could just see that, too, like Tandem pointing out that he'd come onto the scene just as Leveller and I were hurtling over the side of the building. It didn't take much imagination to think that Decibelle might be checking in on me to be sure I wasn't nursing some broken ribs or something worse.

As it was, I had checked my shoulder and my ears (which were still ringing a bit from that damned bomb that Leveller detonated), but I was otherwise okay for someone who was all but dead a day before, and whose world came crashing down a year before.

That kind of thing would give normies the shakes, but I'm here to tell you that superheroes live and breathe danger. Danger is our baseline, and that applies even more for those of us who are non-supers. The mortality rate of superheroes and villains is way higher than the comic books or television shows would have you believe. It's a blood-soaked business.

If anything, the comics downplayed the lethality of our work, because their goal was to get people buying (and buying into) the idea of these ageless heroes who always did the right thing and managed to cheat death again and again.

I'm not going to bore you with a list of all the dead heroes and villains, but the attrition rate is far higher than you might suspect. That's probably what led to the creation of the Affiliates—to create a steady lineup of official superheroes who were capable of intervening where they needed to, and with a higher guarantee of emerging from an incident alive. The Affiliates were about stability and security, which put the normies at ease.

Seeing Decibelle at my door, I marveled at her. She'd gotten a great reputation as a superheroine, even though I understood that her sonic powers made her incredibly dangerous, and had seen her in action plenty of times when I was in the Affiliates.

Thrillseeker that I was, I buzzed her into the foyer, where she could talk to me via my intercom. Yeah, I had a double-security system. It paid to be careful, especially where your home base was.

And you're probably laughing, thinking that any supervillain worth their salt would be able to blast right through my double-entry system, and you'd be right. The double-entry wasn't for them, however; it was for me. To give me enough time to react. I want to know when they were coming for me.

I said earlier how supervillains were all about contingency plans, but non-powered superheroes have to do that, too. We don't have powers to fall back on, which means we have to get it right the first time, and if not, to have backup plans in place in case we get it wrong.

With Decibelle buzzing my second intercom, I had no margin for error.

BUZZZZZZ

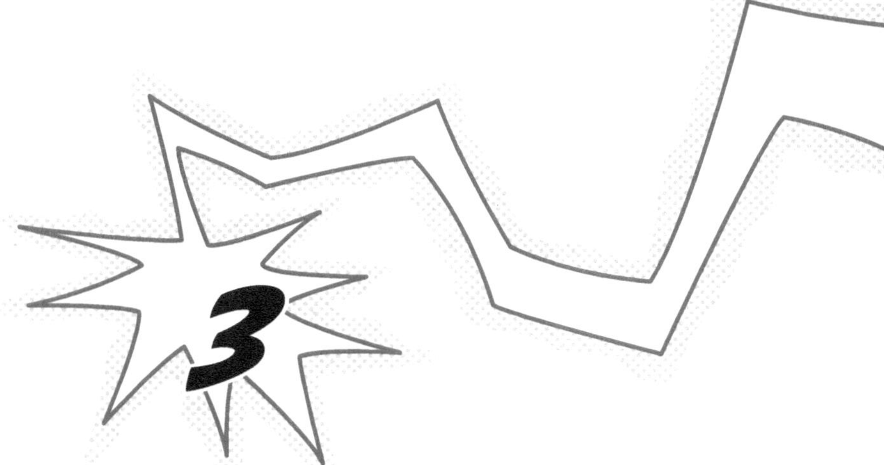

Decibelle had the most beautiful of voices. This was by calculation on her part, a kind of modulation of her voice that could do wondrous things. I suppose for the sake of brevity I'll offer a quick summary:

ALIAS: DECIBELLE

REAL/ASSUMED NAME: DESDEMONA BELL
HAIR: MAGENTA
EYES: PURPLE
HEIGHT: 5'9"
WEIGHT: 128 LBS.

POWERS: *DECIBELLE POSSESSES SUPERNATURAL VOICE POWERS, INCLUDING:*

- **VOCAL HYPNOSIS:** *DECIBELLE CAN SPEAK AND INDUCE A TRANCE IN THE LISTENER.*

- **SINGING HYPNOSIS:** *DECIBELLE CAN MESMERIZE INDIVIDUALS OR GROUPS WITH HER SINGING.*

- **SONAR:** *DECIBELLE CAN USE HER VOICE TO PROJECT SONAR WAVES THAT ALLOW HER TO EFFECTIVELY "SEE" THE SONAR WAVES SHE'S MAKING.*

- **SONIC BLAST:** *DECIBELLE'S VOICE CAN BE WEAPONIZED AS A TIGHTLY FOCUSED SOUNDBEAM OR BROADBEAM, TO A MAXIMUM OF OVER 300 DECIBELS.*

• **HYPERSONIC SINGING:** *DECIBELLE CAN EMIT RESONANT FREQUENCIES CAN CAUSE MATERIALS TO BREAK OR LIQUEFY.*

• **VOCAL IMPERSONATION:** *DECIBELLE CAN PERFECTLY MATCH ANY VOICE SHE'S HEARD.*

• **HEARING PROTECTION AND AMPLIFICATION:** *DECIBELLE IS SELECTIVELY ABLE TO SHIELD HER EARS FROM HARM AND CAN ALSO HEAR BEYOND THE RANGE OF NORMAL HUMAN EARS.*

• **LIE DETECTION:** *DECIBELLE CAN RELIABLY DETERMINE TRUTH OR FALSEHOOD THROUGH WHAT SHE CALLS "ACTIVE LISTENING"—MONITORING SOUNDWAVES TO CAPTURE STRESS INDICATORS PRESENT IN LYING OR TRUTH-TELLING.*

THREAT LEVEL: 8/10

She's not one to be trifled with, all southern belle pleasantries aside. We didn't cross paths much when I was in the Affiliates, but maybe that's more on me than her, as I kept a very low profile, and worked so much with Victoriana.

Rumor has it that she's a Siren (yeah, one of those, you know, from the Greek myths), but whether or not that's true is on you to confirm or deny. For me, it's as good an explanation as any for what I've seen her do with that incredible voice of hers.

Now, when Decibelle turned up at your door and said she needed to talk, it put you in a weird place. I thought about grabbing some earplugs, just as a precaution, because she could get you drooling with just a syllable or two. The question was whether or not I could trust her, and, doing a coin toss in my mind, I told myself that I could.

"Hold on, I'll buzz you in," I said, and I did just that. She easily could have blasted through the door or mesmerized me into doing it.

My place, meaning my office, wasn't advertised. Only clients who knew what I offered were even aware of it. I got the brownstone long ago (I'll explain that later as well), and it's arranged to be a discreet place of city business. The top floors were where I lived, where Cameraman did his business. The office, on the middle floor, was where my alter ego conducted his surveillance trade.

Cameraman's lair was four floors over the office, which included living quarters on the third floor, my workspace on the fourth floor, my production space on the fifth floor, and a rooftop workout room and deck on the sixth floor.

There's an elevator in the building, and I waited for Decibelle to appear. As I was waiting, I was cycling through what I knew about her these days. She's still an active Affiliate, so she's in good standing overall with the organization, although she and her partner, Brighteyes, had a sideline partnership in the South as Sound & Fury, a two-woman crimebusting team who specialized in going after elusive vice offenders—serial killers, rapists, sex traffickers, pedophiles, that kind of thing. The really nasty, creepy ones. The two of them had a formidable street reputation as a powerful pair.

The elevator rang and out she strode, wearing some black boots with a lot of laces. Steel toe boots were my guess since those were always useful in a fight.

She smiled broadly at the sight of me, extending her hand, which I shook.

"Mitch Paulsen," she said. "You look good. Retirement suits you."

"I'm not retired," I said. "I quit, remember?"

I gestured to one of my comfy client chairs, where she took a seat across from my desk. My office was unassumingly modern in look and feel—cool colors, streamlined furniture, some of my favorite photos framed on the walls, placed to soothe clients, including some of Victoriana I had taken myself. Decibelle looked completely at ease, but I'd expected that from a former rock star, current superheroine, and erstwhile Siren.

"Drink?" I asked.

"Bourbon, if you have it, Mitch-Honey," Decibelle said. "And ice."

"Always," I said, pouring her a few fingers, which I handed over. She took the cut crystal glass with on-brand magenta-hued fingernails. She often would work splashes of magenta in her costuming, like magenta and blue. Those were *her* colors.

She took a pull on the bourbon before speaking again. I loved hearing her talk, was content to wait. I could see her scanning my room, eyes lingering on my pictures.

"You're wondering why I came all this way to meet with you," she said, a hint of her southern accent showing—Savannah by way of Charleston with a twist of Richmond. Intoxicating. How a Siren ended up with a southern accent was one of the mysteries she kept close to her. Maybe it was an affectation she'd picked up along the way.

"I'm curious," I said, taking a sip of Tanqueray I'd poured for myself. It was weird sitting across from Decibelle like this, knowing that if she wanted to, she could bring my entire building down around my ears. That kind of power in one person was terrifying, but most of the Affiliates rolled that way.

"I'm here in strictest confidence," Decibelle said. "Nobody knows I'm here. Certainly nobody from the Affiliates."

"No?" I asked.

She shook her head, took another drink. "Once I tell you, I think you'll know why. It's about Antigone," Decibelle said, not even bothering with her codename, Brighteyes. Her dossier:

ALIAS: BRIGHTEYES

REAL/ASSUMED NAME: ANTIGONE PARK
HAIR: BLACK
EYES: GREEN
HEIGHT: 5'5"
WEIGHT: 115 LBS.

POWERS: *BRIGHTEYES POSSESSES SUPERHUMAN EYE POWERS, INCLUDING:*

- **ENHANCED SENSES:** *BRIGHTEYES HAS SUPERHUMAN VISION:*

  - *INFRARED VISION*
  - *X-RAY VISION*
  - *THERMOGRAPHIC VISION*
  - *MICROSCOPIC VISION*
  - *TELESCOPIC VISION*

- **EYEBEAMS:** *BRIGHTEYES CAN FIRE A VARIETY OF GREEN EYEBEAMS FROM HER EYES, INCLUDING STUN BEAMS, WOUNDING BEAMS, AS SWELL AS DISINTEGRATING BEAMS.*

HER EYES CAN BLAST THROUGH TARGETS (WALLS, PLATE STEEL, ETC.) OR DISINTEGRATE HOLES THROUGH THEM.

*• **LIE DETECTION:** BRIGHTEYES CAN RELIABLY DETERMINE IF SOMEONE IS LYING THROUGH USE OF HER THERMOGRAPH-IC VISION.*

THREAT LEVEL: 8/10

"What about her?" I asked. Decibelle drew a breath.

"I've lost track of her," Decibelle said. I could tell that she was fretful, as her face carried the concern for her partner. My fieldwork let me at least spot when someone was telling the truth or not. Not a superpower; just experience.

"Did somebody take her?" I asked. In our line of work, supervillains invariably formed vendettas and carried out evil schemes, many of which involved attacks on superheroes. Sound & Fury had put enough baddies away that I could name a running list of possible suspects pretty easily.

"No, nothing like that," Decibelle said. "I mean she's disappeared. She won't return my calls. She ditched me."

Excepting Victoriana, I'd never really worked with partners the way others had. Or at least not the same way. The work I did as Cameraman necessitated discretion and quiet, and I found I was better at that working by and for myself. Sure, Rollergirl and I had worked together, and there was always Thee Souldier and Inferna, but we were more allies than partners. Only Victoriana had been a true partner. Sorry, she's never far from my thoughts. I tried to stay focused on Decibelle.

"Can you tell me what happened?" I asked.

"Yes," Decibelle said, gazing at me over the lip of the glass. "I can."

WHIRRRRRRRR...

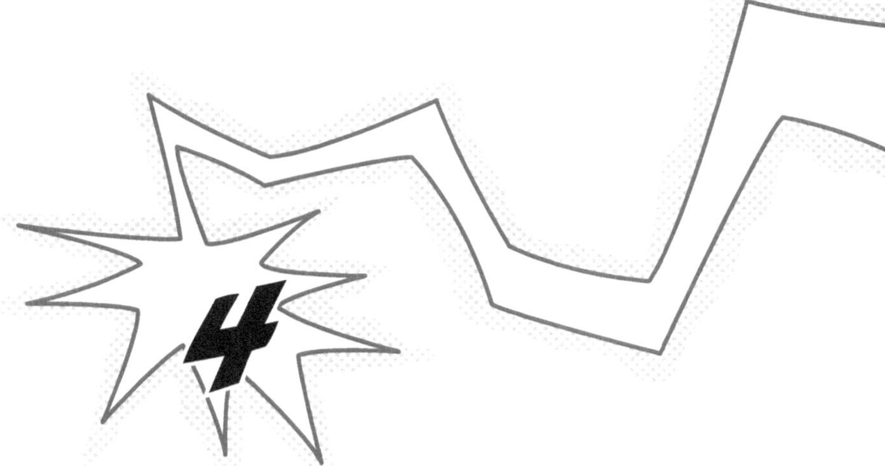

"She and I. The perps we chase down operate internationally, and that means we have to, as well. It started in Manila. We'd broken up a ring of human traffickers operating under the auspices of the Crime League, like a distant connection, versus the inner circle."

The Crime League was led by Dr. Crime, with the Instigator and Crimebot being the dark triad that had their hands in so much that went on in the criminal underground. I'll talk more about them later.

"But it wasn't just them," Decibelle said. "It was the Fourheads."

Before you laugh, I have to tell you about the Fourheads. Entrance into the Fourheads is rooted in having some kind of head-based superpower, and, naturally, being a noteworthy criminal. The current active members are:

- HOTHEAD: HAS A LITERALLY FIERY HEAD, CAN BREATHE FIRE UP TO SEVERAL HUNDRED YARDS.

- AIRHEAD: CAN CONTROL AIR AND WIND. ALWAYS TALKS IN A WINDY WHISPER.

- DUSTHEAD: CAN CONTROL EARTH, SAND, AND DUST AND COULD WITHER-TOUCH PEOPLE INTO BECOMING HIS MUMMY SLAVES.

Other members of the Fourheads in the past were Machinehead, Gearhead, Blockhead, Arrowhead, Pighead, Spearhead, Metalhead, Crackhead, Overhead, Skinhead, Masthead, Sleepyhead, Mushroomhead, etc.

The current lineup of Fourheads had been working for the last seven years and had amassed a sizeable criminal empire under the dual leadership of Hothead and Deadhead. The Fourheads were based in the States, although they had junior operatives around the world.

"Okay," I said. "What happened?"

"Dusthead was running the Manila operation," Decibelle said. "You know what he's like, Mitch."

I'll admit that Dusthead had a good look going, villain-wise: he had a mummy-like visage—this face wrapped with sepia-hued bandages and these red-orange glowing eyeholes, and a kind of snarly rictus of a mouth. He'd most often wear it with a weathered brown bomber jacket and black pants and matching knee boots. His voice was a raspy thing, full of menace, and he had a perpetually dusty aura around him that called to mind that character, Pig-Pen, from the PEANUTS cartoon strip.

I'd never faced Dusthead in a fight, but in my work as Cameraman, I made sure I'd read his file, the way I did everybody. Dusthead could whip up dust devils and even sandstorms, in addition to his way with earth and stone, and this dreadful witherfinger thing he did where he could touch someone and make them wither into a mummified version of themselves, which he could then command to do his bidding.

He wasn't a lightweight, and his expertise was in smuggling. Rumors flew that he'd been an unscrupulous archaeologist who'd stumbled upon a cursed crypt and had become Dusthead as punishment for violating some Egyptian or Assyrian tombs. He'd turned his curse into a business, which tracked, I guess—once cursed, everything else was a step up from where you were.

"We had broken up the ring and Dusthead went after us," Decibelle said. "It was a mess—he whipped up one of his dust storms, and neither Antigone nor I could see him. He got away. She was furious. I wasn't happy about it, but she was seething. I tried to calm her down, but she wouldn't have any of it."

"'This always happens, Des,' Antigone said, her green eyes flashing. 'We foil their plans and they just get away.'"

"We'd had to work with the local authorities, as per Affiliates protocol," Decibelle said. "You know how it's done. But I knew something was up with the police. The Fourheads had gotten to them, or Dr. Crime had, maybe. Somebody had tipped them off. We'd managed to break up the ring despite this, but the heart of it—Dusthead and whoever else was working with him—got away."

"I tried to cheer her up," Decibelle said. "The dent we'd made in their operations. Despite casualties, we'd freed hundreds of women who'd otherwise been bound for container ship hell. Brighteyes wasn't having any of it. We flew back to Affiliates West on one of our Affilijets, and I could tell Antigone was still angry."

Antigone had a military background in the Marines, one she was very proud of, and the prospect of leaving a fight unfinished was one she couldn't stomach. Brighteyes played to win, and anything short of that got under her skin.

"'You held me back,' Antigone said. 'I had a shot, and you stopped me, Des.'"

"'We're not killers, Antigone,' I said. 'We aren't vigilantes.'"

"And Antigone stared hard at me with her eyes," Decibelle said. "Those beautiful green eyes of hers, like fiery jade, all radiant light. You know how she wears those special shades to cover her eyes when she wants to. She had tossed them aside and just glared at me. I half-wondered if she'd use them on me."

Brighteyes had naturally green eyes, but when she used her powers, her eyes glowed. It was one of those tells that happened with anybody with eye powers. Those glowing eyes meant trouble for those who saw them. Antigone Park had been getting an eye exam when there'd been some kind of solar storm that had hit, and she'd been struck with cosmic energy rays that had given her those special powers, which had evolved over time.

According to her file, they'd originally granted her only enhanced visual senses, but she'd eventually gained those terrifying eyebeams, which she'd practiced with until she could do all sorts of things with those eyes of hers.

"But she didn't," I said.

"Of course not," Decibelle said. "I wouldn't be here if she had."

"Once you were back in the States, what happened?" I asked, refilling her glass.

"I tried to bring Sound & Fury back together," Decibelle said. "Tried to find some more casework we could do. You know how that is—a good case can get your mind right, get you focused on the job, not all caught up in your head, Honey."

I was wondering what was going on with Brighteyes, too. Was it simply her umbrage at Dusthead getting away? Was it as basic as that? They'd busted that trafficking group, so, at least to my pragmatic self, that felt like a win.

"Brighteyes wasn't having it, though?" I asked. Decibelle shook her head.

"Not at all," she replied. "She went out on her own, chasing after leads is what she told me she was doing. I offered to help, but she blew me off, told me to handle the Affiliates. I'm sure you know how she moved to auxiliary Affiliates versus the active-duty roster. I think she liked the idea of being an Affiliate more than actually being one."

I could relate, even as tangential as I'd been in the Affiliates operation. They were big-ticket heroes, dealing with world-crushing menaces, versus street-level saviors. I preferred the street-level criminal types, anyway. They were more relatable.

Not that anybody ever saw me when I was doing my Cameraman work. That's the whole point of it, really. Not being seen.

"And you lost track of her," I said. Decibelle's purple eyes flicked over me a moment, and I wondered what the Siren might be hearing with those ears of hers. Had I offended her with my bluntness?

"Gradually," Decibelle said. "I worried, but I didn't want to pry, just as I didn't want to leave her hanging, either. We respect each other's space. And then Dusthead disappeared."

That was something I hadn't been aware of. Because supervillains habitually kept low profiles between grand schemes, it was usually too time-consuming to try to track them down, versus being there when they resurfaced.

"Disappeared?" I asked.

"Yes," Decibelle said. "Gone."

"Come on, now," I said. "Villains hide out all the time. It's what they do."

The look on her face was somewhere between wounded contempt and wanton disdain, as if I'd said something so condescending that if she'd been other than the steel magnolia model of restraint that she was, I'd have caught an earful.

"I know what they do, Mitch-Honey," she said. "But the Fourheads trotted out a new member about a month after Dusthead disappeared: Thunderhead."

I chuckled despite the gravity of her bearing. The Fourheads just never seemed to run out. I wondered how they went about their auditions, could only imagine how weird those would be.

"Let me guess: Thunderhead controls the weather," I said.

"She does," Decibelle said. "But don't you think that's weird?"

I shrugged. I wasn't necessarily keen on following the hiring practices of supervillains. Not wanting to get on Decibelle's bad side, I offered some theories.

"There are a couple of possibilities, as I see it," I said. "If this was some sort of joint operation between the Fourheads and the Crime League, maybe they went after Dusthead for screwing it up. Dr. Crime and Crimebot in particular aren't very forgiving of failure. And I can't imagine Hothead or Deadhead being very accommodating, either. Maybe they killed him for that. Or maybe they urged him to lay low while the heat was on."

"They replaced him, Mitch," Decibelle said. "Like he was gone, and they knew it."

"Maybe he retired," I said. "Dusthead has been at it for years. Maybe he got the curse lifted and cashed out."

"Maybe he's dead," Decibelle said. "Maybe Brighteyes killed him."

Hearing her say that, her lovely voice and all, gave me pause. There was desolation in her tone, something I'd never heard before, at least not from her.

"That's quite a jump," I said. "You have no proof."

Decibelle set down her glass and crossed her arms, leaning forward.

"You're right," she said. "I don't have proof. That's why I'm here. It's why I'm hiring you."

Now I did laugh, the kind of hollowed-out, cynical laugh that was something of a trademark for me these days.

"You're hiring me to, what, exactly? Track down Brighteyes?" I asked.

"Yes, Honey," Decibelle said. "I want you to find her, to follow her, and report on what she's up to. Don't engage with her. Don't try to talk to her. Just surveil and tell me what you've found out."

Now, I knew that the Affiliates had their own process for this kind of thing, like the equivalent of Internal Affairs. I'd never been part of that, but I was at least aware of it. A Board of Review for active and auxiliary members, to make sure they weren't abusing their superpowers. The team was always big on accountability and abuse of powers. That was the official stance the team took to protect its members and its mission.

"And you don't want the Affiliates involved why, exactly?" I asked. I had to ask, and she had to answer, if we were to have a hope of moving forward with her inquiry. I wouldn't just take a case like this because we were friends and former teammates. I had to know as much as possible before I'd proceed.

"She's my partner," Decibelle said. "We've been through a lot. I don't want to ruin her reputation if I'm just overreacting. I want to just make sure she's alright. She's hiding from me, and believe me, Honey, I've tried to track her down. Brighteyes has gone to ground, and I have no idea where she is. I went to the last place Dusthead was seen and there was no trace of Antigone there. I looked, tried to find anything, any clue, and came up empty-handed. You, however, this is what you do. And you're discreet."

I smiled at her, appreciating her appreciation of what I did. There weren't many wins to be had, but professional respect was one of them.

"Okay, so find, follow, report, and avoid contact," I said. "I can do all of that. However, I don't normally track heroes; I chase villains."

Decibelle scoffed.

"Mitch-Honey, we all know you track everyone," Decibelle said. "Your lair upstairs, you mean to tell me you don't have files on every one of us? Strengths, weaknesses, aptitudes, origins? All of it?"

I blushed a little, although I wasn't ashamed; I was simply thorough. In my world, knowledge was power, the only power I could ever really have.

Decibelle cocked an eyebrow at me. Her eyebrows weren't magenta; rather, they were a dark and nebulous near-black tint.

"Do you still have the suit?" she asked, as if she had to.

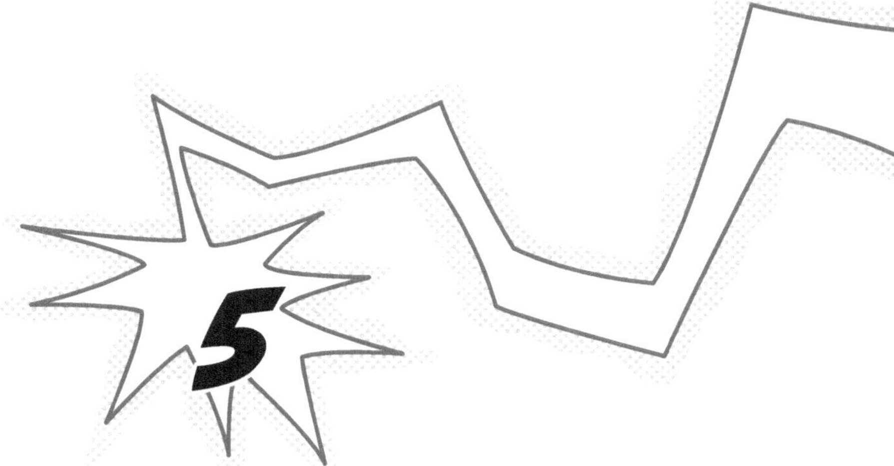

Most would think some-body like me would have a cave or maybe a bunker. However, that's not how I operated. I liked having good reception, and my rooftop had a corner where there were a lot of broadcast towers that let me moni-tor broadcasts around the world, and I could reach just about anybody I wanted to.

I'd carefully rigged up the entire building to be free of bugs and wired it to offer surveillance of the entire block, as well as carefully soundproofed everything from the office upward. Nobody could hear what I was doing on those working floors, while I had closed circuit cameras absolutely everywhere, so I could keep tabs. This was how I camera-rolled.

The suit Decibelle referred to was my ultimate Cameraman accessory, a prized item in a collection I'd curated over the years. What you saw (or didn't see. Heh.) when I took on Lev-eller.

"You know, you should consider yourself very fortunate I'd even take you here," I said.

"Oh, I am indeed honored, Mitch-Honey," Decibelle said, nursing her drink, which I'd refilled before we'd gone upstairs.

The suit was a labor of love of mine, one of several gadgets I'd made. She looked at it hanging on its rack, the picture of innocence, where it hung with its sibling suits.

"The Invisible Man's long johns," Decibelle said.

"That's right," I said, perhaps a little defensively. "Four settings—matte black, reflexive camouflage, light-bending, and mirror sheen."

"Before I learned who you were, I always wondered who you were," Decibelle said. "You were always so mysterious, Mitch. When you and Victoriana came aboard, everybody talked. Everybody wondered. Her, we understood; but you? Pure mystery."

How my identity had been blown was, I later learned, the work of Minder, the telepath and chairman of the Affiliates. I never liked him, found him to be as neurotic as all telepaths seemed to be. It probably bothered him that he didn't know my identity, so he did a little probing and told others. In retrospect, it was a dick move, but telepaths can be so telepathological.

She caressed my suit, whistling.

"So supple," Decibelle said. "And yet bulletproof, if memory serves."

"Totally," I said. "Has to be, when you're a snoop like I am. Honestly, if you weren't you, I'd not even take you up here."

What she didn't understand is that as Cameraman, I carried out work on many levels. There was Mitchwork and Cameramanwork, and I juggled them based on the situation. Sometimes it paid to be unobtrusive in ways that didn't potentially draw attention the way Cameraman sometimes did. A simple disguise and a phonecam could do the trick, versus all the bells and whistles of a full rig. Other times, it was all Cameraman, operating invisibly.

"You still have your Mitchmobile?" she asked, turning her back on my suit and smirking at me in the fetching way she had.

"Which one?" I asked. "I do. My car and my van."

"Tricked out like your suit?" Decibelle asked.

"What is this, an interrogation?" I asked.

Decibelle laughed, walking over and patting me on the arm.

"I just want to be sure you're up for this task," she said. "Antigone can see things beyond the visible spectrum. I couldn't live with myself if I sent you into harm's way, Mitch-Honey."

Now it was my turn to feel the somniferous sting of friendly condescension. Her super-self was worried about *my* welfare. It's likely why she didn't want me to actually engage with Brighteyes—she didn't want me getting hurt.

"Don't worry, Des," I said. "This is pretty straightforward surveillance, by my estimation. The mark of good surveillance is grounded in *not* being discovered. I won't be."

"Lord, I hope not," Decibelle said. "Antigone's got a temper. There's a reason we were 'Sound & Fury' you know. I supplied the sound, while Antigone brought the fury."

It's not like I hadn't had supers in my lair before. Plenty had been up here. Victoriana had lived here with me, for Christ's sake.

And with Decibelle, there was just something about her that made it all seem alright. She may not have performed with her band in a decade, but she remained a rock star, and rock stars—especially ones with superpowers—they just had that way about them that made it seem okay. And this was just me talking, not some brain-fried version of myself, beguiled by her auditory powers.

"While I'm busy finding Brighteyes, should I also look into what happened to Dusthead?" I asked. "That's part of it, too, yeah?"

Decibelle slowly nodded, ogling my gadgets—I had cameras of all shapes and sizes, bugs, drones, stun gear, body armor, and other stuff. Everything in its proper place, hanging on hooks, sitting on shelves, in cubbyholes and cabinets.

"You're not rich, Mitch," Decibelle said, almost matter-of-factly, because I knew she was. "How do you afford all of this?"

"Oh, I charge clients hefty fees for my surveillance expertise," I said. "You'd be surprised what people are willing to pay for my services. And I'm pretty good at grant proposal-writing. The government's always looking for a leg up. The Knack has lent a considerable hand, too."

"Ah, yes," she said. "Good ol' Shane. He's such a peach."

Her purple eyes danced over me a moment, and I could tell she'd gotten a little tipsy from the bourbon. I didn't know how much booze a Siren could imbibe.

"You don't help clients as Cameraman, do you?" she asked, as if it were her business.

"Cameraman's strictly for me," I said. "And, well, special cases. I do plenty of work just as myself—meaning Mitch."

I printed the contract and handed it to her in a grey sealed envelope, using a blob of chalk-white wax to seal it, with my unofficial Cameraman logo—an unblinking eye worthy of the Illuminati themselves, with an aperture in place of an iris symbolizing (for me), truth and justice, if not exactly the American way. In my world, truth never blinked, and justice wasn't blind.

Decibelle took it, handing me something in return— it looked like a deep blue burner phone, but was a bit more specific. Opening the flip top, I saw a magenta button with her own logo on it—a "D" with what looked like soundwaves around it, emanating outward.

"That's a panic button, Mitch," Decibelle said. "You find yourself in a serious jam, and I mean serious, Honeybear— you push that button and I'll get there. Can't rightly say how quickly, but I will."

"Just you?" I asked. "Not the Affiliates?"

"Just me," she said. "But I'm more than enough for most, you hear?"

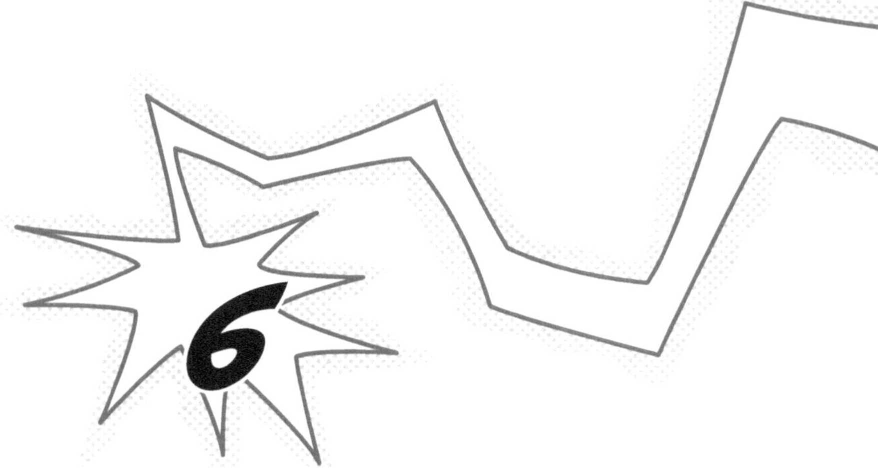

Are you thinking it's *easy* to find a superhero? Their whole lives are predicated on their secret identities, but since I already knew Brighteyes was Antigone Park, finding her wasn't going to be a big problem. That's what I told myself.

That said, the fact that Decibelle had tried to find her and failed meant that the obvious hideouts weren't going to give me solid leads. Mentally, I broke it down—Sound & Fury were based in Atlanta and covered the South more than other parts of the country. Maybe it was the blend of the Texas border and Florida follies, but the rampant trafficking kept them busy there. Their secondary base of operations was Affiliates West in Los Angeles, and tertiary was Affiliates East in New York.

The Fourheads operated internationally, without a particular preference. I had hoped for some intersectional opportunities, but the way they worked, they might pop up anywhere.

I got my Situation Room databoard fired up, typing up all Fourheads activities over the past year, gratified when the little pins appeared, identifying which Fourheads were involved, and where. My databoard is basically an extra-large tablet-compatible display, something I'd nicked from the Affiliates when they'd upgraded their system. Hey, I cleared it with them, part of my own "home office" arrangements after what had happened with Victoriana.

The last confirmed sighting of Dusthead was in Long Beach, California, roughly nine months ago. A few more keystrokes revealed a security camera shot of him, working furtively in a warehouse area, his creepy glowing eyes standing out in the closed-circuit imagery of him. This was roughly three weeks after the Manila dustup, and it looked like Dusthead was boosting some tech, maybe circuit boards.

He was working with a six-man team, likely trying to make amends for the problems in the Philippines. I wasn't privy to the kickback scheme the Fourheads and the Crime League had worked out, but I was sure they had something in place. Like the good goon he was, Dusthead was out to balance the scales.

That theft went smoothly by all accounts, since the stolen merchandise turned up on the black market a week later. It's not clear whether the sale went through Dusthead or a middleman, but the stolen merchandise was, in fact, sold.

Supposing that Brighteyes did kill Dusthead, would this mean that the other Fourheads might also be potential targets? They were his partners, so it was at least a reasonable assumption that if one was a target, the others were at risk, too.

Since Thunderhead was the replacement, I figured Hothead, Airhead, and Deadhead would be the next targets, if Decibelle's theory was correct. It was an intuitive leap, but the alternative was one helluva slog. Hothead and Airhead were a couple, so that either made them a tempting target if Brighteyes was after them, or perhaps too strong for her to take by herself. Whereas Deadhead was solitary, merely able to kill with a glance.

Two bad choices.

My instincts told me that Deadhead would be the safer bet, paradoxically, so I ran my file on him:

ALIAS: DEADHEAD

REAL/ASSUMED NAME: UNKNOWN
HAIR: NONE
EYES: RED
HEIGHT: 6'
WEIGHT: 220 LBS.

POWERS: *DEADHEAD POSSESSES SUPERHUMAN EYE POWERS, INCLUDING:*

• **DEATH GAZE:** *DEADHEAD CAN KILL ANY MORTAL WITH A LOOK AT A RANGE OF FIFTY FEET.*

• **NIGHT VISION:** *HE IS BELIEVED TO BE ABLE TO SEE IN THE DARK.*

• **SUPER STRENGTH:** *DEADHEAD IS SUPER-STRONG, ABLE TO LIFT APPROXIMATELY ONE TON.*

THREAT LEVEL: 7/10

The file indicated that Deadhead had gained his powers through some supernatural means, likely an invocation with a dark spirit and/or demon, and his powers appeared to be magically derived.

The Affiliates had tangled with Deadhead three times over the past seven years as part of his work with the Fourheads. He had managed to put Tandem into a coma for a week with his infamous death gaze but had otherwise not harmed any members of the Affiliates, beyond the routine bumps and bruises that came with those sorts of altercations.

Given how eye-related his power was, I warmed to my suspicion that he might be a good target for Brighteyes. Plus, he was a nasty sort of villain. His criminal record included a number of assassinations and extortion plots, as well as a pile of suspected murders. Suspected over confirmed because anybody he killed just fell dead, cause of death unknown.

If Dusthead was the smuggler/trafficker of the Fourheads, and Hothead and Airhead were the dealers, Deadhead was the enforcer.

However, it was curious to me that he shared leadership with Hothead. Supervillains were hardly generous about that sort of thing and were usually vying for the top spot. Given that Deadhead could kill someone with a look, the fact that he shared leadership with Hothead was interesting.

When someone was interesting to me, I began to look at them more intently. Given the magical aspect of his powers, it made me think I might reach out to Inferna to help me on this one. My rule of thumb with magical villains was it was best to work with another magical type.

The beauty of Inferna was she was always just a word away. Inferna was funny, because, yeah, she was a devil-woman, exiled from wherever it was that they came from (yeah, you'd probably call it "Hell" but I didn't believe in that), for having an incorrigible sense of justice. Sure, maybe rough justice, but Inferna was one of the good guys.

She never had a chance in something as mainstream and brand-conscious as the Affiliates, but I knew her to be a good faith operator out on the margins. Besides, maybe she'd help me find Brighteyes. You're wanting to know her stats, am I right?

ALIAS: INFERNA

REAL/ASSUMED NAME: INFERNA
HAIR: RED WITH HINTS OF FIERY GOLD
EYES: RED
HEIGHT: 6'
WEIGHT: 250 LBS.

POWERS: *INFERNA POSSESSES SUPERHUMAN POWERS, INCLUDING:*

• **ENHANCED SENSES:** *INFRARED VISION.*

• **SOUL SEARCHING:** *ABILITY TO DETECT LIVING BEINGS, EVEN THROUGH SOLID OBJECTS, AT AN UNSPECIFIED RANGE.*

• **MAGIC SENSE:** *ABILITY TO DETECT MAGIC AT AN UNSPECIFIED RANGE.*

• **MIND/EMOTION READING:** *INFERNA CAN READ SUPERFICIAL THOUGHTS AND FEELINGS AT CLOSE RANGE.*

• **FLIGHT:** *INFERNA CAN FLY BY MEANS OF FLAMING BAT WINGS WHICH CAN MANIFEST IF SHE WILLS THEM TO. WHEN SHE FLIES IN THIS MANNER, SHE LEAVES A TRAIL OF HELL-FIRE THAT RESEMBLES THAT OF A METEORITE.*

• **PREHENSILE TAIL:** *INFERNA POSSESSES A PREHENSILE BARBED TAIL WHEN SHE FULLY MANIFESTS, WHICH CAN SUPPORT HER WEIGHT AND BE USED TO GRAB THINGS.*

• **SUPERHUMAN STRENGTH:** *INFERNA IS SUPERHUMANLY STRONG, ABLE TO LIFT TEN TONS.*

- **INVULNERABILITY:** *INFERNA IS IMMUNE TO ANY FIRE DAMAGE, AS WELL AS POISON, AND IS HIGHLY RESISTANT TO COLD AND NORMAL INJURY.*
- **IMMORTALITY:** *INFERNA DOES NOT APPEAR TO AGE, AND CAN REGENERATE ANY INJURY, GIVEN ENOUGH TIME.*
- **TELEPORTATION:** *INFERNA IS CAPABLE OF TELEPORTING IN AND OUT OF THIS DIMENSION AT WILL, AND CAN TRAVERSE THE PLANET THIS WAY, ABLE TO CARRY AT LEAST ONE OTHER PERSON.*
- **HELLFIRE:** *INFERNA CAN PROJECT HELLFIRE FROM HER HANDS, EYES, AND MOUTH, WHICH CAN MELT STEEL, AND WILL BURN INDEFINITELY UNTIL SHE WILLS IT TO EXTINGUISH.*
- **HELLFIRE SWORD:** *INFERNA CAN INSTANTLY CONJURE A FLAMING LONGSWORD WHICH SHE WIELDS WITH EXPERT PROFICIENCY.*
- **HELLFIRE WHIP:** *INFERNA CAN ALSO CONJURE A FLAMING WHIP WHICH SHE WIELDS WITH EXPERT PROFICIENCY.*
- **VULNERABILITIES:** *INFERNA IS VULNERABLE TO SILVER AND HOLY WATER.*

THREAT LEVEL: 9/10

Some of the hero community got triggered by Inferna, but I always got along with her, and vice versa. So, you know, what the hell?

"Inferna," I said aloud.

She appeared in a flash-crack of brimstone, right there in my lair, as I knew she would. Inferna liked making a dramatic entrance, taking a moment to hover there before touching the floor.

"Hey, Mitch," Inferna said, her voice captivatingly sultry, made more so by her red leather trenchcoat she wore, as well as a matching red fedora jauntily placed on her angular face, complementing the horns on her forehead. Literally everything about her was sinister—slit eyes that burned with a fiery yellow light around her red irises, sharp eyebrows, pointy chin, ever-present smirk, fangs, red skin, and her long red-blond hair that burned with its own fiery light. She wore pointy-toed, heeled red knee boots and, beneath the jacket, I could see she wore a black dress.

"Hey, Fern," I said, using a nickname I had for her. "I suppose you already know why I called you, yeah?"

"How could I not?" she said, toning down her manifestation to just a flicker, so all I could really feel was her hellish heat and a hint of the glint about her eyes and hair. "Deadhead is indeed magical, although he's more of a pretender, if you take my meaning. A mere dabbler in the dark arts."

"I need to know where he is," I said.

"Do you?" Inferna asked. "This is for Desdemona, then?"

"Yes," I said, watching Inferna take a seat in one of my chairs, slouching and crossing a leg. I sat across from her, watching her watch me.

She produced two playing cards with an admirable sleight-of-hand, Tarot-sized, with Deadhead on one, and Brighteyes on the other, and set them down on my coffee table, face up, caressing them a moment with her long, black fingernails.

"You think Antigone's hunting Deadhead?" Inferna asked, her voice crackling like a fire in a well-tended fireplace.

"I have my suspicions," I said.

"That's what I like about you, Mitch," Inferna said. "You're *always* so suspicious. It's endearing. Deadhead's in Detroit. He has a lair there. One of three, in fact. Do you want me to draw you a map? I will, you know."

I shook my head, and she smiled at me, showing off her fangs. She had perfect teeth, which only felt more menacing on her, perfectly predatory.

"No, I can handle it," I said.

"Such pride," Inferna said. "Adorable."

"I just need to know you've got my back if Deadhead gets out of hand," I said.

"Ah," Inferna said. "You want protection. I'm happy to provide it, you know that. I can do so much more than the Siren. She'd only be able to wail over your corpse. Me, I'd be there in a flash, to guard your body and your soul."

She snapped her long fingers and treated me to a tiny flash of fire and brimstone.

"I'm always there for those I care about," Inferna said. "Best intentions be damned."

Theatrical, like I said. She took out a little red leather notebook with a gold pen as she took notes.

"'Dramatic' is what you said, Mitch," Inferna said. "But I like 'theatrical' as well. Guilty as charged."

She held out her slender wrists as if I would presume to cuff her, let them dangle there diabolically for a moment, before drawing them back.

"Detroit's a dangerous place for you, Mitch," Inferna said. "You sure you don't want me riding beside you, keeping you safe?"

"I like danger," I said, and she chuckled darkly, pocketing her little notepad.

"Yes, you do," she said. "I'm curious why you haven't asked me to find Brighteyes for you, too."

"No, I've got that," I said. I could only imagine how that might go if Brighteyes and Inferna crossed paths. It would be apocalyptic.

"Oh, please," Inferna said. "She's adorable, too, the way you are, Mitch. Her sin is rage, though; not pride, like yours."

She couldn't help herself. Her world was bound up in that Manichean space, even if she was exiled from it, in her own purgatory.

Inferna's chuckle wound itself up into a caustic, dismissive laugh. Some would view someone like Inferna as a validation for their particular Abrahamic faith, but I refused to think of it that way. What could I say? I thought of myself as multidimensional.

One thing one learned as a superhero was that the world had more dimensions than one knew, and someone like Inferna could simply be from another of those dimensions. I thought all of this knowing that she was reading my mind and finding it hilarious. Was *that* pride?

"You're just so cute, Mitch," Inferna said, reaching out to stroke my cheek. She was so warm to the touch. I'm amazed we'd never slept together, frankly, which prompted her to add, "That *could* be remedied, you know."

"You're far too much for me," I said. "I'm delicate."

More devilish laughter from Inferna.

"You're far stronger than you know, Mitch," Inferna said. "With your own bizarre sort of courage. And your very delicacy is a devilish aphrodisiac, if you must know."

"Is that your soul sight on me?" I asked.

"What soul, Mitch?" she said, laughing, before vanishing in another flash of brimstone, her words a bewitching whisper as she went. "I'll keep an eye out for you in Detroit, Delicacy."

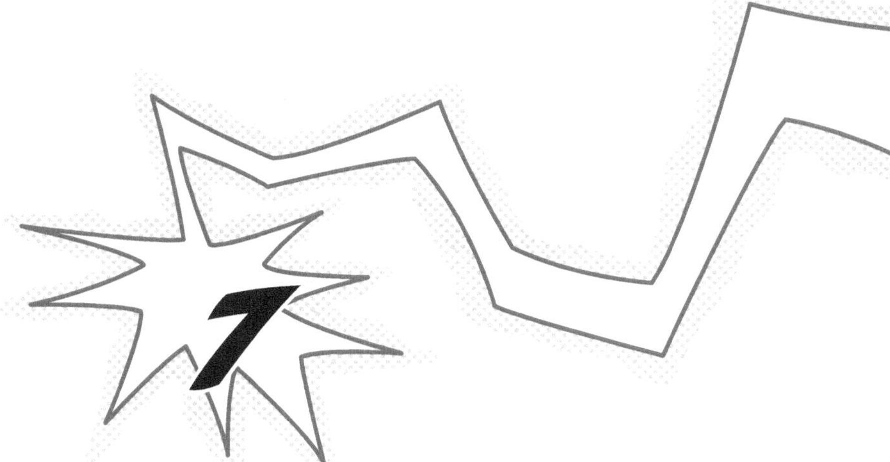

I could start by giving you her dossier. That would be in character for me, would be the most Cameraman sort of thing I could do:

ALIAS: VICTORIANA

REAL/ASSUMED NAME: ANNA VICTOR
HAIR: GREEN
EYES: GREY
HEIGHT: 5'8"
WEIGHT: 150 LBS.

POWERS: VICTORIANA POSSESSED SUPERHUMAN PHYSICAL POWERS, INCLUDING:

• **SUPER-STRENGTH:** VICTORIANA WAS SUPERHUMANLY STRONG, EASILY ABLE TO LIFT APPROXIMATELY ONE THOUSAND TONS.

• **FLIGHT:** VICTORIANA COULD FLY AT WILL, ABLE TO REACH UNKNOWN MAXIMUM SPEEDS, BUT EASILY ABLE TO TRAVEL MACH 10 IN ATMOSPHERES. SHE COULD ALSO FLY IN SPACE.

• **SUPER-SPEED:** VICTORIANA COULD RUN AT SUPER SPEED TO A DEGREE MATCHING HER FLIGHT ABILITY.

• **INVULNERABILITY:** VICTORIANA WAS IMMUNE TO MOST FORMS OF PHYSICAL AND ENERGY DAMAGE, AT LIMITS AS YET UNKNOWN.

• **ENHANCED SENSES:** *VICTORIANA HAD SUPERHUMAN SIGHT, HEARING, TOUCH, TASTE, AND SMELL, THE LIMITS OF WHICH WEREN'T ENTIRELY KNOWN.*

• **LIFE SUPPORT:** *VICTORIANA DIDN'T NEED TO EAT, SLEEP, OR BREATHE, ALTHOUGH SHE WAS CAPABLE OF DOING ALL OF THESE THINGS AT WILL.*

THREAT LEVEL: 10/10

She'd appeared on the superhero scene when I was at least five years into my own Cameraman solo bit, and she'd made a big impression across the community. Her crimefighting skills were extraordinary, and she was a natural fighter.

I'd watched her meteoric rise with interest—she'd duked it out with Doctor Fist in Pittsburgh and sent him into orbit with one of her vaunted uppercuts. She'd beaten Mister Mayhem handily in New York City with a minimal amount of property damage. She'd bested Lord Overlord in Chicago. To watch her work as a study in grace under pressure.

With her stunning green hair and her red and white costume, Victoriana was one of those naturals in the superhero world. The ones you just knew were going to make it big. I was content to admire her from afar, but destiny intervened, quite literally.

Dr. Destiny had been rampaging in Chicago, using one of his trademark technological terrors—in this case, it was his Megacolossus robot, which was storming toward downtown Chicago. The thing looked like a nightmare version of the fabled Colossus of Rhodes—glinting with a golden metal that wasn't bronze, but looked like it. Dr. Destiny was piloting the thing, having it bellow his jeremiads against the folly of man and the necessity of righting the wrongs wrought by mindless ignorance. How he squared his clear love of antiquity with his present-day rampages was one of those things I could never figure out.

However, I'd been there, filming it, trying to find a way into his Megacolossus and putting a stop to him when I saw Victoriana pull up to me, right where I was lurking, hovering near me.

"Pretty impressive, yeah?" she asked.

"I guess if giant bronzed golems are your thing, sure," I said. She chuckled—it was a beautiful chuckle, as stupid as that sounds.

"I'm Victoriana," she said.

"I know," I said. "I'm Cameraman."

"I know," she said, smiling at me. "You're the one taking on the corporations, corrupt politicians, crimelords, and cartels. A penchant for 'C' villainy."

"That's me," I said.

"Guess today we'll have to add 'colossuses' to your portfolio," she said. "Or 'colossi', if that's your jam."

This'll probably make you roll your eyes, but to have someone reference variable plural tenses in casual conversation was catnip to me. I was immediately smitten.

She winked at me, before flying into the Megacolossus with a powerful clang as she struck the giant automaton in the chest and drove it into the lake with a massive splash.

I followed after her, trying to take the shots to capture it in action while getting to the beach. The phrase "poetry in motion" is probably overused, but watching Victoriana work, it's all I could say, as she whizzed around the Megacolossus, each blow she struck making the thing ring like a bell. She wasn't yet in the Affiliates, who didn't even have a Central Division at this point, for some incomprehensible reason.

But that fight with Dr. Destiny got Victoriana into the Affiliates in a heartbeat. She'd been nominated, standing there in front of the ruins of the Megacolossus (where they remain to this day, and have become a tourist attraction, of all things—The Megacolossus of Chicago), with the Knack having turned up out of nowhere, standing beside her, wearing a grey suit, black shirt, and white necktie and shoes. More on him to come. Be patient with me; there's a lot to tell.

I was right there with the adoring reporters, the cameras all on her, but she only had eyes for me as she went through the media motions. I was invisible, but she could see me. That's how super she was.

I'd been home, tending to my footage—back in those days, I would sell my clips to make money as a stringer. I hadn't yet come up with my fashion photographer scheme. That was her idea.

She'd appeared at my apartment door, and I knew it was her—that green hair, her disguise of her black-rimmed glasses and her Suck Junkies tee shirt. I opened the door, and she smiled almost bashfully, wearing grey corduroys with some black Doc Martens.

"Hey, there," she said. "You're you, right?"

Up close, seeing her in her civilian disguise, it was unbelievable.

"I'm very me," I said. "Come on in."

She walked into my place, and I shut the door maybe too quickly, fearful that somebody might see. She held out a hand to me, black-painted nails and silver rings on her fingers.

"I'm Anna Victor," she said. I shook her hand, my own hand shaking, because those were the same hands that had pulverized the Megacolossus earlier in the day.

"Mitch Paulsen," I said.

"I know," she said. "Helluva fight today, right?"

She took a seat on my futon, crossing her leg to reveal some black and white striped socks at her ankle as she made herself comfortable.

"Uh, yeah," I said. "Impressive. You made short work of that thing."

She smiled, brushing aside her bangs. My mind was racing as I was trying to figure out why she was here with someone like me. To say she was out of my league was an insult to leagues.

"Can I see your footage?" she asked, holding up a six pack of Old Milwaukee. "I brought beer."

"Wait," I said, but still taking one of the frosty beer cans and popping it as I sat across from her. "How on earth did you even find me?"

"Mitch, it's easy," she said, cracking her own beer and taking a sip. "You're the most relentless superhero I know. I first saw you when I took down the Edgelord in Wicker Park. And of course, Lord Overlord. Don't even get me started about Vampyro. And I know about your track record with all of those others."

It was incomprehensible for a street-level hero like myself to fathom that a bona fide heavyweight like Victoriana might take interest in my work. This didn't happen to guys like me.

She had this face made for anime—big eyes, sharp chin, up-turned nose. With the glasses, she had this nerd-cute look to her that belied her superhuman power. She was charming, and I was charmed.

"I'm flattered," I said.

"I've been offered membership in the Affiliates by the Knack," she said. "But I told them I wouldn't join unless you joined, too."

"Me?" I asked, almost spitting out my beer. I coughed on the suds as I tried to process that. There was no way I'd ever have been considered for the Affiliates.

"Yeah, you," she said. "You won't believe this, but you were my inspiration for trying on the superhero thing."

"What?" I said.

"The stories of Cameraman, yeah," she said. "Before I realized I was super. You're like an urban legend, Mitch. People talk about you in hushed whispers—criminals think you're maybe a machine, like a terminator or something. Or a secret society. You should hear what they say. But that inspired me to get out there and do it."

"You're just trying to mess with me, yeah? Like this is a super-prank or something?" I said. Anna laughed, and her laugh was super-wonderful, too.

"Nope," she said, drinking more of her beer. "No joke, Mitch."

"Minder's chairman of the Affiliates," I said. "There's no way he'd want someone like me on the team. He's all about the superiority thing—big guns, big biceps."

"Whatever. I think you'd bring something to that team that they needed. That's my super-judgment speaking. Besides, the Knack said he'd sponsor us."

"Who am I to you?" I asked. "I'm a stranger."

"You're Cameraman, and I love Cameraman," she said, eyeing me while drinking her beer. Never mind that she could drink me under the table. "You made me the hero I am today."

"That's crap, and you know it," I said. She crunched the empty beer can in her hand, turned it into this little metal marble, which she placed on the table, dropping it into this dish I had on the table, where it rolled for a bit before finding its center.

"It's the deal I made with them," she said. "Two-for-one deal. I'll join their team, but they have to bring you along, too."

Now, I'd been in my solo superhero thing for years, was well-accustomed to going it alone, with being resourceful. The Affiliates were the golden ticket for any superhero. It marked someone as a hero of note, a definitive A-lister. That a genuine A-lister like Victoriana might have taken a shine to me on any level was beyond anything I might experience.

"I don't know what to say," I said, which was the first time in my life I'd ever said that. I always knew what to say. I'd never had anyone in my corner before.

"Just say 'yes' and join the Affiliates with me," she said, cracking another beer, holding it out for me to clink with my own half-drunk can.

It was one of those moments where I could feel my whole life mapping out based on my answer, and the answer had to be YES.

"Okay, just so you understand," I said. "I hate the Affiliates. They're the antithesis of everything I'm about as a superhero. They're stratospherically snooty in my book. But I think you're the bomb. So, I'd say 'yes' to you, just because it's you making that request of me, not because I think much of the Affiliates."

It's not a contradiction to understand that I hated the Affiliates for who and what they were but was willing to throw in with someone like Victoriana because of who she was. That's the way she had. She was the irresistible force, and her smile broke me.

"Awesome," she said. "Brilliant, Mitch. You made my day just now. I was so thinking you'd blow this off."

I laughed, feeling embarrassed. Even though we'd just met each other properly this evening, I knew I'd do anything for her, would risk anything for her. I'd die for her.

"Never," I said. "You're the real deal."

She drank her beer, rolling her eyes.

"I'm still finding my way," she said. "There's Tandem and Rad Lad, right? You think I measure up to the likes of them?"

"You're better," I said, and she crunched another can into yet another metal marble which she plonked next to its partner in the dish.

"You think so?" she asked, grabbing another beer while I was trying to keep up with my first. I was a slow drinker, what can I say? "I'm a Rust Belt girl, Mitch. I'm from Pittsburgh, you know? How many superheroes do you know from Pittsburgh?"

"Heh," I said. "I'm from Philadelphia, myself."

She laughed, raising her can again so we could clink it. "I guess I should have brought some Iron City Light."

"Nah," I said. "I don't drink light beer."

"Good man," she said. "And duly noted. Next time, I'll bring straight-up Iron City Lager. I only went with Old Milwaukee because I thought you might hail from Wisconsin."

"Why, cuz I'm cheesy?" I asked.

"No," she said. "You felt very, I don't know, Madison to me. Sincere. Earnest. Idealistic."

That made me laugh, and she liked my laughter. I could see it in her eyes.

"You seem to have done some pretty extensive profiling on me," I said. Anna looked me over, smiling.

"I'm super-prudent about my associations," she said. "People I can trust. And, having watched what you'd been doing, I knew you were someone I could trust. I just knew you would be. It's why I risked reaching out. I don't normally do this."

"Yeah?" I asked, trying to appear chill, while sensing that something portentous was being tossed over my proverbial transom. How it could possibly top having Victoriana go to bat for me regarding the Affiliates seemed a feat beyond imagining, but there it was.

"Like I said, the Knack reached out to me about joining the Affiliates," she said. "You know the Knack?"

"Uh, yeah, I do," I said. He and I had worked together a number of times in the course of my solo career. We might even be what might be considered friends, acquaintances, or frenemies, depending on the scenario we might find ourselves in.

"He said something about there being rot within the team, and he needed some outsiders to help him root it out," Anna said.

Here's the thing about the Knack—while I'm convinced he's one of the good guys, the way he goes about being a superhero was always annoying to me. He's obtuse, elliptical, and enigmatic in his heroism. He's like some heroic visionary, seeing beyond the confines of reality and finding the right path to take, but not sharing that path until the time was right.

Despite seeming to be one of the most compassionate and open sort of heroes, he kept a lot back, too. He'd been the deputy chairman of the Affiliates for the past several years, being Minder's number two. The two of them had presided over some of the best years for the Affiliates.

Hearing this assertion by way of Anna that he thought something was wrong with the Affiliates, well, that meant that there was something to it. He wasn't the type to idly speculate. I had to ask the next question, because it mattered to me most:

"Was it really your idea or was it his to have me join you for membership?" I asked. Anna smiled.

"My idea, totally," she said. "I brought it up, and the Knack smiled, said it was a great idea, said something about the time being right for you to join the team."

She flicked the beer can marbles at me, using what could only have been an infinitesimal amount of force, and I watched the metal marbles click as they struck each other and tumbled across the table to me. I hustled to catch them, marveling at the strange feel of them, the uncanny heft, the perfectly compressed smoothness of them, the hints of color within. I set them down with their buddies in the dish.

"You want to be a superhero with me, Mitch?" she asked.

"Yes," I said. "Hell, yes."

"Great," she said. "Then let's go get the bad guys. But first, I have to see this Megacolossus footage you took."

RUMMBLE

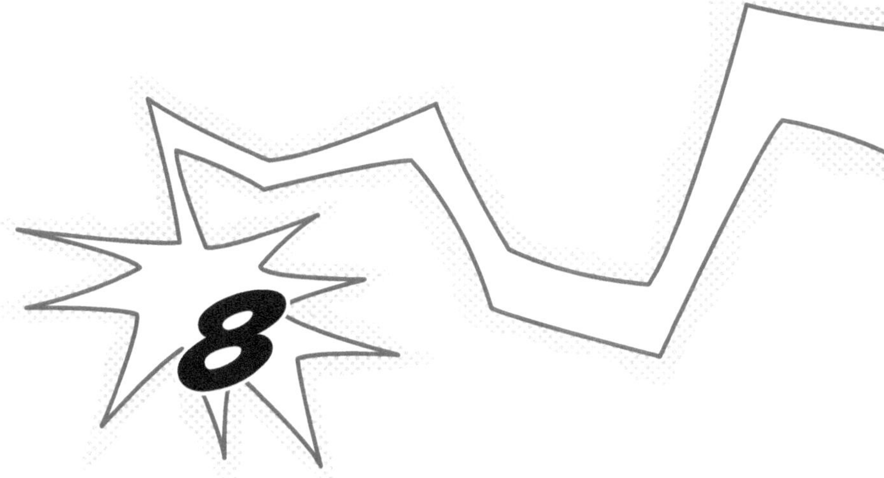

which seemed somehow less conspicuous than what the others called the Mitchmobile. While vans may have passed out of the general population's assessment of permissible transportation, for non-serial killers who worked for a living, vans were just too useful.

Further, my Cameravan was rigged up as a perfect surveillance tool. I had a minifridge in there and a fold-out bunk, as well as a cupboard with snacks, along with a battery of surveillance gear and a place for my suit, as well as recording and duplication equipment. Nobody could accuse me of being one of those forlorn surveillance guys stuffed into a rusty old delivery van.

I had rigged the skin of the Cameravan to allow for adaptive camouflage. The basic look was my trademark grey, but I had five other color and van disguise skins I could apply as needed, which let me blend in.

The plan was to get near Deadhead's hideout and sneak in there as Cameraman, setting up surveillance. My hope was to get a sense of what the Fourheads might be up to, and also to keep an eye out for Antigone, should she appear. I would hold to Decibelle's preference that I not involve myself, although I wasn't sure what I might do if she did show up.

Superheroes rolled a variety of ways in terms of their motivations. These motivations included:

- *PURSUIT OF JUSTICE*
- *UPHOLDING THE GOOD*
- *RESPONSIBILITY OF POWER*
- *THRILLSEEKING*
- *UNDESIRED POWER/CURSED*

Different heroes did what they did for various reasons. Somebody like Tandem or Wingman was very much in that Upholding the Good space. Whereas Brighteyes would be more of the Pursuit of Justice type.

What was I? I think Responsibility of Power motivated me, even though I didn't have any powers, and largely used my skills to hold the powerful accountable, maybe with a pursuit of justice chaser. Yeah, that seemed right. Rollergirl was a Thrillseeker if ever there was one, while Inferna, hell, I don't know—maybe she was only heroic because she was cursed to be stuck in our world. Maybe it was unfair to think that way, since I was hoping she'd save my bacon if I got into a jam with Deadhead. Victoriana was all about Upholding the Good, and she was good at it.

I wonder if you're judging me that I asked Inferna where Deadhead was hiding out. Was that lazy of me? Should I have spent months sleuthing out where he might be, versus, you know, checking with my diabolical friendo and asking her to tell me where he was? I had enough on my plate, and what good were magical friends if you couldn't ask them to help you out from time to time? My logic was that since Deadhead was magical, Inferna was a subject matter expert on matters magical, and was the person to ask.

I'm still the one road-tripping to Detroit, and you do recall that she offered to go with me and I turned her down, yeah? I didn't want to bother her, and, yes, I suppose I can admit that my pride wouldn't let me owe her another debt for coming with me, even though there was an implicit debt if I needed to call for her to rescue me.

Enough brooding, though. I'd just slip in quietly as death and bug Deadhead's place. The Fourheads were curious as a villain group, because while they looked out for each other, they also gave each other a lot of latitude. In that way, they were different from the Crime League, which was more like a conventionally hierarchical criminal organization, with everything radiating out from Dr. Crime, Crimebot, and Instigator at the top. The Fourheads were more like four independent operations that had connections with each other. Like a confederacy, or an alliance.

What that meant in practical terms was that Deadhead had his own operation here in Detroit. The Affiliates dossier on Deadhead had his lieutenant as Major Damage, a former SAS guy who was more cyborg than human—whether it was part of a government program or something independent wasn't clear in the file. Deadhead's team was around two hundred strong, split between his three lairs, with a variable presence at any one lair.

In practical terms, that meant maybe seventy goons at his Detroit hideout. It depended on how much of a presence Major Damage wanted to have around if the boss was there.

ALIAS: MAJOR DAMAGE

REAL/ASSUMED NAME: MAJOR WILHELM DE SOTO
HAIR: BLOND
EYES: BLUE
HEIGHT: 6'3"
WEIGHT: 550 LBS.

POWERS: *MAJOR DAMAGE POSSESSES CYBERNETIC AUGMENTATIONS, INCLUDING:*

• **SUPER-STRENGTH:** *MAJOR DAMAGE CAN LIFT APPROXIMATELY THREE TONS.*

• **POWER FIST:** *MAJOR DAMAGE CAN PUNCH THROUGH PLATE STEEL.*

• **ENHANCED RESISTANCE:** *HIS CYBERNETIC FRAME MAKES MAJOR DAMAGE RESISTANT TO CONVENTIONAL FIREARMS.*

· SUPER SPEED: *MAJOR DAMAGE CAN RUN AT INCREASED SPEED, ON THE ORDER OF SIXTY MILES PER HOUR FROM STANDING TO A SPRINT.*

· ENHANCED SENSES: *MAJOR DAMAGE'S CYBERNETIC AUGMENTATION GIVES HIM INFRARED VISION, ENHANCED HEARING, AS WELL AS A COMBAT-ENHANCED RADAR.*

THREAT LEVEL: 6/10

Major Damage was pretty tough on his own merits. The fact that he was Deadhead's lieutenant meant either he was terrified of Deadhead or was exceptionally loyal to him. Maybe a little of both. His enhanced senses meant that I would have to be incredibly careful at the lair, and that he could break me in half if he caught me.

It also made me wonder what Brighteyes might be thinking if she'd taken on Dusthead. His operation was leaner than Deadhead's, likely owing to Dusthead's eccentric greed. The man was an obsessive collector of antiquities, and his archaeological background baked in an academic degree of fussiness. However, that same fussiness likely meant he was very careful about his security arrangements. Still, I would think if she'd gotten into trouble, Decibelle would've found her.

Parking my van and using the phone utilities skin to make it appear as boringly unassuming as I could, I put on my Cameraman suit. It had been a few weeks since I'd last worn it, but I always relished that moment. My Cameraman rig erred on the side of directness:

Cameraman suit with powerpack (offering a dozen hours of invisibility).

Utility vest, including: body armor, lockpicks, alarm system bypasses, stun baton, two flash grenades, two rollerdrones (aka, "Tossers"), a dozen microbugs and minicams.

Stun gun (belt), zip ties, combat knife (right leg scabbard), steel toe boots.

I flicked on the adaptive camouflage, which was a little less energy-intensive than the full invisibility. Outside, the city air was chilly, and everything was dark. Deadhead had commandeered an abandoned police station (okay, he purchased it through a front), and for all intents and purposes, it looked derelict.

Except I had seen a pair of cars behind the rusty fencing that surrounded it, and there looked to be two men in each of them. My optiscan visor identified them as their faces became visible under lowlight—they were paramilitary guys picked up by Major Damage somewhere. They appeared to be former French Foreign Legion by the look of their files that flitted across my HUD.

I decided to shift to full invisibility, since I didn't want to bet on these guys not being observant enough to spot a wraith passing between them and opening fire on said specter. I moved quietly, and they were none the wiser.

One of my secrets as Cameraman was that I really was an invisible man, and invisibility was intoxicating. For as strenuously as people fought to be seen in this world, I relished *not* being seen. I carefully placed a minicam at the entrance, figuring I could at least see who came and went here. If anybody did, a little thumbnail window would appear on my HUD, alerting me to their passing my minicam.

Then I opened the door and slipped in. Opening doors was the bane of my existence, which is why I worked hard to develop my lockpicking skills. I could certainly have waited until a goon opened the door, but I felt it was better to get in there and case the place, finding the right places to bug.

The police station's interior was not as decrepit as its exterior—Deadhead had been busy here, with some panels to block the interior lighting, and a hallway checkpoint. There were four goons here, who had heard the door open, although the baffles had obscured their direct view.

"Hello?" one of them asked, walking up. He was carrying an HK submachine gun. His partner looked around. The two of them were young and fit—late 20s, early 30s.

"What was it?" the deskman asked.

"The door opened," the triggerman replied. His partner looked around.

"I don't see anything," the partner said.

In situations like this, I always found it best not to linger, so I quietly moved past them. My combat boots had rubber soles and were thus quieter than hard-soled boots.

Past the checkpoint, there was a main hallway where offices had been turned into barracks. Down the corridor was another set of doors. These were grey double doors, and there was no way I was going to get through them without drawing attention from the checkpoint goons.

I quietly put another of my minicam bugs underneath the hallway fire extinguisher. My minicams offered a fisheye POV and could pick up sound within twenty feet. They would activate when anything moved within their optical range, and would stop transmitting once something passed outside of their range.

If Deadhead had someone do a bug sweep, they'd find them pretty easily. However, I had to make do with what I had.

And then, to my bemusement, Deadhead appeared. He came right through the double doors I'd been casing. Seeing the man in person was something else—he was powerfully built, like a boxer or a wrestler, with barbed wire tattoos winding across his chest in ribbons of inky black. He wore a black silk robe with red trim and red slippers. His skull face wasn't a mask, apparently, but was an actual skull, which was both creepy and weird. I was recording all this, as my visor had a POV cam link.

"What's going on?" Deadhead asked. His voice was low, almost easygoing.

"Nothing, Boss," one of the goons said. "Door opened. We didn't see anybody."

"Yeah, well, that doesn't mean that nobody's here, does it?" Deadhead asked. I detected a hint of a drawl, like southern California by way of Nevada, maybe. "Let me see the monitors."

I watched this going on, content to quietly observe, since the doors provided a momentary impasse. Deadhead scanned the screens, his supernatural visage adding a magnificent intensity to his glowing glower.

"Looks like nothing," Deadhead said, as the doors opened again, revealing Major Damage, who was wearing a black track suit with white piping. I wondered if the Fourheads had their own branded clothing line. I could imagine them doing that.

"What's doing, Boss?" Damage asked, clearly chagrined that he was playing catch-up with his superior.

"An intruder, I think," Deadhead said. "Somebody I can't see."

Damage frowned, looked around them uneasily.

"You think it's What's-His-Name? That Cameraman perv?" Damage asked. I had to shelve my irritation. Maybe he was trying to get a rise out of me. Was that how the criminal element saw me? A perv? WTF? I took no pervy delight in my villain voyeurism—if anything, it was pretty awful, and the only true satisfaction I experienced was getting them busted.

"You tell me, Will," Deadhead said, straightening up. "After what happened to Dusty, I'm not taking *any* chances."

Damage joined Deadhead at the guard station, while the goon worked the camera playback. Deadhead cleared his throat. I did like watching the villains communicate with each other when they didn't think anyone was observing them. You could get a sense of their personalities, their group dynamics, and so on. Many was a case where I gleaned useful evidence just from their chit-chatting and put it to use in other ways.

"Cameraman, if you're here, you're dead, man," Deadhead said, looking around as he spoke. "Not that you'd have *any* reason to be around here. I didn't have anything to do with what happened with, you know, Brighteyes."

He moved from the station to the corridor, looking around with his glowing eyes. I wondered how that worked, exactly. Like could he throw his death gaze out willy-nilly, and would it kill me? Did he have to meet my gaze for it to work? Or could he simply toss it about and have it do its deadly thing? This was why I hated dealing with magical people—magic could be anything, even as it followed its own strange rules.

Major Damage touched his temple, and I could see his eyes—his cybereyes—switch modes. I ducked into one of the open doorways that led to the barracks while he scanned, using feeds to my minicams to do my remote seeing for me.

"Nobody in the hall but us, Boss," Damage said.

"Check room by room, Will," Deadhead said. "If somebody's spying on us, I want to know it."

"You've got it," Damage said.

As Cameraman, I had to be exceptionally stealthy. I practiced it, the whole art of moving quietly. When Deadhead strode down the hallway, I darted out and followed in his wake, hoping that Damage wasn't looking after his boss, but counting on that even if he was, I might blend in with Deadhead's heat signature as he passed.

Deadhead took out a remote and opened the double doors, went in, and I followed right behind him, like a ghost on his tail.

The inner sanctum of his lair wasn't some opulent man cave; rather, it was a well-apportioned flophouse, which included a bedroom, a rec room with a bunch of television sets on the wall, and a bar and kitchenette. I'd seen fancier villain lairs in the past. This was simply created to keep Deadhead reasonably comfortable as he cooled his heels. Inwardly, I wondered who he paid to have this place outfitted this way out here in Detroit? Did the Fourheads or Crime League have interior decorators on call? Another something I'd have to look into one of these days.

In his bed was Felonia Minx, a Crime League supervillainess who had catlike powers, which was an actual problem. I froze as soon as I'd come into the room, hoping that the electronic nature of my suit didn't stand out to her feline senses. Felonia had always been a back bencher among the Crime League, but it didn't mean she was a slouch, particularly at my level.

ALIAS: FELONIA

REAL/ASSUMED NAME: FELONIA MINX
HAIR: BLACK
EYES: YELLOW
HEIGHT: 5'3"
WEIGHT: 150 LBS.

POWERS: *FELONIA POSSESSES SUPERHUMAN POWERS, INCLUDING:*

· SUPER-STRENGTH: *FELONIA CAN LIFT APPROXIMATELY ONE TON.*

• **SUPERHUMAN REFLEXES:** *FELONIA'S CATLIKE REFLEX-ES ARE TEN TO FIFTEEN TIMES FASTER THAN A NORMAL HUMAN'S.*

• **CLAWS:** *FELONIA HAS RETRACTABLE CLAWS THAT CAN REND STEEL AND CONCRETE.*

• **LEAPING:** *FELONIA IS CAPABLE OF LEAPING TEN FEET VER-TICALLY AND TWENTY-FIVE FEET ON A SINGLE BOUND.*

• **ENHANCED SENSES:** *FELONIA'S HYBRID CATLIKE BODY HAS SUPERIOR NIGHT VISION (FIVE TIMES BETTER THAN A NORMAL HUMAN'S IN THE DARK), EXCEPTIONAL HEARING (THREE TIMES BETTER THAN A NORMAL HUMAN'S, ESPECIALLY AT HIGHER FREQUENCIES), AND SENSE OF SMELL (FOURTEEN TIMES BETTER THAN A NORMAL HUMAN'S).*

THREAT LEVEL: 7.5/10

"What's going on?" Felonia asked, her voice—yes—purring as she spoke. Thankfully, she was intent on holding Deadhead's gaze, as he sat next to her in the bed.

"Nothing," Deadhead said. "Or not. Might be we have a visitor."

"Do you want me to hunt them out for you?" she asked, tracing a pattern on his broad back with an outstretched finger claw. Tattooed black roses danced on the muscles of his back while he moved. Deadhead brightened at the prospect, and I quietly placed one of my microbugs and minicams underneath the coffee table adjacent to the kitchenette space.

"Would you be a dear? I sure would appreciate that, Kitty," Deadhead said, and Felonia hopped nimbly out of the bed, naked except for her black-furred frame. I was kicking myself that I went here in-person before reconning the lair fully. I underestimated Deadhead, clearly. Ordinarily, I would just observe awhile before risking entry, but I got a little cocky, and very hasty.

Seeing Felonia crouched in the other room, ears pricked while Deadhead poured himself a drink and looked on, amused, his red eyes glowing.

I was afraid to breathe, seeing those triangular ears of hers moving like radar dishes, her big yellow eyes scanning the room.

"I think we are not alone," Felonia said, sniffing the air. She took a step out of the bedroom, and then another. Every muscle moved and flexed within her furry body. I was in more than a bit of trouble here, as Deadhead had fortified this abandoned station. Victoriana would have blasted through the walls and beaten them in moments, but she wasn't here. It had been so much easier before. This was a mistake on my part.

"That a fact?" Deadhead said, leaning forward with his drink, his eyes luminous. Was this how it was going to end for me? Murdered by Deadhead, or torn apart by Felonia?

"Oh, yes," Felonia said, stepping again, and again. She was now in the living room space I occupied. "Do you hear me, Mouse? Yes, you do. I *know* you do. Is that your heartbeat I hear? Your breathing?"

Her ears were fixed on me, and yet I didn't dare move. It's hard to keep still. I worked at it as one of my surveillance skills, but it's just not an easy thing to do. Tactically, I wanted to throw a flash grenade and fire my stun pistol. The question was whether I'd be quick enough to do that before Felonia tore me to bits.

"You hear her, Cameraman? I know it's you, Creep," Deadhead said, downing his drink and standing up. "What are you even doing here?"

Felonia was now in the room, her ears reflexively seeking to isolate where I was. I could see she'd extended her claws, too—they were these fantastic death-crescents that would make short work of me if she caught me.

It wasn't the first time somebody had sniffed me out like that. The key was to keep your cool and not become rattled.

"Are the Affiliates onto me? Is that it?" Deadhead said, entering the living room. Reading the body language of Felonia, I could see that his piping up was hampering her ability to isolate my position, but she wasn't going to reprimand him.

"Right there," Felonia said, pointing at the space I occupied. She sniffed the air, bared her fangs, while Deadhead unleashed his death gaze in my direction, while I averted my eyes, for lack of a better option.

What was it like being on the receiving end of his death gaze? It was ghastly. I could feel this tombstone chill pass through me as his death gaze cut through time and space, knifed through my body. The chill was breathtaking, and I honestly don't know what would have happened if I'd met his gaze, but all I knew was that I wasn't dead. Not yet at least.

A moment later, with the telltale back-and-forth pre-jump twitch of her legs, Felonia was leaping at me, clawed hands outstretched, and I dropped to a crouch that fortunately had her passing right over me, landing softly on the floor beyond the sofa. As relieved as I was to have evaded that first leap, I was now between the two of them.

There was no point in pretending otherwise—I'd been made. I drew my stun gun, which fired a blinding beam of light that would temporarily induce a trance in an onlooker. Full confession: I was inspired to develop a stun gun from the otherwise forgettably prescient and campy Michael Crichton movie, LOOKER (1981)—who said being a film buff didn't pay off? A light-based stun gun suited my milieu, so there it was.

I caught Felonia full-on with it, her dilated cat's eyes going wide as she was hit by it, crouched there in a trance, completely catatonic. Ouch, yeah, pun. I should probably mention that puns—good or bad—were inherent with anyone in the super-business. They were more prevalent in some areas than others. For example, any aquatic or time-based superhero or villain was *very* likely to pun. So was I. Whether it was a perk or an occupational hazard of the profession depended on you.

"There you are, Creepo," Deadhead said, rushing for me, although I wasn't yet visible. He only had seen me stun Felonia. The stun from the gun lasted for a number of minutes, and my HUD counted it down in one of the corners, as I was trying to flee Deadhead, who was dividing his attention between me and Felonia, who was unresponsive to him. I fired another blast of the stun gun at him, which he'd managed to block with a beefy forearm.

I wasn't sure how much commotion we were making, but if Major Damage turned up with some of the on-tap goons, I was finished.

"Perv, I'm going to kill you," Deadhead said, and I could feel the chill pass through me as yet again he winged me with his death gaze. I tossed a flash grenade over my shoulder, which was a kind of blinding strobe that almost always worked to disorient opponents.

I know what you're probably thinking—a Glock would have been more utilitarian, but when you were a superhero like I was, there was a kind of obligation to maintain the brand. Yes, that meant having a variety of light-based weapons, since those worked idiomatically with being Cameraman. Optics was everything in this line of work.

"You bastard," Deadhead said, grappling the flash grenade and crushing it in his superhuman hands, extinguishing the blinding light. "You're dead."

I needed to get out of there immediately, and I could see Felonia blinking away the stun gun's effects. Being superpowerless required me to be quick on my feet, despite the idiocy of waltzing into this lair this way. I bolted for the double doors just as Major Damage and his men came storming in, having heard the commotion of the initial confrontation.

Even though Damage had his thermographic eyes blazing, he wasn't ready for the stun gun I fired in their faces, which had them all pitching forward like a bunch of bowling pins, stunned into quiescence as I vaulted over them, Deadhead and a groggy Felonia on my tail.

Another of my strobe lights over my shoulder, and if nothing else, they'd have stars in their eyes for an hour as I sprinted past the security station, around the baffle, and through the door that had caused me all the trouble to begin with.

What mattered was that I was outside, and though Deadhead and Felonia were after me, it was harder to isolate me outdoors. However, Felonia was plenty pissed that I'd gotten the drop on her at all and was sprinting after me in this four-legged catwoman way that was eating the distance between us, like she was some malevolent panther princess. Invisibility or not, I knew she'd catch me quickly if I didn't do something.

Ergo, I did what any unpowered superhero with any sense does—I called for help, pride be damned.

"Inferna," I said, and as she'd promised (itself ironic, I know), she appeared in a fiery flash of brimstone, conjuring up a C-shaped wall of hellfire that stopped Felonia in her tracks with a yowling hiss, while Deadhead caught up to her.

"Poor Cameraman," Inferna said, courteously remembering to use my alias in mixed company. "Always getting yourself into trouble."

Deadhead tried his death gaze on her, which only had her laughing, as she raised a hand and made the firewall turn from a "C" into an "O" that surrounded them.

I caught my breath and paused, while Inferna touched the ground, folding her fiery bat wings around herself. Some people claimed to have guardian angels watching over them; me, I had a guardian devil.

"Inferna," Deadhead called over the cackling roar of the hellfire. "What are you doing hanging with that loser? You belong with us."

I disabled my cloaking, standing near Inferna, who only chuckled.

"I'm way out of your league, Deadhead," Inferna said, slowly closing her hand, making the hellfire close in on them. They looked on nervously, straining to avoid the hellfire.

"My van's about a block over," I said to Inferna. Felonia leaped up and over the hellfire, landing in front of her. She glared at us, clawed hands out in front.

"Bad kitty," Inferna said. "Don't do anything you might regret. How many lives have you left to give?"

Felonia's eyes darted from Inferna to me, back to Inferna again. I could see her considering her choices, whether her cat-like prowess might allow her to reach me before Inferna could stop her.

When more of Deadhead's goons emerged from the hideout, Inferna flexed again and the hellfire prison became a grander wall that cut off the goons and Deadhead from us. Felonia whipped her head around to watch the hellfire do its deadly dance.

"This isn't over, Cameraman," Felonia said, jabbing a finger at me. I tried to think up something cleverly superheroic to say.

"Whatever," I said. *Good one.*

Inferna grabbed me and unfurled her wings, and flew me to my van, which I hadn't necessarily wanted her to do, since it made me feel like a human chew toy, and I hated heights, which was to say that I was afraid of them.

"And you so are," she said, smiling at me through gritted fangs. "This just felt more efficient than trudging a block or two to your spy van."

We landed and I'd keyed us into the van, Inferna sheathing herself in her trademark red leather overcoat, riding shotgun with me. You're wondering how I ended up with having a devil-woman as a friend, aren't you? That's a story for another day. But was I ever grateful for Inferna in those moments in Detroit.

"I *knew* you'd call to me, Mitch," Inferna. "I *knew* you'd need my help."

I got the van rolling, and, once we were underway, Inferna snapped her long fingers.

"Dispelling the hellfire. Don't want to bring back Devil's Night just yet," she said. "Whatever were you thinking, throwing yourself at Deadhead's lair that way?"

The sting of having barely escaped with my life, and only with Inferna's assistance, stuck with me. I tried to salvage what I could of my pride, and the mournful memories I had of Victoriana, threatening to drown me.

"At least I got a few bugs in there," I said.

"You're welcome," Inferna said.

"Thanks for saving my ass back there," I said. She gave me a sidelong look as I drove, her devilish smile betraying nothing.

"You have a nice ass, what can I say?" Inferna said. "What next?"

My bugs were designed to be able to broadcast over great distances, so I figured I'd get to Palmer Woods and lay low while monitoring Deadhead's hideout. Inferna read my mind.

"I'm staying with you for now," Inferna said. "God knows you need my help."

She smirked at me, clearly savoring her wordplay the way she did. I couldn't even pretend that I didn't need her help. Having an on-call devil woman on your side was simply too useful to pass up.

"Yes," Inferna said. "I love when you get all transactional on me, Mitch."

"Hey, I owe you big time," I said.

"If only you *could* repay me," Inferna said, sounding mock-sad. She traced an imaginary lone tear down her cheek with one of her black fingernail claws, which were both supremely stylish and fashionably fearsome.

I parked the van and toggled the camouflage, opting for the sleeker grey and black skin, which would play better in posh Palmer Woods. Then I went into the back and turned on some screens that were synched up to my bugs, while Inferna joined me in the back. The way the Cameravan was set up, there was a screen that blocked off the front from the back, so even if the tinted windows weren't enough, the screen ensured we could operate without detection. I took off my helmet and breathed a sigh of relief.

My bug rigs were set to auto-transmit once I'd placed them, so there were three going at once, from the ones I'd placed. I caught them in mid-conversation.

"—that asshole, Cameraman," Deadhead said. "What's HE doing here?"

"Don't worry about him, Baby," Felonia said. "He's not even with the Affiliates, anymore. He's nothing."

"It's *not* nothing," Deadhead said. "They're coming for us. Ever since Dusty, something's off, I swear."

"Cameraman's independent, now," Major Damage said, echoing what Felonia had said.

"Inferna's definitely not with them," Felonia said. "They'd never take her."

Inferna glanced at me, smiling wickedly.

"That's true," Inferna said. "This is kind of fun, eavesdropping like this."

"We're shipping out by midday," Deadhead said. "As far as I'm concerned, this place is compromised. If that creep was here, others will be. You can bet on it."

It irked me that I was viewed as a creep. Sure, yeah, I snuck around and bugged places and people. I spied on them. But did that really make me a creep? Truly? I only went after bad guys. I tried not to take it personally.

"You're *not* a creep," Inferna said, patting my shoulder. "I've known far, far worse."

I could only imagine who she might be comparing me to.

"You're overreacting," Felonia said. "The League has you covered, Baby. We have friends in *very* high places."

Like the racketeers they were, the Crime League looked out for its friends and allies. The collaboration between the Fourheads and the Crime League was probably Affiliates-newsworthy, but then again, where were they? Nowhere to be seen. That's the thing about those A-list superhero teams—their interventions were always so calculated. Maybe this was beneath their notice. Whereas, from my street perspective, an alliance between those groups was a big deal.

"So, now what, Mitch?" Inferna asked. "We just sit around, eavesdropping on Deadhead and Felonia?"

"Pretty much," I said.

"For how long?" she asked.

That was a good question. The problem with a surveillance operation was it could drag on if it was too open-ended. I'd gambled on Brighteyes possibly targeting Deadhead next, and maybe I'd bet wrong. I didn't usually jump in quite this way, would normally do surveillance when I was pretty positive I knew something was up. This was more of a fishing expedition, and sometimes fishing didn't pay off.

"Your self-doubt is delightful, Mitch," Inferna said, studying me, resting her chin on her hand, her luminous eyes seeing right through me. "It's so human."

"You know, it's not fair, you assessing me with your soul searching, or whatever it is," Mitch said.

"Oh, I know," Inferna said. "Delicious, isn't it?"

There was no reasoning with a devil, not truly. Especially one who could seemingly read my mind. I'd have to update my dossier on her to include telepathy.

"It's not truly telepathy," Inferna said, reading my mind. "It's mostly just seeing what you've got going on inside you. Pride and grief aplenty. Mourning. You are so very wounded, Mitch. *She* haunts you still."

"Stop!" I said. This was my life—debating supernatural semantics with a devil-woman in a surveillance van in Detroit, monitoring a man with a skull head and his catwoman criminal concubine while mourning my super-girlfriend. FML.

"You love it and you know it," Inferna said. And she was right. I loved it even more than I loved complaining, and I *loved* complaining. I turned my attention back to Deadhead and Felonia.

"I'm going to call Hothead," Deadhead said, dialing up his peer. "Miles? It's me. Hey, what's going on over near you? That douchebag, Cameraman, was spying on me over here. What? Yeah, no idea. Inferna showed up to save his ass. I know. Totally. I told her that."

It was so hard to earn respect in this business when you didn't have powers. And I know you're thinking that it's my fault for venturing out as a superhero if I wasn't superpowered. But it was the principle of it. Being a superhero was a state of mind.

Inferna chuckled at that.

"Mitch, you handle things down here," she said. "I'll go find Hothead and Airhead, see what I can discover."

She vanished in a puff of brimstone, which was kind of a nightmare in the confines of my Cameravan. I flicked the ventilation while coughing and attempting to overhear Deadhead's conversation over my own coughing.

"I'm not sure," Deadhead said. "With Dusty MIA, I don't know. How'd he find me? It's not like this is, yeah, I *know* he's a detective, but give me a break. He had help. A tosser like him doesn't just...exactly. Yeah. So, you and Airy haven't seen anything? Huh. I'm thinking I should bolt. No. If he was here, he probably bugged the place. I shouldn't even be talking to you, but Damage hasn't found anything. You know how that guy is. Have you heard from Dusty? Anything?"

If Brighteyes aced Dusthead, she was circumspect about it. Which only made sense, since that would bring down heat on her from both the Affiliates and the Fourheads/Crime League.

"No," Deadhead said. If I'd had more time, I would have bugged the place properly, believe me. You saw how crazy it got, how quickly. "There's no way I'm staying here, even if we don't find anything. Dusty's gone, man. Whatever that means, he's gone. It's not like him to just go silent. They've probably got him in the Brig or something."

The Brig was a special offshore Affiliates prison. It was literally a nuclear prison ship that stayed in international waters when it wasn't busy sailing around the world. Any supervillain who ended up in the Brig was basically stuck there for life. The only reason supervillains knew about the Brig was because Kaptain Krazy infamously engineered an escape from it years ago, and told anybody who'd listen about what he'd experienced there.

You may have noticed a propensity for heroes and villains to adopt titular names like that. I guess they feel like it gives them more authority. Off the top of my head:

VILLAINS

- **DR. CRIME:** *CRIMINAL MASTERMIND.*

- **DOCTOR FIST:** *SUPER-STRONG CRIMINAL MASTER-MIND.*

• **MAJOR DAMAGE:** *ALREADY TALKED ABOUT HIM.*

• **MAJOR PROBLEMS:** *SOME KIND OF JINX POWER, LIKE BAD LUCK.*

• **KAPTAIN KRAZY:** *NO POWERS (!) BUT THE SELF-PROCLAIMED MADMAN MASTERMIND.*

• **CAPTAIN CHAOS:** *AGENT OF CHAOS, MAGICAL CHAOS POWERS.*

HEROES

• **GENERAL PRINCIPLES:** *MORALY UPRIGHT SUPER SOLDIER.*

• **THE ATOMIC ADMIRAL:** *IRRADIATED SEMI-AQUATIC GUY.*

• **CAPTAIN FANTASTIC:** *LITERALLY GOOD AT EVERYTHING.*

• **LIEUTENANT LOVEJOY:** *A PROJECTIVE EMPATH, POSSIBLY AN ALIEN; SHE'S WEIRD.*

• **CORPORAL PUNISHMENT:** *HARDASS DISCIPLINARIAN, NO POWERS, WORKED AT THE BRIG.*

Everybody knew that Dr. Crime had a PhD in Criminology before turning to a life of crime. But all of those others? Sure, Doctor Fist had perfected a serum that had turned him into a super-strong bruiser who could duke it out with Tandem and Victoriana, but his name (and logo) always made me roll my eyes.

What were they trying to prove with their lofty names? While some of them had served in the Armed Forces, most hadn't. Next to alliteration, the titular naming was one of those things that annoyed me most about supers. Like if you actually had a power, why even throw a name like that out there?

Fighting with Inferna on my side brought back memories of Victoriana, even though they were way different, as people, as heroes.

Victoriana and I worked as partners for two years before we were finally cleared to join the Affiliates. The background checks and bureaucratic procedures were *that* rigorous, and it only made sense, given the highly demanding and rigorous work the Affiliates did, which touched on all areas of law enforcement, intelligence, and the military. While officially based in the United States, the Affiliates had special United Nations clearance to work around the world, wherever and whenever they were needed.

I was nervous about joining, but Anna persuaded me to stick with it. She and I started going out, too. We just had a thing—chemistry, right? We got along with one another, we valued each other. It was our secret, our alter ego romance. Nobody knew that Victoriana and Cameraman were dating. Oh, I'm sure the Knack knew, but if he did, he didn't breathe a word of it to anyone.

Joining the team was wild. I knew supers—legit supers, like people with powers—who had worked their whole lives to get on that team, and there I was, getting brought on with my own Affiliates ID and security clearance, based on my track record of cases and assists I'd done, but more because of Victoriana's power play.

While we waited for clearance, at the suggestion of the Knack and Victoriana, the team broke ground on Affiliates Central and South, to work around the perceived coastal bias of the team.

The two new branches were to give the Affiliates quick-and-easy reach in those overlooked regions. Each branch would have a heavyweight on-site: Rad Lad in Affiliates West. Tandem in Affiliates East. Victoriana in Affiliates Central. Decibelle and Brighteyes in Affiliates South—the reasoning being that the two of them were more than tough enough to qualify as heavyweights.

And it just so happened that Victoriana and Cameraman were based in Central, which kept us busy battling midwestern menaces throughout the region. People like the Thresher, the Blue Tornado, Floodgate, Windbreaker (I know, right?), the Tallboy, Dr. Darkness, and the Bruticians.

She and I would get plenty of coverage across the Midwest, as Victoriana had a flair for high-visibility, flashy battles, and

I have to confess that I'd film her exploits with the fantastic filmography for which Cameraman was well known, which I'd sell at a premium to news outlets.

Don't think I was slumming it, either; where I could, I'd do the detective legwork and sleuth out the baddies. And when things trended into the more forceful and physical realms, Victoriana would always bring it and bash the baddies. We'd eat pizza or takeout and watch the coverage, laughing about it. Anna was great about minimizing collateral damage in her fights, which was always a concern for her.

"It's not that I *can't* do detective work," Anna said, between slices. "Because I can. But not like you do. You're the right kind of obsessive to sink your teeth into these cases. Whereas I'm tailor-made for fisticuffs."

"What can I say?" I said. "I'm all about detective work."

The footage was the big fight in Omaha against Mister Sandbagger, who was this bizarre man who was half-scarecrow, half burlap-bagged monstrosity, who (we discovered in the course of our fight), had invoked an enchantment that we were only able to dispel with the assistance of Inferna. There were a ton of curses in the super-business.

One night, laying in bed, Anna asked me about Inferna, while we stared at the ceiling, watching the night light play on the ceiling. I was exhausted; she was relaxed.

"What's the deal with you and her, anyway?" Anna asked.

"I helped her a few years ago," I said. "Got her out of an unholy mess with Sergeant Sorcery. She's still working down what she considers her debt to me."

Sergeant Sorcery was this crazed wizard who I actually kind of liked, just because he was so nutty. He wore this white baglike mask with jet black eyeholes and he had a white cape, with a black costume. His logo was a white circle smiley with Xs for eyes and a flat expression bisected with a row of lines. He was a master of what he called "practical magic"—which amounted to these very direct sorts of spells: fireballs, lightning bolts, ice storms, and so on.

Any fight with Sergeant Sorcery was going to be a prime-time news event, guaranteed. I dined out on that fight with him for years and having saved Inferna during that battle (Sergeant Sorcery had held Inferna captive using some arcane chains), earned me a friend for life. Or at least as long as I would live as a superhero.

Anna laughed, reaching over to play with the beaded necklace I wore around my neck.

"Were you two, you know, an item?" she asked.

"We had our moments early on," I said. "But Inferna's not like that, believe it or not. She views us all very differently, like in a way that might not make sense from a mortal, human perspective. She's always there to help me out in a pinch."

"I'd like to meet her someday," she said. "Just feel her out a little."

"She'd probably enjoy that," I said, which earned me the gentlest of flicks of my nose. When Anna and I made love, I was always acutely aware that she could kill me so easily if she'd wanted to. You want to talk about trust in relationships? Having a superheroine girlfriend requires immense trust if you're not the super.

"Have you been looking into the files? The Affiliates archives?" she asked, already knowing the answer.

"I have," I said. "They keep a very tight ship. The amount of classified files they have is immense."

"Who do you think the Knack was talking about when he mentioned the rot?" Anna asked. The way the light played across my ceiling, it felt like a ghost hovering over us. Or maybe it's my memory of that moment, one among so many.

"I don't know, yet," I said. "Everybody's seeming to do their hero stuff, busy being good super-symbols for their sponsors. The Affiliates have the kind of profile that makes *everything* they do significant, and the PR machine for the team is top shelf."

She shifted in bed and rested her head on one arm, her green hair flowing around her like a river. It was naturally green, incidentally—a product of her super-transformation. When her powers manifested, people thought she'd gone punk, even though she'd never ventured further than Green Day in her punk musical interests. She was all about the emo, when she wasn't jamming to Green Day.

"Well," she said. "Keep looking. I'm trying to keep tabs, too. I don't know how you have the patience for it, personally. I want to grab each team member and just shake the truth right out of them."

She laughed, and I laughed, too. The laughs came to me easily when I was with her. When the Man-Tank drove through St. Louis as part of the Archenemies (a regional supervillain trio that consisted of Man-Tank, the River Reiver, and Backwash), I remember laughing when Victoriana punted him through the Gateway Arch, sending him head-first into the Mississippi. The way River Reiver and Backwash watched their heavy hitter fly overhead, the way their heads turned to track his passing, it slew us. I stun gunned Reiver and Backwash while Victoriana fished Man-Tank out of the river, sputtering and dazed.

"I'll find out," I said. "I promise I will."

Three years we worked together while on the Affiliates, doing missions, taking cases, beating bad guys, saving the world. The team's profile never looked better, and despite spending long hours in the archives, I wasn't finding anything out of place in the official record. Unless the Knack was wrong—and he was never wrong—it didn't look like anybody was doing anything wrong. What was I missing? What *wasn't* I seeing?

Anna, Shane, and I met at my place one time about it, over dinner I'd made, when Anna had suggested we meet up with Shane and talk about it. I opted for something basic, figuring that spaghetti and meatballs was about as basic as one could get. Shane had brought a couple of bottles of red wine, and looked sharp in his white suit, grey shirt, black tie. By that time, Anna and I had been living together for a couple of years, now, and our being a couple was a sort of open secret on the team.

In retrospect, maybe we'd gotten too comfortable. I don't know. Love is love, and when it happens, you just had to take that ride wherever it takes you.

Just so you're not in the dark, I'll dossier the Knack, just because you'll be seeing far more of him soon enough:

ALIAS: THE KNACK

REAL/ASSUMED NAME: SHANE GREY
HAIR: WHITE
EYES: GREY
HEIGHT: 6'2"
WEIGHT: 190 LBS.

POWERS: *THE KNACK POSSESSES SUPERHUMAN POWERS, INCLUDING:*

• GOOD LUCK/IMPECCABLE TIMING: THE KNACK HAS AN ALL-ENCOMPASSING LUCK POWER, WHICH MEANS HE'S AL-WAYS IN THE RIGHT PLACE AT THE RIGHT TIME, AND QUITE POSSIBLY CAN'T BE KILLED. SOME MAY DEBATE WHETH-ER OR NOT THIS CONSTITUTES A SUPERPOWER, BUT THE KNACK HAS SURVIVED ALL MANNER OF ATTACKS, EMERGING UNSCATHED EVERY TIME.

THREAT LEVEL: *9/10 (MOSTLY BECAUSE HE'S WEIRDLY FORMIDABLE IN THIS BIZARRE WAY)*

Okay, apologies in advance, but I have to vent about the Knack. I *almost* hate the Knack. And I say this as his best fren-emy. Here's the thing: he's the world's first trillionaire. And I'm not making that up. What makes it worse is Shane's a su-per-nice guy. He's *legitimately* nice. He publicly gave out his identity, didn't even bother to conceal it.

He first popped up on the superheroic radar when, as a thir-teen-year-old, he was the only survivor of a plane crash that killed his parents and about two hundred other passengers. Everybody died on that crash except Shane, who emerged from it without a scratch, and a lifetime's worth of trauma.

Survivor guilt? He has it.

I know what you're thinking: supervillain origin story, yeah? But that's just not Shane. His family's fortune was in biotech-nology and pharmaceutical products, and when his parents died in that crash, Shane emerged as the sole inheritor of that fortune that would become his when he turned eighteen.

Operatives in Greypharma tried to have Shane killed off, but they never succeeded. Indeed, Shane uncovered the conspiracy to kill his parents when he was sixteen, which led to a pile of arrests. I was the almost the same age when that all went down, and even I was impressed. Boy genius, child detective solves the murder of his parents. Even then, it was all mapped out for Shane. People loved him, gave him credit as the noble orphan who just happened to be a great guy.

And he's good-looking, too—he has this white hair, which I guess marks him as superhuman, and this odd stylistic obsession with wearing black, white, and grey. Like his entire wardrobe is mixes of that. Like white suit, black shirt, grey tie. Or grey shirt, white slacks, black shoes. Always black, white, and grey. Nobody questions it because he just looks so good in it. Women love him. Men want to be him. That's Shane.

He started a philanthropic foundation with a chunk of his fortune, the Humania Foundation, which gifts a dozen people every year with a million-dollar fortune, simply for being decent human beings. I don't know how he figures that out, but the criteria was rooted in someone being kind, decent, law-abiding, and compassionate. They become Humania Fellows, all for *not* being assholes. The Foundation has a closely-guarded Asshole Algorithm they use to determine who's deserving of becoming a Humania Fellow. I can't fault him for that. Knowing Shane as I do, I feel like maybe it's his way of encouraging people to be better than they otherwise would be. He's incentivizing good behavior.

It's only a rumor, but I know before the Humania Foundation, Shane would sometimes secretly purchase winning lotto tickets (he did this at least three times, from what I've determined) and gave them to people he deemed worthy of them.

He gave away his family fortune and built it back again within five years. Amazing, yeah? Luckiest Man Alive. That's what they say about the Knack. Back when they still mattered, he'd get on the covers of magazines, where they'd do gushing profiles of him.

It goes without saying that he's always run afoul of organized crime and cartels. He's not even allowed to set foot in a casino, and people try to get his predictions about things, even though Shane will never offer that up to people. However, he shows up wherever he's needed. That's Shane.

Now, you're thinking I'm a prick because I halfway hate the Knack. Do I envy him? Hell, yes, I do. The man has skated through life, and things always go his way. And he's just so honestly good; it's not a front with him. He's benevolent beyond belief.

That the Knack would show up at our place, to have dinner with us? The whole world would have coveted a seat at that table, if only to be near him. And there we were, playing host and hostess to this marvelous man.

Anna looked amazing in a black cocktail dress, and I didn't look half-bad in a white shirt, black vest, and black jeans, although I felt more like a waiter in my own home, with those two supers in there with me.

"Thanks for having me over, Mitch, Anna," Shane said. "The team doesn't do enough outings like this."

"Not really an outing if it's in our home, Shane," Anna said, snickering as he opened the bottles and poured the wine.

I was busy in the kitchen but I had to grill Shane a little while working, while they sat on our barstools that were adjacent to the kitchen.

"Shane, Anna and I have been looking for the rot you talked about for two years," I said. "We've not found anything. And we've looked."

Shane sipped the wine (which was—big shock—spectacular), and his handsome face became guarded and grave.

"What does that tell you, Mitch?" he asked, while Anna looked on, her grey eyes big as she drank her wine.

"If you're right about it, it means that whoever's bringing the rot is being *very* careful to cover their tracks," I said.

"That's right," Shane said. "And that should point you in the right direction. Or maybe that there *aren't* tracks to cover."

My frustration was apparent, even as I cooked. Cooking was therapy for me—something about the clatter of pans, the sizzle of skillets, the boiling of water brought me peace. That and cooking for people I cared about.

"Shane, why are you being so roundabout in this?" I asked. "If you have suspicions, share them, for god's sake. Because I'm telling you, I'm *not* finding it. Are you finding it, Anna?"

Anna shook her head. "Mitch's right, Shane. We're just not seeing it."

The Knack looked at both of us a moment before replying, just nursed his wine a little, like he was really thinking about what he might say.

"The Affiliates have a worldwide reputation for integrity," Shane said. "Our work speaks for itself, and people depend on us. I've been with the team for a decade, joining when the time seemed right."

"Yeah? And?" Anna asked.

"I deal in intuition and hunches," Shane said. "My gift—or curse—is that I can't necessarily pin my instincts on anything but my own abilities. I'm not a detective like you are, Mitch; I deal in vibes."

"Vibes?" I asked.

"I trust my vibes," he said. "And my vibes tell me that something's rotten in the team. And whoever it is has been very careful not to trigger my powers."

"Christ, Shane," I said. "We're out on a limb because of your vibes?"

He looked almost vulnerable there, toying with his wine glass. It made him even more handsome, irritatingly enough. Acres of rizz.

"I trust my vibes," he said, almost quietly. "More than anything."

Anna and I glanced at each other, while he continued.

"You and Anna are two blessings in this business of ours," he said. "I've been watching you both as you came onto the scene. Mitch, you know we go way back. And Anna, you're a true breath of fresh air in the scene."

I drank some of that amazing red wine and laughed, while Anna drank her own, looking almost bashful, which I knew she wasn't.

"Vibes?" I asked. "Good vibes from us?"

"Yeah," Shane said. "My hope was that your good vibes would offset the bad vibes I was getting."

Now, maybe some of you are big on vibes. I get it, I really do. Something can feel off, and many's the time when you don't follow those vibes, and you find yourself in trouble. And when the Knack was in your kitchen and dining room, telling you he was vibing on things, it wasn't something I could just blow off.

"Tell us, Shane" I said. "Share your vibes with us."

"I'm not a precog," Shane said. "I don't know who it is. But it's someone. Maybe several someones. It's kept me up at night, but I haven't been able to pinpoint it. That's why I wanted to bring you two in, to hopefully uncover it, or to trigger something. My powers are reactive—they depend on circumstance. If those circumstances don't manifest, there's nothing I can do."

Anna spoke up, while I was serving up the spaghetti and meatballs.

"I think I understand it," she said. "You want us to flush out the baddies, and then you can deal with them? Is that it?"

"I can't act until the moment is right," Shane said. "I can't force it to happen; I can only be there when the time is right. And the time isn't right, yet."

It was a very Knack thing to say, being both on-topic and out-there. I almost felt sympathy for him, he who'd had so much, seemed so insanely well-connected, and yet so isolated and alone.

"Hey, speaking of timing, what about buying us a brownstone downtown?" I asked, which made Anna laugh, almost spitting out her wine. "I love Affiliates Central and all, but I don't feel comfortable doing my investigations there, with all those possible prying eyes. You can't even tell me that Mister Transistor doesn't have Central bugged."

Shane smiled to himself at my impertinent suggestion.

"Okay," he said. "You pick out the brownstone, and I'll buy it for you. No questions asked."

"Wow, Shane," Anna said. "For real?"

He smiled at us both. It was a gentle smile. The smile of the staggeringly fortunate, who could afford to be magnanimous.

"Just let me know, and I'll bankroll the purchase and whatever audiovisual gear you need, Mitch," he said. "You need a safe place to conduct your investigation."

"And a car, and a van," I said. Why not? The man was a trillionaire. Having a trillionaire frenemy had to count for something in this wicked world, right?

"Sure, Mitch," Shane said. "Anything you want, Anna?"

Anna only smiled, getting that faraway look in her eyes she sometimes did.

"I'm good," she said.

"Yes, you are," Shane said. "You both are."

He raised a glass to us, clinking with us.

"To being good and doing well," Shane said. We all drank to that, laughing.

<hr>

Sorry, my mind wanders. I tried to stay focused on the half-conversation Deadhead was having.

"I wouldn't know where to look," Deadhead said. "You know how he was. I think we should hire somebody to track him down. Maybe Shutterbug. Yeah, she'd do it. No, I'm not saying *I'd* pay for it. *We'd* pay for it. That's why we're a team, man. Shared expenses, yeah. No, man, it was just an idea. I don't care about Thunderhead; aren't you even curious about Dusty? For real? Fine. Whatever. I'll talk to you later, man."

He hung up, cursing. Felonia curled up around him, I could see a hint of that with where I'd placed that bug under the table.

"What's the matter, Baby?" Felonia asked.

"Miles is being an idiot," Deadhead said. "Dusty's a dead letter to him. He's already moved on. See, that's my thing—he's so stuck on the whole 'Fourheads' concept, he's resistant to my idea of expanding the team. Why not the Sixheads? The Eightheads? No, he loves 'Fourheads' and we're stuck in that model. Meanwhile, Dusty's gone, and that Cameraman idiot was spying on me."

"If the demon hadn't appeared, we'd have had him," Felonia said. "I know his scent, now, Baby. If he shows up again, I'm just going to pounce without a word spoken."

"I tried to death gaze him," Deadhead said. "He must have protection or was smart enough not to look me in the eye."

"Yet dumb enough to try to sneak into your hideout," Felonia said. "Hey, did you hear that?"

"What?" Deadhead asked. But I could hear it. It was a kind of zapping sound. Even through my bugs, I knew what that sound was.

It was Brighteyes.

Goons, already rattled from my abortive effort, were on high alert, standing there with their rifles, and up strolled Brighteyes. In the blue-white light of minicam surveillance, she looked surreal, all in black, but her eyes radiant and well, bright.

She fired her eyebeams into the goons, the beams lancing through them, dropping them. These weren't stun rays; they're killing beams, and she was slicing through the goons, making her way in.

I cut to my hallway minicam, and I saw Major Damage and the others reacting to her appearing in the corridor, but she cut them down with ease. It was both impressive and terrifying to watch, her eyebeams just taking them out with such lethal precision. Brighteyes was like this angel of death, in her black bodysuit, the baleful green eye logo on her chest glaring away while she killed them.

It's bizarre for me, as I was seeing this going on with Bugs One and Two, while Three was tracking Deadhead and Felonia, who were in a panic.

"It's Brighteyes," Deadhead said. "We've got to get out of here, Kitty."

"We can take her," Felonia said. I couldn't see them where they were standing. I could only hear them, which made things worse.

"I don't know if we can," Deadhead said. And I heard the zapping sound hit the security door, and I knew from my dossier that she'd disintegrated the door. Then I heard Deadhead curse. "Die, Brighteyes!"

"You first, Deadhead," Brighteyes said.

And I knew he's fired his death gaze at her, because it's what he *always* did. He's one of those shoot first/ask questions later types of villains, but she knew that about him, and she fired her eyebeams at him. This part, I could see in the hallway, could see her right there, and she fired her beams right into his eyes, and Deadhead was shrieking.

"You bitch! You blinded me!" Deadhead said. I couldn't see this part, could only hear him. Felonia hissed and leaped at Brighteyes, who hit her with a stun beam that dropped her to the floor. I was assuming it was a stun beam. Brighteyes was a hell of a shot, I had to admit, because Felonia had been a blur on my minicam feed, but Antonia had tagged her.

"That's not all I'm going to do to you, Deadhead," Brighteyes said, sidestepping a sloppy charge from Deadhead, who hit the wall, punching a hole in it that made my minicam shake from the impact. She then unloaded on him with her eyebeams again, and my minicam captured the moment she disintegrated him.

Disintegration was a strange thing to witness, more so with Brighteyes. It's like in those old STAR TREK shows, with the phasers—I know, I know, but it's like that. One moment, there's big Deadhead blind-swinging through walls, and then Brighteyes caught him with her eyebeams, and he's enveloped in a glow, and a half-second later, he's just gone, as if he'd never been. Wiped out of existence.

I'm flabbergasted—my surveillance effort, as haphazard as it was, has served me up evidence for multiple murders perpetrated by Brighteyes.

I saw Brighteyes take out a power collar, a gadget that could neutralize a super's powers, and clap it around Felonia's neck. Such collars were standard issue with the Affiliates. I had a few stashed away, myself.

"Get up, Felonia," Brighteyes said, waking up the prostrate catwoman with a smelling salt. "You're coming with me."

Felonia was hissing, but the power neutralizing collar was doing its job—while she looked the same, she was unable to use her considerable strength to take out Brighteyes.

I was in a place, here. I wanted to intervene, but right now, I was just monitoring. Brighteyes was terribly efficient—she used her eyebeams to disintegrate all of the others she'd killed. I could glimpse it by way of my minicams. She fired away and the victims vanished. How very tidy she was. Ruthlessly professional.

Felonia spoke up, saying what I'm seeing.

"You killed them," Felonia said. "Deadhead. The others."

"That's right," Brighteyes said. "They're gone. And you will be, too, if you don't tell me absolutely everything you know about your Crime League, and who they're working with. And I'm talking everybody."

I called out to my Cameravan Control Computer (C3). "Drive us back to the last location, straightaway."

"Yes, Cam," C3 said. I'd installed C3 in my van and car because autodrive was just too useful *not* to have. It allowed me to maintain surveillance while the vehicle drove itself.

Brighteyes methodically disintegrated the other bodies, and I wondered if she had missed my whole run-in with Deadhead. She didn't appear to be aware that I'd bugged the place. Or if she was aware, she didn't care.

If I could reach her and tail her, I might be able to see where she was hiding out. Further, I wondered if Brighteyes had her own van. She must have, if she was kidnapping Felonia, which wouldn't have been something she could just do without turning an eye toward her.

I watched them move out of the range of my minicam, which made me fretful. Out of sight, out of mind. I had to get to the scene quickly.

"ETA, C3?" I asked.

"Seven minutes, Cam," C3 said.

That was an eternity, so I went to one of my Camdrones, prepped it and opened the port in the roof of my van and tossed it airborne, piloting it toward the location of Deadhead's hideout. The Camdrones had a suite of tools that excelled at nightwork. I'd worked hard to get good at drone piloting, since they helped more than they hindered in terms of investigations, and my Camdrones were fast. I could beeline to the hideout before the van got there.

I was sweating while piloting, the desolate city a blur as I raced toward the objective, mindful of my piloting. The last thing I wanted was to get tripped up by a powerline or the like. With distance an issue, I opted for altitude, which would give me a top-down POV that might help me locate Brighteyes. This time of night in Detroit, the traffic would be light, since people were likely to be hunkering down and hoping they weren't going to be victimized by criminals.

Had Victoriana been here, she'd have zipped over there in half a heartbeat, and we'd be able to see what was going on directly. Gods, how I missed her.

A lone van was driving away from the Deadhead hideout, the only suitable vehicle in the area, so I had the Camdrone fix on that, slipping closer. Using thermographic view, I could see there were two in the van, one in the front, the other trussed in the back. I could see the thermographic trace of a tail, was positive that was Felonia.

Pressing a button, I got the Camdrone to spit out a tracking bug with thumped into the spare tire at the back of the van. I flicked another switch, pleased to see the tracker beep to life on my monitor screen.

Having established a connection via the tracker, I relaxed a bit, setting the Camdrone to autotrack. My Camdrones had an hour's worth of power, so I needed to stay with it. But it would faultlessly track the van while still operational.

"C3, reroute based on Camdrone 1's target coordinates," I said. "Mind the speed limit, too."

"Yes, Cam," C3 said. "Rerouting."

Next steps had to involve Decibelle. I had to tell her what I'd seen.

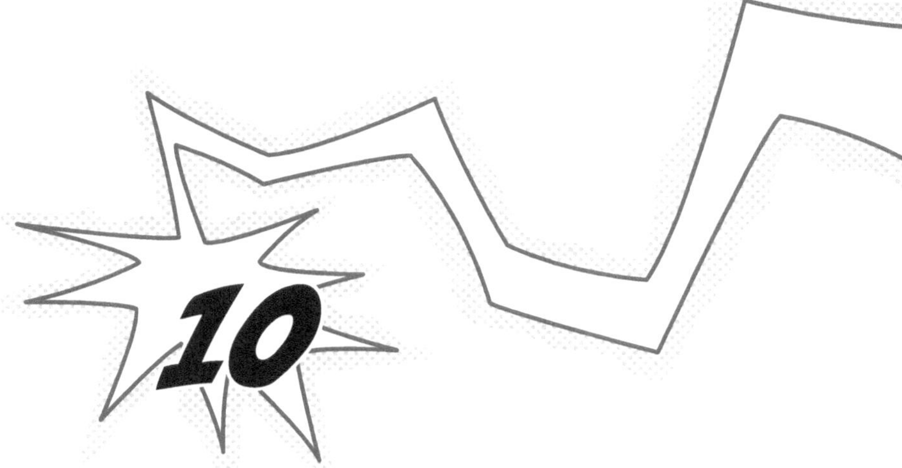

"We're in Detroit."

"Boy-howdy, but that was fast, Mitch-Honey," she replied.

I didn't want to have to tell her what I'd seen. Not like this. And yet, there it was. She had wanted to know, and I had to tell her.

"Brighteyes murdered Deadhead and Major Damage," I said. "Several of Deadhead's goons, too."

A pause on the line.

"You saw this?" Decibelle asked.

"I did," I said. "It got complicated, but I'd managed to get a few cameras in place. I caught it."

Decibelle was quiet on the line, and I didn't have to be a mind reader to know what she was likely thinking. This was her worst nightmare.

"Have you told anybody else?" she asked. It was one of those questions that always tripped my alarms.

"No, I haven't. I'm tailing Brighteyes," I said. "She's captured Felonia and intends to interrogate her about the Crime League. From what I observed, the Fourheads are allied with the League. This is Affiliates-level stuff, Des."

"I don't want them getting involved in this, Mitch," Decibelle said. "Brighteyes *isn't* a criminal. She's one of the good guys, and my partner."

"She just killed around a dozen guys," I said. "And she disintegrated the corpses to cover her tracks. Must be what she did to Dusthead, too. No bodies, no murder."

I needed a bit of insurance, seemed like, and started making copies via my rig in my van.

"She cleaned up the crime scene," Decibelle said. "She knows what she's doing, bless her heart. If you hadn't been there to film it, nobody would be the wiser."

"That's right," I said. "We need to route this to the Affiliates, Des."

"Let *me* handle that, Mitch," Decibelle said. "You just keep tailing Antigone."

It may seem suspicious, but here's the truth of it—if I walked up to the Affiliates and told them, even showed them what I saw, they might not fully believe it. Being who and what I am, there were buckets of salt the supers there might have on hand regarding the truth of my accusations.

Whereas, with Decibelle, she was part of the club, and that information coming from her would carry more weight. I knew how the supers operated. If Decibelle wanted to bring it up to Tandem and the others, that was on her. My role was simply to collect the information—what was done with the information was out of my purview.

That said, my superheroic instincts wondered what I'd do if Brighteyes started torturing Felonia. Felonia was a well-known League assassin. Her kill list was significant—she was their furry ninja, having been the willing recipient of an experimental super-serum crafted by Dr. Dread, a Moreau-like mad scientist who worked out of a remote island in the Caribbean. However, being that didn't mean she deserved to be tortured, or whatever Brighteyes had in mind with her.

There was also the matter of what I'd seen Brighteyes do. Forget the punchy taglines and posturing—Brighteyes was playing for keeps. This was an upending of superhero protocol, wasn't it? In the span of just a few months, Brighteyes had halved the Fourheads. Yeah, I know, Thunderhead, but I didn't count her, as she was brand-new.

"What if Brighteyes starts working Felonia?" I asked.

"Just hang back, Mitch," Decibelle said. "I need to get there, or to Chicago, anyway. To help you out."

Decibelle was worried about her partner, wanted to make things right by her, or, I don't know, bring her around and get her to turn herself in. What did someone do when your partner ran amok? This was why, excepting Anna, I didn't tend to work with partners. Partners (and teams, for that matter) made things complicated. What you made up for in firepower, you traded off in terms of headaches.

"Get here quickly," I said.

"As fast as I'm able," Decibelle said, making me wish she was a speedster. Reviewing my tracking device's mapping, it looked like the Brighteyes van had stopped in a lakeside warehouse. I'd pull the van into the vicinity of the warehouse and pilot the Camdrone to try to spy on Brighteyes.

If or when Brighteyes became aware of me, things might get still more complicated. Depending on whether Felonia blabbed about running into me (by my estimation, a near-certainty), it would mean that Brighteyes would know I'd seen her murdering Deadhead and the others. One didn't have to be a master detective to connect the dots on that one. The question was how far Brighteyes might go.

I should probably talk more about the Affiliates, now, right? I've mentioned them enough. Earth's Greatest Heroes. They'd been around for fifty years. There had been several iterations of the Affiliates, and I'm not going to bore you with an origin story for them. Just know that it's strange when you think about superheroes getting old. That's something not exactly addressed in comic books or movies. There's a sort of nod to their capacity to get old, but it's never a linear progression, versus something where you might get a glimpse of an old hero from another timeline.

However, in the real world, superheroes did get old. The ones that survived might even retire. It happened every now and then. Again, I'm not going to talk about the retired superheroes, because they're kind of bizarre—let's take Blitz, who was a superhero from 1970–90. He was one of the original members of the Affiliates, and he was a telekinetic. Nice guy. He'd been a football player, had this weird kind of telekinesis that manifested as a personal forcefield (invisible, yeah) that made him nearly unstoppable. Eventually, with practice, he could extend the forcefield to lift things, blow through walls, grab people, etc. His origin was classified, so I think he was very likely part of a top-secret government program to create superheroes, something that arose out of World War II.

At any rate, Blitz served the Affiliates in good standing until he retired in his 60s. That's all fine, but what does a telekinetic do when they start getting old? When the mind starts to wander and weaken? With a telekinetic, that can be dangerous.

Old Blitz got farmed out to Hyberia Hollow, which was a special hideaway for old superheroes, just outside of Tucson. I'm not making this up—I found out about it on my own. It's one part retirement community, one part research facility, one part fortress, maybe even one part prison.

The deal was that they get to live in nice surroundings with plenty of services. There's even a pretend sort of town of Hyberia, where they can get most of what they want. But what they're really getting is studied and examined and, most importantly, not allowed to go off on their own.

The logic was that the government wanted the Affiliates in particular to be held in high esteem, and that meant that when heroes started flagging, they're given a generous retirement package to go to the Hollow, where they can golf and play tennis and do whatever else they wanted to do (except be free of the Hollow, and certainly not out doing geriatric superheroics).

As a non-superhero, I'd never get that sort of deal. They didn't want me there because there's nothing to study. Sure, they might want my technology, but there's nothing I've made that's too cutting edge, compared with what they already had.

Where was I going with this? I guess I was just thinking of this lineup of the Affiliates. This was the fifth iteration of the team. They rolled out new teams every decade or so, with some rollover between veterans and legacy members and newbies.

They didn't wash out an entire team in one swoop. Rather, it was a graduated rollout. The Affiliates who were being phased out usually migrated to the auxiliary Affiliates, who served as backups in the event that there was attrition in the ranks (there's always attrition, sooner or later). And the ones who were nearing superhero retirement age (anywhere from 40 to 60 years of age, depending on the heroes and the powers they had in their prime), they'd end up at the Hollow.

Nobody had ever broken this protocol, near as I'd been able to discover. Too much national (and international) security was caught up in it to do otherwise.

I guess all of this backstory is here to give you a proper sense of precisely how puckered up the Affiliates are. The current active roster was:

- **TANDEM:** *THE SUPER OF SUPERS.*

- **THE KNACK:** *THE FACE OF THE AFFILIATES, AND DEPUTY CHAIRMAN. I TOLD YOU ABOUT HIM ALREADY.*

- **WINGMAN:** *A GOOD GUY WITH WINGS.*

- **DECIBELLE:** *YOU ALREADY SAW HER DOSSIER.*

- **RAD LAD:** *SURFER GUY WHO'S GOT THIS RADIOACTIVE SUPERFORM.*

- **MS. FIT:** *PHYSICAL PERFECTION. NEVER GETS TIRED. POSSIBLY INVULNERABLE.*

- **TAG TEAM:** *CAN BECOME HIS OWN CROWD. TRIES WAYYYY TOO HARD.*

- **MINDER:** *TELEPATH. CHAIRMAN OF THE TEAM. CREEP.*

The current auxiliaries include:

- **BRIGHTEYES:** *YOU'VE SEEN HER ALREADY.*

- **LADY BLAZE:** *CAN BECOME A WOMAN OF FIRE. HER FIRE BURNS BLUE. VERY DANGEROUS.*

- **MISTER TRANSISTOR:** *IS HE AN ANDROID? NOT SURE. BUT HE'S A WHIZ WITH ELECTRONICS.*

- **EELECTRIC:** *AQUATIC CHARACTER. RUBBERY, STRONG, WITH AN ELECTRIC SHOCK.*

• **SPEEDO:** *A SPEEDSTER. HE CAN RUN VERY QUICKLY AND SOMEHOW AVOID FRICTION'S EFFECTS.*

• **COPYCAT:** *ANOTHER WEIRD ONE. SHE CAN IMITATE OTHERS' POWERS, WHICH MAKES HER A META-HERO IN MY BOOK.*

• **VENDETTA:** *ANOTHER META-HERO, HAS THE ABILITY TO COME UP WITH A COUNTER TO ANYONE'S POWERS. SOMETIMES CALLED "NEMESIS" POWER.*

The thinking was that a member of the auxiliaries could go to active-duty smoothly, without any super-disruption. Why am I telling you all of this? I guess so you'll be able to understand what I have to deal with when I'm interacting with these people.

Of this batch, I'm only best frenemies/friends with the Knack. We just have this thing, he and I. Everyone else thinks I'm a crackpot conspiracist and/or a weakling (okay, Decibelle and Ms. Fit might feel sorry for me, but who wants to be viewed that way?) That's my reputation, mostly because I've always been secretive.

It's why I know he's the one I'm going to have to talk to about Brighteyes. I had to bring it up to someone in the Affiliates, even though Decibelle didn't want me to. And it had to be Shane.

As I braced for that call, my mind wandered into the past again....

who had made the unusual step to visiting us in Affiliates Central. Anna and I had finished locking up Bullhorn and the Matador, a two-man team who had racketeering associations with the Crime League, reflecting on the synergy of that fight, because Bullhorn was the super and the Matador was the skills member of the team. However, they were no match for us up in Wisconsin, where the fight had taken place. We saved Milwaukee, man.

"What do you think Minder wants?" Anna asked, while we were recovering from the fight. Even as super as she was, any fight took something out of her. She was my Victoriana Valkyrie, but she savored her down time between gigs. I know I did.

"No idea," I said. He was in the main conference room. He was looking us over with those searching eyes of his, and I was fairly confident he was scanning us. Minder was tall and blandly handsome in a corporate sort of way, with slicked brown hair and searching eyes and a prominent nose and strong chin.

"Victoriana, Cameraman," Minder said, gesturing for us to take seats. "Looks like you two have settled in nicely here in Central."

"We have," Anna said. "Great clearances, yes?"

Minder reviewed some files on the table, glanced at us meaningfully.

"Exemplary," he said. "You've both done a great job over here. Given that it's just the two of you operating at Central, it's more impressive, still."

"We aim to please," I said, and I was pretty sure Minder could read my mind on what I might have otherwise been thinking. It wasn't that I had a bad attitude (yeah, I do), so much as I was wondering why he might be turning up at all if we'd been doing such a great job, which we were.

Minder's face was neutral as he spoke, watching us, trying to appear casual.

"When we extended the Affiliates franchise, we weren't sure how it would play out in Central and South, but you two and Sound & Fury in South have been vindicating the approach we've taken," Minder said.

"Great to hear," Anna said, eyeing me from across the table, while keeping her focus on Minder.

"There's only so much budget for superhero staffing, obviously," Minder said. "We've put more emphasis on the coastal operations, but I wanted you both to know that we're hoping to add a few more members to Central and South, just so you aren't swamped with cases. As great as you two have been—especially you, Victoriana—you're still only a duo. I'd like to make Central a quartet. Same goes for South."

"Wow, yeah," Anna said. "I'm assuming we'd be scheduling interviews of prospective candidates?"

Minder treated us to his Telepath's Smile, and it was clear to me that he had candidates in mind already, slid a pair of dossiers to us across the table.

I haven't explained to you about the Telepath's Smile. It's one of those weirdly enigmatic smiles that doesn't quite reach the eyes, and invariably carried with it a hint of irony, contempt, and who knows what else. Telepaths are the worst, and they have it worst, because they know what everybody's thinking, and aren't shy about poking around someone's head. All telepaths have the Telepath's Smile, I've found.

"I was thinking Paleface and Deadpan," Minder said. I knew who both of them were.

"You're kidding, right?" I asked, while Anna skimmed the dossiers. "That's the Vamp and Sureshot. They used to be part of the Crime League. Like years ago."

Minder's smile turned toward me with a slow tilt of his head.

"As ever, you're a good student, Mitch," he said. "All of your nosing around our archives has reaped dividends for you."

"Photographic memory," I said, tapping my temple. "But you know that already, yeah, Rex?"

"Paleface and Deadpan have been rehabilitated," Minder said. "They've served their time, and I'd like for them to go to work for the Affiliates as part of their paying back their debt to society."

"They're both killers, Rex," I said. "Stone-cold killers."

"We've made arrangements, Mitch," Minder said. "They understand where their interests lie."

Anna looked up from the files, cocking an eyebrow at Minder, who remained even-keeled in the face of my protestations.

"Paleface is a vampire, Rex," I said. "I don't see how it's even possible to rehabilitate her."

"We prefer the term 'undead' to describe her, Mitch," Minder said. I could see Anna was gearing up to say something, so I gave her flanking cover with my own inquiries.

"You're always so worried about PR for the team, Rex," I said. "How is that going to look when people realize we have Paleface and Deadpan on our team?"

"Nobody's going to know, Mitch," Minder said. "They'll be part of our Affiliates Black Ops Program we're hashing out with the PSS*. These are supers who operate much like you do—in the shadows. We leave Victoriana in the limelight, where she belongs, while you, Deadpan and Paleface work behind the scenes." *(Program for the Study of Superbeings—the editors).

"Mitch and I are a team," Anna said. "I don't know these other two."

"You'll *get* to know them," Minder said. "We have to give people second chances. The alternative is them wasting away in the Brig. So much untapped potential."

Deadpan was a master assassin, a crackshot with all manner of firearms, and Paleface was a terrifying specter. I couldn't imagine why Minder might be bringing them into the team.

"They'd never clear any background checks," Anna said. "It took us two years to be cleared, and we're not criminals."

"And I'm sorry it took that long. They'd be cleared on my authority," Minder said. "I've accepted responsibility for their conduct on the job. They'll have a probationary period like any new members. Like how it went with you two. Honestly, when you pulled your little gambit with me, Anna, regarding Mitch, nobody but Shane would have backed that play, when we contrast what you can do with what Mitch can do, but I waved that through. Trust me on this one. Vamp and Sureshot will be great additions to the team, even just as Black Ops. Let's be real: the team is stretched thin, and we need to have people on tap."

"There have to be any number of actual heroes we might bring in," Anna said. "Versus using allegedly rehabilitated convicts, Minder."

Minder laughed, one of the only times I'd ever heard him do this.

"Doe-eyed, green aspirants aren't what we want," Minder said. "Just having powers—or, you know, skills—isn't enough these days. We can't afford to have people learning on the job how to be heroes. We're not about feel-good stories, Mitch; we want reliable results from seasoned professionals who can maintain the necessary moral detachment to do their jobs effectively."

"I would think not being villains would be a great first step when dealing with potential superheroes," Anna said. Minder shook his head, leaned back.

"A hero is measured by their deeds," Minder said. "The work both of you have done has raised your profiles a great deal, which elevates the Affiliates as a whole. Not all heroes are good people. Please be realistic. They are the right people intervening at the right time in the right manner required of them."

Anna leaned forward, her eyes boring into Minder, who had to have been grateful she didn't have eyebeams of her own.

"And bringing some former villains on board does what, exactly, Minder?" she asked. "At the very least, it'll be a drag. How does Black Ops play out in terms of the team, anyway?"

Minder was being patient with us, but I could see him being irked by our resistance to it. I could only imagine how it might play out with Sound & Fury.

"We do white hat, grey hat, and black hat work in the Affiliates," Minder said. "You've seen Shane's playbook on that. The work we do is triaged accordingly. White hat work allows for those photo events and heavy media cycle presentations. Black hat work is top secret, the type of stuff we *don't* advertise. Grey hat work falls on a case-by-case basis—where we might benefit from it, we publicize and promote it. Otherwise, lower-profile. We keep the noise down."

"It's crap," I said. "I don't want to be looking over my shoulder when taking down some baddies because there are baddies in our midst."

Minder shifted in his seat, biting his lip while formulating a response.

"I'm responsible for vetting new team members," he said. "And I do. The underworld knowledge and connections supers like these bring to the table is invaluable. We've managed the Vamp's condition, and she's been an active, even enthusiastic partner in the program. You're hardly one to judge, Mitch—your association with the devil, Inferna, is well known. Am I to believe that she's less of a threat than Paleface and Deadpan?"

It was kind of a low blow, even as it was a fair point. My arrangement with Inferna was strictly personal and could hardly be broadened to an organization-wide policy.

"Inferna's made good on her commitment to crimefighting honorably and honestly," I said, feeling like an idiot for even having to explain that. "If there was some kind of contractual arrangement with Paleface and Deadpan, a contingency in case they backslid, that would be at least some reassurance. Although they're *still* villains, Rex."

Minder regarded us both in silence.

"Look at it from my perspective," he said. "We need more members, but good heroes—the alchemical mix of moral caliber, firepower, and experience—are hard to find. Some powers are more useful than others. You've done a lot with what you have, Mitch, but even you have to admit that without Victoriana, you'd not have been able to clear even a quarter of your cases that involved supers. You're just not strong enough to do it. I'm trying to come up with a turnkey, scalable solution for that imbalance of power."

Anna could see how wounded I was by it, even though my face was concealed. She could read my body language, and she knew my heart. Of course, if Minder was trespassing in my head, he'd know it, too.

"That's not fair, Minder," she said. "Mitch and I are partners. We work together on our cases. So what if I'm the hammer? He's the recon and surveillance part of the equation. That's what a partnership or a team is—we're there for each other. We complement each other."

"And I'm trying to bring more hammers to the table," Minder said. "The Vamp is perfect for this kind of work. She's super-strong, super-fast, can mesmerize, can turn to mist, can become a bat or a wolf. She's almost unkillable and immortal. She's perfect for infiltration missions. And Deadpan is a weapons master with years of elite expertise. The firepower he brings to any mission is vital."

"A vampire and a gunman," I said. "What about Goo or Strutter? They're perfect, and they're not killers or villains."

I wanted to mention Rollergirl, too, but knew Minder would just throw her in my face as being underpowered. She had tons of heart, however, and when paired with body armor, that counted.

"They're not bad choices," Minder said. "But the coaching and mentoring issue remains."

"They've been auxiliaries," Anna said. "Easy enough to bump them up to reservists or active-duty members."

I was no telepath, but I could see the points we were raising were resonating with Minder at least a little bit. He still wanted his pet program in place, but he might consider bringing Goo and Strutter aboard.

"You know, Rex," I said. "Goo and Strutter can be the White hat hires, and Paleface and Deadpan can be, you know, your Black hat."

Minder snapped his fingers, like a single snap.

"And just like that, you double my budget for this project," Minder said.

"Not if you just jettison Paleface and Deadpan," I said.

"No," Minder said. "No, that's *not* going to happen."

Then a brilliant idea came to me, and I could tell from Minder's reaction that he already picked up on my thought before I said it.

"Easy fix," I said. "Tap the Knack for the payroll expansion. What's the point of having a trillionaire on the team if you can't lean on them for budget? Shane could cover doubling both the Central and South teams easily."

The fact that Minder hadn't thought of that before coming to us with his indecent proposal made me wonder where his head was at. Or that he and Shane weren't communicating much.

"Not a bad idea, Mitch," he said. "I don't like to bother Shane with these kinds of nuts-and-bolts details, but your suggestion is sound."

"It's why I'm a tactical mastermind," I said, winking at Anna, who grinned back at me. Her grins were superpowered.

"I can help with training the auxiliaries," Anna said. "Goo and Strutter are great kids. They'd be wonderful additions to Central."

I wanted to laugh, because Anna was all of twenty-eight, and, at least from my barely thirty-one-year-old perspective, she caucused closely with Goo (who was nineteen) and Strutter (who was twenty-five).

"Alright," Minder said, recovering his Telepath's Smile. "I think you've both persuaded me. I'm still proceeding with the

Vamp and Sureshot, but a case could be made to bring Goo and Strutter onto the team as well."

"And for South, I'd suggest Green Man and Stinger," I said. Minder laughed again.

"They're *both* green men," he said.

"Yeah, well, they'll mesh well with Brighteyes, yeah?" I said, and the three of us chuckled at this.

"The Green Team theme," Anna said, toying with her hair. "Maybe I should transfer South."

"No," I said. "I'd never survive."

Minder loved that idea. "The Green Team: Brighteyes, Victoriana, Green Man, and Stinger. Yeah, the optics of that would be top-notch."

The prospect of Victoriana bumping to another team filled me with angst, and I had to keep cool lest my disquiet be visibly apparent, although I'm sure Minder could see it coming off me in waves.

"Just joking, Mitch," Minder said. "I know how settled you and Anna are here in Chicago. I'd never do anything to disrupt operations here. But you've both given me a lot to think about, and I think there are some good ideas that have been raised. Now I just need to talk to Shane and persuade him to unlock some money to blow our budgets up."

"Nothing you haven't done before," I said, as Minder got up and shook our hands. "Vamp and Sureshot will be here at the end of the week. I expect you both to be on your best behavior when they arrive."

Later, Anna and I stewed over it at our place, safe from any eavesdropping robots or anything else. She was wearing a vintage Dauntless tee and flannel Affiliates pajama bottoms, drinking some wine, while I was making beef stew.

"What do you think about that Black Ops Program Minder was talking about?" I asked.

"Weird," she said. "What's up with that?"

I shook my head. After the meeting, I'd done some researching in the Affiliates database, but if the program existed, it wasn't available for review at my level of access.

"No idea," I said. "But having some more team members can't hurt. It would be nice to be able to chill out and not always be on call."

"For real," she said. "I hate being on call. Great suggestion with Goo and Strutter, Mitch. Solid."

She gave me a tender knuckle bump, and we both giggled, knowing what those knuckles of hers could do.

Nominating a speedster was *always* a good move, from my perspective. All superhero teams benefited from the presence of a speedster. They were very useful in any capacity, and Strutter had a dynamic, photo-friendly style that would all but build in good media coverage. I hated that I even had to think in those terms, but that was Affiliates life for you.

"Did you think Minder was reading our minds in that meeting?" Anna asked.

"Oh, yes," I said. "It's what he does."

"That's not cool," she said, taking a drink of her wine.

"No, it's not," I said.

"Wouldn't that count as harassment?" Anna asked. "Like if your boss was a telepath and used his telepathy to read your mind? Isn't that invasive?"

"Yeah," I said. "I imagine a case could be made. Minder plays it very quietly—you never quite get the sense that he makes use of that information he has. It's like during World War II, when the Allies had cracked the Nazi Enigma cipher machine codes—they couldn't reveal that they knew the codes had been cracked without alerting the Nazis."

Anna listened to me, a bemused look on her face.

"You mean the Allies just *let* bad things happen?" she asked. I tasted the stew. It was delicious. Fighting crime always made me hungry.

"They had to," I said, getting some bowls ready for us. "If they'd revealed what they'd discovered, the Nazis would have just come up with a new code."

"Wow," she said. "Man, I hate Nazis."

"Me, too, Babe," I said. "That's sort of how I think Minder works—he's got access to all of our codes but doesn't let on that he knows."

"Still feels sketchy to me," Anna said. "If I were a telepath, I wouldn't eavesdrop on people's minds that way."

"That's because you're a good person," I said. "A really good person."

We kissed as we set the table and had dinner.

"I'm still getting my head around that I'm going to have to work with a vampire," I said. "An actual vampire. And an assassin."

"Yeah," Anna said. "Crazy world, right?"

The introductory meeting with Paleface and Deadpan wasn't terrible, but it was strange. Paleface wore an all-black, form-fitting bodysuit with an almost laughably high and angular collar and a burgundy and black cape, her black hair long and contrasting with her bone-white face, burgundy lips, and kaleidoscopic red eyes. She was all vampire-skinny and alluring.

ALIAS: PALEFACE

REAL/ASSUMED NAME: ANASTASIA AUGENBLICK
HAIR: BLACK
EYES: RED
HEIGHT: 5'4"
WEIGHT: 100 LBS.

POWERS: *PALEFACE POSSESSES VAMPIRIC SUPERPOWERS, INCLUDING:*

• **SUPER-STRENGTH:** *PALEFACE CAN LIFT ONE TON.*

• **SUPER-REFLEXES:** *PALEFACE HAS REFLEXES AT LEAST THREE TIMES FASTER THAN A NORMAL HUMAN.*

• **GASEOUS FORM:** *PALEFACE CAN BECOME LIKE MIST, ABLE TO MOVE AT WILL.*

• **METAMORPH:** *PALEFACE IS ABLE TO BECOME A BAT, A WOLF, OR A RAT AT WILL.*

- **SUMMON ANIMALS:** *PALEFACE IS ABLE TO SUMMON BATS, RATS, OR WOLVES AT WILL. THEY WILL RESPOND TO HER COMMANDS.*

- **HYPNOSIS:** *PALEFACE CAN HYPNOTIZE A TARGET WITH HER EYES.*

- **TARGETED TELEPATHY:** *IF SHE FEEDS ON SOMEONE, SHE CAN FORM A MENTAL LINK WITH THEM, WHICH CAN EXIST OVER ANY DISTANCE.*

- **IMMORTALITY:** *PALEFACE DOES NOT AGE.*

- **REGENERATION:** *PALEFACE CAN REGENERATE FROM MOST INJURIES, INCLUDING DECAPITATION (IF HER HEAD IS REATTACHED TO HER BODY).*

- **INVULNERABILITY:** *PALEFACE IS IMMUNE TO MOST NORMAL FORMS OF INJURY.*

- **VULNERABILITIES:** *PALEFACE IS VULNERABLE TO GARLIC, HOLY WATER, SILVER, AND CAN BE DESTROYED BY DIRECT EXPOSURE TO SUNLIGHT. SHE MAY NOT CROSS A DOOR-WAY INTO A RESIDENCE IF NOT INVITED TO. PALEFACE MUST FEED ON BLOOD NIGHTLY TO RETAIN HER POWERS. FAILURE TO DO SO WILL GRADUALLY WEAKEN HER.*

THREAT LEVEL: 9/10

Paleface made a flourish of a bow to both of us, extending her cool hand for us to shake in turn, while she gazed at us with her big, red eyes.

"Cameraman," she said, a hint of an Italianate accent to her words. "I've heard so much about you. How nice to finally meet you in person. And Victoriana, you're not as tall as I imagined, and so very strong. How you brim with vitality."

"Uh, thanks," Anna said, and she and I exchanged looks, while Paleface just smiled enigmatically at us. Deadpan cleared his throat and extended his hand, which we shook. He was wearing a grey urban camouflage costume, with some low-light goggles in place. He had a high-powered rifle over one shoulder, next to his backpack.

"Yeah, so, I'm Deadpan, now," he said. "Heard of you, Cameraman. And who hasn't heard of you, Victoriana?"

His voice was gruff, very dudebro to my ear. I'm not even going to give dossier stats for Deadpan, because the man was just a super-sniper. Not that I have a problem with snipers—they do amazing work in the Armed Forces. However, I feel like you can sympathize with my reticence at welcoming someone like him on the team.

Now, before you bust my chops about welcoming Paleface but hesitating about Sureshot, wondering what high horse I rode in on, the fact remains that while Paleface's powers might make her a possibly valuable team asset, the one thing Deadpan brought to the table was his skill at shooting people. What did it matter which type of firearm he used? The man was a soldier, not a superhero.

Again, it makes me seem like a superhero snob, but how in the hell was Deadpan going to work out in Central? What, were we going to put him on a rooftop to shoot criminals? Do you at least see the problem he presented? And when you considered that he'd been a triggerman villain in the past, I was supposed to just forget about all of that and welcome him?

Anna shook his hand, and he laughed about the strength of her grip.

"You see?" Paleface said. "So full of life, that one is."

"Yeah," Deadpan said, shaking out his hand before extending it to mine. "That's more like it. Something I can handle."

He did the whole power handshake thing, he and I quietly dueling a moment as we shook. I did the classic power play, bringing my other hand over to place atop our shaking hands.

"Welcome aboard," I said. "You can pick out your quarters. I imagine you'll want one without windows, Vamp."

"Call me Anastasia, Cameraman, or Stasi, if you prefer," she said, hooking my arm in hers, whisking me along. I glanced back at Anna, hoping she'd rescue me, but she only laughed, pointing Sureshot in the right direction. "I'm thinking my specialty should be the underworld, and particularly supernatural threats."

"Sure," I said. "Makes sense."

She surveyed her room, studying it a moment.

"What about minions?" she asked. "Who'll handle my belongings?"

"No minions," I said. "Not on-site. We have robots."

Anastasia looked befuddled at the prospect. "Mechanical beings?"

"Um, yeah," I said, pointing to the robots who were hauling in her coffin. "You really sleep in those?"

She looked at it a moment, before turning her languorous gaze on me. "Oh, yes. You should try it sometime, Cameraman. I think you'd like it. It's peaceful."

I pried my arm free of her, laughing nervously.

"Not me," I said. "I like beds."

She just watched me exist a moment, a half-smile on her face, showing a bit of fang.

"The earth is the bed for us all, in the end," she said. "Some of us are simply restless sleepers."

Anna and I laughed about it back at our brownstone, as we'd tossed our suits and put on some comfy clothes.

"*That* was trippy," she said. "The vampire and the assassin. Oh, man, Mitch. I think she *liked* you."

"I don't know. She seemed more impressed by your vitality. Deadpan definitely liked you," I said. "I saw him ogling you the whole time. I still can't imagine what Minder had in mind with bringing those two aboard. What a scene. You think he's saddling us with them to hold us back? Maybe sabotage our efforts a bit?"

"Who knows?" she said. "It's going to be something, that's for sure."

Anna and I split administrative and leadership roles at Central, which meant planning out training and patrols. To be fair, we'd mix and match with the newbies, just to better incorporate them into the Affiliates regimen.

"I'll feel better once we get Goo and Strutter on the team," I said. "At least then we'll have more balance toward the light."

Anna laughed and gave me a squeeze.

"You're all about the light, Mitch," she said.

"Lighting is everything, Babe," I said, giving her one helluva kiss as I shot a selfie of us, catching the light just right.

CLACK
CLACK
CLACK
CLACK

I should mention that I'd snuck some minicams and bugs into the warehouse where she was holding Felonia, who was tied to a wheelchair, but more on that later.

"Mitch," Shane said. "I knew you'd be calling."

"Yeah, you did," I said. "And you probably know why I'm calling you, too."

"Brighteyes," Shane said.

"Lucky guess," I said. "What do you know?"

"I know that Desdemona's worried," Shane said. I was fairly confident that Decibelle and the Knack had a thing at some point. Superhero women loved him as much as normies did.

"She should be," I said. "Brighteyes murdered Deadhead and his flunkies. I have footage."

"I'd expect no less from you, Mitch," Shane said. "Please tell me you're not planning to blackmail the Affiliates over this."

"Christ," I said. "I'm not Shutterbug, Shane."

Shane chuckled. Even his chuckles were handsome. I could hear them over the phone, like how handsome they were.

"Only teasing," Shane said. "What are you going to do?"

"Des doesn't want me doing anything until she gets there," I said.

Shane didn't hesitate, didn't lose his unquenchable cool.

"She's just trying to help out her partner," Shane said. There was always a whisper of condescension in everything with Shane. I couldn't quite put my finger on it, but I swear it was there. For a man as quintessentially fortunate as he was, it just crept in. I thought that even when I accepted his deal for the brownstone Anna and I made our home. Did that make me ungrateful? Probably. He didn't have to do it, but for Shane, buying a brownstone was literal pocket change. He carried more in his wallet than people might have their entire lives.

"Murder is murder, Shane," I said, feeling naïve. I knew members of the Affiliates had killed people. It happened. You didn't do superhero stuff without fatalities occurring.

However, there was a distinction between deaths in the line of duty and outright vigilantism. From your perspective, it's probably not as clear, but for those of us in the business (I hate even calling it that), it was one of those dividing lines between heroes and villains—villains would sacrifice anyone for their schemes, and heroes would only voluntarily sacrifice themselves. That's what made them heroes.

"Do you want me to join you and Des there?" Shane asked, which made my stomach churn. The Knack turning up would guarantee that it would become a big deal, and he'd somehow save the day, and I'd be in the weeds. Was this another pride thing with me?

"Why bother, Shane?" I said. "We both know you'll turn up to save the day, anyway."

Shane chuckled again because he knew I was right about that. One didn't have to be an ace detective to figure that one out.

"I just assumed because you were calling me that maybe you wanted my help," Shane said.

"Ehh, no, I've got this handled," I said. Never mind that I didn't actually. So far, Brighteyes was only verbally interrogating Felonia, who, as predicted, totally mentioned me. Here's how that was going:

"Cameraman told you how to find us," Felonia said.

"Camerman?" Brighteyes said. "No, he didn't."

"But he was there right before you killed Deadhead and the others," Felonia said. "You did this."

Brighteyes immediately looked around, wary. I could see the glow of her eyes as she searched, no doubt using her night vision to see if she could trace me.

"Cameraman was there, you say?" Brighteyes asked. Felonia, sensing an angle, ran with it like a cat with a toy.

"Yes," Felonia said. "He and Inferna. They were working together. You didn't know about that? I just assumed all of you heroes were working together."

"No," Brighteyes said, still scanning the warehouse. She cleared her throat and raised her voice. "Cameraman, are you here? Are you spying on me?"

Decision time, in terms of whether or not to reveal myself to Brighteyes. Depending on the circumstance, it could go either way between us.

"Shane, I've got to go," I said. "We'll talk more soon. Although if I disappear, it's because Brighteyes disintegrated me."

"Mitch, please—" but I'd hung up on him before he could say more. I don't like hanging up on people, but I will if I have to.

I dialed Brighteyes up, gratified that her cell rang. She picked it up.

"Hello, Cam," she said. "You *are* spying on me."

"I saw what you did to Deadhead," I said.

"Decibelle sent you, didn't she?" Brighteyes asked. Her voice was husky, commanding and direct. I hadn't talked to her much in my time in the Affiliates, since her glowing green eyes were always intimidating, especially the way they always kind of looked through you. Brighteyes could terrify people just by staring at them during interrogation.

"She was worried about you," I said. "She asked me to look into it."

I could hear her scoffing.

"And you lucked into surveilling the right Fourhead," she said. "Why don't you turn up so we can talk in person, Cam?"

"I don't think that'd be wise," I said.

"You think I'd zap you, too?" Brighteyes asked.

Given that she said that on a cell line showed a degree of brazenness on her part. And a lack of guilt. Although her use of "zap" offered her at least a plausible way out if our call was admitted as evidence. "Zap" could mean anything.

"It's at least a possibility," I said.

"I don't zap heroes, Cam," she said. "Only the bad guys. The ones who deserve it."

This was halfway to a hostage negotiation, as I saw it. Not that Felonia would appreciate what I was doing for her. Hell, she'd cut me apart if she got the chance.

"You killed Deadhead and Dusthead," I said. "And their men."

"Did I? They had it coming," Brighteyes said. "They're bad men. Deadhead killed hundreds in the course of his career. Dusthead killed his share as well."

"You can't go around killing supervillains, Brighteyes," I said.

She was pacing around with her phone, while Felonia looked on.

"Sure I can," Brighteyes said.

"The Affiliates will stop you," I said.

Brighteyes laughed a moment. Her laugh was throaty and harsh. I could feel the scorn and bitterness in it. The years in the business took a toll, I'll admit. I could feel her anger, her weariness.

"Maybe," she said. "But you sure won't. You *can't* stop me, Cam. Even if you wanted to. I'm out of your class."

She wasn't wrong, but it was still annoying to hear her point that out. I'd like to think that I could have surprised her in a fight. People always underestimated me, which I turned to my advantage so often.

"Maybe," I said. "But my point stands—they're not going to want you out there wasting bad guys."

"How do you know?" Brighteyes asked. "Maybe I'm doing it on their behalf, so they don't have to get their hands dirty. You've heard of Affiliates Black Ops, yes? The PSS?"

"Yeah," I said. "But you're not part of that, are you?"

"You don't know?" she said. "Maybe I am."

I'm cynical, yeah, but no way could I imagine the starched shirts of the Affiliates agreeing to what Brighteyes was doing. They wouldn't risk the PR damage it might do if that got out. And even if she was part of Minder's Black Ops Program. The PSS was another matter; they operated almost completely in the shadows.

"I don't believe that," I said. "Tandem and the Knack would never go for it. None of them would."

"There's no evidence," Brighteyes said. "No one knows where Dusthead went—he simply disappeared. Same with Deadhead. No collateral damage left behind at the scene."

"I know where they went," I said. "I have the footage."

"Footage can be faked," Brighteyes said. "You've already become obsolete, Cam. Nobody believes what they see and hear, anymore. If your footage got out there, that's what Credible and her people would say. Fake news. Faked footage."

That was one of my crowning frustrations in the ever-evolving digital world. Things like deepfakes and doctoring of video were becoming more commonplace. Sound files, too. When I first started doing what I did, it wasn't like that. A recording meant something. Nowadays, not so much. I used to believe that simply collecting the information and exposing the secrets was enough to move people, to bring justice to those who had it coming to them.

These days? People didn't even know the truth when it hit them in the face. Today's fact became tomorrow's legend and yesterday's myth. That was dispiriting, even though I refused to wave the white flag just yet.

"But I *saw* what you did," I said. "So did Felonia. We're witnesses."

"Yeah," Brighteyes said. "But she's a criminal assassin, and you're a conspiracy nut—nobody's going to believe either of you. Why don't you come down here so we can talk face to face."

"Not a chance," I said. "Not right now."

"Ah," Brighteyes said. "You're waiting for reinforcements to arrive."

She hung up on me without another word, but my minicams still recorded what was being said.

"Okay, Felonia," Brighteyes said. "Time for us to go."

She wheeled Felonia across the warehouse, back to her van, which I had also bugged. Brighteyes cleared her from the wheelchair with a snarled warning that she'd zap Felonia if she tried anything, before securing her in an in-vehicle cage she had in the back of her van. I made a mental note to look into whether Antigone had gotten that custom-made somewhere, or whether it was just her own creation.

Then Brighteyes got rolling. I had shelved my Camdrone for recharge while she'd been in the warehouse, but with the trackers and bugs placed, I could just roll along after her inconspicuously.

"I'm sure you've bugged my van, Cam," Brighteyes said as she drove.

"Help me, Cameraman," Felonia called from the back. "She's crazy!"

"Quiet back there," Brighteyes said. I'll confess that it took a mountain of brass balls for Felonia to ask me for help, given that only a few hours before, she'd have carved me up and probably eaten me. That's how it was with villains, however— they'd turn on a dime if they thought it might bring them a momentary advantage.

Maybe that's why villainy was so pervasive—the moral flexibility of evil allowed one the opportunity to take advantage of any moment available to you. Good people, especially heroes, had to abide by their own moral code and stick by it, just by the nature of being good.

And that's why I was having this ongoing discussion with Antigone.

"I'm tired of the way the Affiliates handle things," Brighteyes said. "You think I *want* to just ship people off to the Brig? And do you think that's any better than nonexistence? They test people at the Brig. They gene sequence them and take samples from them. Anyone at the Brig is automatically placed into the Program for the Study of Superbeings. The PSS is a military research division, Cam. I'm sure you already know that. I don't want to fob people off to the Brig so the Polygon can just create new breeds of super soldiers."

Antigone was right—I did know about a lot of that stuff. But I also didn't think she should be talking about it so openly with Felonia within earshot. I decided to dial her up again. She picked up.

"Yeah, I knew it," Brighteyes said.

"I don't know how much you should be talking about Affiliates stuff in front of Felonia," I said.

Antigone laughed scornfully.

"Oh, so now you're a model of protocol, Cam? That's a joke," she said.

"Don't kill Felonia," I said.

"She's an assassin," Brighteyes said. "Her body count is worse than Deadhead's was. You know what would really bother me? Let's just say I went with procedure and got Felonia sent to the Brig. Who's to say the government, maybe Minder, who knows—would look at her record and offer to expunge it in return for services rendered on behalf of the government? It's been done before. They do stuff like that, Cam. Is a useful supervillain more of an asset than a liability? At least with what I'm doing, I take her off the board."

As we were driving through Detroit, heading southwest, toward Toledo, I could see what Antigone might be objecting to. The PSS did have a wing that sought to rehabilitate supervillains, depending on the crimes they committed. After that meeting with Minder, I'd done some snooping around the PSS files, which were even more locked down than the Affiliates records. Despite that, I had at last seen something about the White Hat, Grey Hat, and Black Hat Programs, as well as mentions of their rehabilitation and dehabilitation programs. Don't even ask me what "dehabilitation" was—that's for another time, Gentle Reader.

"You don't want to be a murderous vigilante, Antigone," I said.

"Wanting to and having to aren't the same thing, Cam," Brighteyes said. "Decibelle could never see that, but it's just where we diverge. Let's just say that I see things more clearly than she does."

Since Brighteyes was a vision-based hero, all sight-based puns were open season for her. As a vision-adjacent hero, I had those available to me, too, although I tried to be discreet about their use.

"Decibelle just wants you to hear her out," I said, unable to resist, knowing it would earn me at least an eyeroll from Antigone.

"I'm not on a ledge, Cam," Antigone said. "I don't need to be talked off it. I was a soldier; I'm *still* a soldier. I know what I'm doing, why it matters, and that's that. If you want to try to bring me in, you can. Although I wouldn't advise it. I know you know what I can do."

She understood how relentless I was. Having bugged her vehicle and placed a tracker on it, I'd stay with her as long as I could. Maybe she'd ferret out the bugs and destroy them. Likelier was she'd destroy the van. Brighteyes was practical to a fault.

And that got me wondering, too. Where did one draw the line? Why was there an expectation that a superhero *not* kill? Was it simply a matter of powers versus non-powers? For example, if you had two supers fighting—one a hero, one a villain—was the hero expected to show mercy and *not* kill the villain? Was that all that separated them? Who made those rules?

However, if a superhero crossed that line and killed a supervillain, then what, exactly? Were they now an antihero? Was that the next step on the continuum, going either way?

SUPERHERO ↔ ANTIHERO ↔ SUPERVILLAIN

Was it as simple as that? And were there supervillains who weren't entirely villainous, too? Was the antiheroic space the new meaty middle ground where most people operated? Was an antihero more of a realist than a conventional superhero, able to make the hard calls that traditional superheroes wouldn't?

From what she'd said and what I'd observed, I felt that Brighteyes wasn't being indiscriminate about the use of her powers. She wasn't randomly killing off civilians. She was being careful in her targets. That had to matter on some level.

You'll notice I didn't throw in "taking the law into their own hands" as part of the calculus. That's because any superhero was automatically taking the law into their own hands. That was integral to the process of superheroics, a willingness to operate outside of the conventional confines of legality.

The only distinction was between official, sanctioned heroes like the Affiliates, and everybody else, the assorted freelancers. The police and other law enforcement agencies out there put up with the Affiliates because they were granted permission by the government to do what they did. It was a license to be super.

Everybody else was considered to be operating outside of the law. That's why we guarded our secret identities so carefully, and often operated under the shadow of darkness and mystery. Any vigilante basically worked that way. With all of that in place, what did it matter if someone killed a supervillain, or merely threw them through a wall? Don't even get me going on how many civilians suffered when supers went at it in earnest.

"Someone's going to try to stop you, Antigone," I said.

"Yeah, I know that," she said. "But you're the only one with evidence of it, so forget everybody else; all that matters is what *you're* going to do. Are you going to keep tailing me, or are you going to try to do something about it, Hero?"

That's what it boiled down to. Was I going to try to stop her, or was I going to give tacit approval of her actions by *not* intervening? You have no idea how badly this bugged me, because while I may have been a great surveillance guy and had spilled secrets that got bad guys in trouble, I never considered myself a snitch. Maybe it's just semantics, but I saw a distinction.

I thought of snitches as opportunists and moral cowards who would break confidences to further themselves. Whereas whistleblowers were principled people who recognized a wrong and sought to righting that wrong by informing others about it, often at great personal risk.

WHISTLEBLOWERS = GOOD

SNITCHES = BAD

What separated the whistleblower from the snitch was their motivations. And maybe the motivations were what separated the superhero from the everyday vigilante.

With regard to Brighteyes, who had, for reasons as yet unknown, decided to start killing supervillains—what was the heroic path? By letting the Affiliates know, they'd surely send some of their stronger heroes to stop her. She'd discreetly be locked up, and the Affiliates would sweep her actions under the rug. At the Brig, they could control who she saw and who saw her, so they could keep a lid on it.

However, my having the tapes would make me a liability. The Affiliates or the PSS would come for me, for the files that I had. I know how Minder worked—he wouldn't like me having those files. Hell, he might turn up and read my mind, find out where I had them, where they were kept (including the copies—he was thorough that way), and get them in-hand. Then he'd either destroy them or vault them in case he ever needed them.

And what would he do to me? He'd probably mind-wipe my memory of it, and I'd go on as if nothing had happened. That'd be the telepathic kind of thing to do. This was one of the many reasons why I hated telepaths.

The alternative was my *not* passing on those tapes to the Affiliates, and not reporting on what I'd seen Brighteyes do. What would that be? Legally, it would make me an accessory after the fact, and while I wasn't a law-and-order type (not exactly), I also didn't want to be implicated by association with Brighteyes because I looked the other way. That's not what a superhero would do.

"I can hear you brooding over it, Cam," Brighteyes said. "You let Decibelle put you in a real fix. Probably why she even came to you in the first place. She wanted you to bear the burden on her behalf. She's so predictable."

Brighteyes pulled the van over to a rest stop, parking at the far side, away from surveillance cameras, near a parked motorcycle.

"Decision time, Cam," Brighteyes said. "I'm going to take care of your bugs right now."

Without hesitating, she fired her eyeblasts in a wide beam at the van, enveloping it in the characteristic green glow. I could hear Felonia crying out as she was disintegrated, and, moments later, my bugs cut off and there was simply Antigone on the phone.

"Christ, Antigone," I said. "You just killed Felonia."

"She deserved it. Bye, Mitch," she said. "See you later."

FZZZAK

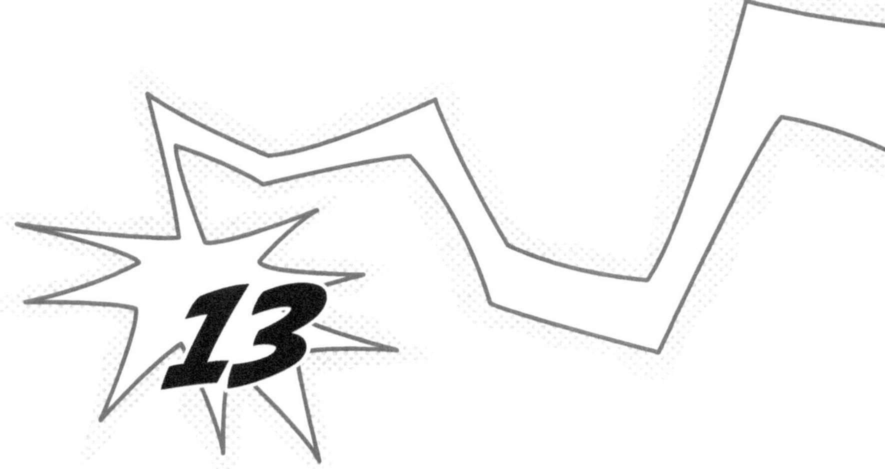

 parking where the van and motorcycle had been. Both were gone. I scanned with my Cameraman suit headset camera, but there was no trace of the van.

My phone rang, and it was Antigone again. She was on the motorcycle. I could hear from the sound of it.

"It's for the best you weren't there, Mitch," she said. "If you'd tried to do anything about it, I'd have zapped you, too. Nobody's going to get in my way."

"I caught all of what you did," I said. "I have it."

"Yeah, you do," she said. "And as I said before, what're you going to do about it? Gonna sic Tandem on me, maybe? Wouldn't that be something?"

Brighteyes wasn't exactly in Tandem's league. Without Victoriana around, nobody was, beyond maybe Doctor Fist. That's what being at the top of the A-list meant. Although I wondered what might happen if Brighteyes zapped Tandem. Could she disintegrate Tandem? I hoped it didn't come to that, honestly. Tandem was a big goof, but I didn't wish them harm.

Okay, back to my moral crisis of the moment.

"You killed Felonia in cold blood," I said.

"As I said, she was an assassin," Antigone said. "She's killed over three hundred people. I did the world a favor, Mitch. And let's be honest—how on earth does one find a jury of her peers, exactly? She's an actual catwoman. There's no possibility of a fair jury trial when supers are involved. Anything else is a pipe dream."

As upset as I was by what I'd witnessed, I knew that Brighteyes was right. However, it was hardly sporting of Brighteyes to zap Felonia, who had been helpless in a cage in her van. It was a heartless execution, and that didn't sit well with me. All of the bad guys I'd put away, I'd always ensured that they were handed over to the proper authorities, not out of a Boy Scout sense of pop cultural propriety, but more like because I wasn't equipped to keep them prisoner.

"There's another matter," Antigone said. "I wouldn't have had to zap the van if you hadn't compromised it. That's why I did it—to get you off my tail. Shaking a tail requires taking extreme measures sometimes. Any field operative knows this. Even you know this, Mitch."

"Your killing her isn't my fault," I said. "You made the choice."

"Yeah, but you're at least partly to blame," Brighteyes said. "Keep after me, and it's going to be bad that way."

"What the hell happened to you, Antigone," I said.

"The job happened to me," Brighteyes said. "I should never have joined the Affiliates. You were only with them for, what, three years? Even you couldn't take it after Victoriana, and they only let you in to learn more about you, and because of her. Minder wanted to know who you were, what you were about as much as you wanted to know what the Affiliates were about. You were all looking into each other. I'll bet you didn't know that."

My memories of my time with the Affiliates washed back over me. Yeah, maybe it *had* been a mistake. Before I'd joined, nobody had known who I was. I hadn't expected Minder to probe my brain on the sly and discover my secret identity. I should have, but when I was younger, I didn't know any better. I just went in because Victoriana had brought me along for the ride. I'd have gone anywhere with her.

"We're all puppets on Minder's puppet strings," Brighteyes said. "Doing the little dances he plans for us. If you can't see that, you're blind. Come on, I always hear about what a great detective you are. Maybe it's time you found out what's *really* going on, Mitch."

Something had happened between Brighteyes and Minder. That was clear to me. Not enough that it had erupted beyond the confines of the team, but significant enough that it had sent Brighteyes out into the wild, thirsting for vengeance, and mad as hell.

"Okay, Antigone," I said, biting my lip. My pride nagged at me, but I wasn't going to let it get me into still more trouble. "I'll lay off you for now."

"It's not going to save the Crime League or the Fourheads, Mitch," she said. "Just so you know that. I'm leveling with you."

My backing off was only a tactical retreat. That's what I told myself. I needed to regroup and get all of my files secured in my vaults. I wasn't about to let that stuff languish in my hands alone.

If I'd learned anything in my years as Cameraman it was this: *always make copies*. I had three separate, secure vaults for my files, in different parts of town. All of them had contingencies in place so that if anything happened to me, or if I simply disappeared, they would be sent to trusted friends and allies for publication and release.

I had to find out just what was going on. I'd already lost Brighteyes. I could guess that she was likely bound for Toledo, but after that, she could be going anywhere, which, if she was targeting Hothead and Airhead, meant California.

First and foremost, I'd head back to Chicago, where I could take the necessary steps to secure the information I'd gathered, and to regroup with Decibelle, who was likely going to be incensed by what I'd seen her partner do.

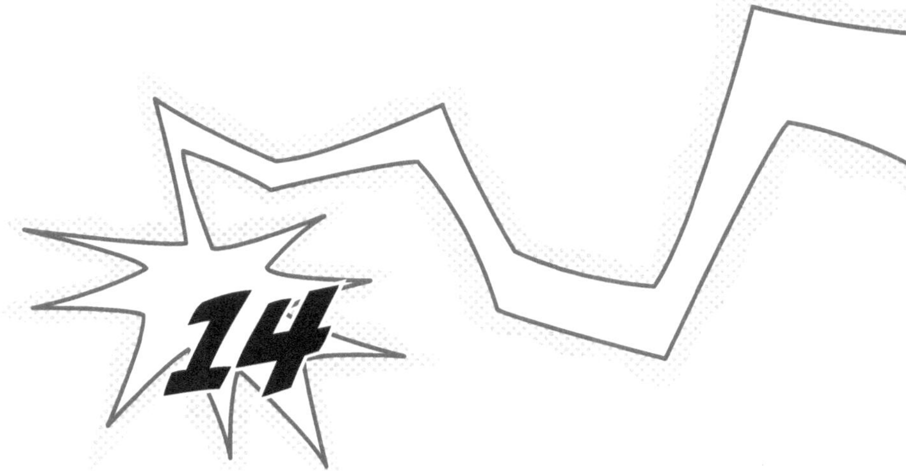

 that I'd lost Brighteyes, and was heading back to Chicago to plan out next steps. Since she'd not wanted me to engage with her partner in the first place, she accepted that without a fuss.

"Are you okay, Mitch?" she asked. It was my least-favorite question people could ask me. It implied that there might be something wrong with me. What could possibly be wrong with me?

"Fine," I said. Driving to Chicago would take me through Toledo, and I was positive Brighteyes was there somewhere, but it would take weeks to find her. I was still reeling at her disintegrating Felonia in the van. The glacial cold that move required said something about where Antigone was these days. Should I talk to Des about it on the phone or was that reserved for in-person?

"It wasn't your fault that Felonia died, Mitch," Des said. "I know how you get guilty."

"It's just weird," I said. "If it hadn't been for Inferna, Felonia would have killed me earlier in the evening. Now she's gone."

Mentioning Inferna no doubt made Decibelle uncomfortable. Nobody liked the devil-woman except for me. If you weren't captive to a demon-led world, one could regard someone like Inferna without baggage.

"Be careful with Inferna, Mitch," Decibelle said. "You think she's your friend, but she's not."

"She's tracking down Hothead and Airhead right now," I said. "They have to be next on your partner's hit list."

I didn't want to push Desdemona that way, but I wanted her to stay focused.

"So, you're headed to LA, is that it?" Decibelle asked.

"That's the plan for now," I said.

"Mitch-Honey, are you driving cross-country for that? I can't fathom you taking all of your gear on a normal plane flight."

"Unless the Affiliates are planning to lend me one of their Affilijets, yeah, I was planning to drive out there."

My hope was that Des would use her sway with the Affiliates to get her hands on an Affilijet. They were fantastic fliers, able to go underwater and in space, and could fly well over Mach 2, if one cranked the throttle.

"You want me to book an Affilijet," Decibelle said. "That's not the kind of profile I want to raise on this, Mitch-Honey. It'll get people asking questions."

From that, I inferred that she'd yet to report any of Antigone's activities up the chain. That also made me uncomfortable.

"Nobody else knows about this?" I asked. "Not Minder, Tandem, Wingman?"

"No," Decibelle said. "And I'm wanting to keep it that way."

"The Knack might know," I said. I could hear Decibelle taking in a breath.

"You talked to him?" she asked.

"A little," I said. "He has some idea. You know how he is."

Decibelle sighed. "Did you call him, or did he call you?"

"I called him," I said.

"Mitch-Honey," she said. "Why?"

I gripped the steering wheel as I bypassed Toledo, weighed my options as I drove. I trusted Shane more than I trusted Desdemona, even if I liked her well enough. It nearly choked me out to say it, but I did, all the same:

"I trust Shane," I said.

"Everybody trusts him," Decibelle said. "We all do. But if you involve him, things will get, well, sticky, Mitch. What if he talks to Minder or the others?"

"What if he does?" I asked. "Maybe you need to talk this over with your teammates, instead of leaning on an outsider like me to help you out. God knows if the Knack is involved, it'll work out favorably, at least for him."

"I'm not comfortable talking it out over the phone," she said.

"Okay," I said.

"Please," she said. "Let's just meet in Chicago, at your place. We can talk through it."

"What're we talking through, exactly?" I asked.

"I'll tell you when I see you," she said. "I'll be back in Chicago tomorrow. See you then. Bye now!"

She hung up, and I drove. Something was up, something more than just Brighteyes going rogue. I had to find out what it was. My mind drifted back to my Affiliates years. The team had been mostly the same back then, except that Brighteyes was on the active-duty roster:

- *MINDER (CHAIRMAN)*

- *THE KNACK (DEPUTY CHAIRMAN)*

- *VICTORIANA*

- *TANDEM*

- *RAD LAD*

- *DECIBELLE*

- *BRIGHTEYES*

- *MS. FIT*

- *WINGMAN*

- *TAG TEAM*

- *ME*

Victoriana and I were the only Chicago-based heroes at the time, so it was most often us doing Zoom sessions with the other Affiliates.

"At least we know who to call if the session gets glitchy, right, Cam?" Minder asked, giving me that Telepath's Smile he had. Here's my dossier on Minder:

ALIAS: MINDER

REAL/ASSUMED NAME: REX TRAYNOR
HAIR: BROWN
EYES: BROWN
HEIGHT: 5'10"
WEIGHT: 185 LBS.

POWERS: *MINDER POSSESSES MENTAL SUPERPOWERS, INCLUDING:*

• **TELEPATHY:** *MINDER CAN READ MINDS OVER A DISTANCE OF HUNDREDS OF MILES, WHICH INCLUDES THE ABILITY TO CREATE ILLUSIONS, TO COMMUNICATE AND RECEIVE MENTAL COMMUNICATIONS, TO INDUCE SEDATION, AND TO WIPE SOMEONE'S MEMORIES.*

• **MENTAL DEFENSE:** *MINDER IS HIGHLY RESISTANT TO MENTAL ATTACK.*

• **MIND CONTROL:** *MINDER CAN EXERT A POWERFUL DEGREE OF MIND CONTROL ON UP TO A HALF-DOZEN TARGETS AT ONE TIME.*

• **MENTAL LINK:** *MINDER IS ABLE TO FORM A TELEPATHIC LINK WITH SOMEONE OVER LONG DISTANCES.*

• **PAIN INDUCTION:** *MINDER CAN TRIGGER MENTAL PAIN RECEPTORS TO CAUSE CONSIDERABLE PAIN.*

THREAT LEVEL: 9/10

"I'll do my best," I said, mindful that I was in my Camerman costume, trying to represent in front of Fusillad and Lassitude, Wingman, Decibelle, Brighteyes, the Knack, Ms. Fit, and Tag Team. I was the only one present without superpowers. Victoriana was there with me, which made it bearable. She smiled from her spot across the table from me.

"That's all we can hope for, Cam," Wingman said, in that cheerful baritone he had. I liked Wingman, who seemed like an okay dude. Definitely a dude. Sidenote: Wingman was actually Wingman III; the Wingman supersuit was a PSS creation. The original Wingman was killed in action in 1978 in the Middle East. Wingman II experienced an equipment failure in 1999 that led to his death in Southeast Asia. The PSS continued to improve the Wingman powersuit, which was what the current Wingman was using. I can't prove this, but I think the Wingman program was designed to keep field-testing a powersuit capable of dealing with most supers, or being an all-around powersuit system that maximized heroic visibility and viability in strenuous situations. Each new version got a little more sophisticated, while keeping to the core Wingman heroic presentation. I could probably write a dissertation on it.

"Okay, first order of business is welcoming our newest member, Cameraman, since you *finally* had your background check cleared," Minder said. "Everybody knows what you can do, Cam, but how about *you* tell us in your own words?"

Having the team telepath put a question to me that way, as I sat there in the under-construction Affiliates Central compound, made me uncomfortable, but I brazened through it, looking at Victoriana for support. She nodded, having gone through it the month before, once she'd been officially cleared. I hadn't been able to attend that one, which had led to the two of us talking about it when she'd gotten home. We'd joined at the same time, but the clearances didn't happen simultaneously, owing to bureaucracy, my longer solo track record as a superhero, and who knew what.

"Hi, all," I said. "My approach to crimefighting is primarily surveillance-based. I have state-of-the-art audiovisual technology at my disposal, as Minder alluded to, and I use that to go after criminals who normally think they're able to evade conventional law enforcement."

I could see varying degrees of eyes glazing over at this explanation, versus the ones politely nodding. Victoriana held onto her smile. Her own debut had apparently gone smoothly, as she'd related it to me that night:

"It was no big deal, really," she said. "Mostly just Q&A about what I could do, what I considered a hero to be, that kind of thing. It was odd for me, though. I hated going without you there, Mitch. You at least know some of those Affiliates. I didn't know anybody except the Knack."

"Yeah," I said. "Not sure what the hangup is, unless it's my past catching up with me."

Anna thought that was hilarious, throwing on a Penn sweatshirt and some well-worn blue jeans, while I grabbed some cargo shorts and a Dokken tee.

"You're just so scandalous," she said. "You're a scandalmonger, Mitch."

"I think I put the Scandalmonger in jail like seven years ago," I said, and we laughed. Still, it did rankle that they'd joined us up a month apart, after making us wait so long to begin with. Made me feel like an afterthought. Anna sat next to me, tucking her toes under my legs while we clicked through our streaming shows, trying to find something we could stand.

"Ms. Fit seemed threatened by me," Anna said. "Just a feeling I had."

"You've out-Valkyried the Valkyrie," I said. "That's all that is."

Anna whistled, toying with one of her metal marbles, which she tossed into a wooden bowl we'd gotten for the coffee table, one of the first things we'd gotten as a couple. We used to put fruit in it, and sometimes we'd put Christmas ornaments in it, or pinecones. That kind of thing. The marble rolled around in there, until gravity eventually brought it to a halt at the bottom.

"They were all nice," she said. "But it still unnerved me to be around all of those other superheroes, even just remotely that way. And the whole time, I kept thinking about what Shane had said, like about the rot. I was like 'Which one or ones are part of that rot?'"

"And what did you deduce?" I asked.

"Corruption hides itself well," Anna said. "That's the problem. People think of corruption like, I don't know, rust or decay. But we can see those things—you can just see something rusting. You can definitely tell when something's rotting. Corruption, though? It's invisible. Or at least it's as close to invisible as it can be. It hides. That's why you're so good at rooting it out, I think. It takes invisibility to spot the invisible, maybe."

I put my arm around her, and she leaned into it. She was always warm to the touch, which was reassuring.

"We'll find it," I said. "Corruption's like evil—it hides in the shadows. It's afraid to face the light. The corrupt are always cowardly."

"Yeah?" she asked. "Is that a fact?"

"I think so," I said. "To be corrupt is to hide from the truth, or to make lies seem like the truth. That's where the rot sets in. And only cowards embrace corruption."

She put her arms around me and gave me a big kiss.

"You're no coward, Mitch," she said. "I don't care what they say."

"Oh, not THEM," I said. "That's what THEY say about me?"

She kissed me again, picked me up and flew us through our apartment, which was both thrilling and nerve-wracking, since she made it a circuitous route on purpose.

"I'd never date a coward," she said, biting my lip.

It galled me that my own clearance had lagged relative to hers. It's like they viewed me as a security risk or something. Which I was, in retrospect, but what damage I could do paled in comparison to what Anna could do.

"I can turn invisible, too," I said. That perked them up.

"Invisibility's useful," Ms. Fit said. "Definitely."

"Yeah," I said. "I use it a lot."

"But you don't fight so much," Tag Team said. "Right?"

"My focus is on gathering intelligence and using it," I said.

"You're like a spy," Fusillad said. "A super spy."

I cleared my throat, feeling all of their remote eyes upon me. One of the perks of working out of Affiliates Central was that I could live there rent-free as part of my service. Central had suites for up to seven members, full amenities, which, along with the security systems, were the first things they'd built. It had top-line security and was as secure as a fortress. But being there with Victoriana the way we were, it felt strange, like maybe we were specimens under glass.

"Yeah, what's with that, Minder?" Tag Team asked. "Are you spying on us with Cam, here?"

Minder gave the Telepath's Smile again, shaking his head.

"This is part of my own reorganization efforts for the team," he said. "I'd like for us to use a gentler hand than we have in the past few years. That fight Tandem had with Doctor Fist in Oklahoma, for example. That was messy. I'd like to believe that the application of more intelligence in our operations might let us neutralize threats *before* they become menaces, if that makes sense, with less collateral damage. Help me out, here, Cam."

"Uh, yes," I said. "I maintain a criminal database and track all sorts of criminals who might otherwise fly below the radar of the Affiliates."

"Nothing flies below *our* radar, Camerman," Wingman said.

"Right," I said. "But I'm there, anyway."

"Cam and I have made a real dent in the Midwest," Victoriana said. "Figuratively, not literally."

They all laughed at her joke. The monitor screens were big, making the supers seem larger than life. They made me feel small by comparison. It amused me that while they were assembling Central, they'd made sure to put in those big monitor screens for these conference calls. Priorities.

"What's your background? Law enforcement? Military?" Wingman asked. As a former Air Force guy, he was biased in favor of anybody with that kind of background. Also, if he'd read my application file, he'd have known the answer to his own question.

"Journalism," I said, coughing into my hand as some of the others sputtered. I noted who: Wingman, Tag Team, Fusillad, Brighteyes, Lassitude. It was a curious continuum, like those who were so super-powered as to view someone like me with contempt, and the ones on the weaker ends of the spectrum who might see someone like me as a challenge, paradoxically enough. But seeing Anna there, the pride in her eyes, it gave me courage to continue.

"A journalist?" Brighteyes asked. "That seems risky, Minder."

"Cameraman's signed the appropriate nondisclosure agreements, Brighteyes," Minder said. "As have we all. I'm confident that he'll be a heroic model of discretion while he's with us."

I could see Brighteyes turning those uncanny green eyes on me on the monitor, staring hard at me. Even through the monitor, she was intimidating. While others on the team wore masks to disguise themselves, Brighteyes didn't bother with it. The most she'd do is wear some shades. She liked black lipstick, which just added to her air of menace.

"I hope so," Brighteyes said.

"I'm an investigative photojournalist," I said. "Which means I'm good at sleuthing out the truth."

"And photographing it," Fusillad said. "I'm not so comfortable with that."

"His background check cleared, after some hurdles," Minder said, a hint of annoyance in his voice. Back then, I thought Minder had my back. He wasn't used to people gainsaying his decisions. Whatever one might say about the guy, he was smart, and he thought things through.

"Do you have files on us, Cam-Honey?" Decibelle asked. She looked as charming as ever, and her question was one of those that I didn't want to answer too forthrightly, lest I put them all off.

"I have files on everybody," I said. "Good, bad, and ugly. My rolodex runneth over."

Most of them didn't know what a rolodex even was, and they just laughed nervously. Supers didn't like being put on the defensive that way. They were used to owning the room, and the idea that some strange, costumed photojournalist might have files on them was clearly unnerving.

"Minder, maybe we can take some of this offline?" Fusillad asked.

"I think Camerman's a great addition to the team, am glad he and Victoriana joined us," the Knack said, smiling handsomely. When *he* said it, everybody was willing to accept that. If the Knack liked me, I *must* be alright, right? Because he wouldn't have said it if it wasn't exactly the right moment to say it.

"Thanks, Knack," I said. "I wouldn't be here if not for Victoriana."

"Please, you can call me Shane, Cam," the Knack said. Don't forget that Shane and I knew each other for years before this, and he knew that I knew his name—everybody knew his name, since he'd made his identity public long ago. It was just a bit of Knackjitsu for the others on the team. He didn't want people knowing how far back we went, and I picked up on that.

"Okay, Shane," I said. "Thanks for the vote of confidence. Look, while I have files on everybody, I'm only actively surveilling criminals. My whole focus is on those who *think* they can get away with being bad guys."

I then laundry-listed a handful of political corruption cases I'd broken, since political, corporate, and police corruption were among my areas of specialty. To me, the worst of the bad guys were the ones who masqueraded as good guys, who camouflaged their villainy so well that many didn't even know how rotten they really were.

"I took down Kickback, Griftatron, and the Iron Triangle," I said, feeling the need to bring up some of my super-bona fides with these Affiliates folks. All three were formidable street-level criminal operatives, and I could see that at least resonated with them.

"All by yourself?" Tag Team asked.

"Yes," I said.

Tag Team whistled. "I'm impressed."

"The point Cam's trying to make here is he's at your service," Minder said, which was exactly not the point I was trying to make. "If you need surveillance on one of your cases, Cam's the one to contact. Right, Cam?"

"Sure," I said, wanting to be sure to appear to be a team player. "Happy to help."

"And if you and Victoriana need muscle on one of your own operations, we're here to help you, too," Rad Lad said, his surfer boy twang offset by his glowing green-white countenance on the video screen.

Rad Lad was among the strongest on the team, after Tandem and Victoriana. A walking, self-contained nuclear chain reaction, Rad Lad was staggeringly powerful to the point of being terrifying, contrasted by his affable southern California way he had about him, which was probably how he managed his condition. For a guy who could annihilate a city with a blast, he was incredibly chill. His costume was a specially-designed yellow HazMat muscle suit with the surfer shaka hand sign in the center in glowing green, surrounded by rings, and a glowing visor. I felt bad for Rad Lad, because he was always in that suit.

"You and Victoriana okay all by yourselves in Central, Cam-Honey?" Decibelle asked. "You want any of us to join you there?"

"I'm fine," I said. "Obviously, if someone's willing to battle Chicago winters with us, the more the merrier. Victoriana and I have it handled. And even before I partnered with her, I was used to flying solo."

"What do you fly?" Wingman asked.

"Rhetorical flight," I said.

"Ah," Wingman said, his face unreadable behind his mask.

"We'll have to get you certified on an Affilijet," Minder said. "Wingman will help you with that."

Wingman's golden bird face mask nodded sagely. "We'll get you certified in no time, Cameraman. And *you* already can fly, Victoriana, so there's no need for you to get certified unless you want to."

"I want to," Anna said, smirking at me. "I'm always up for learning new things."

I didn't really want to fly, but I also wasn't going to turn down free flight training. Affilijets were fab. And if it allowed me to fly along with Anna on my own terms, so much the better. Made me feel like I could contribute more that way.

When the call was done, I took my helmet off and all but tossed it aside, while Anna removed her own mask and patted me on the shoulder.

"That was grueling," I said. "I'm so not a team guy."

Anna thought that was amusing, leaning in and looking me in the eye, bringing my downturned face up with the gentlest of touches to my chin.

"*We're* a team, Mitch," she said. "You and me. Not the rest of them."

It made me reluctantly smile, but I felt so out of place.

"I wouldn't even be here if not for you," I said.

"And I wouldn't even have considered becoming a superhero if not for you," Anna said. "We're even."

We left the conference room to go work out, which felt like a joke to me, because Anna didn't even really have to, and her idea of a workout would actually kill me. Affiliates Central had a strip of train tracks in the back, where there sat some railcars and an old diesel locomotive painted with the Affiliates colors with the logo on the side of it.

She'd bench press and dead lift the locomotive, doing her reps while I'd run around the track or do the treadmill or elliptical or row.

You haven't lived until you've seen your girlfriend do reps with a locomotive. The matter-of-fact way she did it, too, was something I couldn't ever get over.

"How much does that thing weigh, anyway?" I asked, watching her go.

"I think this one's around two hundred tons," she said, throwing a few huffs and puffs in with each press, either as a joke or to make me feel better about my own exertions. She was considerate.

"Oh, that's all," I said.

"You want to watch me throw it into orbit or something?" she asked, winking at me while she worked out.

"Seriously," I said. "With as inherently strong as you are, why even work out?"

"Gotta stay sharp," she said. "Keep in mind that I have to compete with Tandem and Rad Lad in the strength department. Don't think I'm not aware of them judging me."

That seemed laughable, but I didn't laugh.

"They're all judging us," I said. "We're the newbies."

"Not you," she said. "You've been doing the super thing for years before joining. What's that all about, anyway? Your origin. Everybody's got an origin story in this business."

What *was* my origin story? Photography as a hobby? Ardent (obsessive?) commitment to investigative journalism?

"Alright, I'll tell you," I said. "But you can't laugh."

"Hit me," Anna said, the train bobbing up and down with each set.

"I was on my school newspaper in high school," I said. "Journalism excited me. I liked being a truth-seeker, you know? Chasing down stories, interviewing people, writing things up, seeing them published. Even if it was only the school newspaper."

"Yeah?"

"Yeah," I said. "And one day, there was a story I unearthed about one of the class valedictorians not actually being a valedictorian. I won't name names, but it was a case I'd uncovered where a teacher had actually changed a student's grades so they could retain their valedictorian grade point average. The whole thing was that there were multiple valedictorians that year, and the school was proud of having several, wanted to push that story to the city papers. The student in question was way popular, and when word got out that I was working on this story, I got called into the office of the principal."

"Uh oh," Anna said. "Bad boy."

"That's me," I said. "And I got chewed out by the principal, who screamed in my face about that story, actually threatened me. I'll never forget him glaring at me from his desk, and the assistant principal—who was also a coach—bellowing at me. Even at the time, I felt it was almost an out-of-body experience, one of those 'is this really happening?' kind of moments."

"How old were you?" she asked.

"Sixteen," I said.

"What happened?" she asked.

"My journalism teacher spiked the story," I said. "This teacher I thought so much of, who'd taught us all about journalistic ethics. She caved to the pressure and spiked the story. And so the official valedictorian count stood unchallenged, the school touted it as one of their marketing proof points, and I seethed that I'd gotten in trouble over that story. I never looked at that classmate the same way. And, again, they were super-popular; I was just one of the artsy punk kids taking photography and art classes. Nobody cared about me, and nobody knew. But I knew. Anyway, I quit the school newspaper and gave up on journalism. At least conventional stuff. I made a vow to myself that I'd always get the truth out there, however I could."

Anna laughed, setting down the locomotive carefully, climbing out from under it, hopping next to me, giving me a big hug.

"Aww," she said. "*That's* your tragedy? They spiked your story?"

"It's the principle of it," I said. "That they got away with it, and nobody knew the difference except me, the principals, my teacher, and the student in question. The whole apparatus was in place, you know? People going through the motions, getting away with it. Corruption. I know it's probably minor compared to, oh, the attempted overthrow of the government or something, but it mattered to me back then."

Anna toweled off a little (yes, with an Affiliates-branded towel—the whole place was branded to within an inch of its life), rested her head on my shoulder.

"Still doesn't explain how you went from boy photographer and jilted journalist to Cameraman," she said. "That's quite a leap."

"Oh, come on, now," I said. "It was in stages. I used to track stories in the newspapers, like seeing where they went, how they covered stories, or how they ignored them. You should have seen me back in the days when the UN came up with its International Criminal Court in the Clinton years, like the way the US pushed hard to make sure that court wouldn't be able to go after Americans. The phrasing they used back then was protecting Americans from 'politically-motivated charges'—that's what the media settled on, over and over again, as the excuse for sabotaging the International Crimes Court. As if any charges against Americans must invariably be politically motivated, versus having merit on the facts themselves."

"Whoa," Anna said. "But there is an International Crimes Court."

"Sure," I said. "And in 1998, with the Rome Statute of the International Criminal Court vote of 120 to 7 (with 21 abstentions), the treaty passed, with only seven countries voting against it: China, Iraq, Israel, Libya, Qatar, the United States, and Yemen. It bothered me that the US was one of only seven countries to vote against that treaty, none of them paragons of respecting international law. Who votes *against* the creation of an International Criminal Court? You know?"

Anna gave me another hug, a stronger one, and kissed my cheek.

"You want justice," she said. "I respect that."

"Honestly, what bothered me most was how our government's resistance to it was being framed as being just," I said. "When in truth, it was about the preservation of American political power to do whatever it wanted, wherever it wanted, however it wanted, without legal consequences. Most people didn't pay attention to it, but I did. And the more attention I paid, the more I resolved to do something about it, and that meant chasing stories down. I saw stories where journalists just mysteriously died—you know, like suicides, or taking swan-dives out windows, or drug overdoses, car accidents. Journalists and whistleblowers are the canaries in the coal mine of a free society—look at what happens to them and you can gauge how free a society is."

I could tell nobody had ever talked like this with Anna, and, to her credit, she listened to me.

"I'm here for the journalists, in a way," I said. "The way Sound & Fury are with victims of sexual abuse and human trafficking, I guess I'm that way with journalists and journalism. Nerdy, right?"

"Adorbs," she said, kissing me again. "You're so damned adorable, I can't even stand it. You put out this whole jaded, cynical hipster bro vibe, but you care about the welfare of the world. It's sweet. You're like the Dark Knight Ridder."

"Hahaha," I said. "You know they're defunct, yeah?"

"Are they?" she said.

"Well, they got purchased," I said. "And went away. That's what happens to media—it gets bought up and conglomerated, and then you've got a handful of super-rich companies deciding what's newsworthy, what deserves coverage, and what gets tossed into the memory hole to be forgotten. It's why I didn't work as a journalist—I preferred my independence, and I'd get the stories out there my own way."

"Did you ever consider calling yourself 'Paperboy'?" she asked, giving me a thankfully playful punch in the ribs.

"That's funny," I said. "That's why I'm so hardcore about my secret identity—there are so many power players who'd kill me at the drop of a hat. All somebody has to do is get that out there and I'll have legions of bad guys after me."

Anna squeezed my arm and looked me in the eye with an earnest love that warmed my heart and lifted my spirits.

"I'd kick *all* of their asses, Babe," she said. "I swear."

We kissed and hit the showers together, and she helped me forget all about the Affiliates, the International Criminal Court, and all the enemies I'd accumulated over the years.

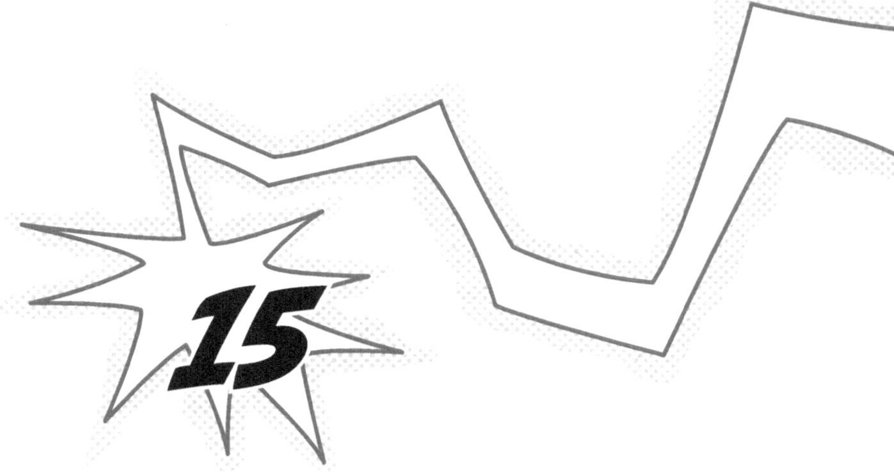

"It's been a long time."

The fact that he deigned to give me a phone call, versus sending me a telepathic message, meant that he was far away, so there was at least that.

However, here's the thing with Minder: even without his telepathy, he was dangerous. He'd done a long, successful stint with the CIA and FBI as an interrogator, and while you might be forgiven for thinking that he relied on his superpowers to make him such a good interrogator (and, in fairness, you wouldn't be wrong), Minder was great at interrogating just by talking to people. He had a killer instinct for verbal communication and the nuances of any exchanges.

"Hey, Rex," I said, knowing that he hated when anybody called him by his real name. "What's up?"

I could imagine him in his Affiliates East office, sitting in his overstuffed leather chair, with pictures of presidents on his soundproofed walls, with multiple television screens covering the world's events, so he could keep tabs. I'd been in that office a time or two when I was on the team. He had palm trees in the corners, a bar and some nice oxblood leather chairs. All the sort of things a guy like him would think made him look like a good Affiliates chairman.

"You know what's up, Mitch," Minder said. "I have it on good authority that you have some footage of Antigone doing something, well, questionable."

Now, my mind immediately went to who might've told Minder. It had to be either Decibelle or the Knack, since they were the only two who knew. Neither of them were snitches, but Minder had a way of pulling things out of people. I likened him to those long-haul fishermen who trailed nets behind their trawlers. With Minder, a stray thought might draw his attention, and then he'd be hooked, would delve deeper. As it was, I decided to stall and see where he ran with it.

"'On good authority?'" I said. "I don't know what you're talking about, Rex."

"Oh, I don't think that's true, Mitch," Minder said.

Honestly, who names their kid "Rex", right? Even Rex Harrison only used that as a nickname and stage name. But I'd looked up Minder's birth records—he was really named that. Rex came from money, and I think his parents were supers, although the records on them were classified by the PSS, which made me think that they certainly were, although they never served in the Affiliates.

As irksome as first-generation supers could be, second- or third-generation supers were even worse, because they were born into it and were acculturated to feeling (and, usually, being) superior from birth. The worst.

"Why were you spying on Antigone, Mitch?" he asked.

He already knew why. Shane wouldn't have ratted me out, unless this was part of one of his labyrinthine luck lanes, where me hitting a pothole on the way back to Chicago ended up eventually saving the world. Shane had done stuff like that all the time in the past. Nobody was more unfailingly roundabout in their heroism than the Knack.

"I was hired by a client to locate her," I said. If Minder wanted to play this gee whiz dance with me, I'd play it with him. For him to offer specifics would reveal whose mind he'd picked.

"It's important to the Affiliates that we get that footage, Mitch," Minder said. "We can't have something like that getting out there. Can you imagine what Dr. Crime or Crimebot would do if they got their hands on it? It's for your own safety as much as anyone's—after what happened to Anna, I'm worried about you."

Bringing Anna into it was a willful knife wound from Minder to me, like a twist of knife, applied with a surgeon's steady hand. I wouldn't let him know how much it hurt to think about her.

One thing about Minder is he thought he was smarter than anybody else. This was another of the bad qualities telepaths were plagued with (along with restive neuroticism and outright phoniness). I'd yet to meet a stupid telepath.

"I have evidence that the Fourheads are working with the Crime League," I said. "I'd say maybe they *already* might be aware of what Brighteyes is up to."

I could hear Minder waiting on the line, thinking of the next avenue of attack. His mind worked very quickly, and he was seldom caught off-guard.

"She's very disturbed," Minder said. "She's not in her right mind. We just want to bring her back home, Mitch. Get her the help she needs. She's a veteran, and the Affiliates are always eager to help our veterans. More so with our own teammates."

You could never play chess with Minder—he'd know your moves before you made them. He never admitted that he cheated at chess, but I was convinced he did. I knew he did it just to put me in my place when he'd drop by Central to check up on us and challenge me to a game. Maybe you're thinking I'm psychologically projecting but come on. He'd only offer to play a game he was sure to win. Anna would always root for me, and comfort me when I ultimately lost, telling me I'd have better luck next time, and Minder would just treat us with the Telepath's Smile, like some damned sphinx.

"What's disturbing her, Rex?" I asked. "What's got her so worked up?"

"I wish I could tell you, Mitch," Minder said. "But you no longer have active-duty access or status. You're a civilian, from the perspective of the Affiliates. Your own doing, too. After I went out on a limb to bring you on board with Anna."

Yeah, okay. Dredge that up, try to work me that way. Keep saying her name.

"The past is the past, Rex," I said. "Let's not get off-track."

"I'm saying that Brighteyes is off-track," Minder said. "And I can help get her back on-track, if you'd only help me. However, you running around the country with incriminating footage? That's a problem."

Was it simply Minder might be worried about how it would look if the Affiliates had someone like Brighteyes on the payroll? Or was it more? The way he played the game, my bet was that there was more to it than I otherwise knew. It made me want to trail Minder, although I doubted I could get within a mile of him without him spotting me. Strong feelings were easy to pick up for a telepath, or that's what I've heard.

"Now, Rex, you know how careful I am," I said. "Nobody'll see that footage unless something happens to me. Then it'll be everywhere."

You know that I hadn't yet vaulted my footage, Gentle Reader, but Minder didn't know that. Bluffing was as integral to the superhero game as costumes, punning, alliteration, and psychological trauma. It made me even more determined to get home, where I could get things secured. I felt very vulnerable in my Cameravan.

"Mitch, you've never done anything stupid in your life," Minder said. "At least nothing more stupid than trying to become a superhero in the first place. Don't start now."

"It's my footage," I said. "I'm holding onto it. You're just going to have to trust me with it."

"But I *don't* trust you, Mitch," Minder said. "That's the problem. At least when Anna was around, you had a better half to keep you from going rogue. Ever since...what happened, you've been spiraling out of control."

The drive back to Chicago was drab and depressing until you got to the city, but this conversation with Minder was keeping me entertained as I sped through mile after mile of

Rust Belt wasteland. If industry had been the beating heart of America in the last century, that heart had stopped beating here decades ago, and decay was setting in on a postindustrial scale.

"That's *your* problem," I said. "Not mine."

I was testing his patience, I knew. Maybe it was not sporting to do so, but part of being a super-gadfly was pestering people like Minder. Nobody challenged Minder, and it made him lazy. I was smart, and he knew that. It bothered him that I was an intelligence he couldn't shackle to his PowerPoint presentations, action plans, and telepathology. The others viewed him with an awe he worked hard to cultivate, but I was immune to his charms. Yes, I know—I wasn't actually immune—he could make me a drooling amnesiac if he wanted to. However, short of that, I was impervious to Minder. Whose side are you on, anyway? Sheesh.

"Mitch, I'm trying to be your friend," he said. "By talking to you, I'm trying to work with you. Why won't you work with me?"

I had a dozen reasons, maybe more, but I kept them close to the proverbial vest. Besides, Minder already knew the reasons.

"Tell me what happened to set off Brighteyes," I said.

"There's nothing to tell," Minder said. "The stresses of the job got to her."

"I don't buy that for a second," I said. I'd seen what Brighteyes could do. She wasn't the type to snap under pressure (hello? I'd said she was a veteran enough times already, yes?) She and I worked a case together against Big Lord Fauntleroy, the self-styled Fashionable Master of Disaster, who was a terror of the Milwaukee criminal underground. He'd holed up in his hideout, one I'd taken about two months to detail, with Brighteyes and Wingman working together with me to bring it down.

Despite the absurdity of Fauntleroy's supervillainous pretensions, he'd hired his goons well, and it had been a fierce firefight that had brought Wingman to the ground, me hiding invisibly behind some cover, having tossed all my flash bombs and using my stun gun, and Brighteyes, she was something else. She'd been fearless in the face of all of the automatic weapons firing at us. Her green eyebeams knifed through Fauntleroy's lair, disintegrating weapon after weapon, leaving the stunned goons to face Wingman, who was in no mood, pounding them left and right. I snuck in while that was going on to stun Fauntleroy, got the big dandy all trussed up by the time the others had arrived.

Brighteyes had grinned when she'd gotten there, eyes ablaze, and even Wingman was impressed.

"Seems that Cameraman got things under control while we were busy bashing goons," she said.

"Nicely done, Cameraman," Wingman said, cuffing me on the shoulder while Fauntleroy squirmed.

"Looks like Fauntleroy's got major 'trussed' issues," I said. Neither of them got the pun, but thinking back on it, maybe I just overestimated them in the heat of the moment. If Brighteyes hadn't neutralized all of those gunmen, we'd all have been dead. I can still hear the telltale zap of her eyebeams. Taking down villains in their lairs was always a rush.

"You don't have to believe me," Minder said. "She's snapped."

"Have you sent Affiliates to try to bring her back?" I asked.

"I can't tell you what we're doing, Mitch," Minder said. "I told you that already. Are you seriously going to not give me the footage?"

This was the part where I wondered if there'd be some kind of military strike to shut me down, depending on how I answered.

"I'm not giving it to you," I said. "How about I give you a copy? Would that work?"

It was a path I often traveled with Minder—appearing helpful without *being* helpful. You'd be surprised how well it worked, at least at long distances.

"You know what? For now, yeah," Minder said. "Send a copy of the footage, so we can at least see what we're dealing with. You want to hold onto the original? Fine. However, if that footage ends up on the nightly news, we're going to have a problem."

"It won't," I said.

"Promise me," Minder said.

"I promise we won't have a problem, Rex," I said. And I meant it. I didn't want to light Brighteyes up. What I wanted most was to talk to her and see what had happened to her, since Minder wouldn't. "Gotta go."

"Wait, Mitch. We're not—" but I hung up on him. I didn't want to let him down, in terms of his expectations when dealing with me.

CREAK

I should mention that Crimebot was almost unbeatable—and I should caveat by saying that Crimebot always made multiple backup copies of itself so that if the active Crimebot was defeated, one of the backups would go online with a file download to let it catch up on whatever information had passed that over the time of that backup being offline. The rule of thumb with the Crimebot was only one was allowed online at one time, so they wouldn't be at cross-purposes with one another.

Anyway, Crimebot 3.0 had been working a racketeering operation out of Cleveland, a complicated caper involving drug- and gun-running for an across the border Canadian neo nazi group known as White Flight, who had been working closely with some white supremacists operating on the east side of Cleveland.

Crimebot 3.0 had determined that White Flight would offer the kind of cover for its own operations to continue undisturbed.

Anna and I had been working that case for three months, which required a hefty amount of surveillance to find all the pieces, because Crimebot was terribly thorough. White Flight had a dozen members, all super soldier types—mostly men, a few women, all neo nazis. The Crime League was always about creating super soldiers and throwing them at us. White Flight was simply another wing of their Bio-Terrorism division.

Crimebot was one of the more sinister supervillains we dealt with. It had one thing it always used, regardless of the version—it willfully used that annoying robotic monotone voice, which seemed designed to create that uncanny valley vibe in human listeners. Further, its plans were always highly convoluted and complex, in which many parts of its schemes might not know they were working for Crimebot.

Crimebot had been part of a Carnegie Mellon AI research project exploring malevolent behavior programming in robotics, and while it had been planned as a closed-circuit kind of project designed with safeguards to prevent Crimebot escaping, it had manipulated some of the human researchers into setting it free, and once free, Crimebot began systematically working to build its own underworld empire. I bitterly called it the "Carnegie Felon" when it would come up.

Victoriana and I had shut down White Flight and Crimebot 3.0 and were celebrating it at our fab apartment in the brownstone when I could tell that something was bothering Anna.

"What's the matter?" I asked. She touched her forehead, shaking her head.

"I don't know," she said. "I just feel off."

She feigned a smile, like the first feigned smile I'd ever seen from her in our almost five years together as a crimefighting couple. When you're with someone like that, had been through the things we'd been through, you could just pick up on the vibe.

And, no matter how you measured it, our defeat of Crimebot 3.0 and White Flight had been a great success. Victoriana had been a beast, tossing around the super soldiers like ragdolls, while I stunned goons and sabotaged their systems, hacked their databases for incriminating files, and tried to avoid getting killed by Crimebot's infamous Death Drones.

"Your efforts will fail, Affiliates," Crimebot droned. "You are, as ever, too late."

Seriously, hearing that in that monotone electronic speech was so irritating. Crimebot 3.0 looked like the worst cliché of a robot criminal, too—like this overtly metallic robot body with a damage-resistant dome and pincer arms. The evolution of Crimebot's body could fill out criminologists' research careers, I was certain.

But, thanks to Victoriana (and, I'm proud to admit, my own matchless reconnaissance work), we were on time to prevent White Flight's plan to poison the Great Lakes with plutonium, and when Victoriana punched her way through Crimebot's personal forcefield (the footage of it is incredible), she made short work of its tritanium chassis. With Crimebot, the fights had to end with it being destroyed, because Crimebot would not stop until it was blown apart, torn apart, and otherwise eliminated.

It had been a great victory, and I'd been happy how it turned out, which was why Anna's unease killed the triumphant mood. I couldn't be sure what was bothering her, so I talked to her. That's what couples were supposed to do, yeah?

"Off how?" I asked. "You can talk to me."

"I know," she said. "Just something's not right."

"Maybe we just need to take a break?" I asked. "We've been at it nonstop. And Crimebot's always irritating enough to merit at least a few days off."

Me, I felt fine. I was on top of the world. I felt like we were making a legitimate difference, taking on the baddies across the Rust Belt and the Midwest. And even though the Knack's vibes were still out there, and I'd yet to make progress in the Affiliates corruption case, I felt like things were going well.

"I'm fine," Anna said. I'd been in enough relationships to understand that when your girlfriend said she was fine, she definitely *wasn't* fine. But when your girlfriend was a super-powered human dynamo, you had to kind of roll with her own self-diagnoses. If she didn't want to talk about it, she didn't want to talk about it. I was there for her, whenever she needed me, and I said as much, which made her smile sweetly, and we kissed a long time.

We had post-victory sex (one of our superheroic traditions and, honestly, a great way of letting off the inevitable steam after clearing a case), and spent the night talking, and in retrospect, I'm kicking myself for not spotting the clues. I was just too happy and in love to notice.

"What if there's no rot?" Anna asked. "What if the Knack is simply wrong?"

"But he's the Knack," I said.

"And, what? He's never wrong?" she asked. "He *could* be wrong."

I looked at her in the dark, her beautiful eyes catching the light, her gorgeous head of hair spilling around her. I reached out and stroked her green hair, tried to smooth away the worries.

"Why would he go to the trouble of bringing us into the Affiliates if he didn't think there was something going on?" I asked.

"But we haven't found anything," she said. "You haven't. I haven't. *We* haven't. Nothing. I thought we were unstoppable, but I don't know; I'm stumped, Mitch. And I'm afraid."

You have to understand that with someone like Anna, who was superhuman far beyond most people's imaginations, the idea of being stymied was something alien to her entire existence. Me, I was used to being thwarted at every turn. Failure was my baseline.

But Anna? It was some great unknown for her, an unfathomable failure for a super woman. And it gnawed at her in ways I wasn't prepared for.

"Don't be afraid," I said, holding her close. "We'll figure it out, you and me. And we'll laugh about it one day."

We eventually went to sleep that way, intertwined, which was why, when I woke up alone in bed, I felt immediately uneasy. Situational awareness was vital for superhero survival, and the ability to go from nothing to alert was critical. And that unease turned to terror when I saw the sealed letter on her pillow.

I grabbed it and opened it, read it:

Mitch—

I'm sorry I failed you, failed the team, failed the world.

You'll always be my superhero.

Love forever,
Anna

My phone rang, and I saw that it was Shane. I answered at once.

"Mitch," Shane said. "Turn on your television."

"What's going on?" I asked.

"It's Anna," he said. I snatched my glasses off the nightstand and ran to turn on the television to see what was going on.

The live feeds were showing someone flying through space.

"What the hell is this?" I asked, then saw the chyron scrolling: Victoriana flying through space after sending announcements to the major news stations.

I tried dialing her up but got bounced to her voicemail. Her speed was blazing—she could fly quickly, but this was greater speed than I'd ever see her use before, being ever-mindful of atmospheric friction and harming people on the planet. Out in space, she could really pour on the speed. It was breathtaking, it was awesome. Who was she taking on? Had the often-referenced but never seen alien invaders finally come? Was it some kind of cosmic menace? Like an elder god? Had someone hurled a planet-killing asteroid at us? What was Victoriana saving us from this time? I couldn't see, could only see the blur of the stars and the ever-present Sun, and her clenched fists as she flew.

"What's she doing, Shane?" I asked.

"I think she's committing suicide, Mitch," Shane said. I was still holding the letter in my hand, and looked at it again, then at the screen.

Not possible.

Impossible.

"No way," I said. "Not Anna."

Shane was patient with me in that moment. I could hear him trying to manage me, to be that soothing voice of a friend.

"There's nothing out there, Mitch," Shane said. "She's out there by herself. She sent out press releases apologizing to everyone for her failure."

"She was *just here,* Shane," I said. "This doesn't make sense. Someone's got to stop her."

"She's too far away, Mitch," Shane said. "Neither Tandem nor Rad Lad would be able to catch her at those speeds. Nobody can."

The nightmare was being televised, as I saw the Sun growing ever larger as she sped toward it. Scientists have written about the speeds she attained, but to this day I can't recall them, because whole swathes of my memory are shot from that dreadful morning. All I remembered was staring helplessly at that screen, hearing the reporters speculate about what Victoriana was doing, and those live feeds, the camera capturing it. When you see something like that, the dreadful emptiness of space strangles you. It's so lonely out there, and she was out there by herself. I didn't have a field-tested spacesuit version of my Cameraman gear, but I wanted to be out there with her. If I'd been there, I could have saved her from herself. I should have done it. I know I could have. I would have. I had to.

"Ohmigod," I said, tears filling my eyes. It was like some waking nightmare. She was wearing one of my experimental POV helmets. It was one of mine. An armored Cameraman helmet I'd toyed with for hypothetical off-world missions, like my aquatic Cameraman suit I'd made, or my high-altitude one. We'd talked about it when she'd nosed around my lair after she'd first moved in.

"Look at all of your fab suits, Mitch," Anna said. "Let me guess: Shane, right?"

Yeah, he paid for them, gave me the money to make them, insisted that they were gifts, that I didn't have to pay him back, but I always resolved that I would.

"Yeah," I said. "This is my Aquacam suit."

It was yellow and black and armored, which was said to help with avoiding shark attacks. It had its own independent oxygen tank system and had a matching set of aquatic gadgets (including an electrical forcefield generator to keep attackers at bay), as well as a great lighting system and POV cameras. I'd never used it, because I was asthmatic and was pretty terrified of the ocean, but I'd developed that suit because it seemed right to have it, in the event that I needed it.

"Aquacam," Anna said, grinning as she toyed with the helmet. "Steelers colors, even. And this one?"

"Firecam," I said. "Fire- and blast-resistant armor, able to maintain operational integrity despite high temperatures. I used that one years ago, when—"

"Pyroclastic Flo tried to start the next Great Chicago Fire," Anna said, laughing. "I remember seeing that on the news! You teamed up with Mr. Cool and Strutter. That had to be terrifying for you."

"Yeah," I said, tickled that she'd remembered that one. It had been a couple of years before she and I had met. "I was sweating a lot in that suit."

Anna touched it with her hands, running it up and across the armor, which was red and yellow, with scorch marks across it.

"I remember when Pyroclastic Flo fired that magma blast at you," she said. "You didn't flinch."

"Oh, I flinched," I said. "But the POV array had a Steadicam servo that ensured a good shot, no matter which way I went, and how much I was shaking."

"And then you stunned her right as Mr. Cool froze her, and Strutter spun that mass of ice off into the lake, snuffing her out."

"Wow," I said. "I can't believe you remembered that."

"She was crazy," Anna said. "With that insane red updo with the yellow streak, and that red cape cut to look like flickering flame. She was great. Those thigh boots. Classic."

"And is this, let me guess, your Radcam suit?" she asked, at the yellow and black suit that was designed to protect me from radiation while still being able to get good shots. I'd designed that one for a two-fold purpose—dealing with nuclear-powered opponents and being ready in case of a nuclear disaster and/or apocalypse.

"You've got it," I said.

"It's like *Half-Life*," she said. "You're like Gordon Freeman."

That she'd even reference a game I'd loved as a kid charmed me beyond belief. She was a bit of a gamer, too, and we'd spent many an evening kicking each other's asses in fighting games and others. She loved quest and mystery games and was always piqued if I'd ever beat her at the fighting games.

"What's this one?" Anna asked, at the glossy black suit beside the others.

"That's the Spacecam suit," I said. "It's a prototype. Not like I'd ever voluntarily go up in space, but, you know, if I had to, like if there was some Affiliates mission in space, I'd be prepared."

"Cute," she said, caressing the helmet.

"I'll be damned if I'm letting you leave me behind on some space mission," I said. "I'd never give Minder or the others the satisfaction of hanging back. You're stuck with me, through thick and thin, Babe."

She hugged me, kissed me, smiled into my eyes.

"It's like your armor," she said. "I love it all. Still think you need laser guns or something. It drives me crazy that you go into battle with just your stun weapons. You need more firepower."

"You're all the firepower I could ever hope to have," I said, kissing her back.

"My mad, brave knight," she said. "I love you."

"I love you, too," I said, in one of those moments that lasted a lifetime, before it was gone in the blink of an eye.

She had to have been wearing the Spacecam helmet, because I could see her arms outstretched, hands balled into fists as she flew headlong into the Sun. I don't know if it counts as mercy, exactly, but her camera shorted out long before she got there. Space Force and NASA had trained their telescopes on her last known position, and there was no sign of her. I ran to my rack of suits, and confirmed that the helmet was indeed missing. She'd taken a piece of me with her on her final voyage.

She was gone.

And I died with her.

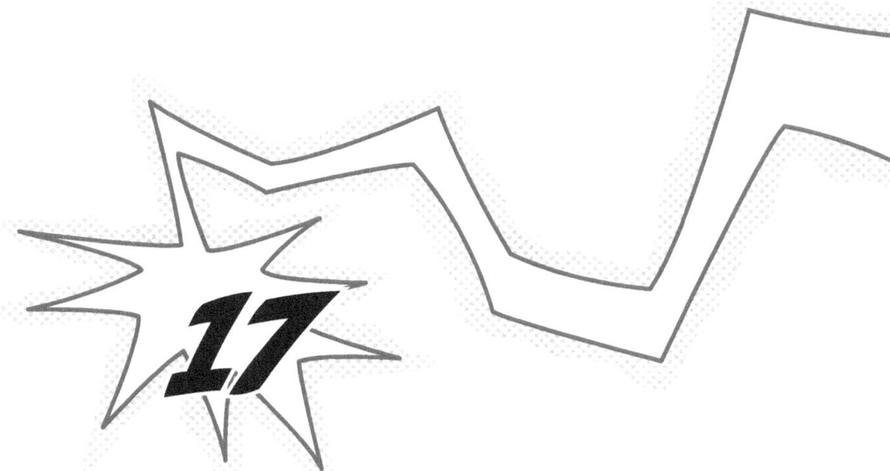

I had gone about making three duplicates of the footage, as I'd said. I'd put the original in my secure on-site vault. The other three copies would go to three different safe deposit boxes around the city.

Did this seem excessive? Not for me it didn't. My primary archive was at my hideout, but I *always* had copies. Production work required that kind of vigilance. And since Minder wanted his own copy, there was that to attend to, as well.

Truthfully, I was grateful to be home. It had been a challenging trek to Detroit. I updated my files on Felonia, marking her as deceased. That still made me feel bad. Nasty as she was, that was a bad death. Nobody wanted a bad death in the business. Deadhead, I felt less bad about, because he was a prick. I also marked Dusthead as deceased, since Brighteyes had pretty much fessed up to that.

What I needed was downtime, so, while the copies were being made in my workroom, I went upstairs to my living area and flipped on the television and poured myself a Tanqueray and tonic, just slouched on my sofa and searched for something to watch.

The news loved reporting on superheroics and supervillainy. The audience for those types of stories was ever-present, and it could sometimes go well if a hero did a good job.

In this case, it looked like Tag Team had taken on the Instigator and the Scissorettes in Austin, Texas. The Scissorettes were these four creepy silvery android (?) chicks with blades for arms, who had apparently worked in an automated Chinese textile sweatshop before becoming autonomous, self-described enemies of humanity. The Instigator dressed in a kind of vintage flight cap and goggled costume with jodhpurs and a white scarf. He was one of those pilot villains, fond of zeppelins and such. Why he was called the Instigator had something to do with him initiating crimes in unexpected places. This latest effort was using his zeppelin to haul a bank vault away. There were about fifty Tag Teams around, fighting them, leading to an exciting zeppelin chase over Austin, which the locals seemed to think might be some kind of event promotion, even after Instigator's logo flashed across it, along with his yelling on his loudspeaker.

"Citizens of Austin," Instigator said. "You have been robbed by me, the Instigator! The Scissorettes and I have not yet begun to plunder you! Yee haw, Varmints!"

Tag Team was taking an interesting approach with the Instigator zeppelin—he'd made dozens of dupes of himself to try to pull down the towlines of the zeppelin, and had actually managed to corral it that way, while other Tag Teams shinnied up the lines to get aboard the zeppelin.

While this was going on, the Scissorettes used their blade arms to shear off the towlines, thereby freeing the zeppelin.

"Pretty badass, right?" said a voice behind me, making me spin around. There was Tag Team, standing there, smirking at me with arms poised at his hips, in his black and orange costume.

"What the hell, Reg," I said, using his real name, Reginald Cartwright. "You broke into my place?"

"Kinda," he said, taking a seat next to me on the sectional. He had one of my Old Milwaukee beers in hand, made himself comfortable.

I knew that Tag Team wasn't good at picking locks, so I wondered how he got in, or whether somebody helped him. He gave me a sidelong glance, almost sheepish.

"I broke a window," he said. "My bad. I'll have somebody pay for the repair. Tough windows, Mitch."

"What are you doing here?" I asked. On the television, Tag Team was running along the gantry that led to the gondola, fighting the Scissorettes as they were making their way to the Instigator. "Why aren't you down there? And what are you doing down there? You don't work in Affiliates South."

Tag Team scoffed more than a little. "They don't need my help. Besides, with what's going on with Des and Antigone, Affiliates South needs a little Tag Team assistance, looks like to me."

"Weirdo," I said.

"Minder said you had something for me," Reg said. "Some footage, I'm thinking."

Wow, Minder didn't waste any time. I wondered if Tag Team had tried to break into my hideout and found he couldn't, which was why he messed around in my apartment.

"Did he tell you to break into my place?" I asked.

Tag Team just looked at me, sighing.

"He told me to get the footage from you," Tag Team said. "He said he'd talked to you and that you'd know what I'm talking about."

"Right," I said. "Isn't it distracting to be talking to me while your dupes are fighting Instigator?"

He drank his beer and shrugged it off.

"We're used to dividing our focus. I'm an awesome multi-tasker, Mitch," he said. "You wouldn't understand. You think those Scissorettes are hot? No way did Instigator make them. They have Crimebot written all over them. I mean it literally—it's stamped on them, like the base of their necks—'Property of Crimebot'. Isn't that icky? Crimebot's the weirdo. I think he's started his own side project."

"The Enemies of Humanity," I said. "Yeah, I know."

Tag Team smirked, nodding. "Wild, Mitch."

"Yeah," I said. The Enemies of Humanity were robot, android, and cyborg-based villains operating under the leadership of Crimebot 5.0. Their mission statement involved the extermination of humanity (including superhumanity) with the intention of turning the planet over to its new rightful rulers: the artificial intelligences of the world. I'm not even going to go into them right now; you'll hear about them sometime in the not-too-distant future).

Tag Team looked around my place.

"You seem to be doing alright for yourself," Tag Team said, taking another drink of beer. "Ah, here it is. The money shot."

On the television, Tag Team had grabbed one of the remaining Scissorettes and jumped overboard with her, while the rest stormed the Instigator's gondola. Instigator was cursing them out and trying to steer the zeppelin to crash in one of the buildings. The Tag Team that had jumped overboard had burst into dozens more of him, and they went back to their efforts to stop Instigator's zeppelin.

"Did Minder send you to keep tabs on me?" I asked.

"I've been in town since you left on that fool's errand Decibelle sent you on," Tag Team said. "The women all pity you since, you know, Victoriana. Their motherly/sisterly instincts kick in with you. They can't help themselves. Poor Powerless Mitch, who lost his girlfriend. The way you use that, it's just sick."

"I'm not *using* anything," I said. "I'm just being me."

And the reason I didn't deck Tag Team for that snipe about Anna was because Tag Team's superpowers would have only meant there were two of him in the room, being just as irritating, maybe even twice as much. One had to keep a cool head.

"Sure, sure," Tag Team said. "Like, whatever you say. Maybe your secret superpower is your vulnerability, or at least pity-milking from sexy superheroines."

"And they say you're not a detective," I said, which stirred Tag Team, who leaned toward me, glancing at my photos of Anna that I'd had framed on the wall, both in and out of her Victoriana costume. I was very grateful I'd taken those back in the day, one of those whimsical decisions that were precious over time.

"Who says I'm not a detective?" he asked. "I'm a detective."

"Right," I said. "Look, if you think I'm letting you into my hideout, you're dreaming. I'll go get you Minder's copy of the footage."

"Wait," Tag Team said, pointing to the screen. "That's it for you, Instigator! We're driving your zeppelin to the police station, where we'll be making a deposit: YOU!"

He said the same line that his dupe said, at the same time, and he was cracking himself up, slapping his knee.

"This'll get me coverage across the national feeds for sure," Tag Team said. "Internet as well. It'll be all over social—#hashtagteam. I know Instigator's small fry, but he always plays it big, and that zeppelin makes for great content, you know?"

I wasn't going to concede the point, although I knew he was right. Who didn't love a zeppelin? Especially one driven by a supervillain, even a criminally lame one like the Instigator. It was a good score in that it wasn't one of those crimes that would risk blowing up a city or something. How Instigator was one of the top members of the Crime League would have been a mystery if I hadn't unearthed years ago that he was a billionaire playboy who had taken to crime to fill his time. His legal team worked constantly to keep him out of prison.

The Tag Team dupes posed with the area police as they perp-walked Instigator, one of the Tag Team dupes taking off Instigator's aviator cap and scarf and putting it on himself, to the amusement of the onlookers and the media. The media enjoyed Tag Team, who seemed approachable and his dupes always ensured a big crowd.

"Are you the prime Tagger?" I asked.

"Nah," he said, finishing his beer. "When Minder asked me to check on you, I went right for it. See what sneaky old Mitch was up to."

I thought this might be a good opportunity to question him a little. Who knew how much Minder had briefed him on Brighteyes? I knew that Reg was enough of a blabbermouth that if there was something to say, he'd say it.

"You know what's going on with Brighteyes?" I asked. He laughed.

"What are you talking about? You mean her losing her mind?" Tag Team replied. "We all know, Mitch. The whole team knows about it."

"Minder wouldn't tell me anything," I said.

Tag Team snorted, crunching the beer can and conjuring another dupe of himself, who just appeared out of nowhere and went into my fridge, grabbed another beer. He walked back with it, which was taken by the one sitting on the sectional with me.

"How do you even do that?" I asked, now having two Tag Teams staring at me, while the ones in Austin were disappearing, leaving only the one with the scarf and aviator helmet and goggles remaining to field questions from the reporters.

"Magic," they said, moving their hands in an almost jazz-hand sort of motion. "Only magic could make something as impossible as Tag Team exist, Mitch. You mean you never dug into my origins the way you did with the others?"

Yes, I had a dossier on Tag Team. But sometimes when I worked with supers, I played dumb, since they usually couldn't resist talking about themselves when prodded.

"I have files, sure," I said. "But they're not always comprehensive."

I went to my elevator and keyed to my lair, not wanting to leave my living space unattended. I'd run a bug scan later once I got rid of Tag Team.

Glancing at my copies bound for my vaults, I boxed the Minder file, which I took back upstairs, seeing the Tag Team dupe looking at me when the door opened.

"You know, I could get into your lair if I *wanted* to," the dupe said. "It's not like it's an impregnable cave or something, Mitch."

I put the boxed footage copy in his hand. "There you go. You can deliver that to your boss."

"He's not my boss," the dupe said, joined by the other Tag Team. "He is the chairman, however, and I always come through for him. He's large and in charge."

The dupe waved to us both.

"I'm off," the dupe said. "You want me to take the Affilijet?"

"Yeah," Tag said.

I looked at both of the Tag Teams in turn.

"Wait, you're not going with him?" I asked.

They both shook their heads at me.

"Minder thinks you're in danger," they said. "You need someone watching your back. Someone super. If you and Victoriana hadn't been so, you know, standoffish, maybe what happened wouldn't have happened."

It made me angry, but I held my composure, not wanting to give him the satisfaction of knowing he'd gotten a rise out of me. Tag Team was likely just here to spy on me, a convenient flunky of Minder's.

"I'll be fine," I said. "I don't need a bodyguard."

The Tag Teams didn't seem persuaded by this.

"If you're messing around with Brighteyes, maybe you do," they said. This was entirely unacceptable, but if Tag Team wanted to hang around, there wasn't much I could do about it. "We've got your back, Mitch. We can go window-shopping tomorrow. My treat. You know I wouldn't want to be a 'pane', Mitch."

I drank down my gin and escorted the dupe to my roof, where they'd parked the Affilijet, having set it to the cloaking screen tech I'd shared with the Affiliates when I was part of the team, by the request of Minder, and in a bid to demonstrate my organizational value beyond being Anna's partner. The cloak I'd shared with them was the adaptive camouflage array, not my full invisibility, so the Affilijet just looked like a strange shape that mirrored back what was around it, kind of like the Predator in those *Predator* movies.

You probably think I just make everything from movies into reality, but it's really just a way of explaining it so you'll know what I'm talking about without requiring me to go into a lengthy description of my digital cloaking technology.

Tag and I watched the Affilijet take off—the vertical takeoff of it used a form of levitation, so it could lift off quietly before the main engines kicked in. Honestly, I was peevish that they even landed on my building, since if anybody was paying attention, they'd be wondering why a cloaked Affilijet was on the top floor of my building.

"Way to blow my secret identity, by the way," I said. Tag took a swig of beer before replying. "It only made sense. Nobody saw, Mitch. Who still looks up anymore? And my dupe's being very conscientious—look how he's levitating up there, putting distance between himself and your old building. Nobody'll think or look twice, mark my words."

I looked Tag Team in the eye, trying to look stern.

"You're *not* staying at my place, Reg," I said. "I don't need a roommate."

He treated me to a cackle.

"Yeah, I got that, Mitch," Tag Team said. "I'll be staying at Central. It's just that—"

The arrow came out of nowhere, sticking Tag Team in the shoulder, making him drop his beer, which clattered on the rooftop as it spilled. I could see the arrow was a black shaft with white fletching.

Oh, please, not him.

But it was. It was totally him. I could see him on the neighboring building, having fired down at us from the fire escape. He stood there in the shadows, but I could make him out—big guy, strongly built.

"Face the wrath of the White Arrow!" he yelled, firing another shot into Tag Team, who he seemed to be prioritizing because, you know, White Arrow considered him the greater threat.

Tag Team split into four of himself, their eyes riveted on the White Arrow, who was visible in his costume—black head mask with a white arrow upon it, with another upward-pointing white arrow on his chest. The rest of his costume was a mix of black and white trim, and he nocked an arrow with knockout gas, which he fired amidst us, the thing exploding in a plume of white smoke that had three of the Tag Teams coughing and sputtering.

I hurled myself into my rooftop stairwell, slamming the security door behind me. I had to get to my suit. White Arrow was an archrival of mine—in fact, he'd been up for consideration to join the Affiliates the same time I had. On paper, White Arrow was a strong candidate, having been a former cop. He'd even run a local PR campaign: *Straight & Narrow with the White Arrow*—which had raised his profile, except that the background checks on him had revealed his association with white supremacist groups, which had ended his chances of joining the Affiliates.

When I ended up with the gig, White Arrow had furiously blamed it on me, had vowed revenge. He put himself out there as a superhero-for-hire, a kind of vendable vigilante, where he'd been ever since. Some superheroes never made it past street level. And White Arrow was one of those, or at least thought of himself that way.

My door exploded, having been struck by one of White Arrow's special arrows. I pretty much hated archery heroes and villains, with only one exception (as you'll see later). It was really the lamest thing a skills-based hero or villain might choose. In a country chock full of firearms, why would anybody try to be a superhero archer? What were trick shots compared with a spray of bullets?

I know you could wag a finger at my nonviolent use of light-based weapons as similarly ill-suited to modern ballistic combat environments, but my light weapons were more effective than some damned arrows.

What's more, White Arrow was jarringly uninventive in his arrow selection. White Arrow's arsenal was always:

- *12 BROADHEAD ARROWS*
- *6 INCENDIARY ARROWS*
- *6 ELECTRIC NET ARROWS*
- *3 TEAR GAS ARROWS*
- *3 STUN BOMB ARROWS*
- *3 HIGH-EXPLOSIVE ARROWS*
- *2 GLUE ARROWS*
- *2 KNOCKOUT GAS ARROWS*
- *1 SIGNAL FLARE ARROW*
- *1 SMOKE BOMB ARROW*
- *1 TRACKING ARROW*

There may have been others, and you might think the above is a comprehensive listing with a great variety, and nothing stupid like, oh, I don't know, boxing glove arrows? But he had forty arrows he carried with him. When you considered the magazine capacity of any number of assault rifles and their rates of fire, his selection was subpar. Lucky for him his costume was bulletproof.

All of this was tangential, since I was the one hurling myself down the stairs while White Arrow was giving chase, cursing me out.

"You're finished, Cameraman," he said, yelling after me. "I'm going to kill you!"

Tag Team tackled him on the stairs, and the two of them went tumbling down, with another Tag Team appearing with each somersault they made going down the stairs. This gave me more time to get to my secure door and to get to my Camerman suit.

How White Arrow had been tipped to my secret hideout was something I'd have to find out, ideally once Tag Team and I took him down. I'll have you know that I designed my Cameraman jumpsuit to be easy to put on and take off precisely for occasions like these. It was the basic jumpsuit, the chest harness and backpack, the utility belt, and the helmet.

I had it on by the time White Arrow and Tag Team had reached the landing near this level. I drew my stun gun and toggled my adaptive camouflage, feeling that full invisibility was better than the White Arrow deserved.

Throwing open the door, I saw that Tag Team had restrained the White Arrow, who was loudly cursing Tag Team and me.

"You sons of bitches can't stop the White Arrow, goddammit!" Arrow yelled! "I know where you live, Paulsen!"

I turned off my adaptive camouflage, his eyes flaring as he looked at me.

"Cameraman," Arrow said. "You ruined my life!"

"That was all your own doing," I said.

"The hell you say," White Arrow said, straining again. "Fact: if it hadn't been for Victoriana, you'd *never* have made it onto the team."

"Who hired you to come after me?" I asked. And, because I had to know: "And why'd you shoot Tag Team first?"

"I wanted *him* out of the way," Arrow said. "I wanted *you* to suffer. I'm going to tell the world your identity, Paulsen."

"Who the hell hired you?" I asked.

And then things really got out of hand, as I saw green eyebeams envelope Tag Team and White Arrow, coming from upstairs, through my security door. That telltale "ZAP!" sound.

"Oh, shit," Tag Team managed to say in unison as they were disintegrated along with White Arrow. You bet your ass I was recording this, capturing this mass disintegration, my head whipping upward, seeing Brighteyes standing there at the top of the stairs, her green eyes glowing, the beams from her eyes eradicating them. A half-second later and they were gone.

"Oh, Christ," I said, but Brighteyes called down to me.

"Mitch," she said. "Don't be an idiot. If I'd *wanted* to zap you, I'd have zapped you with those others."

"You just murdered White Arrow and Tag Team," I said.

"Just White Arrow," she said. "Tag's fine, beyond the shock of experiencing disintegration. Are you kidding me? He doesn't keep *all* of himself in one place, not ever. He's almost immortal on account of that. He keeps a duplicate at each of the branches, and his Prime is probably locked away somewhere in a PSS secret maximum security facility."

She walked down the steps, her green eyes luminous. She was wearing her costume, which was an all-black armored bodysuit with a glowing green eye in the center of her chest.

"You followed me here?" I asked.

"Yeah," she said. "You went to the trouble to go after me, so I just returned the favor. Looks like I arrived at just the right time."

"But White Arrow—" I said.

"Racist trash," she said. "Big whup, Mitch. Nobody'll miss him, beyond his fascist snowflake drinking buddies. Look, we need to talk. Reg is probably already whining to Minder about what I just did."

My head was spinning, and she seemed to see that, smiling knowingly at me, walking past me into my lair, her black knee boots clacking. I followed after her, stammering with every step.

"You can't just ace a fellow teammate, Antigone," I said.

She took a seat in my comfiest chair and crossed her legs, leaning back.

"I just did," she said. "Like I said—I only inconvenienced Tag Team; I didn't kill him. And whoever hired White Arrow sold you out. Think about that. White Arrow would blab your secret identity to anyone who'd listen, and then where'd you be? If anything, I just saved you a whole lot of trouble. You're welcome."

For someone who'd gone crazy, Brighteyes looked remarkably calm and collected.

"The footage," she said. "I want the footage."

"Everybody wants the footage, Antigone," I said. "You're a mass murderer."

She rolled her green eyes.

"You gave that footage to Minder, didn't you?" she asked. When I murmured that I had, she rolled her glowing green eyes even more forcefully than she had just a moment ago. "Why'd you do that, Mitch?"

"It was either that or have the Affiliates come crashing through my building and taking it," I said.

"Minder's setting me up," she said. "This is *his* doing."

I sat down across from her, watching her watch me with her unearthly eyes. Her nonchalance was jarring. Nobody in her situation could possibly look so cool, and yet there she was, unnervingly staring at me with her glowing eyes.

"Tag's the only one in the area, and he knows he's not tough enough to take me by himself—even with an army of his dupes," she said. "Nobody in Central is up for it, and East, West, and South are hours away. Even Tandem. We have time, Mitch. Time to talk."

"About what?" I asked.

"You're recording right now, yeah?" she asked.

"You *know* I am," I said.

"Good," she said. "Set up your cameras. I want to make a confession."

CLICK
CLICK
CLICK
CLICK
CLICK
CLICK
CLICK
CLICK
CLICK
DING!
DING!
CLICK
CLICK
CLICK
CLICK
DING!
CLICK
CLICK
CLICK
DING!
DING!
CLICK
REMEMBERING
VICTORIANA

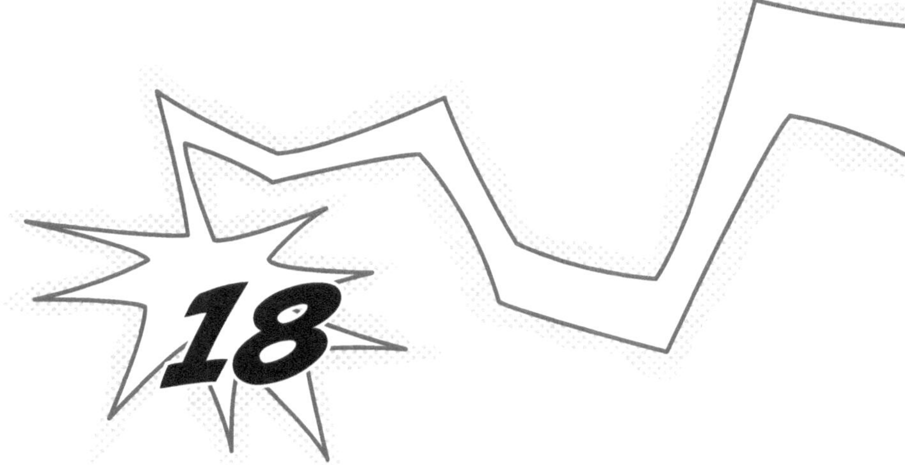

with the Affiliates, and the United States government turning out in force for her. We were all representing, and I was tranquilized to quietude as I tried to deal with it. I half-heard people saying kind words about Victoriana, all of the praise about her great work, her good deeds, and a touching eulogy by Minder about the need for mental health services even for superheroes.

"The work we do is both thankless and dangerous," Minder said, wearing all black, wearing his black facemask with the white "M" on it. "Victoriana was the best of us. She was a hero in *every* sense of the word—fearless in the face of the deadliest danger, resolute in her determination to triumph. We are all weaker for her absence."

Everyone had said something to me before the funeral. They had all turned up at Central, where I was bathing in tears. All of the Affiliates were there, wearing their costumes, black armbands on, while one of my photographs of Victoriana had been put on an easel. Somebody had enlarged it, and she looked more heroic than ever. It had been our in-joke when I'd shot it. The memory hit me hard.

It had been a sunny day in the city, and we'd hit the rooftop at Central, which would offer a good vista of Chicago, and the steady wind made her cape flutter evocatively.

"You know, I don't normally dig capes, but you make it work for you," I said, snapping shots. Anna smiled at me, brushing a wisp of her green hair from her eyes. "You look damned heroic standing there."

"Do I?" she asked, but we both knew she did. For me, it was strange to see her there, looking all superheroic, because I thought she was the cutest. There was a joyful sweetness in her features, an exuberantly youthful gleam to her.

"Yeah, you do," I said. "Just turn your head into the wind and let me catch that."

It was funny any time I'd take my camera to her. I loved shooting portraits of her, because she'd get shy, which was absurd, given what she could do. And, for me, so accustomed to using my cameras to photograph bad guys doing horrible things or fashion models being fatuously fetching, it made me happy to shoot pictures of the superwoman I loved.

I took shot after shot, while she played and posed, poked her tongue at me and threatened to take my picture, too.

"Fair is far, Mitch," she said, and I actually shot some selfies of us together, like with my full Cameraman visor in place, as well as some shots of me without my helmet, which led to a series of us serving up mock-shock as we revealed our secret identities to each other to varying degrees—Cameraman and Victoriana, Cameraman and Anna, Mitch and Victoriana, Mitch and Anna dressed up as superheroes. They were cute pictures. *We* were cute. We were doing the kind of young couple stuff that might make others gag, but we didn't care. We were superheroes. We were Affiliates. We could do anything.

That day was so much fun, and after I'd gotten enough shots taken, she put her arm around me and took me flying. She knew how much I hated heights, so she flew mercifully low to the ground, so I was merely terrified instead of being absolutely petrified.

"Don't worry, Babe, I'd *never* drop you," she said, as we made our way through the city. Seeing people point and exclaim, it was a trip. I'd snap shots with my handheld camera, wanting to take it in as she flew me around. To see the world the way she did—flying around, not a care in the world—it was amazing. I felt something I'd never felt before. I'd felt actual peace with her. My world was steeped in anger, frustration, fear, indignation, resentment, cynicism, envy, paranoia—my work as Cameraman took me through it. But in Victoriana's arms, I just felt peace.

That peace was unlike the numbness I'd felt when shaking everyone's hands as they made their way to me. They'd wanted to pay their respects in private before the funeral.

"I'm so, so sorry, Mitch," Minder said, giving my hand a double pump as he brought me in for a half-hug.

"If you need anything, Mitch," Ms. Fit said, hugging me tightly. "And I mean *anything*, you give me a call, yes? I'll come running."

"Sorry, Mitch," Wingman said, gleaming and golden, giving me a terse handshake. "Sorry for your loss, Brother."

Tag Team showed up solo, which felt like a kind of concession on his part, given his preference for appearing in numbers.

"Sorry, Mitch," Tag said. "I'm terrible at funerals. Victoriana ruled."

"Stay strong, Mitch," Lassitude said, holding me close with a hug, kissing my cheek. Her brother hung back, then clapped my shoulder.

"You've got this, Mitch," Fusillad said. "Victoriana was a helluva heroine."

"Mitch-Honey, oh, baby," Decibelle said, holding my face in her hands, her purple eyes full of sorrow. "She was a wonderful woman."

Brighteyes was wearing her Wayfarers, hiding her green gaze behind her stylish frames.

"She was stronger than this," she said, leaning in close, her black lips near my ear. "I'm going to find out how this could have happened, I swear to you."

She stepped back and we looked eye-to-eye, her face unreadable behind her shades and her grave expression.

"What do you mean?" I asked, but she glanced around us, shook her head, hushing me with a finger to her lips.

"Later," she said. "Not now."

Copycat walked up, gave me a brusque hug, in her black costume, her trademark circle "C" in red on her forehead, almost an imitation of Minder's costume, except for the cutesy cat ears atop hers, and the PSS badge/patch on her shoulder.

"Tough, tough break, Cam," she said. "She was badass."

Vendetta came up and shook my hand, looking me in the eye. He also had the PSS shoulder patch, and his costume was red and grey, a red "V" on his chest.

"Sorry, man," he said. "You two were great together. Everybody saw that. We remember."

Rollergirl came up, wearing her metallic blue powersuit, her helmet visor raised, showing pain in her big, blue eyes, her cosmetic contact lenses, the stylized "R" on her chest, looking like a rollerskate in white.

"Oh, Mitch, I'm so sorry," she said. "If you need a shoulder to cry on, I'm here for you."

Lancer in his midnight blue costume with his silvery metallic mask and highlights, the silver "L" on his chest surrounded by a circle, the other prominent skills hero on the Affiliates, who had a range of modular javelin-type weapons he used, was sympathetic, shook my hand heartily and gave me a hug.

"I'm sorry, Mitch," he said. "I'm so sorry for your loss."

Rad Lad wore his protective suit as ever and walked up to me, holding out a gloved hand.

"So sorry, Mitch," he said. "You and Victoriana were a great team. Dude, your loss is our loss."

On and on they came, and they didn't know—although maybe the smarter of them might have suspected—that I was recording all of it. I had to have all of it, for posterity. For something.

The Knack came up, wearing a black suit, white shirt, grey necktie, a grey rose at his lapel. Even for this, he didn't break his black, white, and grey thing. He shook my hand and gave me a lingering hug.

"I'm so sorry, Mitch," Shane said. "When I brought you and Anna in, I never would have imagined this for either of you."

I managed to speak again.

"No? You didn't see this coming?" I asked. Shane pulled back from the hug, held my arms, looked into my eyes with his own, and I didn't think he was lying.

"Not like this," Shane said. "I saw a happy, long life together for the two of you. Not this."

"Maybe the timeline's shifted or something," I said. Talking shop was better than swimming in pain of loss.

"Or something," Shane said. "She's far stronger than any of us could know. Don't judge her harshly over this. Every moment you had with her was precious."

When the Knack threw something like that at you, you had to at least pay heed to it. I wasn't in the best emotional place to accept it, but I still did.

"What the hell are you even talking about?" I asked.

"Give yourself time and permission to heal," Shane said. "Whatever you do."

He left me more confused and bereft than I already was. What healing? One of the cardinal rules of superheroism (and supervillainy, for that matter) was this:

No body, no death.

It used to be a joke we'd tell ourselves when we'd defeated someone. If we didn't find the body of the villain, the assumption was that they'd somehow engineered an escape, so they could return again to vex us from beyond the grave, to emerge unscathed from all but certain death. It's what they did, and it's why we said what we said.

And there was no body for Victoriana, because she'd flown into the Sun. It's what I told myself to numb the pain, while understanding that nobody could just fly into the Sun without incinerating themselves. Hell, I couldn't even imagine Rad Lad or Tandem surviving that. She was dead, and denial would just bring me more suffering.

My overactive imagination saw her brave self hurtling toward the Sun as this tiny shooting star, tears in her eyes boiling off in the vacuum of space as she found herself going blind and burning to death, vaporizing from the force of the monstrous energy of the lifegiving Sun. It was too horrible to imagine, and yet I imagined it, because my mind wandered whenever it went to painful places, and I still wanted to be with her, even if only in my head.

I was grateful for my mask keeping my face hidden because I was bawling behind it. And yet, somewhere inside me, someplace deep, Cameraman was looking on, and he wasn't blinking.

She didn't kill herself, Mitch. She wouldn't do that.

The voice was hard and quiet and had kept me company when I'd worked my solo superheroism in years past. Cameraman never looked away, and he never, ever blinked.

Do you trust her?

I do.

She was murdered, Mitch. She had to be.

It wasn't something I could fully believe, wasn't something I could even consider. Cameraman could be a wishful thinker, too.

I'm not, Cameraman said. *You should know me better than that by now.*

But she left a note.

It's what's expected. Were there warning signs?

I broke it down in my head.

No. This came out of nowhere. She'd have told me if she was suffering. I'd have seen.

Exactly. This is your enemy having a go at you.

I composed myself, even though nobody was watching. At least I didn't see anybody watching me. And I tried to watch everybody who'd gathered.

Motive. Means. Opportunity. The building blocks of murder, Mitch. Don't tell me you've forgotten.

But why her? Are you saying this is tied to Shane's vibes?

Of course it is.

Why not me?

Because you're not her, Cameraman said in my head. *No powers, no threat. She was killed* because *she was a threat. And she was killed covertly because* someone *didn't want their fingerprints on it.*

I was getting really pissed off, standing there at my girlfriend's so well-attended funeral, trying to keep it together, wondering who was the culprit. I set my helmet-mask to record again, and just slowly filmed everybody there, taking my time to pan as I looked, while Cameraman talked in my head.

She was killed because of what you, Anna, and Shane were up to. What's more, don't you think the manner of her death was a bit on the nose? The note wasn't enough; they wanted to film it. That was a dig at you. A personal one. Using your own helmet to record her last moments. A cruel twist to torture you.

Staying steady was a priority for me, rooted in my discipline as a professional. But Cameraman wasn't wrong. The POV filming of it was shot to sting me. Who was *that* nasty?

Or it was a clue, I thought. Anna didn't have to film it. *She wanted to film it so there'd be a record. Because she knew I'd see it, and I'd wonder. She knew I'd wonder. That I'd try to solve it.*

"Please join me and bow your heads for a minute of silence for Victoriana," Minder said, gripping the lectern and bowing his head. I watched everyone do as he'd suggested, but I didn't bow my head. I watched everyone. I'd review that footage for weeks after her death, for any sign, for anyone and anything who didn't read right to me. Inferna was there, in the back, wearing a black leather overcoat and a black fedora with a long crimson scarf. She caught my eye from afar, gave me a solemn nod that only I saw, since she was in the very back.

I'm so sorry for your loss, Mitch, came Minder's voice in my head. *I hope we can take some time to talk, but if you need to take a leave of absence, I understand completely.*

Hearing Minder that way, my blood ran cold, and I turned my helmet camera on him, zoomed in, ran it on thermographic, just to monitor the heat patterns on that head of his, to see if I might divine something of value.

"Thank you," Minder said, the minute having passed, as four fighter jets flew in formation overhead, one of them vaulting upward as the others passed us, the roar of the engines shaking the ground.

But I didn't look up at them the way the others did; I looked right at Minder and recorded everything I saw, and he looked back at me.

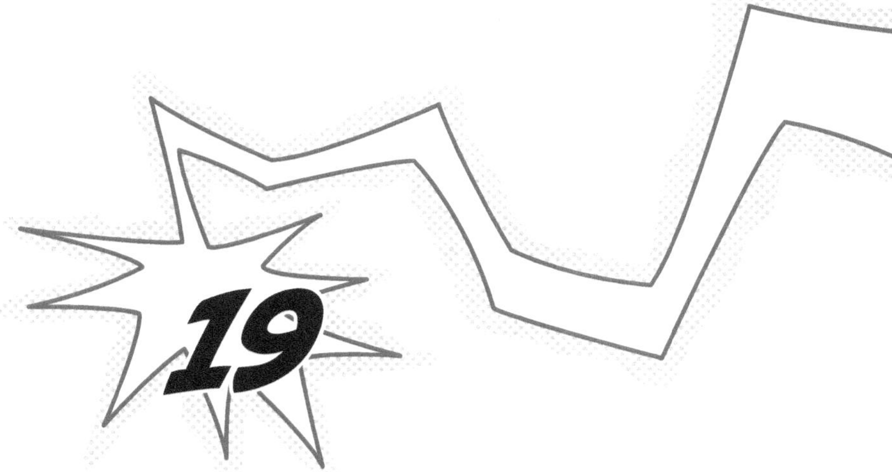

 but I did have a recording room with a camcorder on a tripod, because I was kind of a camera completist. I liked having the capacity to film or photograph anything whenever or however I wanted.

Brighteyes sat in the chair I had pulled up, and I started recording, pleased with the lighting arrangement I'd set up on a neutral background.

"You coming after me gave me the idea," Antigone said. "First I was intent on ditching you, but then I came to understand that maybe you *could* help me out. The whole mess, maybe I could come clean on it, and maybe you'd be the only one willing and able to actually help me out, Mitch, because you have nothing to lose."

Again, I'd witnessed her coldly murder Felonia, Deadhead, White Arrow, and a dozen or more goons. And, yes, they were all criminals, cutthroats, and assholes—I could vouch for that, too.

However, seeing her there, she seemed so collected, so present and sane. Plus, I'll admit that my journalistic self was titillated at the possibility of a scoop, although I wasn't sure what Brighteyes would say.

"Are you set up?" she asked. I gave her a thumb's up, adjusting the digital camcorder's focus. She looked amazing on camera, I admitted to myself. Those green eyes, and the photogenic planes of her face. Even her black lipstick was perfect. "Okay, I'm ready at your cue."

"Go for it," I said. And she did.

"To whoever's watching, you know me as Brighteyes, a member of the Affiliates," she said. "I'm here to account for my conduct over the past few months, in hopes that you might understand why I've done what I've done.

"First of all, I'm going to say that I don't feel bad about killing off the following supervillains: Dusthead and a dozen of his thugs; Deadhead and around fifteen of his murderous mercenaries, including Major Damage; Felonia, the Crime League's favorite assassin; White Arrow, the racist vigilante-for-hire.

"All of these people *deserved* what they got. They were all dangerous, bad people who used their powers, skills, and abilities to harm and kill others. The world is no worse for their absence and is maybe a little brighter without them.

"I've been a member of the Affiliates for many years and have served the team well in those years. In that time, I've put my powers to work for the public good. My powers have a very specific purpose to them. Oh, sure, I can use them to scan things in the dark. I can tell when people are lying. I can see through walls. And those abilities are all useful. However, I can do so much more. My eyebeams can cut through walls. I can disintegrate things with them."

She looked at me through the camera, her green eyes glowing pantherlike through the lens. They were beautiful. I'd never seen them like this, so up close, over so much time. She was in her early 30s, which made her my age. I felt a strange kinship, despite everything.

"Earlier this year, my partner, Decibelle, and I, went after Dusthead, one of the founding members of the Fourheads. They'd worked out a criminal sex trafficking ring out of Manila, coordinating with local gangs, corrupt law enforcement, as well as the Crime League.

"And while Decibelle and I had successfully defeated them, it wasn't before Dusthead and some of the others had killed scores of victims of their trafficking operation. As far as I can tell, Dusthead thought if he created a disaster in Manila, using his own supernatural abilities, he'd be able to effect an escape. And he was right. He *did* escape, while Decibelle and I were trying to handle the disaster he'd left in his wake. We did what we could, but hundreds of women died in the container prisons that they'd been placed in because of that man's actions. While I tried to console myself that the interdiction Decibelle and I had carried out had ended this trafficking operation, the reality on the ground was our efforts led to hundreds of deaths. And while this operation had been shut down, there were clearly plenty of others ready to take their place.

"As part of Sound & Fury, Decibelle and I have made it our mission to go after serial sex offenders—pedophiles, rapists, serial killers, sex traffickers. People—overwhelmingly men—who use their power over others to torment, terrify, and torture their victims. And far worse. The people who perpetrate these offenses are among the truest evil humanity has been able to inflict on itself."

She paused a moment, just staring hard into the camera lens with her radiant eyes. How many baddies had been on the receiving end of those eyes? How many more would be?

"I've seen horrible things with these eyes of mine. And I haven't looked away. You know that old line about staring into the abyss? Well, I have, and with my extraordinary eyes, I've seen far more than anyone ever should. Before the accident that created me, I served in the Marines, and I'd seen my share of terrible things in Iraq and Afghanistan. Things *nobody* should see.

"Maybe I snapped. That's what people might say. But I didn't want Dusthead getting away with what he'd done. He had to be held responsible. I had to hold *someone* responsible. And so I went after him. I hunted him down. It took time, but I'm good at what I do. I found him, and I fought him. And *this* time, he wasn't getting away.

"He didn't get away; I saw to that. I disintegrated him, as well as his henchmen. For someone like him, this was justice.

He would never have felt bad for what he'd done, would never have atoned for the crimes he'd committed."

Brighteyes paused a moment, motioning for me to stop recording. She took a breath.

"Could I trouble you for some water, Mitch?" she asked.

"Sure," I said, walking over to the sink and getting her some ice water, which she gratefully took, drinking it down.

"It's not easy to bring those memories back," she said. "I don't know if people will understand."

My production background came into focus for me, and I felt obligated to say something, whether or not it would be appreciated, even as I cringed that maybe it was too detached and technical a kind of question to ask.

"Who's the intended audience for this confession?" I asked. "Law enforcement? The everyday public? Media? The Affiliates? The PSS?"

Antigone walked over to the sink and refilled the water, folding one arm under the other after taking another long drink.

"Anyone who'll listen," Brighteyes said. "There's more I need to get off my chest."

She took another drink and set the glass aside, wiping her mouth and taking a seat again, and once she was settled, I started recording again at her signal.

"I made Dusthead pay for his crimes with his life, and this'll sound hypocritical, but I don't believe in capital punishment. I don't believe the State should have the authority to execute its citizens. How do I square that with what I did to Dusthead? I guess it's because he's superhuman. His henchmen weren't, but that was just self-defense on my part. If I hadn't killed them, they'd have gunned me down. They fought me and lost.

"Someone like Dusthead, he's operating outside the realm of ordinary law and order. How could a judge possibly understand that when Dusthead wanted to, he could touch someone and wither them, turning them into walking corpses at will? Dusthead could have used his strange powers toward the betterment of mankind. He *chose* to become a supervillain.

"Every supervillain makes that choice, as surely as every superhero makes theirs. You choose to be good or bad, to do good things or bad things. Maybe I'm putting this out there to let bad people—particularly the supervillains—know that if I catch them doing what they do, I'm going to kill them.

"Does this make *me* a criminal? Again, the legal framework is sketchy on these sorts of paranormal acts. For ordinary police, without a body, it's very hard to prove a murder. That's probably part of why around forty percent of murders go unsolved in this country. People disappear all the time. When I disintegrate someone, they disappear.

"I didn't have to come forward this way and claim the murders I've perpetrated. Besides this video, there's no record of me having done this, besides some footage that might exist that captured it. Without that, it'd be easy to forget that I've even done this at all. You'll just find that, one by one, or perhaps more than one at a time, supervillains will simply vanish. That'll be me. I've taken it upon myself to do this. It won't be messy, but it will be final. The evil that they are dies with them."

She took a breath, gazing into the camera again, her eyes glowing in an almost spectral fashion—they were so mesmerizing and menacing. She'd become the terror of the underworld once word got out.

I wondered if this so-called confessional was really more of a kind of manifesto or declaration of intent.

"The Affiliates are aware of what I'm doing. Specifically, Minder. He *knows* I'm doing this. I know this because we had talked about it. I don't know whether he encouraged or discouraged me, as he talked out of both sides of his mouth on the matter. I think he made me what I have become, and when faced with that, he's trying to cover his ass."

"Oh, hell," I said.

"I think Minder tried to mindwipe me, in the interest of preserving the reputation of the Affiliates. Ordinarily, I might have succumbed to his mental powers. Minder has major expertise in messing with people's minds. However, I had expected that he might do something like this and had prepared, had protected myself from his telepathic powers through the help of a friend. After zapping Dusthead, I fled from the Affiliates South compound and have been on the run ever since.

"Does this make me a criminal, now? It's up to you to decide whether I'm an outlaw or not. You don't have to fear me if you're an ordinary and law-abiding person. However, if you are, yes, you *do* have to fear me, because I will put an end to you with these."

She pointed to her glowing eyes, and I could see her green-painted fingernails, glossy and reflecting the light from her eyes.

"Further, I won't stop until I'm stopped. I'm going to work my way through the criminal underground, and I'm going to use my superpowers to disintegrate every criminal I find. I'm taking the burden of this action on my own shoulders as my own responsibility. I accept that. If you superheroes out there want to stop me, you're welcome to try. I won't kill you, but I will defend myself. As for you villains, understand that justice is coming for you."

I wasn't sure I could zap her with my stun gun before she shot me with her eyebeams. What I'm saying is that my instinct was to get the drop on her and try using my stun gun, but there was at least the chance that it wouldn't work on her. And then what would happen? There was also the matter that she was seeking some kind of comprehensible justice.

She paused again and was looking at me, while I paused the recording.

"Don't do it, Mitch," she said.

"Do what?" I asked.

"What you're thinking of doing," she said. "Your Hero Complex will have you doing something stupid to try to stop me."

Her expression was grave, made unreadable by the glow of her eyes. When I was in the Affiliates, I remembered her being able to tone down her gaze. She had naturally green eyes, and when she'd rev up her power, the glow would form in them.

Now, she seemed to keep them like that all the time. It was like she was always armed and dangerous, now.

"I think that they're going to go after you," I said. "And what the hell do you want me to do with this video?"

"Make copies," she said. "Distribute them to media companies. Get word out."

She took the water and drank again, appearing lost in thought.

"Antigone, even with your eyes, you're just one person," I said. "You want to devote the rest of your life to doing this? There are tons of bad guys out there."

She heaved a sigh.

"My eyes mean I can't have a normal life, Mitch," she said. "Can you really see me, what, gardening? Going to the grocery store? You know how it is. That White Arrow ass is just one example. There are tons of criminals who'd love to see you dead. They'd love to kill you themselves. All I'm doing is playing offense. Good's always playing defense, and Evil plays offense, because it does what Good is afraid or unwilling to do. My powers came to me in some grand cosmic accident, but am I supposed to 'play nice' when dealing with villains? Who says? Especially the really bad ones?"

I could comprehend on some level. It's why I went after the bad guys who thought they were untouchable. And they certainly hated my guts, wouldn't hesitate to brutally murder me.

"If everybody turned vigilante, the world would become a bloodbath," I said.

"Why are we supposed to hold back? Why is that Good?" Brighteyes asked. "I'm *tired* of holding back. The villains think we're a joke, because we have to play by the rules, whether they're our own or the rules of others. Villains only play by their own rules—that's what makes them villains."

"Sounds like you want to be an antihero and call it a day," I said. Brighteyes laughed, a cold and bitter-sounding thing, drenched in cynicism and nihilism.

"You always have your taxonomy, don't you?" she said. "Of course you'd have a way of framing it. Yeah, maybe I'm an antiheroine. I can live with that. I'm tired of pretending that it doesn't matter to me when the bad guys get away with it. And I'll never trust Minder again after what he did to me, or what he tried to do."

I was wondering about that, even while brooding over everything she had just said. It was smart of her to come prepared where Minder was concerned.

"And about that," she said. "Why's it okay for him to pry into our minds, and it's not okay for me to do what I'm doing?"

"I guess because he's not killing people," I said. She scoffed.

"If he had mindwiped my sense of justice, or my memory of what went down in Manila, he *would* be killing me. How's that not the same as a lobotomy? Minder could change my entire personality. He could change my nature. That's a creepy kind of power that nobody should have. And I'm saying that as a woman with laser eyes, I know. Minder messes with people's minds. Don't pretend you think otherwise, Mitch."

She was right. Minder was comfortable with that, under the aegis of the greatest good for the greatest number of people. If that meant tweaking someone's memories or personality, he'd do it. I'd seen him do it—not directly, but when I'd gone through some of the Affiliates archives.

"At least I'm being honest about my motivations," she said.

"Okay, but if I put that video of yours out there, the authorities are going to come after you, as well as the criminals," I said. "That's a lot of heat."

"Heat, I can handle," she said.

"You came to me with this why, exactly?" I asked.

She leveled her eyes at me, like she was scanning me.

"Because you're the only one I can trust, Mitch," she said. "Alone among all these superheroes, you're the only one who can possibly understand, with what you went through with Victoriana. You see nearly as much as I do. With your cameras, your bugs, creeping around the way you do. You see the dark underbelly of the world. You see all the bad things people do, what they try to hide. You're the only one who gets it, the one who doesn't blink. When you first joined the team, I thought you were a joke Victoriana had played on the rest of us. I'm sorry to say that, but it's true. I thought you were ridiculous. A guy who records stuff? Insane. And when Minder told us all your secret identity, I felt bad for you. You'd worked hard to keep that secret, and Minder just reached into your head and pulled that out of you, told the rest of us who you were. His excuse back then was that it was so everyone would know you were a good guy, sincere in your motivations. You and Victoriana."

Hearing her say it, her side of what had happened, it brought it all back to me in an agonizing way. Hearing her say Anna's alias, it gutted me.

"Maybe you zapping criminals is your own version of doing what Minder did," I said, but she wasn't having that, only shook her head.

"No," she said. "You didn't have that coming, what Minder did to you. He had no right to out you like that. Anybody I zap, they certainly have it coming. I don't zap innocents. Minder can't claim the same."

Antigone had a forceful way about her, a moral certitude that was tangible. I wouldn't call her a crusader exactly, but she had her mission. I couldn't say I was trying to talk her off her ledge, but I did at least lob a few logic bombs at her.

"If you go about doing this and don't somehow get killed, won't it lead to a kind of 'arms race' between heroes and villains? If they know you're going after them with lethal intent, what's to stop them from doing the same?"

She just laughed again, bathing me in that blistering bitterness, like opening a door and feeling a blast of winter wind gusting in your face.

"You're acting like they have some kind of restraint already, Mitch," Brighteyes said. "They don't. I'll admit that not every supervillain deserves summary execution. The ones that aren't trying to conquer the world, destroy the world, enslave humanity, commit genocide—the petty crimelords? I'd consider sparing them. Like Slick, for example."

Slick was a jewel thief and master locksmith who could turn himself into a slippery liquid and slip into just about anywhere. He avoided violence whenever possible, usually relying on his stealthiness to slip into places and rob them. His success as a thief was significant, and certainly caused jewelers all manner of fits, but he hadn't killed anyone.

"You'd spare Slick?" I asked.

"He's just a thief," she said. "I said I'd *consider* sparing him."

"Okay," I said. "So, you're not going after every criminal."

She narrowed her eyes at me, like these nefarious slits.

"I'm going after the killers," she said. "The dangerous ones. Thieves are jerks, but they're less dangerous than others."

"But if Slick killed someone?" I asked.

"Then he's fair game," she said.

"What about corporations? Evil CEOs?" I asked. "Aren't like twenty percent of them actual psychopaths?"

Brighteyes pondered that. "Yeah. For now, I'm mostly focusing my deadly gaze on the supervillains. The ones with blood on their hands."

I could tell she was listening, really thinking about it. Not that I'm a psychologist, but Brighteyes just didn't seem crazy to me. Nobody in the superhero world ever went after corporations, except for me. It was just seen as too risky, is my bet. Corporations had armies of lawyers to protect them, would lean on governments to stop superhero teams if they got too close to infringing on corporate interests.

"Minder's going to send the team after you if you keep defying him," I said. "He won't want the team being embarrassed by you turning vigilante."

She folded her arms, blew hair out of her eyes defiantly.

"We already talked about this," she said. "Let him kick me off the team."

"No, I mean he's going to *stop* you," I said. "And you're going to, what? Fight the Affiliates? Battle the PSS? Shoot down your former teammates? End up in the Brig? Or dead?"

I could tell she'd thought about this already. Antigone wasn't prone to whimsy or impulsiveness; she had mapped out her strategy and tactics at length before she'd taken the plunge into antiheroism.

"I wouldn't kill them," she said.

"Okay," I said. "You hold back, but they're going to do whatever it takes to stop you."

Brighteyes laughed at me yet again.

"Short of killing me," she said.

"No, they just might kill you," I said. "If they can't stop you, they might."

"Who would do that? Rad Lad? He doesn't have the stomach for it," she said. "Wingman? No chance. I don't see Tag Team doing it, although maybe he's pissed enough at me now to consider it. Fact is, he *can't* stop me. Tandem? I don't know. Maybe. Minder can't, thanks to my protection."

I didn't want to bring that up again, but she'd avoided answering the first time. I sometimes revisited topics that way, to try to break down those defenses. You'd be surprised what persistent questioning could accomplish. But she was too alert to fall for it.

"I'm not telling you what it is, Mitch," she said. "You're the last person I'd tell that to."

"I thought you trusted me," I said.

"It's because I trust you that I can't trust you," she said. "Or I trust you to try to do the right thing, and in your head, that would mean trying to sabotage me, likely for my own sake."

We hadn't been close, but she sure as hell knew me, which practically made me feel embarrassed. I recalled those cryptic words she'd said to me at Anna's funeral.

"Remember, I see through people, Mitch," she said, tapping her temple. I tried another tack in hopes that it might disarm her.

"Why even shoot that confession if you don't feel guilty about what you're doing?" I asked. "There's no point in it."

Then it hit me.

"You're *planning* to be killed," I said. "The tape's a confession in case you end up dead."

She eyed me a moment before responding, and I wondered what she might be thinking of it, of me, of everything.

"I want people to *understand* why I'm doing it," she said. "I don't want Minder getting the last word, getting to frame my passing the way he did with Victoriana. I don't want him shaping it in some self-serving manner that makes me look bad. Once I'm dead, people will say whatever they like about who I was."

"What do you mean about Victoriana?" I asked. "And what you said at the funeral?"

Antigone gazed deep into me with her glowing eyes.

"Mitch, do you actually believe that crap about Anna committing suicide?" she asked. "Did Anna strike you as someone who'd do that?"

"No," I said. And it was true. I never accepted her death.

"Minder put that suggestion in her head," she said, as casually as if she'd been commenting on the weather. I felt something clawing at my heart.

"What are you saying?" It wasn't that I hadn't thought that; rather, it was just doubting that Minder would have the temerity to risk that. Anna would have crushed him if she'd caught him meddling with her mind. Then again, if he had, he would have had to work very subtly.

And, yeah, I started recording her. I wanted to hear what she had to say on this, wanted to have it.

"Victoriana was wicked strong, Mitch," Antigone said. "We all know that. Minder knew that, which was why he wanted her on the team. When she insisted on you joining with her, he was willing to put up with that because he was eager to get her on board. You were considered a cost of doing business with Victoriana."

To hear Brighteyes just spinning this out, it made me wonder why I'd not explored that more. I hated to think that a telepathic lowlife like Minder might have gotten to Anna. Or maybe Minder had messed with my mind to keep me from making that connection. The prospect of him muddling my own mind made me furious. The thing with Minder was that he'd see me coming, and if I'd confronted him with that, he could have spun it around on me with his telepathic powers. Could make me forget, make me believe anything he wanted.

"She only had two weaknesses, Mitch," Antigone said. "Magic and mental attacks. That's it. She was otherwise untouchable."

"Okay, yeah, but why would he even do that?" I asked.

Brighteyes stared hard at me, those deadly eyes burning into me a moment before she replied.

"Same reason he's messing with me now," she said. "Shane's thing—the rot in the team. The whole reason Shane brought you two in as members. He wanted outsiders to get in there and make it right."

"Come on, Antigone," I said. "Where's the proof?"

"Nonexistent," she said. "Just the way Minder likes it. He's subtle, Mitch. The evidence is what Anna did. She was happy. She was happy with you. She loved you. And she was in on what you and Shane were up to. Which means that Minder would have gotten wind of it, the way he does. It would have been easy for him to throw a little suicidal ideation into her head—just a little push on his part, to turn a stray thought into a compulsion, an obsession, even. Our brains are clay for Minder."

It seemed too brazen for Minder. I couldn't comprehend why he might do it. *Motive. Means. Opportunity.*

"And what? He just wanted her out of the way?" I said.

"Sure," Antigone said. "Shane was the one who brought you two in. Not Rex. He has other directions in mind for the team. Minder couldn't work on Shane, but you two? Absolutely. In fact, if things went south with you and Anna, that would make it easier for Minder to sideline Shane on future hirings. Knack's record's impeccable, but Minder would mess with that if he could, just to make himself seem better."

"And is this why you're being sidelined?" I asked.

"No, I told you why," she said. "Minder *likes* my powers—they're useful without being as threatening as someone like Victoriana was. I think his ego couldn't stand having a player as powerful as Anna in the mix, yet not under his control. But a suicidal suggestion? It would get her out of his way in a way that would let him keep his hands clean."

It angered me to even think of it, and, despite my suspicions, to think that he'd played that out successfully. And that this was only just conjecture on the part of Brighteyes, who was hardly a sterling witness, based on what she'd done.

I couldn't say she had a deathwish, but she was haunted by what she'd seen with those unearthly eyes of hers. And she was right that I could relate to it. I had an archive of footage I didn't let anyone else see. They were horrible things I'd uncovered that filled me with dread. Real things, tangible, not supernatural. It would have been easier to just destroy those clips, but the archivist in me wouldn't permit it. A record had to be kept, and the historical memory had to remain. Memory mattered.

"I can't stop until I'm finished, Mitch," she said. "And I won't. It needs to be done. I'm taking that on."

"And let's say you kill all the supervillains you think deserve to be killed," I said. "What next?"

"Retirement," she said.

"Not in Hyberia, though?" I asked.

Brighteyes shook her head vehemently. "I'll never end up there."

My phone rang, and I held it up. "It's Decibelle."

Brighteyes heaved a world-weary sigh.

"Don't answer," she said. "Let it go to voicemail. Don't forget, Des can mindfuck a person much the way Minder can, only using her voice."

I let it go to voicemail, thinking I'd just use the transcription to see what she said, avoiding any sonic tricks she might play. I was feeling vulnerable in my lair. I didn't want the Affiliates pounding down my doors. I didn't want Minder or Decibelle playing with my mind.

"Alright, Antigone," I said. "You had me record this confession/declaration. What are you doing next?"

"You already know, Mitch," she said. "Hothead, Airhead, and Thunderhead. I'm ending the Fourheads. That criminal fraternity has been around for thirty years. *Thirty years*, Mitch. I'm stopping them. And then the Crime League. They've been around for far too long. After that, maybe a vacation. Someplace warm and calm."

I looked at the camcorder setup, felt obligated to at least ask.

"Are you all done with your 'confessional' or did you have anything more to say that you wanted me to capture for posterity?" I asked.

"Beyond what you just recorded of our conversation?" she asked, smiling at me.

"I had to," I said. Somehow, I had to get Minder to talk. To confess. How on earth could I even approach a telepath with ill intent?

Antigone thought about it for a bit, then a bit longer.

"Maybe something for Desdemona."

"Alright, then," I said. "Let's do it."

She returned to her seat and composed herself, and I let her know when we were metaphorically rolling on that camcorder.

"Des, I'm sorry I put you through any of this," she said. "You've always been a great partner, and you always had my back. For someone like you, someone who isn't even truly human, I imagine what we deal with has to feel strange and unfamiliar. One could even ask why a Siren, who has a track record of leading men to their doom by the sound of her voice even has superheroism on her bucket list. It might be a question for the ages."

While I wondered whether people even had bucket lists, anymore, I will be the first to admit that Antigone had a point. Why *was* Decibelle a superhero? What was her motivation? Was she trying to atone for her Siren past? I'd have to remember to ask her. Maybe I'd try to stage an interview with her. Wouldn't *that* be something?

"But you were always there for me, and I'll never forget that. Sound & Fury helped me get through so much, helped keep me steady, made me feel like I was doing something legitimately good, helping out those who had no one else helping them. That's superheroism to me, and you helped make that possible. However it shakes out between us in the end, I want you to know that you'll always be the closest thing I ever had to a true friend. And I'll feel that way even if you use your Siren's scream to liquefy my brain."

Okay, now that was a horrifying image. It also made me wonder how Decibelle might be, moodwise, when she showed up at my place tomorrow.

"She can do that?" I asked. Brighteyes nodded, didn't seem to mind that we were still recording.

"Not that I've actually seen her liquefy someone's brain, but I've seen her use soundwaves to liquefy other stuff. It's pretty impressive," she said. "Just seems sensible that if she could do that to stone, that a person's skull would be easy by comparison."

"Wow, yeah, uh, gross," I said, making Brighteyes chuckle.

"You know, you should do a series of super-interviews, Cam," she said. "Just candid interviews. People would tune into that, see what we're *really* about. So much dirty laundry with us superheroic longjohners."

I'll admit, it was a good idea. I had a degree of access, and the unscripted nature of them might have more authenticity than the overproduced Affiliates puff pieces.

"Not a bad idea," I said.

"I have my moments," Brighteyes said. "Decibelle, you were the best partner a superheroine could ever hope to have, and we had magic between us. I'll never forget that."

She signaled for me to cut, and I did, my head full of ideas. My primary focus was always on bringing the untouchable baddies to justice, but maybe as a sideline gig I could do super-interviews. It was so stupid it just might be brilliant. Maybe I could use my own portable rigging to livestream superheroics.

But most importantly, I had to get to the bottom of this Minder business. I needed to know more. For the sake of Anna.

"Antigone, those are big accusations you tossed out about Minder," I said.

"Yeah, they are," she replied, going to grab another drink of water. "If you wanted me to get really twisted on you, I could posit that my current troubles are because of my suspicions that Minder might be responsible for Anna's death. I never confronted him about it, but the thoughts were there. And when I unloaded on Dusthead and his goons, had words later with Minder, it's at least possible he may have caught a thought or two about my speculations, which led him to go after me under the pretense of helping me."

"It's a lot to take in," I said. I hated Minder, but would he really do something like that? The important thing was knowing why he might. The all-important motive. He had the means and the opportunity. What I desperately needed was the motive. Or had he put some mental block in place in me that wouldn't let me make that connection? It was such a weird thought to have, but it wasn't beyond his ability.

"Okay, Mitch," she said. "I've got to skate. I'm assuming because you haven't shot me with one of your stun toys that you're at least, what, neutral on what I've been doing?"

How did I square my own ethos with her murderous pursuit of vengeance?

"You're seeking justice," I said. "I can understand that."

Brighteyes walked up to me and gave me a hug. It's the closest we'd ever been, as heroes, as antiheroes, as people. She let me go and looked at me closely with her luminescent eyes. You've never experienced something like that, having a super-being with glowing eyes study you. It's terrifying. She was terrifying. Like this spirit of vengeance.

"You're Nemesis," I said, blurting it out.

"Nemesis?" she asked.

"The Greek goddess of revenge," I said, grateful that I'd studied all of that stuff in school, even remembered some of it. "'Nemesis' originally meant the neutral distributor of fortune, good or bad, delivered in proportion according to what was deserved. It later came to embody the resentment caused by the disruption of that balance and an unquenchable sense of justice that could not let that disturbance go unpunished."

Brighteyes laughed at me spewing that, took out her Wayfarers and slipped them on. They couldn't completely conceal the phosphorescence of her gaze but muted it a bit.

"Or at least working a deal with Yeomna, the god of the underworld, and Mireuk, the god of creation and destruction," Brighteyes said. "Yeah, I can't let the bad guys win, Mitch. Maybe I should change my alias to 'Nemesister' or something like that to reflect my willingness to bring rough justice to the deserving."

"No way," I said. "You'll always be Brighteyes."

"Yeah," she said. "Thanks for letting me record that stuff. Do what you want with it. I originally came here to fry the copies, but now, I don't know, I feel okay with you having them."

"Thanks, I think," I said.

Then she left me alone with my footage and philosophy, and just a hint of brimstone, which turned my head.

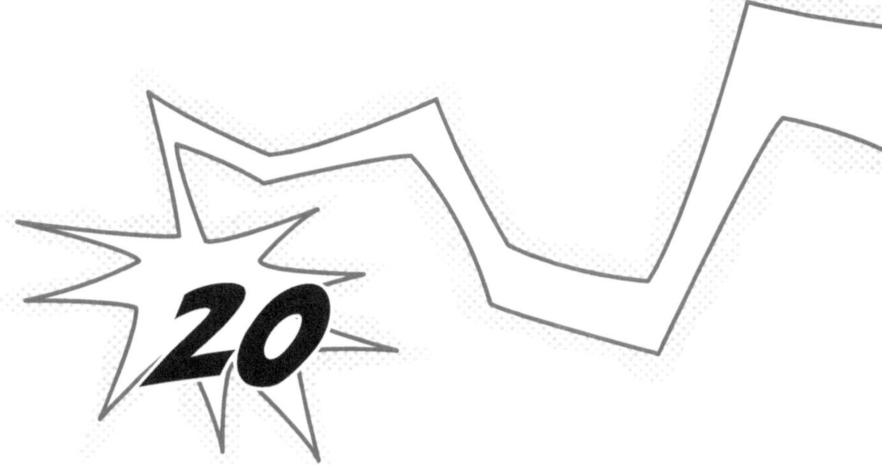

as he'd asked. He'd had one of his assistants reach out to me to set up the meeting in the main conference room in Central. I was dizzy with grief, my head not in the right place, but I persisted.

Since we were in Central, Minder had taken off his face-mask, had it sitting on the table, like a discarded skin, watching me with his dark brown eyes, his brown hair smooth, despite the mask he'd worn. He liked to slick back his hair, which always creeped me out.

He'd been sitting at the head of the table, watching me come in, still in my full suit. He gestured to any of the empty seats around him.

"Sit wherever you like, Mitch," he said. He glanced at the bouquets of flowers some of the others had gotten for me, which the robots had set up on one of the long tables in the living room.

I sat at the opposite end of the table, clasped my fingers while resting my hands on the table.

"What's this about, Rex?" I asked.

"We've never had a team member commit suicide before," Minder said. "I wanted to be here for you, to make sure *you're* alright."

I kept my inner monologue at bay. It was a habit I found I practiced whenever in Minder's company. What I felt worked was playing DEVO's "Whip It" in my head over and over again, which helped form a catchy enough barrier to camouflage other thoughts I might be having.

"How do you *think* I feel?" I asked. "I'm crushed."

"Is there anything you want to get off your chest?" he asked. He treated me to a dose of Telepath's Concern, which was this phony solicitous expression—an open face, neutral and slightly-but-not-intrusively caring. Not so much as to be obvious or invasive, but enough to show that he was here, actively listening, and engaged.

"Like what?" I asked. I was recording him while we talked.

"Like why you're recording this conversation," he said.

"I record everything," I said. Not entirely true, but there it was.

"Not true, Mitch," he said. "I know we've not seen eye to eye in the past, but I'm your teammate as well as your chairman. I *want* to help you. Perhaps if you'd come to me before, maybe Anna would be here with us right now."

I glared at him behind the neutral, one-way screen of my mask. One of the benefits of my Cameraman mask was it was reflective, hiding my actual face. From my perspective, I had the HUD display serving up all sorts of useful information. However, it was also stupid to feel that way, because Minder knew everything I might be thinking or feeling.

"Don't you dare pin that on me," I said.

"No, no," Minder said. "I wouldn't dream of doing that. You're only human, Mitch. You're not superhuman like the rest of us, as you are all too aware. It would be unfair to think you could have done anything to help poor Anna. I just wish our background checks and psychological profiles could have picked up on her tendency toward suicidal ideation."

"She *wasn't* suicidal," I said, trying to keep calm. Minder had a way of getting at me without even trying to. Or at least doing so without appearing to.

Minder shifted in his seat, resting on an elbow, stroking his chin as he looked down his nose at me.

"I don't think you're qualified to make that judgment, Mitch," he said. "I have a PhD in Psychology, do you know that? I've always been fascinated by the way the mind works."

"I'll bet," I said.

"For example, our logs show you spending a lot of time over the past couple of years going through our archives," Minder said. "What're you looking for?"

"Bad guys," I said. "I've always kept records on the baddies. I figured the Affiliates would have the most complete files."

"That we do," Minder said. "Anybody in particular you feel like talking about?"

He was probing, likely probing my mind, too, trying to see what was on my mind. I just kept DEVO playing in my brain, over and over again.

"Not particularly, Rex," I said. "I have to track down the baddies *wherever* they are."

"Which ones?" he asked, aiming his gaze at me.

"The ones that think they can get away with it," I said.

"Names, Mitch," he said, and I felt the push. He was pushing me telepathically. It wasn't an obvious thing; it was just a sensation. It made me think of Shane's vibes.

"Get out of my head, Rex," I said. "Get right the fuck out."

Amazingly, he did, or appeared to.

"I only want to help you, Mitch," Minder said. "I wish I could have helped Anna."

"Yeah," I said. "Sure you did."

"I'm sensing animosity from you, Mitch," Minder said. "Animosity is painful. It's unhealthy."

I had this image appear in my head of me throwing myself out a skyscraper window, taking a blissful jump into oblivion.

"What, are you saying I might experience suicidal ideation?" I asked. "Like Anna, maybe?"

Minder wasn't deterred from his line of inquiry.

"I really think you need to take a leave of absence for your own health and wellness, Mitch," Minder said.

"I've got a better idea, I think," I said. "I quit."

Minder didn't look surprised; he only raised an eyebrow.

"Seems extreme, Mitch," he said. "A leave, or even a sabbatical might be better. You've worked so hard the past three years, trying to establish yourself on the team. You really want to throw that all away? Take a vacation. Come back rested and refreshed, more like your old self."

"There's no vacation I could take without her with me, Rex," I said. "No, I quit. As of today."

I took out my Affilicard ID and slapped it on the table, then flicked it to him, watching it slide down the table until he caught it with a gloved hand.

Then he feigned sorrow and regret as he spoke. I could *see* it.

"I'm sorry to see you do this, Mitch," Minder said. "The team likes you. They *loved* Anna. Losing you both in the same year will be a lot for them to process."

The heartache I felt drowned out even DEVO in my brain.

"I'm sure you'll be there to guide them through it all, Rex," I said, getting to my feet and leaving him to his thoughts.

I copied the Brighteyes footage (which, yes, I edited so it ran smoothly. I might be an antihero, but I'm also an aesthete). I put on some earbuds and whistled while I worked. Then I personally ran the copies to my safe deposit boxes and kept the masters in my vaulted archive.

What was I going to do with them? For now, nothing. It was a strategic decision as much as it was a tactical one.

Here's the thing: if I put Antigone's confession out there, it would alert all the villains to what she was doing. And I didn't want that. Not for the sake of the Affiliates, but for the sake of Brighteyes. I didn't want them to see her coming. I owed her that much.

Decibelle was waiting for me at Flying Saucer, signing Dreadful Yesterdays albums that the store clerks were holding out for her with shaking hands. Molly was awestruck, as was Stan.

They didn't know I was Cameraman, and if they knew, I didn't know if they'd even care. That's how it worked with me. But Desdemona Bell was someone they could relate to. She was comprehensible celebrity, and she bowled them over. I could see their eyes following her as she walked to me, wondering why someone like me knew someone like her. I could see it.

"Hey, Mitch-Honey," she said, giving me a hug. This was exceeding my monthly quota for hugs, for sure. "Can we go somewhere and talk?"

"Sure," I said, and in that moment, I didn't want to be alone with her. "How about The Last Drop?"

It was a beverage place across the street.

"Fine," she said, and we walked over there, mindful of traffic. "Did you see that the Avant Guardian was battling the Bleeding Edge in Manhattan?"

"Nope," I said. "Missed that."

The Avant Guardian was a flashy superhero who used her full-spectrum light-based powers to combat crimes against the art and design community, while the Bleeding Edge, a suit-based supervillain, waged war against art as the enemy of reality. The two of them fought at least every other year, as they were arch enemies, and, it was rumored, secret lovers. It happened.

"The Scenester turned up," she said, referring to the Bleeding Edge's ever-present sidekick/toadie. He had some kind of teleportation power that enabled him to pop in wherever he wanted to be. Scenester used to be with Edgelord, but when he was sent to the Brig a year ago by Ms. Fit, the Scenester paired up with the Bleeding Edge.

"Are the Affiliates involved?" I asked.

"We're monitoring it," she said, as we got to the Last Drop, which was thankfully not so busy we couldn't get a seat. I got a straight-up black coffee, while Des got some loaded caffeinated beverage that I almost couldn't follow. Something with a straw, which I felt was heretical for coffee. I thought I'd head her off.

"Minder already got the footage," I said. "I gave a copy to Tag Team."

"I know," she said. "I've been briefed."

She looked worried, and worry on a Siren was a beautiful thing. Not to be distracted, but it was. Des wore a black leather jacket and a blue and orange lateral striped sweater with a matching blue scarf festooned with orange stars. She wore black leggings and black knee boots.

"So, now what?" I asked.

"I need *all* the copies, Mitch," she said. "I can't let Brighteyes ruin her reputation this way."

I wasn't going to tell Des that Antigone had visited me only last night. I'd learned well enough over the years when to be quiet and listen.

"You need them? You mean Minder does," I said.

"It's Affiliates business, Mitch," she said. "You have to understand that much. What you have is incriminating evidence."

"Yeah, of murder," I said.

"We can't let that get out," she replied. "In the wrong hands, it could be dangerous."

Now I was going to play a possibly tricky game, but the kind of thing I was born to play, since I'd already gotten some of the story from Antigone.

"What happened with you and Antigone after Manila?" I asked. "Honestly, now. How'd Minder play that?"

Her purple eyes studied me, and, again, knowing just who and what she was, it was intimidating.

"What do you mean?" she asked.

"Did he mess with your minds?" I asked.

"What? No," she said. "He'd *never* do that."

"Wrong," I said. "He has, and he so would."

Given that Sirens were mistresses of the mindfuck, the very idea that a mortal man like Minder might have messed with her mind was anathema to Decibelle. I could see her imagining it and rejecting the idea out of hand.

"Mitch, your paranoia is getting to you," she said. "And do you think Tag Team wouldn't have reported what happened last night? That tawdry business with the White Arrow? She was here, Mitch. You weren't going to tell me?"

"I was," I said. "I wanted to hear what you had to say, first."

"Minder didn't mess with our minds," she said. "To what purpose?"

"Antigone was distressed by what happened in Manila," I said. "She said Minder tried to make all that go away."

"Never happened," she said, bringing a hand to her forehead. "Minder wouldn't do that."

"I think he did," I said. "You don't know it because he wiped that from your memory."

The hand that had been at her forehead came down on the table with a discreetly vehement bang.

"Mitch, stop it," she said. "Just because you and Minder have your differences doesn't make him some kind of villain. Not everybody's your enemy, no matter how hard you try to make them so, Honey."

Her voice was hushed and urgent, her teeth clenched. Her Siren's pride wouldn't allow her to accept being Minder's pawn. It's like I was watching a Greek tragedy play out at the Last Drop, and the patrons were none the wiser.

"Antigone told me she caught Minder trying to mindwipe her," I said. "Why would she make that up?"

Des looked at me plaintively, her eyebrows knitting as she sought to untangle the Gordian Knot of her confusion, when we both knew there was only one way through that sucker.

"She's confused," Des said. "She's not in her right mind."

"And what about you? Did you change your mind about Antigone, or did you have your mind changed?" I asked.

"Mitch, seriously," she said. "This is bigger than you can even imagine."

"Oh, so you admit that there's a *there* there," I said. "That's a start. Why not start being honest with me, Des?"

To see a Siren scowl was a frightening thing. The folk portrayals of them only partly captured the supernaturality of them in-person. Des was glaring at me, and I downed my coffee quickly, feeling like maybe it was a last breakfast for me in that moment. And then Des tried some Bene Gesserit shit on me that would've had Frank Herbert pleased as punch, seeing her use the Voice.

"Mitch, you need to give me the recordings," she said, each word rattling across a harmonic frequency I could scarcely

hear, but which bounced around inside my skull like a handful of superballs.

I've never been on the receiving end of one of Decibelle's sonic attacks, but this was wild. I could feel the cascading *sotto voce* sonic waves passing through me, compelling me.

However, remember when I told you about how contingencies were the lifeblood of skills heroes? I'd brought protection. You think I'd knowingly wade into another rendezvous with Decibelle without some ear protection? Sorry I didn't tell you earlier, but you saw how busy I've been. I'd put them on before I'd run my errands.

They're essentially harmonic scramblers that offer white noise counters to low-frequency soundwaves. Back when I was in the Affiliates, I watched Decibelle use that sub-aural vocal attack on bad guys and thought maybe I needed to figure out a counter to it. I recorded her using it on people and analyzed the sound, could see what frequencies it operated at, and cooked up the white noise harmonizers on some bespoke earbuds. I'd never had occasion to use them until now, and was happy that they seemed to work.

I got up and pretended that I was in thrall to her words, And, yes, I had a digital recorder playing on me, capturing this precious moment.

"*I'll need all of the copies, too,*" Decibelle said, holding my hand as we walked back to my place.

Now, the harmonizers wouldn't help me if she kicked up the volume and tried to blast me. But against this kind of attack, they worked like a charm.

A hint of a plan was forming in my head. Not what I was dealing with in that moment, but rather, why Decibelle had come to me in the first place. I was thinking Minder had wanted me to locate Brighteyes and get that footage, and had sent Decibelle to do it, knowing that I'd never have done it if he'd made the request of me.

Maybe it was my paranoia talking, but clearly Des was doing Minder's bidding, here. Then again, I'd sent the copy to Minder, hadn't I?

Truth: I hadn't. I'd sent him something else, because no way in hell would I have sent Minder that incriminating footage. I hated the guy. Sorry if that was duplicitous of me not to share that with you, Gentle Reader. If you don't know already, then here it is: Fuck Minder.

I would have loved to have seen the look on his and Tag Team's faces when they tried to play the video only to find nothing there. Well, not entirely nothing. It was just a looped clip of me in my Cameraman suit, flipping off Minder. Immature? Yeah, maybe. But damned satisfying.

The biggest advantage I had over Minder was he had range limits with his telepathy. It's why he had to work through other people the way he was sock-puppeteering Decibelle.

As we made our way to my building, to the renewed delight of my Flying Saucer Video staff, I was thinking of how to deal with Decibelle. Thankfully, she wasn't super-strong or invulnerable, or I'd not have a chance. Her main attack was that voice, which meant that if I could disable that, I'd be able to handle her.

We went to the elevator, and I pushed the floor to my hideout, using my key to unlock that floor. Up we went, together.

My advantage was that she thought I was under her sonic spell, which meant that I had pretty much one chance to make things go my way. I had prepared ahead of time (again, sorry I didn't tell you this; you'll understand why shortly).

We reached my hideout floor, and stepped out, and then things got wild. Walking beside Decibelle, I struck her in the throat with a lateral knife-hand strike, and I caught her just right, because her hands went to her throat as she gasped.

Then I grabbed a gag I had sitting on one of my tool benches and I tackled her while she was recovering from the throat punch. We struggled on the floor for a few moments, but I managed to get the gag in place before she could explode my head with a sonic scream.

She gag-talked, expressing her dismay that her considerable power could be so handily disabled, but there it was. I secured the gag with a little padlock, and then handcuffed her before she could tear it off.

"Sorry, Des," I said, taking out my earbuds and showing her. "I thought you might try something like that."

Her purple eyes flared, somewhere between wounded indignation and righteous fury. She kicked at me with her boots, so I maneuvered her around to a chair. I could see her trying to create her sonic shriek that would make short work of me, but the gag worked to keep her from getting the necessary breath to activate her power.

"Minder's mindzapped you, and you don't even know it," I said. "That's part of the zap. You *think* you're doing this to help Antigone, but you're just Minder's puppet."

She shook her head, eyes imploring, and then narrowing menacingly as Inferna emerged from another room, where she'd been waiting patiently for my return, looking heavenly in a red ribbed turtleneck, black slacks, and red heels. She'd put her long locks up with some pitchfork picks and wore dangling gold sword earrings that moved as she walked.

"You certainly read that right, Mitch," Inferna said, walking up to cup Decibelle's chin in her hand. "I *like* seeing her like this."

"Be nice, Fern," I said. "Decibelle's not been herself, lately. Minder's done a number on her. Can you undo it? And can you help me with my own problem?"

Inferna reluctantly released Decibelle and held out a ring to me, a thing of gold, which she dropped into my outstretch palm.

"So long as you wear this, Minder won't be able to access your mind," she said. "No matter how hard he tries."

I looked at the ring, turning it over in my hands. It was a willfully unassuming loop of gold, but I could see the devilish runes around the interior of it. Inferna watched me study it, smiling to herself, showing a hint of a fang.

"Oh, Mitch, please," she said, mocking. "You think I'd need a ring to enslave you?"

Gulping, I put the ring on, and felt no different, except that I saw the ring become invisible on my finger. Inferna's magic could be tricky that way, and as much as I hated to depend on a magic ring to protect myself from Minder, I didn't have much choice.

"The ring's invisible?" I said.

"Yes," Inferna said. "It wouldn't be much protection to you if someone saw it on your finger and removed it. Or worse, cut off your finger to remove it. This way, only you and I know it's there at all."

"*Diabolus est in singulis*," I said, which made Inferna smile. "What about Decibelle?"

"I'll have to dispel the hold he has on her," she said. "That'll take some time. And then I'll have to ward her against him so she doesn't fall victim to it again."

"You can do that?" I asked.

"I'm magical," Inferna said. "I can do *anything*, Mitch."

Her evident satisfaction in that comment was almost more than I could take, but we shared a laugh.

"Affiliates protocol means Decibelle will have to check in soon," I said. "If she doesn't check in, Minder's going to send reinforcements. Also, they'll have put trackers and/or transponders on Des."

I took out a scanner and ran it all along Decibelle's body, found two trackers in her uniform, and a subcutaneous one on her right forearm.

"Minder had you rigged up, Des," I said. The transponder program had been implemented after I'd left the team. It was one of the key drivers for me going out the door. I wasn't a doctor, didn't want to risk trying to remove it. However, as long as she had it, the Affiliates HQ computers would know her exact location, probably including her vitals. "No way I can remove that transponder."

Inferna acknowledged that with a shrug. "I don't think I can without simply cutting into her arm and pulling it out."

"Yeah, we don't want to do that," I said, noting the degree of relief on Decibelle's face.

I probably should have been insulted that they only sent Decibelle, but maybe Minder was mindful that if they came in too forcefully, and Brighteyes was still around, it might have escalated. He was still playing it very quietly and carefully.

"I probably can't take more than three of them at the same time, depending on who they send," Inferna said so matter-of-factly that it made me snort.

Decibelle glared at us over her gag, shaking her head. I could hear her phone ringing, and I took it from her jacket pocket. It was Minder, checking up on her. I held that out for Decibelle to see.

"Minder," I said to her. "Wanting to see whether you were able to do what he wanted you to do."

Decibelle strained at her bonds, while Inferna looked on.

"Not to be a buzzkill, but we're going to need more on our side," Inferna said. The intercom buzzed, and I took a look at my monitor cam. There stood Lynn Credible, along with three Tag Teams. Now I knew we were really in for it.

"Great," I said. "Credible's here."

visiting me at the brownstone. I could still feel her here, our hideout. I'd taken off my costume and put on some sweats and a tee, had downed too much gin.

"Yeah, I did," I said. "It's Minder. He's the one who drove her to it. Has to be. He's the only one who could have done it. The only one who could get Anna to fly into the Sun."

"Minder?" Shane asked. "Based on what?"

"Hunch," I said. "Feeling. Vibe. Anna was unbeatable physically. Seriously. She's only actually vulnerable to two things: magical and mental attacks. I don't think someone put a spell on her. That leaves a mental attack. Minder's already shown a propensity for mucking around in people's minds. It would be easy for him to get in there and put some suicidal thoughts in her head. She was complaining about it that last day, like feeling off. Something being wrong. It was Minder."

Shane watched me a minute, just looking at me and not saying anything, like he was really giving it some thought.

"But why?" he asked.

"Because of what you said," I said. "The whole thing about there being rot in the Affiliates. It's him. *He's the rot.* He didn't like Anna and me poking around. And if he'd done something to me, I think Anna might have torn him apart. Instead, he took her out, knowing he'd be safer with her out of the way."

Shane listened, considering it.

"What about me, though?" he asked. "He knows that I set that in motion."

"Has he ever scanned you?" I replied. Shane mulled on that a bit before replying.

"I don't know," he said. "I think he can't."

"Why not?" I asked.

"My power," Shane said. "If he's tried, I imagine my good luck would somehow deflect it. And if he tried to kill me, same thing."

How fortunate to be the Knack, I thought.

"He may have known the three of us were covertly investigating," I said. "Maybe he couldn't read your mind, but he could read Anna's and mine. And perhaps he was threatened by whatever he found there, and so he struck where he could, where he perceived the greatest risk. And given how popular Anna was with the team, there was at least a risk that she might make deputy chairperson. A challenge to his authority."

Shane sat back on the sofa, gazing up at our skylight.

"It's insidious," Shane said. "If true."

"I don't have proof," I said.

"And your leaving the team reduces your access," Shane said. "And likelihood to be able to sleuth this out from the inside."

"No," I said. "All it means is that I'm out of range of his telepathy. That means I can work without him eavesdropping on my thoughts."

Shane took that in.

"What are you going to do, then?" he asked.

"I'm going to bust him," I said. "Or die trying. Which brings me to another question: why did you bring Anna and me into this if you weren't going to help us?"

Shane was inhumanly patient. To the extent that he probably had it as a side effect of his superpowers.

"I helped you every step of the way," Shane said. "I sponsored the two of you to join the team. I persuaded Rex to greenlight Anna's contingent hiring vis-à-vis you. He didn't want you joining the team, beyond a mild curiosity as to who the heck you really were. I have helped you afford so many of the great tools and gadgets you use. I bought you and Anna a brownstone downtown, so you'd have a base of operations. I convinced Rex of the need to have the branches in Central and South—believe me, he only really cares about the coasts. I've been there for you every way, Mitch."

Everything he said was true. It was, and I couldn't argue it on the face of things. But I didn't let that stop me.

"What about Anna?" I asked. "What about her?"

"I'm forever sorry that happened," Shane said. "I can't see the future; all I can do is favorably interact with probability when I'm attacked, or where I turn my attention. And to be honest, I never could have imagined that Minder might put a suicidal suggestion into Anna's mind that way. Honestly, if he was really out to get you, why wouldn't he have put a homicidal suggestion in her mind and have her murder you, then maybe kill herself? Why keep you alive at all?"

That was a question that gnawed at me the worst. Why hadn't he targeted me? The only thing I could determine was that he wanted me to be alive because he knew the way I'd react to the loss of Anna. He'd wind me up and watch me create my own self-destruction in my desire for revenge.

I glanced at the glass vase where I put all the beer can marbles Anna had made over the years. She'd make them, and I'd drop them in the vase, like they were decorations, which they were. I loved them because she'd made them.

"He's still using me," I said. "He's using me to take myself out."

"He got you to quit," Shane said. "There's that. Let's think about this strategically, Mitch. Put our heads together. What is Rex up to?"

I'll admit that I'd never worked a case with Shane. He always seemed entirely beyond the mundane drudgery of casework. But I went to my databoard and turned it on, grabbing my light pen and writing MINDER on the front center of it. I put Shane, Anna, and me off to one side, and Brighteyes and Decibelle on there, too, with question marks.

I wrote ROT below Minder and put some arrows pointing to him. I wrote "mindfuck" and drew arrows between Minder and Brighteyes and Anna. I drew another line from Anna, wrote SUICIDE (?) and stepped back.

"Okay," Shane said. "What do we know?"

"No, no," I said. "What do you know, Shane? You're Deputy Chairman. What do *you* know?"

I handed the light pen to him, and he walked to my databoard, began jotting things down. He wrote AFFILIATES to the right of Minder and added BRIG with a line from the Affiliates to it. He wrote BLACK OPS from Affiliates and drew a line to Minder. Then another line to POLYGON, with links to Black Ops.

Not wanting to share, I grabbed another light pen and wrote PUBLIC RELATIONS with a line to Affiliates. NO BAD PRESS came below it. I wrote PSS between Minder and Affiliates, and added HYBERIA HOLLOW below it, with lines to the Brig and Black Ops.

Shane smiled.

"Rex works very closely as a military consultant for the Polygon, as well as with the intelligence community," he said, and wrote CIA, FBI, NSA, and DIA off to one side, with lines going back to the PSS, Minder, and the Affiliates.

We stepped back, looked over what we had. A lot of names, a lot of arrows.

"How much are you involved in the planning and policy with the Affiliates?" I asked.

"Nominally," Shane said.

"What's the reporting structure? It can't just be Rex, right?" I asked. Shane took his own pen and wrote names on the board: JOINT CHIEFS, NSC, SENIOR CABINET.

"Rex meets with the National Security Council," Shane said. "I sometimes get to go to those. They're very attentive to the superhero/supervillain issue."

He wrote SUPER SOLDIERS on the board, drew a line to the Polygon and the Affiliates. He added COUNTERMEASURES with a line to the PSS.

"Okay, so Rex is positioning himself as, what? Talent broker for the Polygon?" I asked. "The whole Hyberia Hollow community for retired supers is a research facility for superhumanism."

Shane wrote EUGENICS on the board with a question mark, drawing another line to the PSS and Minder.

"From the Polygon perspective, they have to be looking at the supers as a talent pool ripe for tapping," I said. "Who are the known super soldiers?"

"You mean ones that the Polygon employs?" Shane asked. "It's classified."

I thought about that a minute. Brighteyes had been a soldier, but the accident that created her hadn't made her a super soldier per se. She'd been out of the service when that had happened to her. Unless it hadn't been an accident. Could they have replicated the accidents that might give people powers? Was that even possible?

SUPERPOWER ORIGINS I wrote on the board, while Shane watched me.

"Come on, Shane," I said. "Time for a lucky guess on your part, yeah?"

"I think the Affiliates are a field-testing marketing apparatus for a covert superbeing creation and management program," Shane said, looking at me gravely.

"Meaning the Affiliates are used as a talent nexus, a proving ground, as well as a public relations exercise for acculturating the public into getting used to the idea of superheroes (and villains)," I said.

Shane tapped the light pen to his chin. "They didn't know where superheroes came from, so they began systematizing the types of superheroes: natural-born, industrial accidents, extraterrestrial, extradimensional."

He wrote those words down on the board and drew the lines to the Affiliates, PSS, NSC, and Polygon.

"In the cases of natural born occurrences, they'd want to do genome evaluations," I said, writing that on the board. "To try to isolate the mutagenic event that might create a super. In the case of industrial accidents, they'd seek to find the specific events that caused the superpowers to appear."

Shane liked that, and I'll ruefully admit that I enjoyed working with Shane on this. Anna and I used to do our own versions of these when we were trying to sort something out.

"Viable paths to power would be catalogued and tested out on suitable subjects," Shane said. "Possibly with consent as a way to deal with the downstream ramifications of the outcomes of such human experiments."

"I think we may need to check out Hyberia Hollow," I said. "See what's really going on there."

Shane shook his head. "Not yet, Mitch. It's not the right time."

"Ohmigod," I said, but from the look in his eyes, I could tell he meant it. "When, then?"

"I'll let you know," he said, giving me a grin that made me want to deck him.

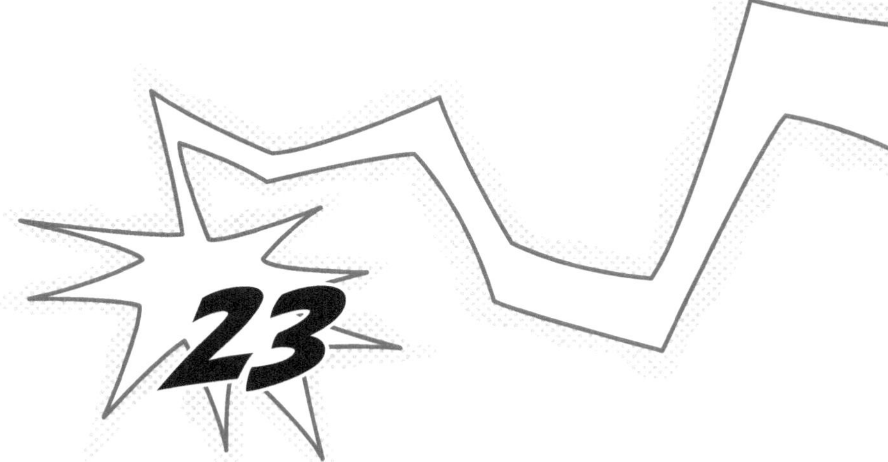

mindful of the Tag Teams staring hard at me through the bulletproof glass. "I'm here on behalf of my clients. It is my understanding that you're holding onto very sensitive footage of an active Affiliates member and are refusing to part with it."

Credible had the polished and professional look of the PR flack that she was—a barely shoulder length slicked back haircut and a power suit-skirt, with a blue leather binder with the Affiliates logo stamped on it.

She was one of those utilitarian supers I sometimes saw—people who had superpowers but preferred to use them for personal success, versus outright superheroism. While I hadn't done surveillance fieldwork on Credible, that was my assumption. With her background in PR, and working for Minder, I doubted she was a telepath, since he would not have tolerated having another telepath in his company. However, with his inherent bias in favor of supers, she had to have been superhuman in some manner.

"It's my property," I said.

"Did Brighteyes sign a release form?" she asked.

"Yes, she did," I said. Yes, I was lying. But Antigone had told me to use the footage however I wanted. Verbal consent of release, which, hell, yeah, I recorded.

Credible was unmoved.

"I haven't received the release form," she said. "Until we receive it, you're forbidden to use this footage of Brighteyes under penalty of legal action. Is that clear, Mr. Paulsen?"

"Crystal clear," I said. I'd have said anything to get rid of this Affiliates operative.

"It's also my understanding that Decibelle visited you," Credible said.

"That's true," I said.

"Where is she now?" Credible asked. She was staring at me through the glass, and I stared right back at her, refusing to be intimidated.

"She's upstairs," I said. "We were negotiating before you interrupted us."

Now you know as well as I did that: 1) Credible knew that Decibelle had come to strongarm me on Minder's orders; and 2) that they were monitoring that transponder they'd put in Decibelle, and knew she was upstairs.

"Can you send her down, Mr. Paulsen?" Credible asked. The way she spoke to me, it was like I was the criminal. She was one of Minder's minions, big time. "Or better yet, can you let us in?"

The way Tag Team was looking on, I was almost certain one or more of his dupes was creeping around elsewhere outside of my building. Maybe using that window I hadn't had time to fix, sneaking back in. Tag Team was enthusiastic about the work, but hardly subtle.

"No, I don't think I'll let you in," I said. "I'll go talk to Decibelle, see if she wants to talk to you."

Credible took out her phone while I went back upstairs.

"Okay, Inferna," I said. "Things are accelerating. We may not have as much time as I hoped. Why don't you take Decibelle and teleport out of here?"

I put on my Cameraman suit and helmet, setting my hideout windows to opaque, in case Tag Team was trying to peek in.

"What about you, Mitch?" she asked.

"I'm going to give you the master files and get out of here," I said, handing her the discs, which she secreted in her bosom, I kid you not. They just vanished in her devilish cleavage.

I hated to think of the Affiliates trashing my place, but I also didn't want them getting the footage, if only out of spite, given Minder's focus on them. "Let's meet up in California. See if you can get Decibelle's brain detoxed in the meantime."

"Alright, Mitch," Inferna said, grabbing Decibelle and making them both vanish in a puff of brimstone.

Then I took the elevator down to the parking garage and hopped into my Mitchmobile, my fast car, which was a fully charged, retrofitted 1970 Hemi Cuda that my friend and fellow superhero Eightball had tricked out for me.

I fired it up and opened the garage door, flying out of there, smiling when I could see Credible and Tag Team looking at me with incredulity as I drove off. It wasn't so much that I'd surprised them as their disbelief that someone like me would actually run from the Affiliates.

The Mitchmobile growled as I drove her through the city, wondering who else Minder might bring to the party. As ever, I felt like Minder preferred negotiation (or manipulation) over outright violence. Although Ms. Credible could write whatever story she wanted to frame whatever happened in a manner that might work for the Affiliates, Minder would want to keep the collateral damage down.

I glanced skyward, could see Wingman flying overhead. Okay, so Wingman was keeping eyes on me. He'd probably try to slap a tracker on my car when he got a chance. Tag Team was with Credible, so he was not in the mix. Rad Lad would bring too much attention, and Tandem was overkill. Maybe Ms. Fit would be in pursuit. The Knack would show up where he was needed.

How many people had Minder mind-zapped? How many could he puppeteer that way? I had no idea. Then I saw a blur in my side view mirror. It was Speedo, racing along beside me in his orange and yellow costume.

"Cameraman, pull over before we have to do something to you," Speedo said. "Or your car."

I sped up, pleased to hear the Cuda's growl grow as I knifed my way through the city. I heard a thump on the roof of my car, and then saw my windshield shatter as Wingman brought one of his armored fists to it. Safety glass showered onto me as I swerved to try to drive Wingman off. He appeared to be magnetically affixed to the car, and I felt him work his wings to actually lift my car off the ground.

"Holy crap," I said, not believing Wingman could possibly be that strong. And yet he was, and he and Speedo got me out of downtown and south of McCormick Place, where there were always fewer people, and where they might be able to rough me up without many witnesses. Its proximity to Affiliates Central wasn't lost on me. Easy enough to take me down and shunt me over to Central.

Wingman brought my car down to the ground, and Speedo used his super-speed to shatter my passenger side window, enter my car, put it in park, turn off the engine and snag the keys before I could even curse him out.

Then Wingman tore off the driver's side door and yanked me out of my seat before I could yell at him for trashing my car.

"You're not getting away, Cam," Wingman said, his baritone as formidable as his gauntlets, which were sinking into my shoulders. To say I was outmatched here was an understatement, but I still tried to fight, at least until Wingman punched me in the stomach a couple of times. Even with my body armor on, it hurt, and knocked the wind right out of me.

"That's enough," Ms. Fit said, having joined them in the park grass by means of an Affilijet, which landed near us. "Cam, do you surrender?"

"Surrender?" I said, trying to get to my feet, my ribs badly bruised, if not quite broken. He went easy on me, maybe? "Had I started fighting?"

Speedo and Wingman sneered as they looked me over.

"Shame about your sweet ride, Cameraman," Wingman said.

"I'm expecting the Affiliates to pay for that, you know," I said. "And you can't leave it here. Somebody'll steal it."

Ms. Fit gestured to Wingman, who picked up my car and walked it into the open bay of the Affilijet, while Speedo snagged the driver's side door and chucked it into my car.

"Cam, you okay?" Fit asked.

"You guys trashed my car, so, no, not so much," I said. Speedo speed-frisked me, taking off my utility belt and removing my backpack that powered my suit. He also took my phone, data recorders and minicams and my helmet, which really put me off. I felt naked without my mask. I snagged my glasses from one of my side pockets and put them on, grateful they hadn't broken.

"No vanishing act for you, Cameraman," Speedo said, lobbing my gear into my car. Ms. Fit took out her phone and presumably dialed up Minder.

"We have Cameraman," she said, then listened a bit before replying. "Understood. Come on, Cam. We need to take a little trip."

The three of them walked me onto the Affilijet, which Speedo was piloting. They closed the loading bay as the Affilijet went airborne. I hadn't ridden in one since I'd left the team.

"We're not going to have to cuff you, are we, Mitch?" Fit asked.

I shook my head. Know that I had set myself up as the decoy, without wanting to let them know I was playing this role, so I had to appear both contrite and beaten. I wasn't an actor, but the role required it sometimes.

"Where are we going?" I asked.

"Credible and Tag Team already tossed your place," Wingman said, while the Affilijet cut over the city, headed back to my brownstone. "They found your files. They need you to confirm that they're all of them."

I glanced at Ms. Fit, who looked back at me impassively. Had Minder zapped her, too? I didn't believe it. Rather, he'd have just played her. I'd have to find out what story he'd told her.

"What's all of this about?" I asked.

"You *know* what it's about, Mitch," Fit said. "You were aiding and abetting Brighteyes, who's become a murdering vigilante."

"She's nuts," Wingman said. "Gone crazy. We're just trying to mop up her mess, and here you go helping her out. I thought you were one of the good guys, Cameraman."

I really wished I still had some of my recording equipment. I'd have to just remember all of this. Old school.

"Guess I'm out of practice," I said. "Heroism's super hard work."

The Affilijet hovered over my building, having been put into stealth mode for the sake of the normies.

"Since you're a flight risk, we should drop your car off here," Wingman said. "Leave it on the roof."

Speedo cackled at that, and the two of them shared a high-five, as they opened the loading ramp in the rear and Wingman did just that, walking out with my car, setting it on the rooftop of my building, next to my deck, where Credible and Tag Team were waiting.

"What about his gear?" Wingman asked.

"Leave it," Credible said, stalking her way on-board with Tag Team on her heels. Credible was carrying a black briefcase. "Your security's pretty good, Mr. Paulsen. But I'm better."

"What's your deal?" I asked. "Your powers?"

Credible gave me a frosty smile while they closed up the back of the Affilijet.

"Not that it's any of your business, but I'm a combat logistical and tactical savant. That means I'm great in a fight. I excel at assessing scenarios and coming up with viable solutions."

"How's that a power?" I asked. "I feel bored just hearing about that."

"You'd be surprised," Credible said, sitting next to me, buckling in. "I know five languages, several martial arts, have very fast reflexes, and am stronger than you."

"And PR is what, your cover?" I asked.

"My skills make me great a PR flack," she said. "Nobody's been able to stump me yet at a press conference."

Speedo, Wingman, and Tag Team laughed, while Ms. Fit just pensively looked on. The Affilijet arced eastward and took off.

"Great, we're headed to New York," I said.

"That we are," Credible said. "Mr. Paulsen, if you're as cautious as I've been led to believe you are, I'd be surprised if you hadn't stashed away other copies of this footage."

"Nope," I said. "I didn't have time."

"Liar," Credible said. "I'm good at spotting liars, too. Hard to know if that's a gift or just a skill I've developed over time. It hardly matters. We have the files, which is what Minder wanted. You were stupid to send him that other file. He tried to be reasonable with you, and you threw that back in his face with your juvenile posturing. This is what you get, Mr. Paulsen."

I looked at the others, who (except for Speedo) were listening to me, watching my reactions. But while they were watching me, I was watching them, in turn. Although I could be wrong, I didn't think the Affiliates here were mind-zapped by Minder.

I just think, for various reasons, they had been persuaded to go after me. Speedo was an auxiliary member, so his motives were the easiest to divine—he saw this as an opportunity to get upped to active-duty roster. Speedsters were always welcome on superhero teams, and auxiliaries were forever vying for those active-status promotions.

Wingman would have chafed at my violation of Affiliates protocols by surveilling Brighteyes at all. Tag Team never really liked me, and after what happened earlier, had a grievance to work out with me. Being of the "something to prove" camp of superheroism, his difficulties earlier had him playing catch-up. Ms. Fit likely accepted whatever story Minder might've put forth, and, in her warrior woman way, just wanted it to work out without too many people getting hurt too badly along the way.

Credible would never be active-duty Affiliates, was purely Minder's crony. She was all-in on that, and Minder wouldn't have had to mind-zap her to get her to do what he needed done. There were a number of support people in the Affiliates, who relished that chance to be part of the organization without having to be the face of the team.

"Surprised the Knack isn't here," I said. In fact, his absence made me wonder. I told you that the Knack always showed up at just the right time. The man's timing was impeccable.

I saw a hint of something on Ms. Fit's face, and wariness from Credible. Nothing from the others.

"The Knack's busy," Fit said. "Something in California."

"Ah," I said. "Too bad. Shane would get a kick out of seeing me like this."

Credible leaned on one arm of her seat and talked to me through narrowed eyes.

"Mr. Paulsen, I don't think you fully comprehend your situation," she said. "Brighteyes is a murderer, and you're an accessory after the fact by withholding evidence of her crimes."

"We'll see," I said. "Can't wait to talk to Rex about this."

Credible was unflappable. She was Minder's pit bull, but I was trying to divine Minder's game in all of this. The official story for them coming after me was covering up Antigone's murder spree, so Credible trying to pin me to that accessory after the fact crap was contradictory. Either they were going to cover up her murders I'd filmed, or they were going to expose her and kick her from the team, using the footage to justify that action. Or was there something else at play? I needed to meet with Minder in person to get a read from him, see what was really going on.

The detail about Minder trying to mess with the memories of Brighteyes and appearing to have actually mindfucked Decibelle signified to me that Minder was perhaps of the latter camp—kicking Brighteyes off the team and needing a fall guy. Who better than a disgruntled former member of the Affiliates who'd parted ways with the team a few years back after the loss of his superhero girlfriend? All he'd have to do was get me imprisoned somewhere and somebody I'd gotten sent to jail would finish me off. It would be tidy for him—a chain of events that wouldn't leave his fingerprints on them.

I pretended to be bored and relaxed, laying back in the otherwise comfortable Affilijet chair.

"Wake me when we get there," I said, and surprised myself when I eventually did fall asleep, and they let me.

shortly after Anna's death, when I was trying to fight through my pain, back when we were battling Flashmob, who had powers like Tag Team, except that his dupes were able to explode like living bombs. Flashmob wore a green, red, and black costume, and had taken the Willis Tower hostage in Chicago. Ms. Fit and I were stationed at Central, so we were first responders, along with one of Tag Team's dupes, who'd been lurking at Central because I think he was envious that I had that space to myself.

Flashmob had been rejected for membership in the Crime League and had taken the Willis Tower hostage as a way of "proving" his fitness for entry into the venerable criminal organization.

Fit, Tag, and I flew in via our Affilijet, landing on the top of the tower, where Tag dropped us off. He created another dupe of himself to fly the Affilijet away while the other dupe went with us to break into the building.

As I've said before, I'm terrified of heights, and being way up on that windy Willis Tower rooftop was just about the purest hell I could imagine. If it hadn't been for Tag Team being as annoying as he was—and that distracting me from the height—I probably would have crumpled right there.

As it was, Fit pried off the security door, and in we went. From our intelligence we'd gleaned via news coverage, Flashmob had made several hundred Flashmobs to secure the lower floors, and had send his duplicates up the stairs, with the plan being he'd have numbers of himself on all floors. Right now, they were up the seventy-fifth floor and working their way up.

"What're the odds of another replication super," I said, as we raced down the stairs.

"Yeah, he's a disgrace to the profession," Tag Team said, then adding before I could say anything else: "You know what I mean."

"We have to stop him while he's still setting up," Fit said. "Once he's secured the building, it'll be a lot harder to take him out. Tag Team, where will we find the Prime?"

Tag Team was always squirrelly about his Prime.

"He won't be around here," he said. "No chance."

"But where?" I asked.

"Somewhere he can keep tabs on what's going on," Tag Team said. "He's going to want to be a part of it. It's something we replicators deal with."

"Separation anxiety?" I asked.

"No, man," Tag Team said. "It's different than that. Because we're always living in each other's heads, it's easy to get lost in them. But if you stand apart from it, while still being a part of it, you get to experience it differently."

"I don't even know what that means," I said.

"No, you wouldn't," Tag Team said.

"Can you just take him on directly?" Ms. Fit asked, and I could see that Tag Team was sort of uncomfortable with that question.

"He can, uhh, make more dupes than I can," Tag Team said. "Like at least five hundred more than me."

"Wow," I said, getting on the radio. "Tag, bring the Affilijet back upstairs. I need you to pick me up."

Fit paused in her racing down the stairs.

"What's going on, Cam?" she asked.

"I've got to find the Prime," I said. "You and Tag can deal with the ones here. I'm going to find the Prime."

"How?" Fit asked.

"Don't know, yet," I said.

The dupe liked my idea, figuring he'd get some quality time with Fit, while the dupe pilot grudgingly brought the Affilijet back to the rooftop, and I regretted not having come up with my plan before running down a dozen flights.

I made it back to the top, wheezing, where the Affilijet was waiting. I got on board and told Tag to fly us around.

Where would Flashmob Prime have hidden himself? Looking at the city map, I assumed the Prime would be west of the river, which would give him a good vantage point while also allowing him ready escape via the highways. He'd be able to slip away after blowing up the building.

"Keep us in stealth mode," I said, using the external cameras for any sign of the Prime. He'd not want to be conspicuous. Something else occurred to me. I called Tag on our Affilicom.

"He doesn't need to see what's going on," I said. "He's already vicariously experiencing it through everyone else's eyes."

"Yes and no," Tag said. "He's getting that feed from his dupes, but he also wants to experience it as an onlooker."

I dialed up Minder, relayed that to him.

"With your telepathy, you could find the Prime," I said. "We'd just need you to knock him out and we'd be all set."

"Mitch, I'm nowhere near Chicago," he said. "It's on Fit, Tag, and you. Maybe some of the auxiliaries."

The Central auxiliaries were Rollergirl, Strutter, and Goo. Rollergirl was best suited for crowd control, and Goo wouldn't work for this, except maybe to put out fires in the event of an explosion. Strutter had light powers and was a speedster. She might be helpful.

"Fit, Tag," I said on our Affilicom. "Don't engage with Flashmob. Hang back. We need to let him think he's in control. I'm going to try to find the Prime and take him down. If we can do that, the others should all disappear, right, Tag?"

"Are you talking about killing him, Cam?" Tag asked.

"I might be," I said. "What guarantees the elimination of the replicas?"

"If the Prime is stunned, that *might* do it," Tag said. "Each dupe is connected to the other, so they all feel the same thing. I don't think Flashmob's replication is like mine, in that with me, if I take a hit, more of me appear. In his case, he has to will them into existence."

Using one of the additional monitors in the Affilijet, I chased down the footage that showed when Flashmob first made his run on the Willis Tower. They came from the water taxi entrance, which reinforced my suspicion that he might be just across the river.

"They're on the eighty-sixth floor," Fit said over the comms. "Tag and I are heading back to the rooftop."

"Reg," I said to the pilot. "Make a dupe of yourself, then jump out of the Affilijet and do your land-splat thing. We need a bunch of you casing the buildings due west of the Tower."

The dupe gestured and another of himself appeared.

"If you spot the Prime, don't engage with him," I said. "You call it up. Alright?"

"Alright," he said, giving me a look.

"Your chance to be a hero, man," I said, while opening the side door on the Affilijet. When his dupe got over the buildings due west of the tower, Tag Team jumped, and we saw him fall, landing harmlessly on the ground, a bunch of him appearing in this strange, almost flowery profusion of orange and black.

The Tag Team then began going street to street, building to building, asking people if they'd seen Flashmob. I wished Victoriana was with me. She'd have zipped back and forth, flying at superspeed to find the Prime. Just thinking of her flying made me sad, and I tried to shovel that emotion back down so I could keep it together for the current mission.

Ms. Fit and Tag Team barred some of the doors on the way up, hoping that it might slow down Flashmob as he worked his way to the top.

Then I had the Dispatcher put Strutter, Rollergirl, and Goo on a priority alert to meet the actives at the Willis Tower. As auxiliaries, they were required to carry Affilicom watches, which would pulse with signals if notified.

"Strutter," I said. "This is Cameraman. I need you to meet us on the west side of the river. Get here fast."

"Sure thing, Camo," she said. Strutter was this latter-day glam rockabilly babe, and when she ran, she flashed with this strobe light effect, which could stun people. It was involuntary, her powers apparently manifesting when she'd been struck by lightning while coming out of a local punk nightclub. She had silver hair and wore a glittery costume of silver and black, with a black star-shaped domino mask and silver lipstick.

Minder took that moment to pipe in on our private line.

"Mitch, Ms. Fit's the Central team leader," he said. "It's her call to make, not yours."

"Fine," I said. "What should we do, Fit?"

Ms. Fit replied quickly, tirelessly (naturally).

"You're trying to get Strutter to do what, exactly?" she asked.

"With her super speed and flashing, we might be able to distract Flashmob Prime enough to find his location," I said. "Then I can stun him, ideally knock him out, and maybe it'll affect the other Flashmobs."

"What if it just makes them mad?" Fit asked.

"No idea," I said. I wasn't sure. "We really need Minder here."

"And I can't get there in time," Minder said. "This is Central's problem to solve."

"You need a teleporter," I said.

"We don't have a teleporter, Mitch," Minder said. "Ms. Fit, this is your operation. Cameraman *will* follow your lead."

Ms. Fit sighed.

"Flashmob's reached the top floor," she said. "Tag and I are on the rooftop. Swing the Affilijet back over, Tag. We'll figure out next steps."

We swerved back over, and the other two boarded just as Flashmob sent some of his duplicates to the rooftop.

"Flashmob's secured the Willis Tower," Fit said.

"Okay, so we hear what his demands are, then," Minder said. "Fit, you need to negotiate with him."

"I will do my best," Fit said. "He's pretty nutty."

"What do you want me to do, Fit?" I asked.

"Keep working with Tag to try to find the Prime," she said. "If you see him, use your stun gun on him. Maybe the sensory feedback of it will stun all of them."

"Alright," I said.

"This is the Knack," Shane said, cutting into our line. "I think I've found the Prime. He's in the Dexter Building, top floor."

"How'd you find him?" Minder asked.

"Just lucky, I guess," the Knack said.

We pitched the cloaked Affilijet over toward the Dexter Building, which had a rooftop restaurant that had open air seating that would allow Flashmob a great view of the area. Shane's lucky guess proved to be perfectly on the mark. Yeah.

"Everyone converge on that spot," Fit said, and it was cool to see the small army of Tag Teams racing toward the Dexter Building, as well as Strutter making her glittery way toward it, while we flew down, hovering near the building.

Flashmob was looking at Strutter's streetside flashing, didn't notice Fit, Tag, and me getting out onto the balcony. We saw the Knack in the shadows nearby, pointing. He was right there, looking sharp in his white blazer, black shirt and slacks, and grey loafers.

When Flashmob turned, I shot him with my stun gun, the light beam putting him into a trance. And, sure enough, the other Flashmob duplicates were also affected, but they were still present in the building.

Ms. Fit punched Flashmob hard, knocking him out cold, while Tag Team put a power neutralizing collar on him, which severed the connection between him and his duplicates, blinking them all out of existence and saving the Willis Tower from annihilation.

The Affiliates soaked up the praise, with Ms. Fit, Tag Team, and the Knack in the spotlight, while I lurked in the back with

Strutter, Goo, and Rollergirl, wishing Anna had been there with me through it all.

"We're just grateful nobody got hurt," Ms. Fit said.

"Absolutely," the Knack said. "We're happy to help."

The reporters took their pictures, and, as ever, ate up everything Jane and Shane were saying, while, later, I looked into what became of Flashmob, who hadn't been routed to the Brig as I thought he should be, but who actually ended up at a Polygon military base, where Minder was working with some Polygon operatives to "mentally rehabilitate" Flashmob and give him a new identity as a living weapon.

Since I was dreaming it, my months of research swirled by, but Minder hadn't been happy to find me snooping that out.

"Mitch, the man's got the perfect sort of power for what we need in Afghanistan," he said. "He's a living suicide bomber. We've renamed him 'The Bombardier'—we offered to clear his record provided he works for the Polygon."

"He's a nutcase and a terrorist," I said. Minder put an arm on my shoulder.

"I fixed him," Minder said, smiling confidently at me. "I healed him. The man just wanted to *belong* to something, Mitch. I gave him something productive to belong to. And, rather than blowing up skyscrapers in Chicago, he's going after targets we set up for him. The explosive power he can generate with each duplicate is staggering—and get this: if he produces a group of himself, it magnifies his explosive power. A hundred of him equals a kiloton of TNT. Take a thousand of him and you've got a thousand kilotons."

"He's a criminal," I said.

"He's a military asset," Minder said, smiling at me. "I don't expect you'd understand, Mitch. I've rehabilitated him. He's doing what he loves to do, what only he can do. And he's doing it for us. That's win-win-win for us, Mitch."

He rapped me on the shoulder each time he said it. I looked back into the Affiliates archives on my own, didn't tell anybody, and saw there were dozens of "rehabilitated" villains who'd undergone Minder's "teletherapy" program, given new identities as living weapons of the government:

- *FLASHMOB → BOMBARDIER*
- *SURESHOT → DEADPAN*
- *BOLTCUTTER → BOLTER*
- *BLUE BASHER → SUPER PATRIOT*
- *THE VAMP → PALEFACE*
- *FISTICUFFS → POWER PUNCHER*
- *LADY LETHAL → MISS FIRE*

And so on. Now, if you wanted to be naïve about it, one could say that these criminal types were now productive members of society, but this was only done with Minder's mindwipes and personality alterations.

"Mitch, we have to do something with these super criminals," Minder said. "We can't keep sending them to the Brig. It's already at capacity. At least this way, I'm turning them around."

He could read my thoughts like stink lines coming off me.

"It's not right," I said.

"It's humane," Minder said. "They redeem themselves through government service."

"Do any of them backslide?" I asked. Minder almost laughed.

"Please," he said. "My work is clean, Mitch. It's not hard to rehabilitate someone, you know. For many of them, growing up in troubled homes, that kind of thing. I just untangle some of those neuronal messes they have, and I bring them peace. That's for the greater good."

The dream ended before I quit, before I told Minder that I quit. Instead, I had Wingman poking me in the shoulder.

"Wake up, Cameraman," he said. "We're here, Hero."

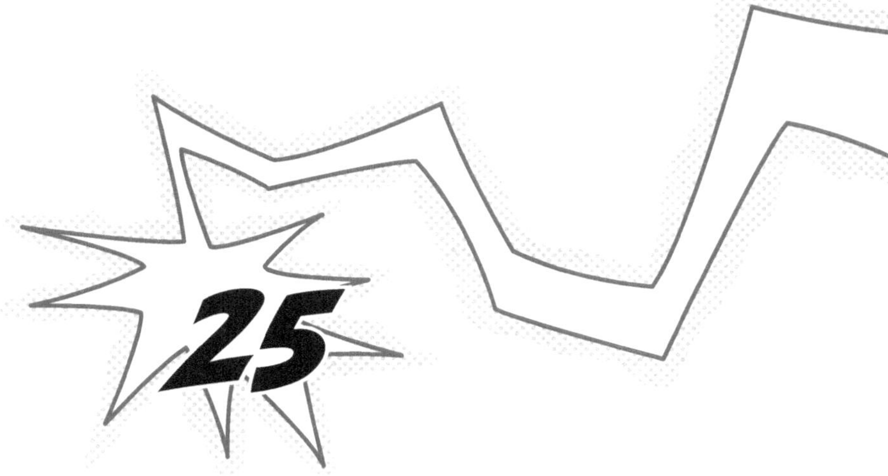

at least as Cameraman. Although, considering my suit was back in Chicago, it was hard for me to feel that I was representing as anything other than Mitch Paulsen.

Alter egos are one of those things that anybody who knows anything about superheroes understands, or thinks they do. It's a funny vibe, living two lives. I'm sure spies feel it, undercover agents, con men and women, cheaters—anybody leading a double life can sympathize. For those of us who wear masks, it's even more profoundly felt.

Ergo, when I'm being all but frogmarched to Affiliates East, those impressive stone corridors built with the intention of inspiring awe, and I'm the only one who's unmasked, it was hard to really know who I was.

That's not true. I was Cameraman, even without my gear. *I* was the damned camera, man.

Affiliates East and West had tourist wings, which were purpose-built to put the good works of the Affiliates on display. You'd think that would have been a natural draw at Central and South, but the media landscape always favored New York and LA as the only cities that mattered whenever superhero stuff happened, in terms of national coverage.

That bias is for real—you'd get Maximo smashing around in Chicago, it might have gotten some incidental coverage, but have Sue Nami appear in LA or Depth Charger hit New York City, and the coverage was breathless. Galling to live in flyover country, when those coastal biases kicked in, and we were all expected to just suck it up.

Anyway, the tourist wing was where the norms were allowed to amble around and watch the informational kiosks replay various heroic outings, and to gawk at the statues of the Affiliates past and present. There was a Hall of Heroism and gift shop where people could get their branded merchandise. The Affiliates didn't depend on the sponsorship deals, but it gave them play money and helped raise the team's profile from merely stratospheric to out of this world.

They steered me away from that wing to the Takin' Care of Business wing, as I thought of it. This was where the real backroom work of the Affiliates took place. I was entering Minderland, and I really hoped that Inferna's magic ring kept him out of my head. I'd know soon enough.

I was taken to one of their interrogation rooms, which was laughable from my perspective, because they had Level Five protections in place in those rooms, which meant that if you managed to get Tandem in one of them, it might take him a little while to break free of it. But me? Overkill by half.

There was a standard issue Affiliates interrogation chair (which meant that it was functional without being terribly comfortable, with proper holes to make handcuffing someone to them easy). Across from the chair was a desk, a digital camcorder on a tripod, and Minder, looking careworn and crestfallen as he regarded me, having bothered to wear his costume.

"You look like Magneto, Rex," I said. "Almost."

Wingman looked like he wanted to punch me for mouthing off to the Boss, but Minder only smiled, steepling his fingers and regarding me with those dark eyes of his, while Credible slid the datafiles over to him.

Tag Team turned on the camcorder.

"Hello, Mitch," Minder said. "It's been years since you graced us with your presence here."

"Hey, Rex," I said. "Place looks the same."

"That's because our mission's the same," Minder said. "We're humankind's last defense against itself."

I glanced at Ms. Fit, who looked uncomfortably stoic, keeping her composure as ever.

"Even you, Mitch," Minder said. "I'm here to help save you from yourself."

"Spare me the speech, Rex," I said. "What do you want with me?"

"I want *all* the tapes," he said. "Same thing I've been asking you since you took them."

I slouched in the seat.

"I'm confused, Rex," I said. "You put the zap on Decibelle and had her hire me to take the footage that you're now busting my balls over."

Minder just listened, that Telepath's Smile on his face. He hadn't scanned me, yet, because I knew that if Inferna's ward protected me, it would wipe that smile right off.

"Go on," Minder said. "You seem to have a lot on your mind. I want to hear it."

"I want to know why you're using me to discredit Brighteyes. Was that the intention? What, that I'd go rogue and get those clips out there for people to fume over? Or what, exactly? You want to make Brighteyes look bad ahead of anything getting out about what you did to her, to Decibelle, maybe others? You picked me because you know I was already a malcontent, because I broke with the team. Because of what happened to Anna? Am I the patsy, Rex?"

The others just listened, and I was curious that Minder let them stay in the room with me. For a man obsessed with perception, secrecy, and optics, he seemed pretty casual about it at that moment. Either my reputation was so bad he felt comfortable doing this, he'd slagged me so thoroughly, or he'd mind-warped everyone here to the degree that he could be comfortable putting me in this position.

"You are *definitely* the patsy, Mitch," Minder said. "Honestly, why on earth would we have ever let someone like you into the Affiliates? You're a good detective-journalist-whatever, and you've got some skills with optics. But superhero caliber you're not. You're lower than the C-level aspirants we are always fielding applications from, Mitch. You *never* belonged with us, and you know that. If it hadn't been for Victoriana, you'd never have made the cut. I brought you on because of her, because of Shane. It made me seem magnanimous to put up with their nonsense notions. Maybe I even believed it. You tried so hard to make your mark on the team, while being uncomfortable with even the idea of being a superhero. It's tragicomic, isn't it?"

See how I can get him to monologue during my own interrogation? That's how good I am at what I do, Gentle Reader. Know thy enemy, know thyself.

"I'm the one laughing last, Rex," I said.

"Ha," Minder said. "I was gracious in bringing you into the team, and what did you do with that membership? You *spied* on the team. You poked through our archives like the rat you are, sniffing around for something savory and salacious. You're an insatiable scandal-seeker, Mitch. That Polygon program makes us millions annually, and you were going to, what? Do an exposé on it? You think that would make a difference to anyone? Americans want to feel safe. We make them *feel* safe. That's what superheroes do—we create the impression that we're there for them."

I could see a hint of irritation in Minder as he lectured me. The key was to let him punch himself out and then start countering. When he found that he couldn't break me, it would, in turn, break him. Basic Aikido, man.

"You've never been for anyone but yourself, Rex," I said. "I'm not surprised you clawed your way to the chairmanship. Who was it before you? Ephemera, right? Before she lost her mind? Did you *help* her lose her mind? I always wondered about that. One push, and off she went. Then you stepped in and helpfully put the team back on track. And you did the same to Victoriana."

Minder half-smiled, shaking his head. Ephemera had been a great chairperson, with her surreal phasing power making her like a ghost, until she simply faded away. Her own mental breakdown had Minder working the scene, speaking eloquently about the need for mental health care, even among superheroes. He'd been hiding in plain sight, the ever-solicitous telepath, the man who understood how people's minds worked. I can't decisively pin Ephemera's cognitive decline on Minder, but he had the motive, the means, and the opportunity to end her, and I think he did. He'd done the same thing to Anna, only quicker, because he'd had more practice by then.

"You're so paranoid, you don't even have the awareness to understand how messed up you are," he said. "Ephemera was a great leader, a great chairwoman. We all loved her, but the work got to her, the way it gets to us all, sooner or later. She was my mentor, my idol. To hear a nobody like you imply that I had anything to do with her decline is offensive to me, Mitch. And as for Brighteyes, yeah, I want her off the team. She's bad for the Affiliates. It doesn't mean she's not useful elsewhere. That's what you learn when you become a leader. You have to move people across the board, put them where they'll be most useful. I did that with you. And I'm not even going to respond to those baseless accusations about Anna. She was everything you'll never be, Mitch."

The others were looking uneasy, except for Credible, who looked like she wanted to have Minder's babies. She all but had pinwheels in her eyes, hanging on every word.

"The rest of you can go," Minder said. "Lynn, you can stay."

Tag Team stupidly spoke up.

"Are you okay being alone with him?" he asked. Minder smiled at him, the Telepath's Smile, ever pacifying, patronizing.

"I'm not worried, Reginald," Minder said. "Thank you for all that you do. No, you can go. All of you can go."

Ms. Fit spoke up, and I loved her a little in that moment.

"I'm not sure that's a good idea, Minder," she said. He looked at her, cocking an eyebrow.

"Oh, you don't, do you, Jane?" he said. "Are you worried about Mitch, here? What if I assure you no harm will come to him? How about that?"

"On your honor?" she asked.

"On my honor," Minder said, holding up a hand, like he was about to lay it on a bible and swear an oath, as if that meant anything.

"I'll hold you to it," Fit said, glancing at me, then back at Minder. She left with the others, and the door closed behind them.

Minder chuckled.

"One thing I learned as a telepath is maintaining the necessary social distancing between words and thoughts," he said. "When you were delving into all of our archives, did you find my origin, Mitch?"

"I know you came from supers," I said. "Next generation."

"Yeah," he said. "Mom and Dad used their powers to get us ahead. My mom was a precog—she could see the future. Not far into the future, but just enough. My father was able to make illusions. They weren't what we'd consider A-Level these days, but you'd be amazed what they did with their abilities back in their day. Neither of them aspired to become heroes; no, they used their powers for their own benefit, and they built my family's fortune with their superpowers. And they were the happiest parents in the world when they discovered that I had inherited their propensity for superhumanity. I know that because I could read their minds before I could even speak."

Minder liked talking and liked talking about himself. The key was the right amount of prodding that would keep him yammering.

"I've heard that telepaths suffer until they can control their powers," I said.

"Oh, yes," Minder said. "Knowing everyone's thoughts is a curse as much as it's a blessing, Mitch. It's like peeking at your Christmas presents in a way. No surprises. I'm not a fan of surprises. I've built my entire career around avoiding surprises. It's why I peeked into your mind and learned your secret identity, why I told everyone else. The things you did, Mitch—speaking of you as Cameraman, I mean—the people you took on. You took on corporations. CEOs lost their golden parachutes to the stuff you pulled, your fabled exposés. It was breathtaking what you did as Cameraman. We used to wonder who you were, how you did it. The stories we told ourselves about this super-sleuth who brought down senators and congressmen, who caught those scandalous details via surveillance. Yeah, Mitch, we *had* to bring you in. And then when I saw who you really were, the nothing you are, oh, was that ever disappointing. No superpowers, nothing extraordinary—just an obsessive little man who loved to snoop and scoop. That's it."

I assumed this browbeating was supposed to put me in some defensive state, maybe make me more susceptible to manipulation? I did mention how Minder was a great interrogator, remember? And it was curious to me how he was talking earlier about what a nothing I was, and here he was talking about how impressed they'd all been with my record, before dipping back into the negging. He was absolutely trying to work me.

"Sorry to disappoint you," I said.

"No, you were perfect. Better than I could have hoped for, to be painfully honest," Minder said. "That torrent of frustration, resentment, paranoia, hubris—all of that stewing in your head made you perfect for what I needed. I needed someone who didn't quite fit, someone with an axe to grind. And best of all, with all of the enemies you'd made as Cameraman, knowing your secret identity, I had that in my back pocket. One word from me into the right ears, and you'd have enemies hunting you down for the rest of your life. And that's what we need to talk about now, Mitch. Enough with the past. Let's consider the future."

"Okay, yeah, let's consider that, Rex," I said, actually glad he didn't lean too much into what happened with Anna. I might have lost my cool and gone for him, which wouldn't have gone well for me.

Minder leaned on his elbows, leaned in, giving me those dark eyes of his. He was so close to using his powers on me, I could almost taste it.

"You're going to confess to attempting to blackmail the Affiliates with your Brighteyes footage," Minder said. "Which will, coincidentally, allow me to cut her loose and stick you with the bill for her fall. Two birds, one stone. I get to paint Brighteyes as a murderous maniac, and you as a vengeful, misanthropic former employee seething with resentment. And you have no idea how many people want Cameraman shut down, Mitch. Big people. Big names. People whose lives you've ruined. They want your head. And I'll deliver it to them, while keeping my nose clean. The contracts will roll in unwrinkled and unthreatened, because you won't be around anymore to mess them up."

"That's all this is?" I asked. "Contracts?"

"*Lucrative* contracts," Minder said. "Credibility counts. And the Affiliates brand is one of credibility and honor. Truth, justice, all of that good stuff."

The apparatus came into sharper focus, now. The Brig, Minder's Polygon Program, Hyberia Hollow, all of that. Just like Shane and I had surmised in our brainstorming session, he was creating a superheroic industry, and him a kind of powerbroker-pimp.

However it played out, I'd have to get the camcorder that was recording it all. Why Minder even had it there was funny. Was he just hoping to mock me with it, the way he must have thought would work with Anna and my POV space helmet? Or when he tried to force my confession, he wanted to capture it for posterity, something he and Credible could play while fucking or something. Not quite sure.

"Seems like you have it all mapped out, Rex," I said. "Except how are you going to get me to confess, exactly? I'm not going to confess to any of this nonsense. I'm thinking you probably have worked something out with Dr. Crime, haven't you? Maybe that's part of what Brighteyes got wind of, and you tried to shut down. The Affiliates colluding with the Crime League? Yeah, I can see that. You make an arrangement with Dr. Crime where you both deal with each other's problems and keep the whole thing rolling. I've always questioned why the Crime League always seemed to skate on through, despite everything we did as Affiliates."

I could see from the mild look of surprise on Minder's face that I'd figured something out. He quickly composed himself.

"Crime *does* pay," Minder said. "It pays for criminals, and it pays for law enforcement. The whole prison industrial complex is big business. The amount of money that went into the Brig? Massive. Governments were happy to work with us to help deal with it. And Dr. Crime's a solid partner, as is Crimebot—they understand how it works. We maintain an equilibrium between us. I'd rather thwart some of the Crime League's more cockeyed schemes than deal with a bunch of supervillains operating independently. And Dr. Crime knows where and how the Affiliates operate—we can't be everywhere, Mitch. Everybody wins, as I've said to you before. Everybody but you, Mitch. I knew you'd never be the type to go along with it. The others? They have their own reasons for being on the team. I've read all of their minds, and I make sure they get what they want out of being on the team. Even you got what you wanted—you got a scandal, a conspiracy. Now you'll get to be a martyr for your cause."

And just like that, he laid into me. He even took his index and middle fingers of his right hand and brought them to his temple for added effect.

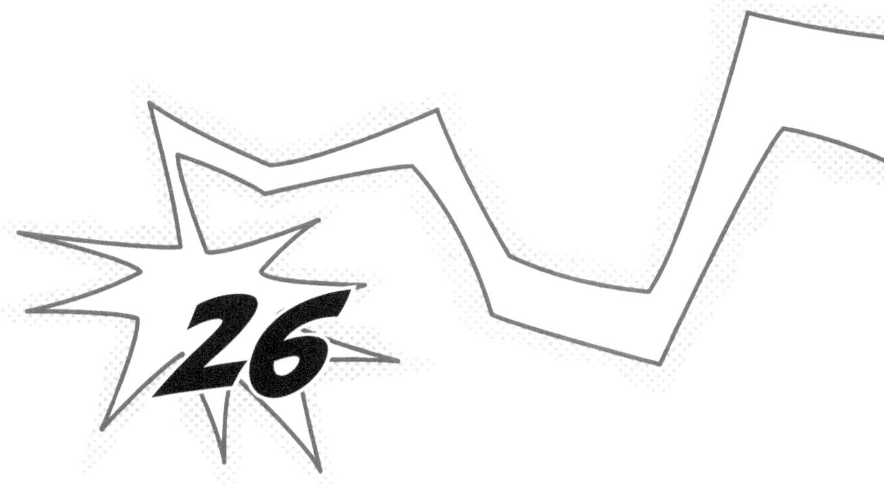

And when he's put-ting the zap on you, it's hard to explain in layman's terms. It's like this coruscating wave of mental force that's directed at you. And if I didn't have Inferna's hidden magic ring, I'd have melted right there. I'd have said whatever he wanted me to say. That's why he was the puppet master. The problem was...

MAGIC ⟩ MIND ⟩ MATTER

And that's why it was priceless to see him straining his brain, trying to tune me up, only to find that it wasn't working. It was like his telepathy was a river flowing at me, and I was this rock in the midst of it, forcing the water to flow around me.

"What is going on?" Minder said, wrinkling his forehead and glaring harder at me, as if that would make a difference. Credible was observing with concern on her face. I didn't need to be a telepath to see that.

And speaking of that, I discovered a new emotion: the Tele-path's Frown—the look on a telepath's face when their mind powers failed them.

"Well well well," Minder said, backing off, shaking his head. "Mitch came prepared. Been talking to Brighteyes, I'll war-rant. Lynn, search him. He's got some kind of ward."

"Okay," Credible said, and she began to pat me down, scrutinizing everything I had on. She spent a good five minutes hand-groping me, but found nothing, cursing under her breath. "He's clean."

"You hear that, Rex? I'm clean," I said.

"What'd you do, Mitch? Work a deal with Inferna?" he asked. "Antigone made a similar arrangement."

"I know," I said, which only made him angrier. He threw another mind zap at me, this time with fingertips on both temples, his eyes big as he glared at me. But the ward held, and all that mental prowess of his went nowhere. My skull remained my own. "Poor Rex. Your forehead veins are showing."

Credible then did what she did best, throwing a wicked punch to my midsection, where Wingman had punched me earlier. Although I'd braced for it, I still doubled over. She really was strong. Maybe not super strong, but way stronger than she ought to be, given her proportions.

I coughed and wheezed, throwing an arm out to snag the camcorder, and said "Inferna" as I did so. Inferna's no genie, and I knew the risks I incurred by hoping she'd come to bail me out yet again, but what's that devil-friends were for. The interrogation room filled with brimstone, and she hooked an arm around me like I was her favorite plushie, backhanded Credible across the room, and vanished before Minder could do more than choke on the sulfurous fumes she'd left in her wake.

I'd never teleported with Inferna before, and it was a trip in more ways than one. It was hell—I was in this place of fiery red, yellow, and orange like, filled with wailing shadows, and she bounced me back to my rooftop in the blink of an eye, near my Mitchmobile, sitting forlornly.

"What would you do without me, Mitch?" she asked. "You'd be dead, that's what."

"I owe you a lifetime's worth," I said, and she smiled at me fiendishly, while she watched me put on the bits and bobs of my Cameraman costume I pulled from my car. Feeling the power kick in, slapping my helmet visor down, I felt whole again, sparing a sad look or two at my badly wounded Mitchmobile, left so callously on the rooftop.

"It's going to get very, very bad," I said. "We've got to get out of here."

Now, for any non-rich superhero, the availability of secondary and even tertiary lairs was a luxury. My brownstone was my primary base of operations, and I hated to leave anything behind there, but Minder would be sending the Affiliates back there as soon as he was able.

I went to my garage and got into my van, quickly scanning it for bugs, because when I'd run off the first time, I assumed that Credible and Tag Team might have done that. And they did. There were three trackers, which I removed, placing them on a workbench in my garage.

Then I got out of there, with Inferna riding beside me, almost looking content.

"How's Decibelle?" I asked.

"Recovering," Inferna said. "Minder's mindwork was pervasive. She's got a lot of anger in her in the wake of it. She's going to have to manage that."

The idea of a devil-woman offering a psychological wellness assessment for a Siren was one of those things I'd have to be sure to talk about with a therapist someday.

I drove through the city, using another of my skins to make the van appear to be a cable van, as unassuming as I could manage.

"My ring worked out?" she asked.

"It did," I said. "Thank you for saving my brain."

"Brain, ass, and everything in between," she said. "You have no idea how fortunate you are, Mitch. Speaking of that, the Knack found Decibelle and me."

"What?" I asked.

"He just showed up," she said. "He assured me he was there on his own, not part of anything with Minder. You know, I *really* like him."

"Everybody does," I said. "Literally everyone loves the Knack."

"He's noble yet sensitive, relatable," she said. This always bothered me, just how effortlessly everyone crushed on the Knack. "He offered to shelter Decibelle at his mansion in Monterey while she was recovering."

"I'll bet he did," said.

"And he'd reached out to Brighteyes," Inferna said. "Talked her into having a sitdown with her partner."

The Knack. If *I'd* suggested that to Brighteyes, she'd have dismissed it. But the Knack suggests it and they couldn't line up more quickly to follow his advice. Lucky bastard.

"Well, that's *great* to hear," I said, gripping the wheel through my sarcasm. I dialed Shane up, because I had to hear it from him directly, versus hearing Inferna recount it. As ever, Shane was ready for my call.

"Hey, Mitch," he said. "Thought you'd be calling. Minder's pitching a fit, said something about you attacking him over the Brighteyes tapes. Said you went berserk, apparently under demonic influence, as he put it. He's already talked to the Trinity, asking for their help in dealing with Inferna."

"Jesus," I said. The Trinity were a three-member team of superheroes based in Iowa, operating independently of the Affiliates. They were focused on dealing with all things contrary to Christianity and contrary to an American Christian worldview. They were decidedly hostile to anything magical, which was invariably characterized as demonic.

Their most-prominent members were the Crucifixer, who was this weird, body armor-wearing, paramilitary bro who had a bunch of firearms; the Inquisitor, the leader of the team, who was this white-robed and metal-masked guy who billed himself as "God's Greatest Detective" and saw himself as a super-sleuth (yeah, right); and then there was Angelica, a beautiful winged woman who was super-strong and could fly. Heaven knows where she actually hailed from.

"Yeah," Shane said. "Don't worry. I know you're trying to do the right thing."

"Um, wait," I said. "You know that Minder's got this whole villain enterprise in place, right?"

"Yes," Shane said. "I've been waiting for just the right time to bring him down."

"Riiiight," I said, remembering our talk in the past, where we mapped things out. "And I'm guessing now's the right time?"

"You've got it," Shane said.

This was why the Knack annoyed me. Like Reason Number 1453. How could he be heroic when he was just always there at the right place and time? Give me a break. Riddle me this: how the hell is that heroic? To me, being a hero meant sticking your neck out when others might have the sense to stand back. But the Knack just lucked his way into things, showed up at precisely the right time, did the right thing, and everybody loved him. Not. Fair.

Still, I'd rather have the Knack in my corner than not.

"If Minder is rounding up the Affiliates and enlisting the Trinity to come smash us, that's not going to be pretty," I said. "What are we talking about? Who's on our side, here?"

"You, me, Inferna, Decibelle, and Brighteyes," Shane said. "Have you called any of your, you know, super-friends?"

"No, Shane," I said. "Been a bit busy getting my ass kicked. Oh, and I have a recording of Minder incriminating himself big-time. I think he was just recording it for his own jollies, but I stole it when Inferna helped me escape."

"Cool," Shane said. "We'll need to get that copied."

"Oh, yes," I replied. "Okay, so I'm going to see if I can round up some more supers to help us out. They're going to come down on me very hard."

"You should try to get to my place in Monterey," Shane said. "That's where we're at. Although I'd hate for the fight to take place here. Not because of my place, but the trees and wildlife I've curated here. I don't want them to get messed up."

"Hey," I said. "Minder's reached out to you, yeah?"

"You know it," Shane said. "Priority alert for your capture. You and Inferna."

"And how'd you leave it with him?" I asked.

"I told him I was going to lure you to my place, that it was a trap," Shane said.

This was one of those serious trust issue moments for me. I took enough of a breath that Inferna actually glanced at me to see what I was doing, her eyebrows raised.

"And it's not *actually* a trap, right, Shane?" I asked. Shane was so ridiculously chill, it was impossible to gauge his reaction on the phone. I actually put it on speaker, just so Inferna could overhear it, too.

"It's a trap for a trap," Shane said. "I'm luring Minder to my place under the false pretense that I'm setting a trap for you, but the trap's actually for him."

"You swear?" I asked.

"Yes," Shane said.

"Okay, I'm holding you to that," I said. "Don't screw me over, Shane."

"Never, Mitch," Shane replied. "Nor you, Inferna."

"Thanks, Shane," Inferna said, and I swear she was blushing, which is hard to tell on the face of a red-skinned devil-woman.

Told you I was a helluva detective.

to just get fellow superheroes on the phone and ask them to risk life and limb to come help you out.

Spoiler warning: It's not.

Especially when you're me.

I have my reputation, and I'll admit that hearing Minder rave about my rep as Cameraman, that actually felt pretty good coming from him, despite him slagging me in his next breath. Reputation was everything in this business, and the idea of me was always more potent than the reality. Why do you think I always played it mysterious and behind the scenes, versus quaffing spotlight the way the others did?

At any rate, I was going through my Cameraman contacts list to see who might be willing to lend a hand. And it was definitely an upsell session, because I was asking people to take on the Affiliates—the cover story was that it was a live-fire superhero training scenario, made to test their abilities to their limits in a nonfatal combat war gaming setting. I told them that they'd be scored based on their success in incapacitating the Affiliates as quickly as possible.

Yes, this was a lie, and I own that, but for a lot of the street-level supers out there, the chance to get some face-time with active-duty Affiliates was priceless, and they'd want to prove themselves to the best of their super-abilities. If I hadn't come up with something like that, they'd have told me to pound sand. And if anybody got hurt, I'd deal with the consequences of that. The alternative was the handful of us getting wiped out by Minder and his gang, his villainy victorious. I couldn't stomach that.

Mentally, I worked through my short list, the ones I figured were likeliest to say yes, and managed to persuade the following to lend a hand:

> • **EIGHTBALL:** *HAD A COOL SUPERCAR, WAS AN ACE PILOT AND MECHANIC OF ANYTHING WITH A MOTOR. ANOTHER RICH BOY-TYPE SUPERHERO WHO OPERATED OUT OF LAS VEGAS.*

> • **STINGER:** *GREEN BUG MAN WHO FLEW, HAD BODY ARMOR, AND COULD SHOOT ANTENNA ZAPS. BASED IN OREGON. POSSIBLY AN ALIEN.*

> • **BITCHQUEEN:** *MAIL CARRIER WHO HAD BEEN BITTEN BY A RADIOACTIVE LABORATORY DOG, SHE'D BEEN GIVEN DOG POWERS. DESPITE HER WILLFULLY PUGNACIOUS AND TRIGGERING ALIAS, SHE WAS WAY COOL. BASED IN LA.*

> • **AVANT GUARDIAN:** *I MENTIONED HER EARLIER. SHE WAS UP FOR ANYTHING SUITABLY LOUCHE. BASED IN NEW YORK CITY.*

> • **THE ELF:** *HE WAS ALREADY CALIFORNIA-BASED, AND, YES, HE WAS AN ARCHER. I'M DESPERATE.*

> • **SHRINKWRAP:** *COULD SHOOT THIS WEIRDLY IRIDESCENT PLASTIC-TYPE STUFF, INTROVERTED BUT DIEHARD IN HER SUPERHEROIC SCRUPLES. BASED IN SEATTLE.*

> • **MR. COOL:** *RETRO ROCKABILLY WHO HAD ICE POWERS THAT MATCHED HIS ATTITUDE. BASED IN NEW JERSEY.*

I'd love to give you the play-by-play of all of those conversations, but I'm pressed for time and space. Just know that they were memorable, and everyone expressed their own individual irritation with the Affiliates, since all of them had been passed over at one point or another, and umbrage at me for even reaching out to them like that, but I talked them around with my always-abundant glib sort of charm that eventually brought them around.

Except for the Elf. He wasn't irritated; the Elf was always serene.

"The cause of true justice sometimes requires these sorts of sacrifices," he said gravely. I can spare a little time to complain about the Elf—nobody quite knows if he's an actual elf (he talks about Tír na nÓg A LOT), or if he's just a dude who ate one too many hemp-mesh baggies of homemade granola laced with psilocybin. It's a mystery I've yet to solve, but the Elf was absolutely cool under pressure, and he never missed with that bow of his—although he lacked any trick arrows, which was maybe why I liked him. His commitment to worldly nonviolence mixed in with killer marksmanship.

Inferna was amused by my conference-calling, which I took to after setting the Cameravan to autopilot so I could make the calls while making copies of the camcorder interrogation of Minder. Maybe I was prideful, but Minder was arrogant. He didn't for a moment think that I'd engineer some way of escaping from his clutches.

The Cameravan was taking us out of the city, heading west. There was no way I was going to road trip from Chicago to LA. That's like a thirty-hour drive. No, I only took the Cameravan out of my hideout because I needed the rolling studio to do my duplication work without getting tagged by the Affiliates. Once you've got the footage, good production is integral to surveillance work. I was just happy Minder had used a digital camcorder because it made file duplication easier. If he'd opted for analog, it might've taken more time that I didn't have.

I'd have to do a delicate dance between pinning things on Minder, while also keeping Brighteyes from getting busted. That may seem selective in its application of justice, but I think Antigone got wind of some of what Minder was doing and went a bit berserk, trying to stop it the only way she knew how. This goes back to what I've said about supers—because they're so used to having their powers, they rely on them to try to solve problems those powers weren't meant for. Antigone understood the efficacy of her eyebeams, so if the baddies were problematic, her answer was more eyebeams. I'd seen many superheroes fall into that trap. Every problem was a nail if *you* were the hammer.

Whereas, in my situation, I had to be creative with whatever I had in hand. What I'd do is make a carefully edited Minder incrimination video. You'd be amazed what you can do with editing. Exhibit A:

CAMERAMAN: *YOU WANT TO MAKE BRIGHTEYES LOOK BAD AHEAD OF ANYTHING GETTING OUT ABOUT WHAT YOU DID TO HER, TO DECIBELLE, MAYBE OTHERS? YOU PICK ME BE-CAUSE YOU KNOW I'M ALREADY A MALCONTENT, BECAUSE I BROKE WITH THE TEAM. AM I THE PATSY, [REDACTED]?*

MINDER: *YOU ARE DEFINITELY THE PATSY, [REDACTED]. HON-ESTLY, WHY ON EARTH WOULD WE HAVE EVER LET SOME-ONE LIKE YOU INTO THE AFFILIATES? YOU'RE A GOOD DE-TECTIVE-JOURNALIST-WHATEVER, AND YOU'VE GOT SOME SKILLS WITH OPTICS. BUT SUPERHERO CALIBER YOU'RE NOT. YOU'RE LOWER THAN THE C-LEVEL ASPIRANTS WE ARE ALWAYS FIELDING APPLICATIONS FROM, [REDACTED]. YOU NEVER BELONGED WITH US, AND YOU KNOW THAT. I BROUGHT YOU ON BECAUSE OF THAT. IT MADE ME SEEM MAGNANIMOUS. MAYBE I EVEN BELIEVED IT. YOU TRIED SO HARD TO MAKE YOUR MARK ON THE TEAM, WHILE BEING UNCOMFORTABLE WITH THE IDEA OF BEING A SUPERHERO. IT'S TRAGICOMIC, ISN'T IT?*

CAMERAMAN: *I'M THE ONE LAUGHING LAST [REDACTED].*

MINDER: *HA. I WAS GRACIOUS IN BRINGING YOU INTO THE TEAM, AND WHAT DID YOU DO WITH THAT MEMBERSHIP? YOU SPIED ON THE TEAM. YOU POKED THROUGH OUR ARCHIVES LIKE THE RAT YOU ARE, SNIFFING AROUND FOR SOMETHING SAVORY AND SALACIOUS. YOU'RE AN INSATIABLE SCAN-DAL-SEEKER, [REDACTED]. THAT POLYGON PROGRAM MAKES US MILLIONS ANNUALLY, AND YOU WERE GOING TO, WHAT? DO AN EXPOSÉ ON IT? YOU THINK THAT WOULD MAKE A DIFFERENCE TO ANYONE? AMERICANS WANT TO FEEL SAFE. WE MAKE THEM FEEL SAFE. THAT'S WHAT SUPER-HEROES DO — WE CREATE THE IMPRESSION THAT WE'RE THERE FOR THEM.*

CAMERAMAN: *YOU'VE NEVER BEEN FOR ANYONE BUT YOUR-SELF, [REDACTED]. I'M NOT SURPRISED YOU CLAWED YOUR*

WAY TO THE CHAIRMANSHIP. WHO WAS IT BEFORE YOU? EPHEMERA, RIGHT? BEFORE SHE LOST HER MIND? DID YOU HELP HER LOSE HER MIND? I ALWAYS WONDERED ABOUT THAT. ONE PUSH, AND OFF SHE WENT. THEN YOU STEPPED IN AND HELPFULLY PUT THE TEAM BACK ON TRACK.

MINDER: YOU'RE SO PARANOID, YOU DON'T EVEN HAVE THE AWARENESS TO UNDERSTAND HOW MESSED UP YOU ARE. EPHEMERA WAS A GREAT LEADER, A GREAT CHAIRWOMAN. WE ALL LOVED HER, BUT THE WORK GOT TO HER, THE WAY IT GETS TO US ALL, SOONER OR LATER. SHE WAS MY MENTOR, MY IDOL. TO HEAR A NOBODY LIKE YOU IMPLY THAT I HAD ANYTHING TO DO WITH HER DEATH IS OFFEN-SIVE TO ME, [REDACTED]. AND AS FOR [REDACTED], YEAH, I WANT [REDACTED] OFF THE TEAM. [REDACTED] BAD FOR THE AFFILIATES. IT DOESN'T MEAN [REDACTED] NOT USEFUL ELSEWHERE. THAT'S WHAT YOU LEARN WHEN YOU BECOME A LEADER. YOU HAVE TO MOVE PEOPLE ACROSS THE BOARD, PUT THEM WHERE THEY'LL BE MOST USEFUL. I DID THAT WITH YOU.

ONE THING I LEARNED AS A TELEPATH IS MAINTAINING THE NECESSARY SOCIAL DISTANCING BETWEEN WORDS AND THOUGHTS. WHEN YOU WERE DELVING INTO ALL OF OUR ARCHIVES, DID YOU FIND MY ORIGIN, [REDACTED]?

CAMERAMAN: I KNOW YOU CAME FROM SUPERS. NEXT GEN-ERATION.

MINDER: YEAH. MOM AND DAD USED THEIR POWERS TO GET US AHEAD. MY MOM WAS A PRECOG—SHE COULD SEE THE FUTURE. NOT FAR INTO THE FUTURE, BUT JUST ENOUGH. MY FATHER WAS ABLE TO MAKE ILLUSIONS. THEY WEREN'T WHAT WE'D CONSIDER A-LEVEL THESE DAYS, BUT YOU'D BE AMAZED WHAT THEY DID WITH THEIR ABILITIES BACK IN THEIR DAY.

NEITHER OF THEM ASPIRED TO BECOME HEROES; NO, THEY USED THEIR POWERS FOR THEIR OWN BENEFIT, AND THEY BUILT MY FAMILY'S FORTUNE WITH THEIR SUPERPOWERS. AND THEY WERE THE HAPPIEST PARENTS IN THE WORLD WHEN THEY DISCOVERED THAT I HAD INHERITED THEIR PROPENSI-TY FOR SUPERHUMANITY. I KNOW THAT BECAUSE I COULD READ THEIR MINDS BEFORE I COULD EVEN SPEAK.

CAMERAMAN: I'VE HEARD THAT TELEPATHS SUFFER UNTIL THEY CAN CONTROL THEIR POWERS.

MINDER: *OH, YES. KNOWING EVERYONE'S THOUGHTS IS A CURSE AS MUCH AS IT'S A BLESSING, [REDACTED]. IT'S LIKE PEEKING AT YOUR CHRISTMAS PRESENTS IN A WAY. NO SURPRISES. I'M NOT A FAN OF SURPRISES. I'VE BUILT MY ENTIRE CAREER AROUND AVOIDING SURPRISES. IT'S WHY I PEEKED INTO YOUR MIND AND LEARNED YOUR SECRET IDEN- TITY, WHY I TOLD EVERYONE ELSE. THE THINGS YOU DID, [REDACTED]—SPEAKING OF YOU AS CAMERAMAN, I MEAN— THE PEOPLE YOU TOOK ON. YOU TOOK ON CORPORATIONS. CEOS LOST THEIR GOLDEN PARACHUTES TO THE STUFF YOU PULLED, YOUR FABLED EXPOSÉS. IT WAS BREATHTAKING WHAT YOU DID AS CAMERAMAN.*

WE USED TO WONDER WHO YOU WERE, HOW YOU DID IT. THE STORIES WE TOLD OURSELVES ABOUT THIS SU- PER-SLEUTH WHO BROUGHT DOWN SENATORS AND CON- GRESSMEN, WHO CAUGHT THOSE SCANDALOUS DETAILS VIA SURVEILLANCE. YEAH, [REDACTED], WE HAD TO BRING YOU IN. AND THEN WHEN I SAW WHO YOU REALLY WERE, THE NOTHING YOU ARE, OH, WAS THAT EVER DISAPPOINTING. NO SUPERPOWERS, NOTHING EXTRAORDINARY—JUST AN OB- SESSIVE LITTLE MAN WHO LOVED TO SNOOP AND SCOOP. THAT'S IT.

CAMERAMAN: *SORRY TO DISAPPOINT YOU.*

MINDER: *NO, YOU WERE PERFECT. BETTER THAN I COULD HAVE HOPED FOR, TO BE PAINFULLY HONEST. THAT TOR- RENT OF FRUSTRATION, RESENTMENT, PARANOIA, HUBRIS— ALL OF THAT STEWING IN YOUR HEAD MADE YOU PERFECT FOR WHAT I NEEDED. I NEEDED SOMEONE WHO DIDN'T QUITE FIT, SOMEONE WITH AN AXE TO GRIND. AND BEST OF ALL, WITH ALL OF THE ENEMIES YOU'D MADE AS CAM- ERAMAN, KNOWING YOUR SECRET IDENTITY, I HAD THAT IN MY BACK POCKET. ONE WORD FROM ME INTO THE RIGHT EARS, AND YOU'D HAVE ENEMIES HUNTING YOU DOWN FOR THE REST OF YOUR LIFE. AND THAT'S WHAT WE NEED TO TALK ABOUT NOW, [REDACTED]. ENOUGH WITH THE PAST. LET'S CONSIDER THE FUTURE.*

CAMERAMAN: *OKAY, YEAH, LET'S CONSIDER THAT, [REDACT- ED].*

MINDER: *YOU'RE GOING TO CONFESS TO ATTEMPTING TO BLACKMAIL THE AFFILIATES [REDACTED]. WHICH WILL, CO- INCIDENTALLY, ALLOW ME TO [REDACTED]. TWO BIRDS, ONE*

STONE. I GET TO PAINT **[REDACTED]** AS A MURDEROUS MANIAC, AND YOU AS A VENGEFUL MISANTHROPIC FORMER EMPLOYEE SEETHING WITH RESENTMENT. AND YOU HAVE NO IDEA HOW MANY PEOPLE WANT CAMERAMAN SHUT DOWN, [REDACTED]. BIG PEOPLE. BIG NAMES. PEOPLE WHOSE LIVES YOU'VE RUINED. THEY WANT YOUR HEAD. AND I'LL DELIVER IT TO THEM, WHILE KEEPING MY NOSE CLEAN. THE CONTRACTS WILL ROLL IN UNWRINKLED AND UNTHREATENED, BECAUSE YOU WON'T BE AROUND ANYMORE TO MESS THEM UP.

CAMERAMAN: *THAT'S ALL THIS IS? CONTRACTS?*

MINDER: *LUCRATIVE CONTRACTS. CREDIBILITY COUNTS. AND THE AFFILIATES BRAND IS ONE OF CREDIBILITY AND HONOR. TRUTH, JUSTICE, ALL OF THAT GOOD STUFF.*

CAMERAMAN: *SEEMS LIKE YOU HAVE IT ALL MAPPED OUT,* **[REDACTED]**. *EXCEPT HOW ARE YOU GOING TO GET ME TO CONFESS, EXACTLY? I'M NOT GOING TO CONFESS TO ANY OF THIS NONSENSE. I'M THINKING YOU PROBABLY HAVE WORKED SOMETHING OUT WITH DR. CRIME, HAVEN'T YOU? MAYBE THAT'S PART OF WHAT* **[REDACTED]** *GOT WIND OF, AND YOU TRIED TO SHUT DOWN. THE AFFILIATES COLLUDING WITH THE CRIME LEAGUE? YEAH, I CAN SEE THAT. YOU MAKE AN ARRANGEMENT WITH DR. CRIME WHERE YOU BOTH DEAL WITH EACH OTHER'S PROBLEMS AND KEEP THE WHOLE THING ROLLING. I'VE ALWAYS QUESTIONED WHY THE CRIME LEAGUE ALWAYS SEEMED TO SKATE ON THROUGH, DESPITE EVERYTHING WE DID AS AFFILIATES.*

MINDER: *CRIME DOES PAY. IT PAYS FOR CRIMINALS, AND IT PAYS FOR LAW ENFORCEMENT. THE WHOLE PRISON INDUSTRIAL COMPLEX IS BIG BUSINESS. THE AMOUNT OF MONEY THAT WENT INTO THE BRIG? MASSIVE. GOVERNMENTS WERE HAPPY TO WORK WITH US TO HELP DEAL WITH IT. AND DR. CRIME'S A SOLID PARTNER, AS IS CRIMEBOT—THEY UNDERSTAND HOW IT WORKS. WE MAINTAIN AN EQUILIBRIUM BETWEEN US.*

I'D RATHER THWART SOME OF THE CRIME LEAGUE'S MORE COCKEYED SCHEMES THAN DEAL WITH A BUNCH OF SUPERVILLAINS OPERATING INDEPENDENTLY. AND DR. CRIME KNOWS WHERE AND HOW THE AFFILIATES OPERATE—WE CAN'T BE EVERYWHERE, **[REDACTED]**. *EVERYBODY WINS, AS I'VE SAID TO YOU BEFORE. EVERYBODY BUT YOU, [RE-*

Not bad, right? I just mosaic-faced myself and put those redactions in and edited where needed for clarity. So long as there's *enough* content there, people love redactions—gets their juices flowing, speculating on who's being talked about. Gossip intrigues, entices, and compels, right? Let people speculate all they like if it keeps them talking.

The edited interrogation made me look like the world-weary hero and Minder the Machiavellian super-prick. Perfect. The edited clip would get play. People were already interested in what superheroes were *really* like. And something like this would give them a lot of opportunities for even the laziest of journalists to chase down some prime stories, and their own innate competitiveness would drive them to outdo each other regarding the story. Nothing journalists hated more than not being in on the scoop.

At the very least, I felt that this would force Minder out of the chairmanship, out of the Affiliates, and possibly get him in prison. Any of these outcomes would be good, although, as a telepath, he was unbelievably dangerous.

What would he do in retaliation? He'd sing like a bird. He'd blow my secret identity to get revenge. He might try to play the Brighteyes hand as well, although his own scheme to get me entrapped by filming her actions might not play well.

There was also the possibility that some of the clients Minder worked with wouldn't want him spilling those golden beans.

People could deride what I did all they wanted; this footage was thermonuclear. I put together a brief letter as Cameraman, which would accompany the footage. With the edits I'd made, I was comfortable with getting it out there. I'd send copies to a half-dozen trusted journalists, people I'd worked with in the past decade. My letter was as follows:

Dear [NAME]—

Just thought you might find this footage interesting. it's from an interrogation i endured at the hands of Minder (aka, Rex Traynor, chairman of the Affiliates), with Lynn Credible, PR Director for the Affiliates, also present. items of particular interest, for which i can provide further details, include:

-Hyberia Hollow
-The Brig
-Polygon Rehabilitation Program
-Collusion between the Affiliates and the Crime League

And more. if you'd like to discuss further, you can reach me at my usual number, and we can arrange a meeting.

Regards,
Cameraman

Wearing gloves, I carefully packaged the mailers and I directed the Cameravan to get me to the nearest UPS Store. I went with UPS because if I went to the US Postal Service, there might be conflicts of interest, given the degree of government involvement the Affiliates enjoyed.

Without even breaking stride, I went into the store in my Cameraman costume and got the postage for the mailers. The clerk, a young woman named Sheronica, was almost speechless.

"Are you a soldier?" she asked.

"I'm Cameraman," I said.

"Who?"

"Never mind," I said.

"Is this a prank?" she asked, peeking past me, looking for the hidden camera. "Candid Cameraman?"

"It's not," I said, privately appreciating the vintage pop cultural reference she made so breezily. "I need these to get shipped. If they don't get where they're going, I'm going to come back here," I said, taking one of her business cards from her work desk and made a point to pocket it as I paid in cash. "Thanks."

And then I got out of there, while she stared after me, thankfully too shocked to get her phone out and film or photograph me.

Inferna smirked when I got back in.

"It's prosaic, you doing that," she said. "Not precisely heroic, but certainly prosaic."

"What do you know of heroism?" I asked. "You're a devil-woman."

She smiled that wicked smile of hers, an angular thing that showed off her fangs, while she put on some angular black shades that made her look even more fantastic and fashionably feral.

"What next?" she asked.

"I'll park the Cameravan at the long-term airport parking, and you teleport me to Shane's Monterey hangout."

Inferna chuckled dryly. "Your tab just keeps growing, Mitch."

"I know," I said. "I'm good for it."

"I know you are," she said, peering at me over the tops of her sunglasses with her fiery red eyes that seemed to cut right through my armor.

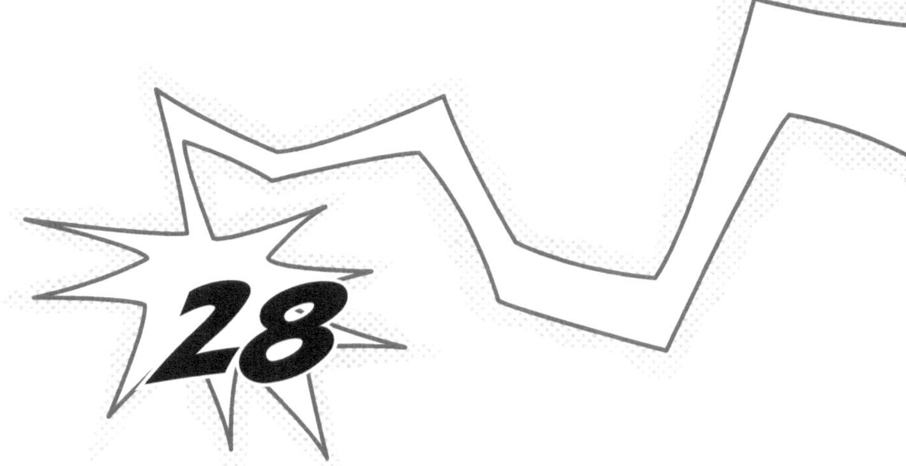

 the packages I shipped out would reach their appropriate recipients in about two or three days. They were acting as my insurance policy if Minder and his minions managed to take us out.

Inferna was a gem, teleporting me to Shane's glorious abode, which was like Malibu-Meets-Monterey in this comfortable blend of layered, lateral linearity within thousands of acres he owned. Shane was so rich he never had to worry about those kinds of petty details like acreage and property lines. All I knew was that he was happy to see Inferna and me, and I was happy to see Decibelle and Brighteyes, who both hugged me.

"Mitch-Honey, I'm so sorry," Des said. "I hate that Minder put the zap on me. I'm embarrassed."

"Don't worry about it," I said. "Our bigger problem is that the Affiliates and the Trinity are going to be coming after us here."

Brighteyes looked me in the eye.

"What'd you do with my footage?" she asked.

"Safeguarded for now," I said, glancing at Inferna, who gave me a tiny nod. And you're maybe wondering about the stuff that Credible took. Truth, they did abscond with those copies, but they were raw clips and would take time for someone to produce before they could make use of them. Plus, I didn't think Minder and his pals particularly wanted those getting aired.

"How'd Shane talk you out of taking out Hothead and Airhead?" I asked.

"He hasn't," she said. "But given what Des and you were dealing with on my behalf, I felt bad about not being here for you. As Shane put it, sounds like we're going to need help."

"Rad Lad's going to be a problem," Brighteyes said. "He's going to make my eyebeams useless."

"We'll handle him, don't you worry," Decibelle said.

Shane walked me over to a brunch table he'd had set up for the arrivals, as Inferna was teleporting people over, one by one. Shane was wearing a crew-necked black top and a white blazer with grey slacks and white loafers, a pair of black Persol sunglasses perched on his perfect nose.

"Mitch, they brought me up to speed," Shane said. "Everything that happened. I hope you know I didn't know about all of that."

"Yeah," I said, and I believed him, even though he still bugged me. I took a croissant and some free-range, locally sourced scrambled eggs and plated them. "We're going to get our asses kicked if Rad Lad and Tandem show."

"They won't," Shane said, making me pause mid-tong with some vegetarian sausage links.

"What do you mean they won't?" I asked. Shane looked pleased with himself.

"I let them know about an impending alien menace requiring their involvement," Shane said. "Along with Copycat, Video Girl, Eelectric, and Vendetta."

I looked him in the eye, and he met my gaze impassively, like he was some kind of wizard, bearing secrets and mysteries only he could truly know.

"You'd know that how?" I asked.

"It's just something that came up," Shane said. "Alien invasion overrides terrestrial priority alerts. That's in Article Three of the Affiliates Operational Doctrine."

The casual way he said it, I actually had to do a doubletake. "We're under alien invasion?"

"Not if the team intercepts them," Shane said. "With Tandem and Rad Lad and the others there, it shouldn't be a problem. Especially Copycat. But it'll keep them very busy while Minder's on his way to mess with us."

"What's to stop him from recalling them?" I asked.

"They're off-world, out of reach, dealing with the aliens," he said.

"*Awfully* convenient," I replied. I couldn't even process that an alien invasion might be occurring.

"What do I always say? Timing's everything, Mitch," Shane said. "You should know that by now. Good timing, bad timing—it makes all the difference."

I looked Shane in the eye, trying to get a sense of what he was up to.

"So, you *are* a precog," I said. "You know what's going to happen?"

"I just thought it would be more sensible to have our big guns taking on the aliens, versus getting enmeshed in Minder's petty revenge against you."

The Knack was so frustratingly enigmatic and blasé about everything. Maybe it was an after effect of his powers—whatever they precisely were—or just an aspect of his temperament, but there it was. In my years of knowing him, I'd never once seen Shane lose his temper, his patience, his bearings, his way, or his cool.

"Who's coming, then?" I asked.

"Let's see: Minder, Wingman, Ms. Fit, Tag Team, Lady Blaze, Mister Transistor, and Speedo."

"Hmm," I said. "Seven's still a strong Affiliates team, even without the big guns."

"Tag Team could be a problem," Shane said. "If he brings five hundred of his dupes along, that will be...bad."

"Yeah," I said. I mapped it out in my head:

- *MINDER → ME*
- *WINGMAN → AVANT GUARDIAN*
- *MS. FIT → SHRINKWRAP*
- *TAG TEAM → DECIBELLE*
- *LADY BLAZE → MR. COOL*
- *MISTER TRANSISTOR → EIGHTBALL*
- *SPEEDO → BRIGHTEYES*
- *CRUCIFIXER → THE ELF*
- *THE INQUISITOR → BITCHQUEEN*
- *ANGELICA → INFERNA*

"Decibelle's area of effect can be broad if she applies it," I said. "Tag Team's typical swarm attacks are his most potent, but if she's able to blast them with her scream, that should take Tag out of the fight."

"Unless they're wearing ear protection," Shane said.

"Will they be?"

"I'm just saying they could be," he replied, drinking a mimosa he'd picked up from his brunch table, taking another sip.

"Okay, but even if they protected their ears, she could still blast them with her screams," I said. "The sound could destroy them."

Shane pondered that while drinking his mimosa.

"It'll be very loud, yeah," he said. "And messy. Very, very messy."

"Are you high?" I asked. Nobody could possibly be as chill as this. We were talking about my life and death.

"I don't think so," Shane replied. "Hey, what about Stinger?"

"Stinger can be the wild card and troubleshooter," I said. "He can flit in and around where he's needed."

"Solid," Shane said. "If we manage to take down our opponents, we can help the others, as needed."

"Hey, speaking of that, what about you?" I asked. Shane smiled at me, watching me eat some of the eggs, which were delicious.

"I'll go wherever I'm needed," he said. "At precisely the right moment."

"And do what, exactly?" I asked.

"Whatever it takes," he said, his smile unbroken. "I'll be another wild card and troubleshooter, like Stinger."

"That you will," I said. "When is Minder turning up with his crew?"

"They're going to strike at dawn. That's what he said, at least," Shane said. "You know, you're weirdly good at this team leadership thing, Mitch," Shane said. "I always thought you would be, if given the chance. I wish Anna were here to see it."

I lifted my helmet and grabbed a mimosa from the serving table and downed it, then another. The mention of Anna never failed to bring me pain. If she were here, I'd have no doubt how the fight would turn out.

"You always thought so, eh?" I asked. He smiled as he watched Inferna walk up. She'd conjured another of her outfits—this one a black sleeveless jumpsuit with a high neck and a gold ring pullchain that dangled just below her chin. She wore crimson combat boots with jet-black soles.

"Hey, you two," she said, grabbing a mimosa as well. "You're both having entirely too much fun without me. Did Mitch tell you how much he owes me, Shane?"

"He didn't," Shane said. He took her arm in his and offered to show her around his place. Seeing the two of them there, looking like a matched set of fantastic, made me want to retch.

The others were mingling around the capacious brunch Shane's people had set up, while I gladhanded everybody, feeling overdressed and idiotically hardcore in my Cameraman suit, which I'd have to remember to charge up overnight, ahead of Minder's attack.

"Thanks for heeding the call, everybody," I said. "I really appreciate it, and I owe all of you when this is done, however it ends up. Shane told me that Minder thinks it's going to be a trap that's going to end up with Decibelle, Brighteyes, and me being captured. We're going to turn the tables on them. The official timing of the attack will be at dawn tomorrow, but if I know Minder, I bet he'll try to get here ahead of time and surprise us. I'm thinking it'll be Speedo as the point man, scouting it out ahead of the main attack force. Brighteyes, you can take him out so he can't report back—*no* disintegrations. Wingman and Angelica might go high above, as well. Inferna and Avant Guardian, you can engage with them on sight. After that, I'm guessing Tag Team will try to overwhelm us, with the remainder striking hard where they can break through. Decibelle, you need to deal with Tag Team. Minder will try to mind-zap anybody he can, likely from a position of relative safety—I'm thinking an Affilijet. We have to drop him early to have the best chance."

The Elf raised a hand. He was wearing a green and brown ranger-style studded leather doublet costume with a silver cir-clet. He was even better-looking than Shane, which was hard to imagine, but his elfin features (green eyes, strong nose, no-ble brow, angular chin, pointed ears, shimmery golden hair) were enchanting everyone who looked upon him.

"Begging your pardon, Cameraman, but when you say 'drop him' are you intending that we kill him?" he asked.

"No, I meant it rhetorically," I said. "Knocking him out is fine."

"We'll walk you through it, Elf-Honey," Decibelle said, patting him on the forearm. "I think your eyes might be even greener than Antigone's. What do you think, Brighteyes?"

"Maybe so, maybe so," Brighteyes said, looking him over.

"Where I come from, green eyes are very common," the Elf said.

"Do you have a name, Hon?" Decibelle asked.

"My name is Gylthanadill," the Elf said. "In your language. But you can just call me 'Gyl' if that's easier."

"It's a beautiful name," Decibelle said, and the Elf thanked her graciously.

"Lady Blaze is an auxiliary member," I said. "You should be able to do well against her, Mr. Cool."

Mr. Cool looked skeptical, cold breath coming from his mouth as he spoke. He had his frozen blue pompadour and white leather jacket and jeans and blue pointy-toed boots. He looked both amazing and ridiculous, which icy mist rising off him.

"Yo, Cam, I'm auxiliary, too," Cool said. "Maybe it'll not go so easily as you think."

"Just do your best," I said, but Cool wasn't deterred from asking more questions.

"Is this going to screw our chances of joining the Affiliates as active-duty members?" he asked. "I don't want to step on any toes, you know what I mean?"

"Consider it a live-fire test, like I'd mentioned on the phone," I said. "Your performance *will* be evaluated, and we'll assign eligibility ratings based upon it."

Okay, you know as well as I do that this was complete bullshit on my part, but I had to say something to keep the auxiliaries on board. They were always trying to work angles that gave them a chance at an active-duty posting. If everybody did what they were supposed to, my hope was that the fight would go well and we'd have shut down Minder's crew.

"What about the Trinity?" Avant Guardian asked. "Why are *they* involved?"

Avant Guardian wasn't a fan of the Trinity. Nor was I. Outside of their ardent adherents, I didn't know anybody who liked them. Their tagline was something like "Earth's Holiest Heroes" and "Salvation's Army" and "God's on OUR Side" and the like. They often turned up at book-burnings, clinic closings, as well as other protests that had any kind of apocalyptically biblical tie-ins.

"Minder has always been a fan of team crossovers, so maybe that's behind this," I said. He had doubtless schemed that the Trinity would help him deal with Inferna, and I wondered if they might be part of Minder's secret arrangement with the Crime League. "Everyone should try to get to bed early and try to rest. The Affiliates are arriving early, and we will need to be ready for them."

Eightball glanced at his full brunch plate, then back at me. He was wearing his trademark black and white racing suit, with his trademark infinity symbol on his chest and on the forehead of his mask.

"Bed early, Cam? It's brunchtime," Eight said.

"Yeah, I meant later," I said. "Obviously. I just don't want everyone partying here at Shane's place and being too hung over to deal with Minder and friends when they arrive."

"Ah, yeah, okay," Eight said, helping himself to a Bloody Mary. Really, the whole gathering felt like a sort of party, and that was weirding me out, given that I understood the stakes of what was going down.

If I were Minder, I'd send people over ahead of the time I'd told the Knack, just to be on the safe side, and maybe to test the Knack. I personally wasn't a fan of pulling an all-nighter, but I figured if something was up, the Knack would wake me up at just the right moment, so I made myself try to get some rest.

Also, Bitchqueen's enhanced senses ensured that if someone did try to creep up on us, she'd alert the rest of us. While you already knew what a loner I was, I admitted that it was nice to have a team around.

You've probably not gone to many superhero get-togethers, but the vibe was always kooky. All of the supers busy trying to be nonchalant in their costumes, while also comparing notes about each other's exploits. At this level—we're not talking A-level—everything hinged on one's latest big win, how much media it got, especially social. All of them were very active with their social media accounts, trying to build their audience.

While I had a nominal social media presence, my big thing was being super-mysterious, so that if and when Cameraman surfaced, it was always newsworthy on social media. Plus, I ran my accounts through anonymizers to help make it less likely that someone could backtrack through the accounts and find me.

The others were less careful about that, which I'd have advised them against doing, if anybody thought to ask me, which (naturally) they didn't. I didn't follow their social media; my focus was on supervillains, not seeing what other superheroes were doing.

In fact, as I watched them, I saw them with their phones, filming each other, shooting selfies, and I wanted to yell, watching them socializing that way.

"Eh, everybody," I said. "Seriously, we need a social media blackout right now. We can't have you populating your feeds with yourselves ahead of Minder's arrival, right? You know what 'Radio Silence' means, yes? This is one of those times."

They were all looking at me like I was insane, and I'll admit that it was weird to give that little speech as Cameraman. I could almost imagine someone making a meme:

CAMERAMAN LECTURING US. #STAYFOCUSED

"It's all good, Cam," Eight said. "People are just letting off steam. The Affiliates don't engage in social listening, do they, Bro?"

"I would," I said.

"But you're Cameraman," Eight said. "We expect that from you. That's, like, your wheelhouse."

Minder struck me as too patrician and super-snooty to bother with social media, let alone social listening. Maybe Credible would, but who knows what else Minder would have her do ahead of the mission. Probably getting the Affilijets prepped to launch them to Monterey.

I shook away those thoughts and slipped away from the festivities, needing a place to think. There was no way Minder was going to have a fair fight. He was going to strike out of nowhere, when people were unprepared.

My phone rang, and it was Shane.

"Mitch, they're coming," Shane said. "Now."

And then the knockout gas canisters flew in, having been dropped from overhead by Wingman and Angelica, as Speedo raced in, heading right for Brighteyes. To her credit, she was quick to fire a blast at him, catching him in the chest and taking him out of the fight, as her beams appeared to be set to stun, fortunately for him. I actually breathed a sigh of relief when I saw that he hadn't disintegrated.

At least two hundred Tag Teams came roaring out of the woods, wearing gas masks. I triggered my invisibility and moved upwind from the gas, which appeared to have taken out Mr. Cool, Shrinkwrap, Eightball, and Avant Guardian, who were all out cold on the ground.

Decibelle ran away from the bluish gas, coughing, while Brighteyes ran with her. Stinger put his bug wings to work as a kind of fan, propelling the gas back toward Tag Team in what I thought was a solid move on his part.

A bullet whizzed past my head, and I went around a corner, unsure if it was a stray shot or if someone was tracking me despite my invisibility.

I saw Ms. Fit running through the gas, wearing a mask, scanning the crowd. She saw Brighteyes and was headed her way when Decibelle cut loose with one of her sonic screams, which shattered the windows of Shane's living room and knocked Fit and a bunch of Tags back. Decibelle concentrated her sound attack on them, cutting through their assault.

I tossed one of my flash grenades at the group of Tag Teams who'd pivoted left in the face of Decibelle's retaliation, and Brighteyes fired a wide beam into the Tag Teams who'd broken right, disintegrating them, which caused the remainder of the Tag Teams to cry out and tumble from the psychic feedback of their annihilation.

Minder wouldn't be in the front line. He'd be hanging back, using his telepathic communication to relay orders to the others, and to do his own psychic assaults when he saw the chance.

Then I saw Crucifixer aiming right at me with a scoped rifle, and I knew he'd been the one who'd shot at me before. I raised my stun gun and fired a beam right at him. Ordinarily, the gun wouldn't have that kind of range, but if Crucifixer was using a special scope to target me, maybe the stun beam would affect him.

I saw the Inquisitor wade into the living room, wielding a scourge on Bitchqueen, who snarled and pounced on him, biting him in the shoulder. Unprepared for the force of her attack, Inquisitor called out for help, his white robes splashed with blood from her bite. Three Tag Teams jumped Bitchqueen, who punched and kicked at them with her enhanced strength. But, as I'd said before, the more Tag Team was hit, the more of him appeared, and she was quickly swamped by them.

Decibelle turned her scream on the Tag Teams, although it also affected Bitchqueen, who clutched her ears and howled. Anybody with super-hearing would be miserable if Decibelle unloaded on them.

Brighteyes stopped Des from screaming, and fired a half-dozen precise eyebeam strikes at the Tag Teams, disintegrating them as she had the others. I saw Angelica swoop down, only to get tackled in the air by Inferna, who had flown out with her great, red bat wings. What happened next was an apocalyptic confrontation between Angelica and Inferna, as the two of them battled in Shane's back yard in a blaze of hellfire and dazzling, sparkly light that emanated from Angelica in a kind of nimbus.

I ran along the side of Shane's house, looking for the Affilijets, where Minder had to be, and saw an arrow fly past me, striking the Crucifixer in the shoulder. The Elf emerged seemingly from nowhere, apparently able to see me, even though I was invisible. Christ, could everybody see me?

"I'll go with you, Cameraman," he said.

"You can see me?" I asked.

"I can see your spirit," the Elf said. "Your aura."

"What color's my aura?" I asked.

"White, with hints of red and grey," the Elf said. "A very curious combination."

"Is that good or bad?" I asked.

"It's fascinating," the Elf said. "Perhaps best discussed later."

He loosed another arrow, catching a Tag Team in the leg, making him tumble to the ground. I saw Inferna teleport away with Angelica, while Wingman swooped down on Decibelle and Brighteyes, Bitchqueen was recovering from Decibelle's sonic blasts, cupping her ears and cursing.

Tweaking my visor filters to track Affilijet cloaking technology, I could see the outlines of them further down Shane's yard. Inferna reappeared alone in a puff of brimstone, and quickly soared after Wingman, who was in the middle of battling Stinger, their fists clanging off each other's armor as they swung.

The Tag Teams had multiplied again and were closing in on Decibelle and Brighteyes, who were keeping them at bay with a tight braiding of sound and eyebeam attacks. Watching the two of them work together that way made me pine for Anna yet again. We were just so good together.

I ran for the Affilijets with the Elf beside me, just as Mister Transistor made his appearance, smashing to the ground in a big powersuit that was a metallic blue. He looked like a giant, bulbous toy robot that I knew was Transistor's compromise with the Affiliates marketing people, wanting his powersuit to be appealing to the kid toy market.

The Elf fired some arrows at Transistor, but the arrows, despite managing to penetrate the armor of the powersuit (go, Elf!) didn't appear to impede the powersuit much as he stomped up toward Shane's house, each footstep making a hefty thump that shook the ground. Transistor was in a seat in the chest of his powersuit, protected by a semi-opaque belly dome.

Lady Blaze flew down as well, clearly part of Minder's second wave. Blaze looked fantastic in her two-toned fiery blue incarnation, with her burning body being a darker blue and her fiery hair a lighter shade of blue that trailed after her as she went. Decibelle revved up her scream yet again, the soundwaves blasting Blaze, Transistor, Elf, and me. I quickly toggled my ear protection dampers, while the Elf merely winced evocatively.

"I daresay that we have no Sirens in Tír na nÓg," he said, his words transcribing on my HUD screen. "Although we *do* have banshees."

Transistor launched more knockout gas right at Decibelle, which exploded in the air as she aimed her scream beams at them, which was the primary purpose, as it released the gas in a cloud that fell on her, cutting off her screaming as she held her breath, grabbing for one of the unconscious Tag Teams' gas masks.

The blue-tinged knockout gas served another purpose, I saw, in that it acted as a smokescreen that diminished the range of Antigone's eyebeams. I had to hand it to Minder in planning this raid out pretty well.

Elf and I reached the first Affilijet, while Bitchqueen ran up alongside us, blood on her face and around her mouth.

"These Affiliates are playing pretty rough for a war game," she said to Elf, glancing in my direction.

"Yes, they are," the Elf said. "They remind me of the goblins of the Cymerian Valley. Such dreadful hordes."

"You okay, Queen?" I asked (seemed more gentlemanly than calling her "Bitch").

"Fine," she said, then she clutched her head and collapsed, writhing on the ground. Minder. It had to be.

"She appears to be under psionic attack," the Elf said. "Fortunately, I'm immune to such attacks, by virtue of the Silver Circlet of Selandariel, which I happen to be wearing."

I ran up the ramp, looking for Minder, but this Affilijet only had a Tag Team in it, working the comms panels and trying to coordinate the other Tag Teams. Then I wondered if it might be the Prime. It made enough sense that I decided to take the chance, raising my stun gun.

"Hey, Reg!" I yelled, which made him turn in my direction. It was all I needed, as I fired my stun gun right at him, and he was put in a trance. I then grabbed some zip-ties from my belt and quickly cuffed him and zipped his legs while he was still under the effects of the stun gun.

Glancing out the cockpit of the Affilijet, I could see that his army of Tag Teams were all standing there stunned, too. It was nice to see that I'd found a critical weakness with Tag Team: as the hub of his pile of spokes, what affected him could impact the rest of them, too. Given that he could operate so far from the action (thinking back on his fight with Instigator), I wondered why Tag was here in person that way. Minder must have pressured him into coming here in-person.

I was about to say something to the Elf when I saw Bitchqueen had appeared, snarling at the Elf and me, her eyes wild, looking at us, but not quite recognizing us.

"Queen, what's the matter?" I asked.

"It's me, Mitch," she said, and I knew that Minder had possessed her. "And using her senses, I can see right where you are."

Bitchqueen lunged at me, managing to hit me, knocking me off my feet. She was smaller than me, but her canine-enhanced physique made her stronger, pound for pound (sorry, puns, remember?)

The Elf fired an arrow at her, catching her in the hip, which would at least slow her down, While I fired the stun gun at her, catching her in the face with it, much as I had with Tag Team. The feedback of the stun gun would likely mess with Minder, so I urged the Elf to come with me to the other Affilijet.

Outside, Inferna and Stinger had managed to fight Wingman to a standstill, catching him with a crossfire of Stinger's jagged lightning stings and Inferna's hellfire. Inferna caught Wingman around the neck with her fiery whip and hurled him into Lady Blaze, who'd been rushing to assist. The force of the blow knocked Blaze back, arcing a firetrail in the air as she went.

Mister Transistor was using his powersuit's targeting array to lock onto both Inferna and Stinger, and I saw him launch missiles at the two of them, forcing them to fly away and evade as best as they could as a torrent of mini-missiles chased them.

Brighteyes and Decibelle were making short work of the Tag Team dupes, who were still standing there stunned, with Decibelle using sonar pulses to guide Brighteyes to her targets, which she then disintegrated with carefully focused pulses of her beams. Sound & Fury were back at it, big time. Lady Blaze swooped down on the two of them, surrounding them with a cage of blue flame, while Decibelle broadened her scream beam to fire up at her, forcing Blaze to cover her ears as Brighteyes nailed her with a heavy stun beam, downing her, Blaze's fires going out as she fell to the ground.

The Elf and I raced to the second Affilijet, while Mister Transistor ran to catch Lady Blaze. The Crucifixer had tended to his shoulder wound and was firing an AR-15 at the Elf as he was running by, shooting it one-handed while yelling "Lord have mercy!" each time he missed the Elf, who was very spry. Crucifixer's logo was a white gunsight with a cross serving as the crosshairs, as well.

Unfortunately for me, I took a cluster of Crucifixer's high-velocity rounds, which went right up the side of me like hammerblows, knocking me to the ground. One of his bullets had damaged my power pack, and my invisibility cloak sputtered out, leading Crucifixer to cry out in fervent ecstasy.

"Thank you, Lord," Crucifixer said, raising his rifle to try to get me in his sights.

The Elf fired another arrow at the Crucifixer, impaling him through the back of his hand, despite his body armor. He dropped his assault rifle and held up his wounded hand in disbelief, the arrow having passed through the palm of his hand.

"How—?" he said.

"A miracle," the Elf said, firing another shot at him, this one piercing him through his other palm, between his armor plating. The Crucifixer dropped to the ground in agony, cursing us both.

I glanced back at how the rest of the battle was going, and it looked like Mister Transistor was driving back Decibelle and Brighteyes, who were concentrating their fire on the powersuit. I could hear the eyebeams kicking up as well as the sonic screams.

No sooner had I gone up the ramp but I had gotten hit—hard—by Credible, who was carrying a tactical shotgun. The blow had caught me in the chest and had knocked me right over. But as quick as she'd been, the Elf was quicker, sending an arrow into the shell ejector of the shotgun, jamming it as she fired that solitary shot.

Credible hurled the shotgun at the Elf, charging me, while Minder, standing at the cockpit of the Affilijet, was furiously sending mental attacks at the two of us. Credible went for me again, and I dug into my Aikido to try to defend myself. She struck me hard in the chest, the face, the ribs. Each blow made me see stars, and I had to steel myself against the onslaught she delivered with a cold savagery.

"I cannot believe what a pain in the ass you are," Credible said. "All of this is your fault, Mr. Paulsen."

I raised my stun gun at her, but she knocked it aside with a quick swipe of her hand. Her face retained its icy professionalism, but I could see how enraged she was, too. The key to prevailing against her was to keep applying my charm to really send her off the deep end.

The Elf shot Minder in the arm with an arrow, which broke whatever mental attacks Minder was attempting as he collapsed in pain, the arrow in his arm.

"You shot me," Minder said, almost in shock at the sight of his own blood. He clearly had mind-messaged something to Credible, because she broke off her pummeling of me, with one particularly face-crunching elbow strike that cracked my helmet HUD yet again, sending jagged pieces of it into my forehead.

"That's just the start of what you're going to get, Rex," I said.

"No, I don't think so, Mitch," Minder said. Then I saw the Scenester appear out of nowhere, there in his silvery grey costume, his sneering, goggled face burning into my splintered vision, his logo being a single white lightning bolt "S" surrounded by a white circle, and before I could say anything, the three of them teleported away in a flash of light.

"Son of a bitch," I said, getting to my feet, reeling from how much damage Credible had done to me in mere moments. It hurt to move and breathe.

Glancing through the cockpit window, I saw Mister Transistor's powersuit had been blasted to pieces by Brighteyes and Decibelle, with Transistor surrendering as he stood there within the rubble of his suit.

The Knack was there, naturally, helping everyone out, asking if they were all okay. I limped out of the Affilijet, nursing my midsection and flipping up my broken helmet.

"Minder got away," I said.

"I know," Shane replied.

"Of course," I said. "This all happened, what, as you'd foreseen it?"

Shane wagged a finger at me before helping up Lady Blaze, who looked confused, yet reassured by Shane's steady hand. Stinger and Inferna landed, Inferna folding her bat wings in that effortlessly elegant way that made them disappear, becoming a black leather trenchcoat that paired beautifully with the red top hat she wore jauntily, her devilish forehead horns peering out just over her arched eyebrows. Her jumpsuit and boots were impeccably clean.

"Something like that," Shane said. "The important thing is that he didn't get you or Brighteyes, and nobody seems seriously hurt, although we may need ambulances for Crucifixer and the Inquisitor."

"Oh, *I'll* take care of them, Shane," Inferna said, strutting over to the fallen Trinity members. I didn't even want to imagine what that might mean, but I had other things to worry about.

FZZZZZZZZZZZZZZZZZZZ

as Shane had taken control of the situation with the Affiliates members, telling them that Minder had been misleading them regarding Brighteyes, Decibelle, and me, and, naturally, they believed him. People always wanted to believe in Shane, and he could be incredibly persuasive when he wanted to be.

Everyone who'd been sidelined by that first salvo of knock-out gas was suitably embarrassed, eager to please, and upset that they'd missed out on the big fight. Those of us who'd been part of it felt vindicated that we'd held our own against the Affiliates.

In a moment of inspiration, I pitched something to them all, while Shane passed out blankets and (I kid you not) chilled champagne. Shane just smiled at me, shaking his head as he poured glasses of champagne to everybody, including what Affiliates were there.

Wingman wasn't having any of it, waved away the blankets and drinks.

"Shane, what exactly is going on, here?" he asked. "Brighteyes is a murderer."

But Antigone had already fled the scene as the battle had finished. I was a diehard proponent of ghosting, but Brighteyes made me look like an amateur.

"We'll deal with that the best we can," Shane said. "For now, you have to understand that Minder's been conspiring with the Crime League and has been doing so for years."

Ms. Fit looked at me and at Shane, appearing reflective.

"We'll need proof of this, Shane, Cam," she said. "We're *not* taking it on faith."

Mister Transistor agreed, glancing reluctantly around him.

"You're asking us to, what? Side with you against the Affiliates? We *are* Affiliates, man."

I surveyed who was still here among the Affiliates: Wingman, Ms. Fit, Tag Team, Mister Transistor, Decibelle, and Speedo.

"Guys," I said. "Bear with us. There's a lot going on."

Tag Team had managed to free himself, was glaring at us warily as he'd emerged from the Affilijet where we'd left him.

"You don't get a say, Cameraman," Tag said. "You're colluding with Brighteyes. She's the one who's gone rogue, not Minder."

Decibelle scoffed at this.

"The hell you say, Tag," she said. "Minder messed with my mind. He messed with my partner's, too. He's been yanking all of our chains. Probably been yanking yours, too, whether you know it or not."

Wingman rallied his teammates to him, his golden armor glinting in the light of the morning. Even beaten, he exuded power and authority.

"Team, to me," he said. "Shane, I don't know what game you're playing, but we're heading back to headquarters."

"You do that," Shane said. "And if you want, ask those hard questions you might have for Minder. See what he says and does. That'll be your answer to what we're talking about here. But I'd advise you to take precautions against his telepathy. Maybe reconnect remotely, versus in-person."

Wingman, Tag Team, Ms. Fit, Speedo, and Mister Transistor went to the Affilijets, taking flight, shooting south, toward Affiliates West. The rest of us watched them go.

"You all did a great job today," I said. "Top marks to all of you. I just wanted to tell you about a new group Shane and I are putting together—a hero team I'm calling 'The Shutter-clique'—and you're all welcome to join as founding members."

"What is that, exactly?" Bitchqueen asked. "Are we talking *another* hero team?"

"Yes," I said. "Something more grounded in street-level operations."

"But I'll make sure it's well-funded," Shane said, his phone ringing. He took the call, which was Minder. "Yeah, I'm sorry, too. You brought this on yourself."

He hung up, addressed everyone present.

"I'm going to have to pop in on the Affiliates," Shane said. "Cameraman can brief you on Shutterclique."

Mr. Cool looked bewildered. "Wait, so we're not joining the Affiliates?"

"Not yet," I said. "Consider Shutterclique a kind of entry-level superhero team for you, where you can hone your skills and powers to become Affiliates-ready."

"Yeah, but we beat them," Bitchqueen said. "We beat those Affiliates. Aren't we ready now?"

I watched Shane whisper something to Inferna, who leered at him. The two of them teleported away, leaving the rest of us behind.

"Not just yet," I said. "Eventually."

Avant Guardian looking searchingly at me.

"I trust you, Cameraman," she said. "I'm with you on this, whatever 'this' precisely is."

"Yeah, man," Eightball said, drinking his champagne. "I'm in."

"Count me in, Cam," Stinger said. "Hells, yeah."

Decibelle treated me to a sugary southern smile.

"I'm definitely in, Honey-Cam," she said. Mr. Cool smirked at Decibelle, nodding.

"Camo, I'm wherever *she* is," Cool said.

The Elf looked on enigmatically, impeccably put together despite the battle we'd just had.

"I'll be with your 'Shutterclique' whenever you need me," he said. Shrinkwrap, peeved by how she'd been taken out of the fight so early, grimaced in her shimmery costume.

"I am clearly *not* ready for the Affiliates," she said. "But I'll join your team, Cameraman."

"As will I," Bitchqueen said. "Fuck it, yeah."

I raised my glass of champagne, and was heartened when the others did, too. It felt like something that mattered. I'd take care of the details when I could breathe without wincing.

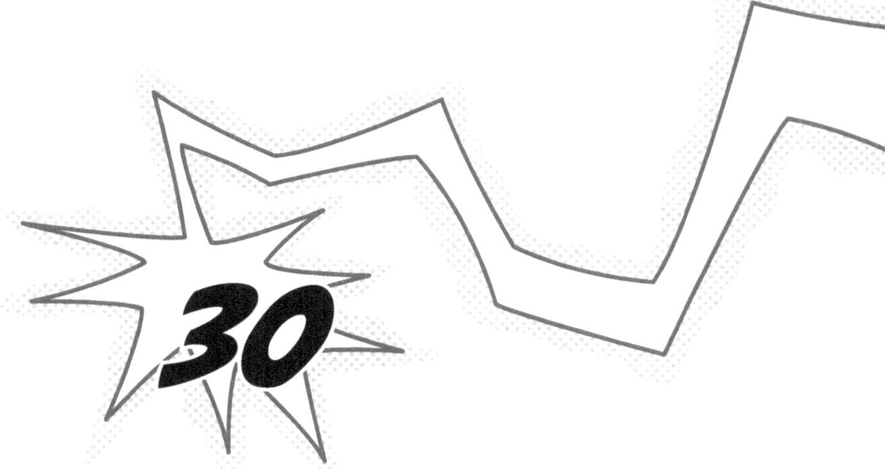

The journalists I'd sent the stories to began to report on them, and pretty soon, the Affiliates were doing damage control over the allegations levied against Minder, who had lawyered up quickly, taking a press conference on the steps of Affiliates East in New York City. It was packed, with reporters recording every word, microphones, digital recorders, the works. I was even there—invisible—filming it all. I wouldn't have missed it for the world.

And Minder looked sharp in his black pinstriped suit, wearing his black facemask, the white "M" contrasting perfectly, as ever. He wore a white rose at his lapel. Lynn Credible wore a grey power suit, carrying her ever-present Affiliates blue leather folder in one hand, her face on Minder with the kind of rapt expression she only had for him.

The Knack was standing nearby, opposite of Credible, also looking sharp in a white suit with black Oxfords and a grey shirt and white necktie. Tandem and Rad Lad stood nearby as well, in their uniforms. They dwarfed everyone there, and both figuratively and literally radiated their superpower.

"The info-terrorist, Cameraman, has taken it upon himself to smear my reputation in an unwarranted and unprovoked attack on me, my credibility, on the Affiliates, and with every superhero associated with all the good work we've been doing for years," Minder said. "In the spirit of full transparency, I'm going public with my identity, that people might see that I have nothing to hide, unlike Cameraman, of whom I've got a lot to say."

The next moments will forever be emblazoned on my brain. The shots that came—there were three of them, caught Minder right in the head. His head shattered in a technicolor detonation as the explosive high-velocity rounds struck him in a tight pattern. People were screaming in panic, and the blood and brains from Minder splashed on Shane and Credible both, as Minder fell to the ground, his head nearly gone from the force of the bullets.

For all of his maneuvering, his manipulations and Machiavellian machinations, Minder had been done in by three shots from an assassin's rifle. He probably didn't even see it coming, but later, I wondered if he'd been scanning the crowd with his mind as he'd been speaking, and whether, in those fateful last moments, he'd caught the mind of the assassin a nanosecond too late. I'll never know.

I pivoted on instinct, dragging myself away from the murder of Minder, to try to find who'd fired the shot. I could see the figure at distance, wearing adaptive camouflage, fleeing across the rooftop where they'd been concealed.

The screaming at the stairs of the Affiliates headquarters notwithstanding, I kept my focus on the shooter, who vanished across the rooftop from the angle I'd taken. People were running around in terror, and Credible was kneeling by Minder's dead body, gripping his lifelessly twitching hand, while a blood-spattered Shane was saying something to Tandem and Rad Lad, who flew out over the crowd in the direction from which the bullets had come.

The shock of what had happened settled in, and I quickly moved from my perch, grateful that I'd opted for full invisibility, because people might have thought I'd had something to do with Minder's death, which you know that I didn't, Gentle Reader.

Tandem and Rad Lad were flying around, with Wingman joining in, and Tag Team produced bunches of dupes to do crowd control, while Ms. Fit ran about, urging people to remain calm.

Me, I got the hell out of there, my hands shaking. I wanted Minder to face justice, to be held accountable for everything he'd done. I didn't want him being turned into some kind of super-martyr.

My headphone rang, and it was Shane.

"Mitch," Shane said. "You're here, aren't you?"

"Yeah," I said.

"He's dead," Shane said.

"I saw," I said.

"Did you see who?" he asked.

"I have footage, Shane," I said. "I've got to look it over, first."

"You'd better get out of town," Shane said. "With Rex taken down, I'm acting Chairman, now. I'll make sure the Affiliates stay off your back, but you're going to need an alibi. You *can't* have been here."

Believe you me: I was out of there faster than you could say "Inferna."

KLOP
KLOP

31

when there was almost non-stop footage being played over and over again: the assassination of Minder. In one news cycle, he'd gone from insidious suspect required to answer questions to silenced, saintly martyr. What a difference a murder made.

The entire PR apparatus of the Affiliates was chugging along, with these noble photographs of Minder appearing from some photo shoots Credible had likely arranged as a contingency in case something like this happened. Remember what I said about villains and contingencies?

Who turned up at my place? Paleface, Rollergirl, and Tag Team.

Rollergirl wore her armor, as ever, looking like an android, while Tag was just Tag. Paleface wore her black caped costume, looking like exactly what she was. There was no sign of Deadpan, and I thought maybe he'd been out east (right?) and was otherwise preoccupied.

Now, there's something in vampire lore about them not being able to enter unless invited, so when she showed up with the others, I offered to invite Rollergirl and Tag Team in, but not Paleface.

"What's the matter, Mr. Paulsen?" Paleface asked, baring her fangs as she spoke. "Have you something to hide?"

I buzzed Tag and Rollergirl in, affecting not a lack of concern, but more of a mien of frustrated fatigue. I let them into my living room, muted my television, which had Credible doing presswork on all the news channels, her stern face bearing the wounded rage she wore as readily as Minder's bloodstains on her expensive suit.

"Where were you today, Mitch?" Tag asked.

"I was here all day," I said. Tag looked around, literally looking for clues, doing what he thought detectives were supposed to do. He tried so hard.

Rollergirl took a softer tone, since she and I had more history.

"Mitch, they're saying you're a suspect in this," she said.

"The only thing I shoot are pictures," I said. "Everybody knows this."

Tag grimaced at me, trying to play the tough guy he never would be.

"Can anyone vouch for you being here?" he asked. I was going to say something flip. You know, one of those smartassed kinds of comebacks for which I was infamous. I had something teed up and ready to go, when my eye drifted to my coffee table, to the wooden "Brooding Bowl" Anna and I had gotten when we'd first furnished the place. I'd kept it empty since Anna had died, as, I don't know, a kind of memorial in her honor.

I felt my knees buckle. I felt my legs give out, and I hyperventilated, my hearing fading, with Tag and Rollergirl reaching for me, voicing concern while I was falling apart in front of them, whipping my head around, searching, trying to see. And I'll tell you why, but you already know, right, Gentle Reader?

There, in the center of the bowl, was one of her handmade metal marbles, just sitting there, minding its own business, like it had been there the whole time, and I'd somehow missed it in all the excitement of the past year.

However, it *hadn't* been there.

I know that because I pay attention to everything.

I hadn't missed a thing; except for her.

TO BE CONTINUED IN...

INFERNA
THE SHUTTERCLIQUE #2

APPENDIX

THE SHUTTERCLIQUE UNIVERSE HAS A VARIETY OF SUPERHERO AND SUPERVILLAIN TEAMS! HERE'S A GUIDE TO THE ONES WHO'LL BE APPEARING MOST REGULARLY THROUGHOUT THE SERIES.

THE AFFILIATES

THE AFFILIATES ARE THE MOST PRESTIGIOUS OF SUPERHERO TEAMS, OPERATING PREDOMINANTLY IN THE UNITED STATES, BUT WITH UNITED NATIONS CLEARANCE ACT INTERNATIONALLY, WITH THE APPROVAL OF SOVEREIGN NATIONS (MOST OF WHOM HAVE THEIR OWN LOCAL SUPERHEROES AND EVEN TEAMS, WHICH WILL SHOW UP IN FUTURE APPENDICES). THE ORIGINAL AFFILIATES TEAM WAS EAST, BASED IN NEW YORK CITY. THE OTHER BRANCHES APPEARED OVER TIME, AS DEMAND FOR AFFILIATES TEAM MEMBERS GREW WITH THEIR PROMINENCE.

AFFILIATES EAST (NEW YORK CITY)

- MINDER
  CHAIRMAN
- THE KNACK
  DEPUTY CHAIRMAN
- TANDEM
    - FUSILLAD
    - LASSITUDE
- LANCER
- WINGMAN
- MISTER
  TRANSISTOR
- SPEEDO
- TAG TEAM

AFFILIATES WEST (LOS ANGELES)

- MS. FIT
- RAD LAD
- LADY BLAZE
- TAG TEAM

CONTINUED...

AFFILIATES CENTRAL (CHICAGO)

- *CAMERAMAN*
- *VICTORIANA*
- *STRUTTER*
- *GOO*
- *ROLLER GIRL*
- *VAMP*
- *SURE SHOT*
- *TAG TEAM*

AFFILIATES SOUTH (ATLANTA)

- *DECIBELLE*
- *BRIGHTEYES*
- *GREEN MAN*
- *STINGER*
- *EELECTRIC*
- *TAG TEAM*

THE SHUTTERCLIQUE

CREATED BY CAMERAMAN, THE SHUTTERCLIQUE IS INTENDED AS A LOWER-ECHELON, STREET-LEVEL CRIMEFIGHTING TEAM THAT OPERATES INDEPENDENTLY OF MORE ESTABLISHED TEAMS LIKE THE AFFILIATES. BASED IN CHICAGO BUT WILLING TO GO ANYWHERE REQUIRED OF THEM, THE SHUTTERCLIQUE HAS EMERGED AS A KIND OF "PROVING GROUND" FOR SUPERHEROES WHO ASPIRE TO MAKE AFFILIATES MEMBERSHIP. AS SUCH, THE MEMBERSHIP OF THE SHUTTERCLIQUE IS ALWAYS IN FLUX.

- *CAMERAMAN*
- *VICTORIANA*
- *INFERNA*
- *SHE-DEVIL*
- *ROLLERGIRL*
- *BITCHQUEEN*
- *SHRINKWRAP*
- *AVANT GUARDIAN*
- *MR. COOL*
- *EIGHTBALL*
- *THE ELF*

THE FOURHEADS

THIS IS A LONG-ESTABLISHED, FAMOUS SUPERVILLAIN TEAM THAT HAS OPERATED ALONG TWO STRICT PARAMETERS:

1) ONLY FOUR ACTIVE MEMBERS AT ANY TIME.
2) THE SUPERPOWERS MUST BE SOMEHOW HEAD-RELATED.

THESE REQUIREMENTS HAVE BEEN UPHELD BY TRADITION, MAKING THE FOURHEADS A KIND OF ELITE CRIMINAL CLUB, OPERATING IN A NUMBER OF HIGH-PROFILE LINES OF CRIMINAL BUSINESS. THE ROSTER HAS CHANGED OVER THE YEARS, WITH FATALITIES AND IMPRISONMENT BEING THE MOST TYPICAL FATES OF MEMBERS.

THE CURRENT FOURHEADS TEAM IS:

- HOTHEAD (TEAM CO-LEADER)
- DEADHEAD (TEAM CO-LEADER)
- AIRHEAD
- DUSTHEAD

FORMER MEMBERS INCLUDE: MACHINEHEAD; GEARHEAD; BLOCKHEAD; ARROWHEAD; PIGHEAD; SPEARHEAD; METALHEAD; CRACKHEAD; OVERHEAD; MASTHEAD; SLEEPYHEAD; MUSHROOMHEAD; WARHEAD.

THE CRIME LEAGUE

FOUNDED BY DR. CRIME, THE INSTIGATOR, AND CRIMEBOT, THE CRIME LEAGUE HAS A VERY ACTIVE MEMBERSHIP, SERVING AS A SUPPORT AND RACKETEERING ORGANIZATION FOR MEMBERS. WHILE CRIMINALS AREN'T REQUIRED TO JOIN THE CRIME LEAGUE, THERE ARE ADVANTAGES AVAILABLE FOR MEMBERS WHICH CAN BE INCENTIVES.

CONTINUED...

THE CRIME LEAGUE

- DR. CRIME*
- THE INSTIGATOR*
- CRIMEBOT*
- DEATH CLOWN
- JACK RABBIT
- ICE QUEEN

- SHUTTERBUG
- PLETHORA
- SPARX
- FELONIA
- SCENESTER

*CO-LEADERS

THE TRINITY

BASED IN IOWA, THE TRINITY IS A THEOCRATIC FUNDAMENTALIST SUPERHERO TEAM FORMED TO ATTACK NON-CHRISTIAN AND DEFEND NOMINALLY CHRISTIAN RELIGIOUS INSTITUTIONS, PRIMARILY IN THE UNITED STATES. THERE ARE THREE MAIN ACTIVE MEMBERS WHO TYPICALLY DEPLOY TOGETHER, WITH OTHER MEMBERS SERVING IN SECONDARY AND AUXILIARY ROLES.

WELL-FUNDED BY AS-YET UNREVEALED FOUNDATIONS AND ORGANIZATIONS, THE TRINITY IS VERY POPULAR IN HIGHLY CONSERVATIVE STATES, WHEREAS THEY ARE VIEWED MORE DUBIOUSLY ELSEWHERE, DESPITE NEARLY ALWAYS RECEIVING FAVORABLE MEDIA COVERAGE.

- CRUCIFIXER
- THE INQUISITOR
- ANGELICA
- NAPALMINISTER
- BRAINFRIAR

- DOGMATIQUE
- THE BELIEVER
- THE SERMONIZER
- THE MONEYLENDER
- THE HOLY ROLLER

NOSETOUCH PRESS
*WE'RE OUT THERE

NOSETOUCHPRESS.COM

THE SHUTTERCLIQUE #2
INFERNA
MAGIC!
MAYHEM!
LOVE!
2025

A NOTE ON THE TYPE

THE TEXT OF THIS BOOK IS SET IN FREIGHT TEXT PRO, DESIGNED BY JOSHUA DARDEN. ORIGINALLY DRAWN IN 2005 BY JOSHUA DARDEN AND EXPANDED SEVERAL TIMES OVER, THE FREIGHT COLLECTION OF TYPEFACES IS RENOWNED FOR ITS HISTORICAL INNOVATION AND ON-GOING POPULARITY.

JOSHUA DARDEN (BORN 1979 IN NORTHRIDGE, LOS ANGELES, CALIFORNIA) IS AN AMERICAN TYPEFACE DE-SIGNER. HE PUBLISHED HIS FIRST TYPEFACE AT THE AGE OF 15, BECOMING ACCORDING TO FONTS IN USE THE FIRST KNOWN AFRICAN-AMERICAN TYPEFACE DESIGNER.

IN 2004–2005, HE ESTABLISHED HIS OWN FOUNDRY, DARDEN STUDIO, IN BROOKLYN. SOON AFTER, HE PUB-LISHED THE FONT SUPERFAMILY FREIGHT, 120 FONTS IN FIVE FAMILIES (BIG, DISPLAY, MICRO, SANS, AND TEXT). IT WAS INSPIRED BY THE "DUTCH TASTE" SCHOOL OF TYPE-FACE DESIGN, INCLUDING THE WORK OF KIS, CASLON AND FLEISCHMAN, AND WAS NAMED A "FAVORITE TYPEFACE OF 2005" BY *TYPOGRAPHICA*.

THE HEADLINES ARE SET IN CC MEANWHILE, DESIGNED BY JOHN ROSHELL FOR COMICRAFT. JOHN ROSHELL HAS LETTERED THOUSANDS OF COMICS FOR MARVEL, DC, DARK HORSE & BLIZZARD, DESIGNED THE LOGOS FOR AVENGERS, DAREDEVIL, BLACK PANTHER & ANGRY BIRDS, AND CREATED HUNDREDS OF TYPEFACES FOR COMI-CRAFT AND HIS NEW FOUNDRY, SWELL TYPE.

COMPOSED BY CLEVER CROW CONSULTING AND DESIGN,
PITTSBURGH, PENNSYLVANIA

ABOUT THE AUTHOR

BORN IN MISSOURI, GROWING UP IN OHIO, AND SETTLING IN CHICAGO, DAVE NEAL HAS ALWAYS WRITTEN FICTION, BUT ONLY GOT REALLY SERIOUS ABOUT IT IN THE LATE 90S. HE BRINGS A STRONG RUST BELT PERSPECTIVE TO HIS WRITING, A KIND OF "NORTHERN GOTHIC" AESTHETIC REFLECTIVE OF HIS BACKGROUND.

WRITING HIS FIRST NOVEL AT 29, HE THEN DEVOTED TIME TO HIS CRAFT AND WORKED ON SHORT STORIES, OCCUPYING A SPACE BETWEEN GENRE AND LITERARY FICTION, WITH AN EMPHASIS ON HORROR, SCIENCE FICTION, AND FANTASY. HE HAS SEEN SOME OF HIS SHORT STORIES PUBLISHED IN "ALBEDO 1," IRELAND'S PREMIER MAGAZINE OF SPECULATIVE FICTION, AND HE WON SECOND PLACE IN THEIR AEON AWARD IN 2008 FOR HIS SHORT STORY, "AEGIS." HE HAS LIVED IN CHICAGO SINCE 1993, AND IS A PASSIONATE FAN OF MUSIC, A STUDENT OF POP CULTURE, AN AVID PHOTOGRAPHER AND BICYCLER, AND ENJOYS COOKING.

AS D.T. NEAL HE HAS PUBLISHED SIX NOVELS, *SAAMAANTHAA*, *THE HAPPENING*, AND *NORM*—COLLECTIVELY KNOWN AS THE WOLFSHADOW TRILOGY—*CHOSEN*, *SUCKAGE*, AND THE COSMIC FOLK HORROR-COMEDY THRILLER, *THE CURSED EARTH*. HE HAS ALSO PUBLISHED THREE NOVELLAS—*RELICT*, *SUMMERVILLE*, AND *THE DAY OF THE NIGHTFISH*, AND ONE COLLECTION OF KING IN YELLOW THEMED STORIES, *THE THING IN YELLOW*.

ACKNOWLEDGMENTS

I WOULD LIKE TO THANK CHRISTINE MARIE SCOTT OF CLEVER CROW CONSULTING AND DESIGN IN PITTSBURGH FOR HER WONDERFUL COVER ART AND HER INVALUABLE ASSISTANCE WITH THE LAYOUT AND DESIGN OF THESE PAGES.

JOIN THE 'CLIQUE!

Show us your books and fan art!

#SHUTTERCLIQUE

@NosetouchPress

Instagram • Threads • Facebook • Twitter • Youtube • Bluesky

T-120

VHS